For my father-in-law

'Pigeon Bus' most o

written, and my lovely wife Ali.

Baby One More Time

November 2005

When I was growing up, my dear old mother – God rest her soul – tried her very best to get me to live by just two principles. One was from the bible and one was from the Beatles, though she wasn't particularly a fan of either. The first was: 'Do unto others as you would have done to yourself'. The other was: 'All you need is love'.

If you've got someone you love, she used to tell me, *and that person loves you back, you don't need anyone or anything else.*

Sounds simple enough, doesn't it? Sounds reasonable, right? It won't be long until I'm able to tell her, in person no less, that she failed – or should that be, I failed? Perhaps we both failed, I don't know. I'm quite sure she'll let me know soon enough. See, while she was still around, I seemed to be doing her proud – a good kid at school, conscientious and clean-living, popular and polite. I was every mother's dream – moreover, I was every potential girlfriend's mother's dream. With my twinkling blue eyes, boyish good looks and impeccable manners, who wouldn't have wanted to take me home? Then, when I turned seventeen, two things happened.

First of all, mum's Austin Allegro was involved in a head-on collision with an articulated lorry and she died instantly. I was devastated, and in truth, two decades later, I'm still not sure my heart is completely mended.

Second of all, I actually started *having* girlfriends rather than occasional post-cinema gropes up blouses on a Friday night, or hand-jobs behind the sixth form block at lunchtimes or – the best I could have hoped for at that point – sweaty two minute exchanges of saliva and semen in some seedy darkened corner of the park. Suddenly, the girls seemed to want to offer me more. I think they felt sorry for me; worse still, I think I *let* them feel sorry for me – played on the grief I felt on a daily basis. Played the vulnerable victim, the helpless little sad sack. Come on now, you remember being seventeen – if your conscience and your libido are doing battle, you know as well as I do it's a pretty one-sided contest. All I knew is that I was suddenly getting a *lot* of sex, and the pain I was feeling seemed – well – just a little less intolerable, just for a little while. It quickly became an addiction – like morphine or something. So here I am, still playing the field in my late thirties – still yet to find true love. Still yet to start *looking* for it in anything other than a half-hearted way. And now it's too late. I suppose really, then, it's not true to say I'm playing the field - I've left the field. It's Game Over.

This is not my life story - rather, it's the story of a particularly interesting and eventful few weeks in what will be the latter days of that life. However, I'll continue with the potted version before we get to that. So back to being seventeen. Still being a minor, I was taken into the care of my Auntie Barbara - my mum's sister - and her husband, Colin. I never knew my dad, you see, so all of a sudden I found myself both parentless and homeless. Barbara and Colin were amenable and hospitable, all that sort of stuff, but I think all three of us were relieved when the arrangement came to an end - which it did less than a year later, when I went off to university.

I hadn't exactly passed my A Levels with flying colours - mum's death and my nascent sex life were not a good combination where my studies were concerned. I ballsed up my Biology and Social Studies completely, not even scraping a pass. However, I'd always had a natural aptitude for Maths, so I got an 'A' without even trying. Technically, this wasn't enough to get me into any of my choices of university, but the good folks at Sheffield Hallam wrote me a letter informing me that they were aware of my 'mitigating circumstances' and were prepared to offer me a place studying Applied Mathematics, with the proviso that I, well, applied myself. I took them up on their offer of a place but did not make good on my promise to try my hardest. I went through the degree on autopilot. I had lots of fun, though - I was classed as an orphan (though I'm technically presumably not one), which meant they threw a heck of a lot of money my way in terms of grants. This paid for my rent and upkeep and still left me lots of money to spend on partying. I also had lots of girlfriends. Truly, they were salad days where my love life and / or sex life were concerned. Since I'm likely to have popped my clogs before turning forty, I suppose this phase of my life could technically be termed my mid-life crisis. I started going through girlfriends, flings and one night stands at an alarming frequency. My whole personality was changing – I was, at times, a rather heartless little bastard.

I lived in a house rather than the Halls of Residence during my first year - a house of women, in fact, though I made it my business not to try sleeping with any of them. I knew full well that I would soon be finding a new house if I did - my track record was already pretty terrible at that point. With only one notable exception (more of her later), I'd not managed to keep a relationship alive for more than a month, and I needed this arrangement to work out for ten of them. I quickly discovered I had another reason to keep my hands off the girls I lived with - they turned out to be excellent tutors where my love life was concerned. They taught me lots about how women think and act, sometimes intentionally and sometimes simply by virtue of me sitting back and observing them.

In the spring of that first year, on a night out with mutual friends, I met a girl called Helen Braithwaite, an adorably feisty lass from West Yorkshire. We clicked immediately and it was the start of a formidable friendship – with my limited time left on Earth I can say with relative certainty that a lifelong friendship was born that night. It was never anything sexual – as I discovered during our first conversation together, she had a boyfriend, an aspiring musician named Jeff Barraclough, back at home. Three years later, she became Mrs Jeff Barraclough (I was an usher) and, two years after that, Mr and Mrs Jeff Barraclough jetted off to the States where Helen writes a fashion column in a top Chicago newspaper.

Anyway, back to the story of our university days, Helen and I decided to move in together in our second year, finding a new house with different housemates - a couple this time, who were perpetually perplexed by our situation (*So you're just friends? And he's not gay?*). Jeff wasn't exactly tickled pink by the living situation, but he soon got used to it. As Helen would say, he had two choices. We found another house, just the two of us, for the final year of our undergraduate courses (a situation which several of my girlfriends / potential girlfriends at the time found very difficult to grasp, let alone embrace).

I scraped through my degree, gaining a 2:2 I really didn't deserve. Helen got a first class degree that she did deserve. She moved to London for a while and became a journalist. I stayed at Sheffield, this time living with three blokes I never really took to, and did the only thing I felt I could - a one year teaching degree spanning the end of the 1980s and start of the 1990s. I trained, somewhat begrudgingly, to be a Maths teacher - it was not something I'd ever considered or wanted, and indeed I felt it a bit beneath me. For the first time in a long time, though, I really had to knuckle down - I did not find it easy. I knew loads about Maths, of course, but nothing about transmitting that knowledge to kids. It came naturally to me, meaning getting to the heart of their misconceptions did not. So, for that academic year (and that academic year only), my love life took a back seat. That's not to say I didn't have girlfriends - I just didn't put that much effort into finding or keeping them. I passed - just - and moved back home to find a place to live and a job.

So - I was a Maths teacher. It was official. The most complimentary thing I can say about my career - from those early days right til the end - is that I didn't hate it. I didn't love it either. I wasn't one of those larger-than-life inspirational teachers you see in movies - I didn't touch hearts or minds. Did I love my job? No.

Did I like it? Sometimes! Parts of it. Did I think it was my calling? Not for a nanosecond. It was therefore just like so many of the women you will read about in this book - except I didn't have the same choices in my career as I did in my love life. I had to stick with it, because I didn't know what the heck I would do that wasn't teaching. I think initially I saw it as a 'starter' career, that as I grew older and more experienced, I would move onto something bigger and better. Even if the cancer hadn't put paid to that, I still think I would have seen out my working life as a secondary school maths teacher. I had resigned myself to it: settled. Maybe I should have done the same thing where love was concerned.

So I sort of ambled along half-heartedly, doing just enough to get by and not to get sacked (although, in all honesty, if you don't touch up the kids, hit any of them or turn up drunk, it's pretty bloody hard to get sacked - there were plenty of teachers at my school more apathetic and less talented than I, who were there before me and are probably still there now). I settled into the career, which remained a kind of constant in my life even as my love life continued to be erratic, unpredictable and eventful. I have to admit there was something oddly reassuring about that.

I lived this life of fleeting, sometimes rather chaotic relationships against an unchanging backdrop of Maths teaching for about thirteen years.

Then I got...The News.

It was the first month of 2003. I'd noticed a bit of swelling down there and was having these sharp, shooting pains. Had I been overdoing it a bit with my new girlfriend, Angela? That was my first instinct, so I ignored it. Then I began to feel really tired, and I could tell something wasn't right. It was Angela who encouraged me to visit the doctor. I was diagnosed with germ cell testicular cancer. I lied to Angela. Told her the tests came back clear. Then a couple of days later I repaid her encouragement by dumping her, just a few short weeks into our relationship. My sexual appetite quickly waned and I never dated again.

I've always had an odd, almost geeky sort of fondness for percentages – that is until a few of them bit me in the ass. Here in the Western World, a man has 0.4% chance of contracting testicular cancer. Only 10% of those cases turn out to be incurable. Allow me to do the Maths for you here – that means that only 0.04% of men end up dying from testicular cancer. That's 4 in every 10,000, or 1 in every 2,500 - and you're talking to that one right now. I'm dying. Chemotherapy was, for me, not successful. But I'm not going to talk too much more about the ins and outs of the cancer itself. Let me tell you now that if it's an account of the trials and tribulations of terminal illness you're interested in, you might as well save yourself the bother – this is not that kind of story. Likewise, if you want to learn more about cancer, and testicular cancer in particular – again, this is not the story for you (although I can recommend several excellent books which serve just those purposes – Adrian Jowett's *Nuts, Balls and Rocks* is very frank and funny, and does have a happier ending than mine, and Paul Scotting's *Cancer: A Beginner's Guide* is short but, as the title would seem to suggest, very factual, if you're interested in the science behind it all). No, I stress once more that this is not a story about cancer. It's not intended to teach you about cancer, or indeed to tug at your heartstrings. Rather, this is a story about someone who happens to have cancer.

Mine is a tale of a crazy idea, an idea I got when I found out I was dying, and more specifically the adventures I experienced in realising that idea. It's a tale of redemption, reminiscence and romantic misadventures.

It's also a tale of Hula Hoop wedding rings, cheap cider, seaside dance-offs, embarrassing bathtub incidents, fingernail clippings and Rock, Paper, Scissors, to name but a few.

You might also treat this as something of a handbook, for scattered throughout my story I will be listing my ten Top Tips for pulling. Each one is personally tried and tested. It's not like I will be needing these tips anymore, so feel free to either use them or pass them on to someone you think might need them – in the absence of the children I should have fathered or any significant contributions to my chosen professional field, you could even consider this my legacy.

Enough of that for now – welcome to my apartment. It's the same one I got when I returned from university. Nice, eh? How did I afford it? I think many have wondered that. Am I also an international drugs trafficker? Super spy? Did I win the lottery? No, no and no. The truth is that I was able to pay for the flat outright with the money left over to me in inheritance and the insurance money from the accident, which came through during my second year in Sheffield. Keeping a promise I made to Auntie Barbara, I didn't touch any of it until I bought the apartment.

You might as well get well-acquainted with the place because a good part of the story I'm going to tell you happened right here between these four walls. Over there in the corner is my precious vinyl collection, organised first by genre and then alphabetically. Oh, and the genres themselves are, of course, organised alphabetically. Some of the genres are ones I've made up myself – for instance, right next to 'Soul' there's 'Seduction' – a collection of records I use when I've – you know - got company. I really must thank Sinatra when I see him up in Heaven (and when Al Green joins us, I'll thank him too – those two chaps have worked their magic on many an occasion for me). I love vinyl - it just sounds so much *warmer*. So much sexier. I reckon my vinyl collection must be worth at least £20,000. They're my babies, although Lord knows what's going to happen to them when I pop my clogs, because I've got no intention of getting rid of them before that happens, and I don't really have anyone I can give them to. I'm not some anachronistic throwback, mind you – a very large proportion of my vinyl collection is also to be found on the hard drive of my computer, and a large proportion of that on my iPod.

Yes, I love technology. You've no doubt spotted my 70 inch plasma screen television. You'll probably hate me for saying this, but I don't actually watch a great deal of TV – but it was watching TV one night on this very set that gave me my big idea, to which I'll be coming shortly.

I'm into art, too. That may sound strange when you consider my educational background, but check out that painting on the wall – that's called *Circle Limit III* by M.C. Escher. I love it. I could bore you for hours on end about his use of tessellations and polyhedrons, rotational symmetry and infinitesimal size. I'm a geek, and I make no bones about that.

So that's my place, and it's all thanks to my mum that I've got it. There's a canvas picture of her over on that wall there. This probably sounds crazy, but every morning I take a minute out of my day to thank her for the luxuries she has afforded me. And every morning I have to fight the thought that I would swap it all for just one more day with her.

I've no doubt you'd quite like to hear about The Plan. We'll start with two words.

Rod Stewart.

Thursday, 16th June, 2005

He was the one that started all of this. Not that I know him personally, you understand – rather, it was watching a documentary about him on that night in June that gave me the idea. You know, of course, that Randy Rod's got a bit of an eye for the ladies and that he's been married a few times. At the time of writing this, his seventh child was born a mere matter of weeks ago, and who knows if the old codger's going to stop there? That's seven children from five different mothers. The man's practically Henry VIII in spandex. You also doubtless know that he loves his blondes, which is where he and I differ (okay, we also differ on our musical abilities, our bank accounts and our footballing skills, but we definitely overlap somewhat when it comes to our colourful romantic histories). I don't dislike blondes, mind. I just like all the other hair colours, too, and a pie chart illustrating this would look something like this:

Hair colours of Will Jacob's ex-girlfriends

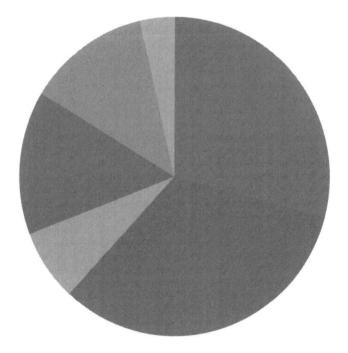

Anyhow, what you may not have known about Rod is that, from time to time, always at Christmas time, his current wife rounds up all of his ex-wives and the whole lot of them sit and eat together. Oh yes. Picture that for a minute – all peroxide, pouting and party poppers. The idea, bonkers though it seemed, sort of warmed my heart. I liked the notion that any wrongs Rod must have committed were now either forgotten or forgiven. I was also intrigued by the idea that everywhere he looked, he was staring a different part of the past in the face. I imagined it was like a little trip through time. I switched the TV off, made a beeline for the 'Soft Rock' section of my vinyl collection and stuck Rod's *Every Picture Tells a Story* and *Atlantic Crossing* LPs on back-to-back, and drifted off into daydream.

I pictured myself sat there, at the head of the table, surrounded by my ex-girlfriends. I don't know if Rod is that way inclined or not, but I would have my table organised systematically, either chronologically from first girlfriend to last girlfriend (or vice-versa - I'm easy), or at very least from shortest relationship to longest (again, I don't mind it being the other way round). It's just good sense to have a system, isn't it? I wondered what we would talk about – would we reminisce? Would there still be a spark? What surprised me was that my daydreams never ended with me taking one, several or all of them to bed at the end of the night. Instead, those daydreams ended with a sense of resolution, forgiveness and affection. Fondness. *Friendship*.

I just couldn't shake these images from my cycle of thoughts. As the days rolled by, daydream turned to obsession, and obsession to plan. Where I would out-trump dear old Rod, though, would be that I would have a series of 'dates' with each of the ex-girlfriends rather than a big dinner party with all of them. That way I wouldn't have to share myself round and would get some good quality one-to-one time with each of them.

You're wondering what my motives could possibly have been, aren't you? Why would I *want* to be in contact with women I've had past relationships with? Break-ups happen for a reason, right? I know exactly what you must be thinking – but this was not some last-ditch attempt to win St. Peter over when I got to the Pearly Gates. Aside from the fact that I might have been a bit of a Lothario from time to time, I really don't consider that I've had too disrespectful a life. Have I spent my Sundays cooped up in some church singing hymns and praising Jesus? Well, no. Have I devoted my days to helping those less fortunate than myself and handed over big wads of cash to charitable causes? No again. But, because of my former teaching career, I feel like I've paid my dues when it comes to playing my part. I've done *something*. No, as I say, that wasn't what my little quest was all about. I just wanted one last trip down memory lane; maybe take a glimpse at what might have been.

Friday, 1st July, 2005

And so I put pen to paper. Or rather finger to keyboard. It was action time.

Job number one was deciding who qualified as an actual girlfriend. But what is a girlfriend? Where does the line lie? Without meaning to boast, the list would have been a bit long and unmanageable if I had included each and every woman I had lured into bed. Okay, I'm boasting a little. Besides, I've forgotten most of their names. And some names I never even knew. And, doubtless – because there are plenty of women out there just as morally dubious as me – some names weren't even real. Likewise, the list would have been a bit skimpy if I had only included those girls who said they loved me (skimpier still if it was just those girls to whom I had said it back). What was needed here was a spot of precision and some boundaries. So the criteria for appearing on the list were as follows:

a) There had to have been a period of at least one month between first kiss and last kiss;

b) We had to have gone on at least five official dates. Don't ask why it was five. It's just a nice round number;

c) I had to still be able to recall her first name AND surname. Not either / or. Middle names were unnecessary. I don't even know Helen's.

The following women satisfied all three of those criteria (and, by the way, don't get me started on the trouble I had putting this table together. Do I sort it alphabetically by first name? Alphabetically by surname? By relationship length? In which case, short to long or long to short? As a cumulative score of looks and personality combined? Pardon the expression, but what a ball ache):

Name	Year(s)	Relationship length	Marks out of 10 for looks	Marks out of 10 for personality
Harriet Hamilton	1986-7	5 months	8	8
Samantha Biggins	1988	1 month	3	2
Patty Bronson	1988-9	9 weeks	9	4
Narinder Takkher	1989	2 months	8	7
Rachael Rothstein	1989	1 month	6	6
Elodie Dupont	1989	1 month	7	4
Rhonda Patterson	1991	4 months	9	8
Katie Kapowski	1992	3 months	9	7
Florence Black	1994	4 months	6	7
Maria Jenkins	1996	4 months	7	9
Mandy Singleton	1997-8	9 months	8.5	7
Tracey Fenton	1998	5 weeks	7	6
Zoe Johnson	1999	2 months	4	8
Kayleigh Law	1999	2 months	7.5	5
Rachel Hadley	2000	9 months	9.5	7
Louise Stanhope	2000	1 month	6	7
Donna Barton	2001	7 weeks	8	3
Janice Gregory	2001	4 months	7	7
Suzie Dewhurst	2002	5 months	10	3
Averages	n/a	12 weeks	7.7	6.0

This was the table staring back at me from my computer screen. I should clarify, perhaps, my ratings system – it is based on my own experiences of women and not on women generally. So a zero for looks wouldn't be as damning as it sounds – rather, it would mean that person was the least attractive person I had ever dated. Which, admittedly, still sounds rather damning, but please bear in mind I have never gone out with someone who would be considered unattractive. Likewise, the ten on my scale – occupied, as you can see, by Ms Dewhurst – represents the most attractive person I have ever dated, and so the score is relative to those two markers. I see that my average ex-girlfriend scores higher on looks than on personality – not the greatest surprise in the world if I'm completely honest.

I admit that, like so many statistics, some of the figures here are a little misleading – it's not really true to say my average relationship length is around three months. Hell, that makes me sound like Mr Commitment. If I had included all the one night stands, flings and those dalliances that fizzled out in less than a month – and I wouldn't be chasing up anyone who fitted into any of those three categories – it would be significantly less than that.

Regardless, what I had here was a list of nineteen potential candidates to fill in seven vacancies. Tracking down these old flames was my next challenge. Sometimes it *was* a challenge; sometimes it was simple.

I started off with only a vague plan of action - that being to find the women one-by-one, repeating this until seven of them had agreed to meet up with me again. Simple? Yes, but it called for a kind of ranking system, and here is where the table came in useful. Deciding who to tackle first proved more problematic than you might imagine. My options were thus:

(a) Start with the longest relationship first and work downwards. Which is all well and good, but quantity doesn't always equate to quality, does it? I had some pretty mediocre relationships which were fleshed out long past their expiry date - and likewise, plenty of great ones which burned bright but ended quickly;

(b) Start with the ones who were geographically closest and work outwards. A solution steeped in practicality if nothing else. I didn't particularly want to be traipsing halfway across the country to meet up with someone for a few hours (though this would disadvantage the five women on the list who I met during my university days – in particular Elodie, who moved back to France. Would I have the time to hop over the channel and back in the space of a single day? It sounded fun but highly implausible). Nor did I particularly want to spend ages tracking someone down if I no longer had their address. It wasn't like I had forever;

(c) Start with the ones I liked best and work downwards. Sounds like a sensible approach, but it wasn't quite that straightforward. Liked what? Her company? Her looks? The sex? I could compile that list ten times and come up with ten different answers;

(d) Start with the ones I knew most recently and work backwards. Again, a good practical solution - I had a greater chance of still knowing their whereabouts. However, this approach carried plenty of disadvantages - I did like the idea of reconnecting with the distant (more so than the recent) past, seeing how time had changed the women in question. In which case I had to consider the opposite approach:

(e) Do it chronologically. Just like in the table. All well and good until you get to the university section which, as I have already explained, was potentially very problematic.

In the end I plumped for a kind of hybrid of all of the above, starting with someone with whom I had a fairly long term relationship, who lived fairly nearby, who I liked quite a lot and of whom I had a fair amount of fond memories, and who came along at around the midpoint of my love life.

Florence Black.

I knew exactly where to find her. She owned her own business - a little coffee shop, just off one of the side streets in town, of which she was the sole employee. It was called *Black Coffee*. I knew she still worked there because every now and then I would take a detour down the side street to capture a fleeting glimpse of her, walking quickly enough to see but not be seen. I still cared about her - not enough to actually talk to her or acknowledge her, obviously, but enough to want to know that she was alive and well.

No time like the present. I slipped out of my dressing gown and showered (mid afternoon showers were and are not uncommon since I gave up work). A dash of aftershave, a comb through the hair and a quick swill of mouthwash and I was good-to-go. I got in my car and drove into town, making a beeline for *Black Coffee*. All told, it was a ninety minute timeframe between picking her name off the list and arriving at the door of her store. I didn't feel at all nervous – if only that fearless audacity had lasted.

As I walked in, she was customerless and running a tea towel around a coffee mug.

'Well, well, well! It's Will, Will, Will. Long time no see, young man!'

'Erm...quite!'

'And what can I do for you today?'

I ordered a cappuccino I didn't really want. She joined me at my table as she brought it.

'This one's on the house. So how are you, my love? You're looking well!'

'Ah well, that's good news, since I'm dying of cancer!' She put her hands to her mouth and fixed her unblinking eyes on me. 'And that's what I came to tell you.' Still no words. Still no blinks. This was starting to feel uncomfortable. 'So...that's...about the size of it really.'

She pushed my coffee to the side and leaned over the table to hug me. 'I'm so, so sorry.'

Right, time to move in for the kill while she was still hugging me. 'So what I'd like to ask is - would you like to spend the day with me? Just for old times' sake. A final goodbye.'

She unclasped her arms, sat back down and eyeballed me. 'Are you trying to get back in my pants? You're not dying at all, are you?'

'I am! Dying that is. Not trying to get into your pants. I swear on my life. What's left of it, anyway. I just want to spend some time with you. Nothing sleazy, I promise.'

'Oh God, you are telling the truth. Oh, honey - no. I'm sorry, but no! I can't spend any time with you!'

My cheeks flushed. I wasn't used to rejection. I felt an uneasy mixture of embarrassment and anger. I unsuccessfully fought the urge to ask the same question I'd been asked countless times as I ended a relationship.

'Why?' It sounded as pleading and desperate as it usually did.

'Why? I'm married! I've got two kids! I can't just go gallivanting off with an ex-boyfriend for the day. That wouldn't be fair on anyone. I'm really...'

'Sorry. Yes I know. You mentioned. And I'm sorry for wasting your time.' I got up to leave.

'Stay and finish your coffee! Or at least start your coffee! Please.'

'It's okay. Thank you. It was nice seeing you again.'

And with that I walked out the door I had entered not two minutes earlier with what remained of my dignity. It was pretty brutal, a game-changer - I resolved, as I returned to my car and headed for home, not to talk to any more of my exes face-to-face. A rejection over the phone would be a much less bitter pill to swallow than one in person.

Saturday, 2nd July, 2005

New day, new approach. Whilst meeting face-to-face had been something of a misjudged strategy, I still had faith in my hybrid system of picking the next potential (for want of a better word) date. I stared at the list on my computer screen, and the name that seemed to jump out at me this time was Rachel Hadley: a little more recent than Florence, but considerably more attractive (and, according to my marks system, neck-and-neck in terms of personality). Rachel was – and as our relationship was only half a decade ago, I could only presume still was – drop dead gorgeous. Despite her rather bland name, she had this lovely Mediterranean sort of complexion and big hazel eyes. She was sweet, too – she was a nurse, and you could tell. She oozed compassion and selflessness. If a face-to-face rejection from Florence had been a bit of blow, a face-to-face rejection from Rachel – *those* eyes looking at me, *that* voice telling me no – would have knocked me out cold.

I still had her number in my phone (anal retentive? Keeping my options open? Too lazy to update my contacts? Your guess is as good as mine). It was with more than a little nervousness that I hit the green call button – clearly yesterday's episode had taken the wind right out of my sails.

Burrrrrrrrrrrrr. Burrrrrrrrrrrrr. Burrrrrrrrrrrrr. No answer. *Burrrrrrrrrrrrr. Burrrrrrrrrrrrr. Burrrrrrrrrrrrr.* Was she screening my calls? *Burrrrrrrrrrrrr. Burrrrrrrrrrrrr. Burrrrrrrrrrrrr.* Voicemail. I had the time it took the non-personalised generic message informing me that the person I was trying to call was not available to decide what to do. Try again later? Wait for her to ring back? Leave a message? I decided a monologue was potentially better than a dialogue – at least I could put forward my case without being interrupted or shot down. I left her the following message:

'Hi Rachel! It's Will Jacobs. Remember me? Listen, I've had a bit of bad news recently. I've got testicular cancer and it's terminal. I don't know how much longer I've got to live. I know I mistreated you when we were together and I'd love for nothing more than to say sorry to you face-to-face. Please say yes. Hopefully I'll speak to you soon. Bye.'

I felt a little nervous and tense, so I took a bath to calm myself down. When I got out, I checked my phone and noticed I had a missed call and a voicemail, both from Rachel:

'Will, hi! It's Rachel.'

So far so cheery!

'I just got your message. I'm so sorry.'

Sorry about the cancer or sorry you can't meet up?

'It's such terrible news.'

Okay, that's promising!

'I'm afraid I can't meet up with you.'

Nuts. It was both.

'Listen, though, I want to thank you. When we split up, I was absolutely distraught. I thought we'd be together forever, which I know sounds crazy after – God, what was it? Less than a year? But then, a couple of months later, I met Ben at work. He's a doctor. He's my soulmate. I don't know if it's because we both work in the same field, but we've just got so much in common, in a way that, looking back, you and I never did. I think I was settling with you - I just didn't know it. I'm realising I'm sounding petty here, but I mean it - thanks for bringing Ben into my life. Thanks for splitting up with me when you did - it's like fate or something. I don't know. All I know is that I wasn't about to break up with you, ever. And no, I don't really want to meet up, but, you know, good luck with everything, if that's the right phrase to use. Bye.'

I was starting to think this was a bad idea. Not twenty four hours ago, I had been utterly cocksure, feeling I was spoiled for choice – now I could easily envisage all nineteen women turning me down. Meeting in person hadn't worked. Phonecalls hadn't worked. I wondered whether it would be okay, ethically speaking, to text someone to tell them you're dying - a rejection text would be even less unpleasant! I would use a little sad face to express the gravitas of the situation - nothing says heartfelt sorrow like a colon and an open bracket. Hmm - maybe email would be a better option. At least then I could articulate the situation a little better, write something a little longer and more heartfelt than:

Dyin of cncr :(Meet l8r?

The more I thought about this email thing, the more I liked it and the more I managed to persuade myself that it was less dubious than it seemed. It would mean a slight shifting in my selection method, giving a kind of weighting to those women I could contact by email. Not that it was the ideal solution – there were a great many women whose email addresses I did not possess. It's not exactly a pre-requisite of a relationship, is it? I decided to sleep on it – if it still seemed like a good idea in the morning, I would do it.

Sunday, 3rd July, 2005

It still seemed like a good idea. Or, at least, I still didn't have a better one.

I got my first and only email address way back in 1994, at a time when no one else I knew seemed to have one. The earliness enabled me the now unthinkable luxury of having my whole name, without any numerical suffixes or the need for strange nicknames, as my address. It was – is – willjacobs@aol.com. In much the same way that Alexander Graham Bell must have struggled to find people to ring up and chat when he first invented the telephone, it as a long while before I could use it to actually correspond with people I knew. Therefore, anyone who came into and disappeared out of my life pre-1994 would prove a challenge and even those who were around a few years after that would be difficult – not that I was completely discarding any of them. They would form what I would refer to as the 'Challenge Pile'. A quick glance of my trusty table showed that eleven women came along after I got an email address – although two of them had already knocked me back. So that left nine – about half of the list. The other eight I would put on the backburner for now.

Who to contact first of the nine? It struck me that there was a quick way to whittle the list down to an even smaller number – either I still had their email addresses or I didn't. It would be an advantage for those who fell into the former category. It also occurred to me that I could sub-divide each group by creating a sort of league table. If her cumulative looks and personality score was equal to or greater than my arbitrarily chosen score of 13, she was in the 'Premiership' section. Anything lower than that and she would be relegated to the 'Championship' section. I, by the way, do not follow football myself, and can quite honestly say that I've had more girlfriends than match tickets. What I do follow is the league tables, which are just manna from heaven when it comes to statistics. I love statistics. You know that of me already. I could happily sit for an entire day looking at the statistics involved in football matches. All of which makes it a small wonder I even have nine women on the list, I realise.

I created the following Carroll Diagram:

	In my address book	Not in my address book
Premiership exes	Tracey Fenton Mandy Singleton Maria Jenkins Janice Gregory	Suzie Dewhurst
Championship exes	Zoe Johnson Louise Stanhope	Kayleigh Law Donna Barton

As you can see, this rather helpfully shortened my shortlist even further, putting the spotlight on four particular women. They were easily contactable AND of high calibre. There were seven slots up for grabs and these four could have all of them if they wanted. I would decide what to do with however many slots were remaining afterwards – whether a Premiership ex not in my address book (i.e. Suzie) trumped a Championship ex not in my address book was a matter of no small consideration.

One of the many advantages of the email plan was that, through the modern day wonder that is copy and paste, I could contact all four of them more or less simultaneously. The email I knocked out was as follows:

From: willjacobs@aol.com

Subject: Big news

Hi {insert name of ex},

How have you been lately? It's been a while, hasn't it? You may or may not want to hear from me, but I feel I have to share with you some sad news. I have been diagnosed with testicular cancer and have no more than a couple of years to live. It would be one of my dying wishes to see you just once more. If you feel like you can't do that for whatever reason, I totally understand. I also understand that you may have a boyfriend or be married by now – that's okay, as that's honestly not what this is all about. As I say, I'd just like to see you; I just want to say goodbye properly.

Hope to hear from you soon,

Will

I hadn't expected to get any immediate replies – but I was wrong. Mere moments after sending this first batch of emails, I got an email back – a 'failure notice' informing me that there was no such user as angryrabbit38@google.co.uk – that was Janice's address. No such user? Had she changed her address? I supposed women would do that if they got married. Or had I typed it in wrongly or something? It was worth double-checking – but, alas, no. Undeterred, I added her to my challenge pile. Technically, it was my third knock-back in a row, but I still had plenty of reasons to be hopeful.

I played *Minesweeper* in a bid to distract myself – it would stall me for a couple of minutes at a time, after which I would hit 'Refresh' to see if Tracey, Mandy or Maria had replied. After an hour-and-a-half of this increasingly rhythmic routine, I decided to call it a night. It was now 9pm – I set myself a deadline of exactly 48 hours from now for the three ladies to reply, and I would check my emails next in exactly 24 hours.

I collapsed on my leather sofa and stared at the ceiling. I could read. I could watch something on the television – I still had Friday's *Countdown* to watch. I could listen to music. I could tackle a Sudoku. Still, all I really wanted to do was strategise. The ball was rolling. Step 1 was complete. But what next? What would be my Step 2? What would I do when either the 48 hour deadline had elapsed or all three had replied, whichever came soonest? It seemed to me that two options presented themselves:

- Try the Championship exes whose email addresses I still had – a nice easy option, but was I going for quickness or quality? If the answer was 'quickness', there was nothing stopping me logging back on to my computer and emailing them immediately. Even with the best case scenario of Tracey, Mandy and Maria all agreeing to meet up, this still left four spare days to fill, and there were only two women who fell into this category;

- Try my Challenge Pile. Perhaps revert to the hybrid strategy which had so far proved so massively unsuccessful – perhaps try something new. Or perhaps employ something more akin to the Premiership / Championship ranking system to narrow it down to a select few. I would work my way down the list until I had found my Magnificent Seven. I would take the rejections on the chin, safe in the knowledge that whilst my options were dwindling, I still had them. Surely – *surely* – out of this long list of women, seven of them would want to see me again? As soon as I had my Magnificent Seven, my next step would be to actually go ahead and arrange the – for want of a better word – dates. They weren't going to be dates in the sense that I was used to, mind. Whereas previously my dates had all involved me trying to have sex at the end of the night, these dates would involve me trying *not* to have sex at the end of the night, which frankly was going to be a much stiffer challenge. Pardon the pun. I'd have to try to arrange it so that each day was allocated to a specific date. Clearly, the Saturday and Sunday were going to be the most in-demand days, but it was going to have to be on a first-come-first-served basis. If anyone else requested those days, I'd have to fob them off and hope they could reschedule. I'd just make up something to do with cancer - a doctor's appointment or something.

I was getting ahead of myself. I still hadn't decided what Step 2 would be.

I weighed up the possibilities. Quickness or quality? Quickness or quality? My brain seemingly fit to burst, I eventually plumped for a third option – drink enough Jack Daniels to knock me out. I would cross that bridge when I came to it.

Monday, 4th July, 2005

My vow to check my emails only once daily at 9pm lasted for less than twelve hours. As soon as I awoke the next morning, fuzzy headed as an old drunk but excitable as a small child on Christmas morning, I scrambled frantically over to my computer and logged on to my account, wearing only my boxer shorts and my duvet draped around my shoulders. I just couldn't wait; I was too curious. Too obsessed – already.

Buried amidst my usual email offers of Viagra (how dare they! Didn't they know who they were dealing with?), penis enlargements (ditto! I certainly never had any complaints!) and timeshares (definitely wasn't going to be taking them up on that, what with the imminent dying and all), there was one genuine email. It was from one of the Magnificent Seven:

Sender: Tracey Fenton

Subject: re: Big news

I got that fluttery feeling in my stomach – half nervousness and half excitement. The subject header gave no clues whatsoever about what the tone of the message was going to be. I opened the message up, which I am now going to present to you verbatim:

WANKER!!! it was bad enough that u treated me the way u did when we were going out. Now ur making up ridiculous stories to lure me back into bed? u must think I was born yesterday. get out of my life forever u pathetic creep, or i'll send my boyfriend round to kick the crap out of you. SICK BASTARD.

Reading between the lines, I think that one was probably a no.

The brutality of the message made me buckle – I turned to the Championship section, looking for a quick fix. Tracey was out, so I'd replace her with either Zoe or Louise. Lucky Louise was the recipient of the same email I had sent yesterday, by virtue of the single point she had over Zoe in the looks / personality stakes. I noted the time and, as before, set a 48 hour deadline.

I checked my emails with an almost obsessive frequency, and a couple of hours later, I got a reply from Louise – her swiftness was encouraging. Wasn't it?

From: Louise Stanhope

Subject: What?

What is this? Is this one of those scam things? Every other day I seem to get an email from some Nigerian bloke who's just inherited a million quid and needs help transferring the funds. But this - this is a new one. So let me guess here - you've hacked Will's account and you're sending out this spam email to everyone one his contacts list. You're hoping some poor sucker will respond then when you've got them in your grasp, you'll hit them with some bullshit guilt trip story, something to do with helping to pay for treatment for this very obviously imaginary cancer. I'm contacting the police, scumbag.

P.S. - If the real Will was dying, he'd at least have the decency to telephone me or meet me in person to tell me as much.

I decided I'd better not respond to that one.

Christ. This was not going well. So then Zoe – your turn! Once again, I fired off the same email. My day was pretty much a write-off – I did not leave the house and nor did I bother to shower. No activity distracted me for more than half an hour at a time, and after I had tired of whatever it was I was doing, I was straight back on the computer, checking for replies. None arrived during the remainder of that day.

Tuesday, 5th July, 2005

I needed some good news and I needed it fast. My hopes were sinking. It was just after six o' clock in the evening – just three hours before the deadline for my first batch of emails. I was desperately hoping that I'd get a reply from Maria and Mandy, my remaining hopes from the Premiership pile. Actually, that's a bit of unnecessary hyperbole, since I still had plenty of other irons in the fire - I wasn't desperate. But I was hoping - there was a reason why they were in the first wave of attempts. At some point, though, I would have to draw the line. Rules are rules. As I booted up my PC, I tried to come up with a list of reasons why they might not have replied (for it was for the worst that I was preparing myself). Perhaps they were mulling it over. Who could have blamed them? A great many relationships end with a sense of bitterness, even hatred, as we've already seen from some of the responses I had already received. I could well understand the dilemma some of them might be experiencing. *On the one hand - he's terminally ill. On the other - he broke my heart into a thousand pieces.*

Just three hours for Maria and Mandy to respond to my email. If they didn't, I would have to put them on the backburner while I tried to fill the remaining spaces. Finger crossed...

And there it was.

Maria's name in my inbox.

Still pessimistic, I realised that my hopes were possibly about to be shattered. I gulped audibly and clicked on the email to open it, looking at the screen through my fingers.

From: Maria Jenkins

Re: Yes!

Will! How absolutely lovely to hear from you. I wish it was under different circumstances. Yes, I'd love to meet up. You just let me know when you're free and I'll clear my schedule for you.

See you soon,

Maria

X

Hallelujah! Praise be! The adventure was back on. My spirits were lifted once more. I dragged my fist downwards and let out a little 'Yes!' to no one in particular. My fortunes must have been turning because, about an hour later, I got this reply from Mandy:

From: Mandy Singleton

Subject: re: Big news

Hello, Will! Wow, long time no see. Or hear. Bloody hell, that's such sad news about the cancer. I lost an aunt to cancer last year. It spread really quickly, before I had time to visit her to say goodbye. Anyway, that's not what you want to hear, is it? What I'm trying to say is - yes, okay, so things ended a bit badly

between us, and yes, okay, I thought Hell would freeze over before I wanted to see you again. But life's too short, isn't it? So, sod it, let's do it! A lot has changed in my life, too, and I'd love to catch up. Let's make a plan.

Bye,

Mandy

Xx

I hit the hay that night with a smile. The glass-half-empty Will would say I was failing – so far in my quest, I had scored a measly two out of eight. He would also grumble that I had filled only two out of seven of the days in the week I had envisaged – an only marginally better proportion. The glass-half-full Will was in the house tonight, however, and he was chuffed to bits that two of his exes had agreed to see him one more time. It was two more than he had when the day started.

I was just drifting off happily, aglow in this new-found positivity when it dawned on me – I was going to have to reply to Maria and Mandy. After much deliberation, I decided the best course of action would be to reply thusly:

From: willjacob@aol.com

Subject: Fantastic!

Dear Maria / Mandy *{delete as appropriate}*,

Thank you so much for agreeing to go meet up again. I'm really looking forward to it. I've got a few tests and doctor's appointments over the next few days – how are you fixed for the week beginning 10th July?

See you soon!

Will

X

     This way, I had a little bit of time to organise five other dates, without it being so long into the future that either would lose interest.

Wednesday, 6th July, 2005

Ding ding! Round Three. I took a few nasty blows in the first two rounds, but I was still standing and definitely not ready to throw the towel in yet. Yes, I've switched from football analogies to boxing ones and, no, I don't like boxing, either, but it's given the world some cracking idioms.

     I switched on my computer again and loaded up my emails for the millionth time this week. More emails with offers to enlarge my penis. And more emails for triple-x porn sites. More usefully, both Mandy and Maria had replied, both telling me that they were perfectly happy to wait and that I was to contact them nearer to the time, whenever I was ready. Good news indeed. There was a third email of note awaiting me – Zoe's. She had finally replied. Whether I was feeling quite buoyant from my recent successes or whether her status as a Championship ex gave her message a little less gravitas I couldn't say, but I seemed to have a little less trepidation as I opened it.

From: Zoe Johnson

Subject: FU

     I hoped that stood for 'Fully Understandable' or that she was going to type FUN IDEA but forgot to finish the subject header. I doubted it. I'll preface her reply by saying that the modern world has gifted us with so many opportunities to be very rude very easily – one only has to look at the plethora of expletive-ridden forums littering the internet, with strangers turning on each other in a way they simply wouldn't do face-to-face. As an early pioneer of using technology in this insensitive way, I'm not proud to say that at the dawn of the mobile phone explosion at the end of the century, I dumped a girlfriend by text. I can't remember the exact message, but I may - may - have typed it in text speak: 'i h8 2 leave things this way' or something of that ilk. There may - may - have been a sad face on the end. That girlfriend was Zoe and as you are about to discover, she had not forgotten that rather unceremonious ending.

Well, well, well. Look what the cat dragged in. Or in this case, look what the mouse dragged in. An email from the great Will Jacobs. King of the Heartbreakers. What kind of douche bag dumps someone by text? Well, it gives me great pleasure now to return the favour, only by email. Here goes:

Fuck you, Will Jacobs. I don't care if you're dying or not, you've been dead to me for years.

See ya.

I know I should have taken the high road. I deserved my berating. But I couldn't help myself. Now, just to backtrack a little, at the time of going out with Zoe, I was already in the throes of what I shall call my 'Mrs Robinson phase'. It always seemed to me that it was easy enough to be an attractive young woman when you're not long out of your teens, when gravity is on your side and you still have the flush of youth. Those women who had managed to hold onto their beauty, whose sexiness shone through the crow's feet and the beginnings of a wrinkled neck - they were the ones most deserving of our admiration. I know, I know - paging Dr Freud. I was clearly in need of a replacement mother figure or something. After that less-than-friendly email, I couldn't resist firing off one final pot-shot, petty though I know (and knew) it was:

From: willjacobs@aol.com

Subject: your mother

Right, well in that case I might as well get this off my chest after all these years. Your mother was red hot, and all the time we were together, I fancied her more than I fancied you. Phew! That feels so much better! Tata now!

Yes, this redemption thing was going really well, wasn't it?

It was time to try my hand with another round of exes. With all the easily reachable ones now messaged, I turned to my challenge pile – which was basically my original table minus the ones I had tried. It struck me that they were rather like Top Trumps cards, and deciding which the best one was would depend on what category you had chosen. For ease of comparison, I added a final column to the end which totalled looks and personality, then ordered them by how easy I thought they would be to track down, starting with the one I considered to be the easiest (time was against me now, so I had to strike a balance between convenience and merit):

Name	Year(s)	Relationship length	Marks out of 10 for looks	Marks out of 10 for personality	Total
Suzie Dewhurst	2002	5 months	10	3	13
Rhonda Patterson	1991	4 months	9	8	17
Katie Kapowski	1992	3 months	9	7	16
Kayleigh Law	1999	2 months	7.5	5	12.5
Donna Barton	2001	7 weeks	8	3	11
Harriet Hamilton	1986-7	5 months	8	8	16
Rachael Rothstein	1989	1 month	6	6	12
Narinder Takkher	1989	2 months	8	7	15
Patty Bronson	1988-9	9 weeks	9	4	13
Samantha Biggins	1988	1 month	3	2	5
Elodie Dupont	1989	1 month	7	4	11

It was looking bleak for those uni girls – I could have spent weeks trying to track down Elodie in her native France. I pictured her cycling through some rustic French village on a bicycle with a basket on the front, flicking her tumbling auburn hair about as her white skirt billowed in the breeze. *Au revoir ma chère.* With her painfully low combined score, Samantha stood little chance too. Patty fared slightly better on that front, but as I could remember nothing of her original whereabouts other than that it was south of the Thames Estuary, locating the proverbial needle in a haystack would have been a quicker task. I at least knew roughly where Rachael, Narinder and Patty were originally from – Northumberland, Northampton and Huddersfield respectively – but those are still big places. And who was to say they still lived there now? They could have been scattered far and wide – but still, they would have made viable reserves if I failed to secure all seven dates. The other six were all plausible candidates. Suzie – whose mobile number I still had, whose address I still knew and who I dated relatively recently, so relatively little chance of those details changing – would be a cinch to reach, but there's no more unhinged lady on that list, so I was hesitant to try her. I really wanted Harriet, with her high score and long absence, to be one of the seven, but I had no idea how I would get hold of her nowadays, hence her relatively low placing on the list.

My next try, then, was going to be Rhonda, my gorgeous music loving girlfriend from the early nineties – high up on the list despite our relationship being such a long time ago. The reason? I still had her parents' phone number on an old Rolodex I had managed to dig out believing it might have been a rich source of old information. As it turned out, hers was the only number on it that I needed. Maybe she still lived nearby, maybe not – but if that number still belonged to her parents (and I reckoned there was a fair chance it did) then they could hopefully put me in touch with her. I didn't ideally want to speak to her on the phone, not after what had happened with Rachel, but she seemed like just too good an opportunity to pass on.

I could not possibly have envisaged the conversation that ensued.

'Hello?'

I recognised the voice on the other end of the line straight away.

'Mrs Patterson! How the devil are you? I don't know if you remember me, but this is Will Jacobs – I used to go out with Rhonda about fifteen years ago? Anyway, I'm trying to track her down and I wondered if you might be able to give me her address or phone number?'

'Is this some sort of horrible joke?'

'Joke? What? No, this is really Will Jacobs and I really want to track her down! I mean, I understand she might not want to speak to me, but please tell her that if she will only give me a chance, just to say hello...'

Silence.

'Mrs Patterson?'

More silence, at least ten seconds of it, followed by the sound of sobbing. I followed my instincts and waited until the sound subsided and finally Mrs Patterson's voice became audible again.

'Didn't you hear? My Rhonda died two years ago.'

Yet more silence. This time I initiated it. My heart seemed to sink down my chest and into my stomach.

'She was having a bad time of it...She jumped from her apartment window, just outside of Birmingham, where she was living.'

My next two words seemed to come instinctively rather than by choice – because they were a bad choice. 'You're joking? I mean, sorry, no, of course you're not joking; I just meant...I don't know what I just meant. I'm sorry. I'm truly, truly sorry.'

'I do remember you, Will. Rhonda really, really loved you. It was probably one of her happiest times, when the two of you were together.'

'Oh wow. Really? Thank you.'

'Don't thank me. Because then when you left her she was a mess. You really broke her heart.'

'Oh. I'm really sorry.' I felt flushed with shame. I did, of course, have an ace up my sleeve which would unburden me a little, and I was going to use it. 'Listen, Mrs Patterson, I'm going to be completely honest with you here. There's a reason I wanted to get in touch with Rhonda – it was to say goodbye to her. I've got cancer. I haven't got too much longer to live.'

'You're not serious, are you?' There you go, you see! Her response was just a slightly more articulate variant on 'you're joking?'

'I am serious, yes.'

'Oh, you poor dear.' There was another little pause. I wasn't really sure what I expected her to do with this information. As it turns out, the silence was a pregnant one, as Mrs Patterson was ruminating on a little plan. 'Can you come to my house, do you think?'

When our chat was finished, I returned to the computer, the screen of which was still displaying the newly-rearranged table, and deleted Rhonda's row, slightly cold and callous though it seemed. It was probably somewhat disrespectful of me to continue with my quest – doubly so to do so immediately after I had found out about her death – but that's what I did. If anything, the experience had reinforced my own mortality – that I was still alive but that my time was short. I had to do this.

Katie seemed like a good next choice – but how to track down someone I had not seen for well over a decade? I didn't have her email address and I didn't have her phone number. She lived fairly locally and though the name of her street wasn't quite on the tip of my tongue (let alone her house number) I reckoned I could find it if I drove there. A few problems – firstly, this was a house she rented and shared with a couple of her friends, when both were young adults – it was hard to picture her still there now. Secondly, as I didn't know her house number, it would mean knocking on every door in the vicinity until I hopefully found her. Finally, the whole Florence episode had really put me off face-to-face meetings.

I needed a new strategy to try to track her down, and I believed I had one. Have you ever used that website, www.bestdaysofyourlife.com? Millions of people have, so you probably know of it even if you haven't used it – it's the one where you type in your name, what school you went to and when, and what you're doing now. It's basically a good way for people who are doing well for themselves to show off about just how well they are doing – most of the rest don't bother. The beauty of this website – the advantage it had over regular email – was that married women had to put down their maiden names, and were searchable by those. So if Katie was a member, with her fairly distinctive maiden name she ought to be fairly easy to track down.

It seemed like a gift from the gods, then, when I typed her name into the website's search engine and only one Katie Kapowski came up – moreover, she was still local. She hadn't uploaded a picture of herself, and nor had she opted to include anything on her profile blurb, but it just had to be her. I forked over the £9.99 joining fee that would enable me to send her a message – and that message, you will not be surprised to hear, was the same trusty old message I had been sending all week, copied and pasted once again. While I was on the site, I searched for Kayleigh, Donna and Harriet, but to no avail – there were no Kayleigh Laws whatsoever, whilst the opposite problem faced me with the other two – there were scores of Donna Bartons and just as many Harriet Hamiltons. None of them appeared to be the ones I was looking for – certainly none were even remotely local, and none of the profile pictures even closely resembled the images I had in my head. I was tempted to search for the university quintet while I was at it, but figured it would be a good strategy to which I could revert if need be at a later date.

It was getting on a bit, but I was loathe to shut down my computer just yet. I would leave it for half an hour just in case I got a reply from Katie. What to do to pass half an hour on the internet? No, not that! *Minesweeper* was losing its appeal, so I went on a website I'd read about a few days earlier that sounded like a bit of fun – www.ageyourself.com. Basically, you upload a photo of yourself, choose which option you want - +10, +20, +30, +40 or +50 - let the computer do its magic. It will generate an older version of you, up to 50 years older. I suppose it's much like those computer-generated pictures showing what children who have been missing for years might look like today. I went straight for the +50 option, seeing what I would look like as a man in his late eighties, who's had a full life. I could see there was no great science or art to this artificial ageing process - they'd simply used Photoshop-style effects to add more saggy jowls, deep-set wrinkles and liver spots, dulled down the skin colour to something slightly more ashen, then used that same ashen hue to colour over the hair, giving the (not particularly convincing) illusion of baldness. I smiled as I gazed at my so-called future self. Gazed at the reflection in the mirror that I would never see. Old man Will Jacobs. I wondered what stories the old codger would have to tell his grandchildren and possibly great-grandchildren. Maybe how he found love a little later in life than most, put his roaming days behind him and settled down with the love of his life. The old geezer and I - we've got something in common. We both know death's on the horizon. He's ready for it, though. He's had a good innings. I printed the picture but left the paper in the tray.

Half an hour had passed and, to my great delight, when I returned to bestdaysofyourlife.com the little envelope icon was flashing, indicating I had received a message. It was Katie! Okay, so the Rhonda news had been a heartbreaking setback, but clearly my stars were realigning! I had located Katie and she had responded swiftly. My luck was definitely in. This is what she had to say for herself:

Hello Will. How nice to hear from you.

Ouch. I mean, I realise that on paper that reads as a friendly enough introduction - but you don't know Katie. I could hear her saying it, her voice drenched in sarcasm, her intentions barbed.

Yes, how awfully nice to hear from the ex-boyfriend who, completely out of the blue, abandoned what seemed to me - erroneously, clearly - to be a perfectly promising relationship with no word of an explanation.

Told you.

So, you're dying, are you? And you want to meet up? I presume you've sent this exact same message to your scores of other ex-lovers. I've got your card marked. I know what you're doing. I'll wager you've suddenly found God, now that the threat of judgment is suddenly looming. So you're rapidly repenting before your visit to St Peter. All of a sudden, you've developed a conscience, now that it's to your advantage to have one. You're being nice to all those women to whom you were such an utter bastard (because I'm as certain that I wasn't the last as I am that I wasn't the first). Well, sorry to say this, but it turns out I *don't* have a conscience. Turns out I'll be perfectly at ease with myself reading your obituary, knowing that I could have made amends but didn't. I hate to say this, but maybe the cancer is your just desserts – you stole months from my life, probably stole months and years from dozens of women's lives. Maybe the cancer is stealing the months and years from your life: what goes around comes around.

I don't want to help you and I don't want to hear from you again. I'd say 'go to hell', but I suspect you'll be heading that way soon anyway, you pathetic scumbag.

Crikey. It was one thing being torn to shreds by women who - like Louise - didn't believe I was dying. It was quite another being torn to shreds by women who did believe me, like Zoe and Katie. I couldn't believe the vitriol I was receiving; the vitriol I had created, really.

I decided to retreat to the safety of my bed.

Thursday, 7th July, 2005

I awoke with my usual thought: was today going to be my 'Deathday'? I don't mean was I going to die that day - I had a bit of time left on this Earth, I was sure about that and, unless I get hit by a bus before the cancer gets me, I'll see it coming. No, it's something else. Even before I found out about the cancer, I was always intrigued by the idea of one's 'Deathday'. One of the year's 365 / 366 dates is going to be the one on which you eventually die. Just as loved ones associate you with your birthday, those who outlive you will also come to associate you with your Deathday (unless, like Shakespeare's, they're one and the same). They'll either celebrate or, more likely, commemorate the life you had when that day rolls around each year. Their grief will be slightly heightened, and that day will remind them of you. It happens to me when the anniversary of mum's death comes - that date, which had no special relevance to her whatsoever, is now inextricably linked to her. So I wonder - what's my Death Day? Is it today? Will my gravestone read: *Will Jacobs. 6th June 1969 – 7th July 20XX?*

A cheery start to the day I'm sure you will agree! Deathday or not, I had work to do. I still only had two of the seven days sorted, and time was ticking.

Mid-table Harriet seemed to be drawing me in today; my big teenage romance. Tricky to track down but worth it, as her high scores suggest. I'm afraid I don't buy into that 'first cut is the deepest' nonsense (sorry, Rod!), but she made a big impression on me. Much like the Katie situation, I had a rough inkling where her parents used to live, having been there on a couple of occasions (taking advantage of the fact that they weren't in, naturally) – and for the same reasons, I did not feel it a particularly viable option to try to track her down that way. Not that my Plan A and subsequent Plan B were any less ostentatious. I suppose it's a measure of just how much I cherished our time together back when we were teenagers that I went to the lengths I did in order to locate her.

As I'm sure you can appreciate, the phone book has a multitude of Hamiltons. After checking to see if any of them still lived at Queensbury Road where she had lived with her parents – they didn't – I did a quick calculation of how long it would take me to telephone all of them and ask if they had heard of Harriet. I estimated there to be around two hundred different Hamilton families in my phone book. Let's say each telephone conversation had taken thirty seconds, including dialling the number, waiting for a response, asking the question and waiting for the person on the other end to say 'no'. That's a hundred minutes right there. And it's exceptionally unlikely that all of the Hamiltons would have been in, so I'd have had to try them again another time. And of course we'd have been presuming she still lived in the area, or at least that a Hamilton to whom she was related did. We'd also have been presuming she wasn't ex-directory. No, there had to be a better way – a more efficient one. As a master in the art of copying and pasting, I reckoned there was. I stood a better chance of tracking her down, I hypothesised, by trying to figure out her email address. I realise that sounds like madness, but it was worth a shot – I had a system, you see.

I started with the rather hopeful but at the same time not unlikely assumption that all or part of her name would form part of the email address, whether capitalised or not, initialised or not. Mine did. I did a quick tally of the different service providers represented by my email contacts, then cross-referenced it with a Google search of the most popular service providers in the UK. Between them, I managed to form what I considered to be a top five (it was not a great surprise to me to find out that Hotmail was Pick of the Pops). If it had transpired that Harriet's address was not with any of those, it would have been back to the drawing board – I could have been there forever. Onto the end of each address, I would add either .com or .co.uk.

I tabulated the possibilities thusly:

First name	Surname	Number	@	Service provider	Extension
harriet	hamilton	No number		hotmail	.co.uk
Harriet	Hamilton	1		yahoo	.com
h	h	2		ntlworld	
H	H	3		msn	
		4		gmail	
		5			
		6			
		7			
		8			
		9			
		68			
		69			
		1968			
		1969			

All I had to do was try to mix and match the possibilities, like one of those cylindrical wooden child's toys where you twist round different heads, torsos and legs to make different people. It would create lots of different combinations, but if Lady Luck was on my side, one of them would be Harriet's. I figured she owed me one, what with the cancer and all. Lady Luck, that is – Harriet owed me nothing. On the contrary.

There were lots of possible approaches to this, the one to which I was initially drawn being to go across the top (so harriethamilton@hotmail.com), then the next one after that working downwards (harriethamilton@hotmail.co.uk). Then I'd try the next service provider down (harriethamilton@yahoo.com) and keep going in that fashion until I'd exhausted all the service providers, trying .com and .co.uk for each. That would be all the harriethamilton possibilities. I'd do the same with harriethamilton1 and repeat the process. Pretty soon I'd have all the harriethamiltons. Then I would do the same with the implausible-looking harrietHamilton, and so on and so on until I'd tried every possibility starting with harriet. Then I'd repeat all that with all the possibilities starting with Harriet. I could keep going, but I'm hoping you get the gist. So - that way would have been systematic (an approach to life to which I'm always drawn) but inefficient. Instead I leaned more towards likelihood and probability. Some combinations were more plausible than others. For example, it seemed implausible that both her first name and surname were initialised (ruling out overly abbreviated addresses like hh1@hotmail.com). I would start with the more plausible ones. To each of those would-be addresses, I sent this email:

From: willjacobs@aol.com

Subject: Here's hoping...

This is a real shot in the dark, but I'm trying to reach Harriet Hamilton, and I'm hoping you might be her. This is Will Jacobs – remember me? You and I were something of an item. If this isn't Harriet, I'm terribly sorry, but if it is I'd really love it if you could get in touch with me. I've had some bad news – I'm terminally ill, and I would love to see you one more time, just for old time's sake.

Will

It was, I admit, a ridiculous ploy. Underscores, dashes, nicknames, abbreviations, and the fact that, rare as it is in this day and age, she might actually not have an email address – these were all potential spanners in the works. And what about the numerical suffix? I had chosen those numbers in the hope that she was either using a single digit or her year of birth (which I had narrowed down to a 50-50 – more of that later). What if it was another kind of number – her whole date of birth? Her wedding anniversary? Her house number? If my first round of combinations proved unsuccessful, I was prepared to go from 10 to 100, but I would have to draw the line there.

As well as being ridiculous, it was also massively painstaking, and more than a little dull, so I tried to alleviate the repetitiveness of it all by turning it into a game – how quickly could I fire off a new email? I got it down to just six seconds – a heck of a lot quicker than the time it would have taken to make a phone call. A horrid realisation dawned on me about halfway through the process – there was a very good chance she was married. I had come too far to back down now, though, so I ploughed on, clinging to the hope that she was still unmarried, or married and divorced, or married but still using the email address from her maiden days.

In most cases, the email bounced immediately, suggesting that, as with our angryrabbit from earlier on in the week, there was no such email address. I did get one reply as I was in the process of sending the emails out.

From: Harriethamilton8@msn.com

Subject: Mistake?

I'm really sorry to hear about your illness, but I think you might have intended this for someone else. I am called Harriet, but I've never met anyone called Will Jacobs. I hope you find the Harriet you're looking for.

God bless,

Harriet

I received around a dozen of these sorts of emails over a period of about three weeks. I liked this one:

From: Hhamilton7@yahoo.co.uk

Subject: Not me

There seems to have been some misunderstanding here. You intended your email for someone called Harriet. I am Herbert Hamilton. I'm 72 years old. I suggest you exercise a bit more care when typing.

Regards,

Herbert

However – and the serendipity was my reward for what turned out to be a good couple of hours' work - one of the emails did reach its intended recipient:.

From: HarrietHamilton9@aol.com

Subject: Meeting up

Wow! Will Jacobs! I never thought I'd hear from you again. What tragic news about your cancer. I'm really sorry. If you want to talk about it, I'm all ears. Or not. Whatever. Either way, I'd love to see you again. When did you have in mind?

Regards,

Harriet

Xxx

Result! Thanks Lady Luck! I rehashed my message with the 10th July deadline.

It turned out to be a great day all round as I got a nice surprise that evening – a phone call from Helen, who told me to load my computer up and get on the webcam as she hadn't seen my face for ages.

H: *Rain Man! Good to see you old chum. What the bloody hell have you done to your hair?*

W: *Ah, a typically warm-hearted greeting from my best friend. Anyway, what do you mean? It was a very expensive haircut, I'll have you know. I'm going for the spiky-messy look.*

H: *Well, the good news is you're halfway there. And not just messy - you seem to have grey hair now!*

W: *No. I've got grey hairs. There's a difference.*

H: *Potato pot-ah-to.*

W: *Tom-ay-to tom-ah-to.*

H + W: *Let's call the whole thing off!* (Both laugh)

H: *Listen, matey, you're turning into a bit of a stranger. Sort it out. Anyway, how's tricks?*

W: *Good, good. There's the dying of cancer bit, obviously, but apart from that – tickety boo! How come you're up? Isn't it two in the morning?*

H: *Sprawl McCartney up there is wriggling. My choices were to give him a swift kick to the shins and reclaim my half of the bed or to come and make a bed on the sofa. I took the high road...this time.*

W: *You're softening in your old age.*

H: *YOU'RE softening in your old age.*

W: I presume that's an erectile dysfunction joke.

H: I presume the cap fits.

Silence.

H: Are you trying to think of a witty comeback?

W: Yes.

H: Are you failing miserably?

W: Yes.

H: So what's what?

W: Well, I'm going on a date.

H: Ooooooooo!

W: In fact I'm going on seven. In seven days. Or that's the plan anyway. I'm up to three so far.

H: Come again? I bet you will knowing you, you mucky little article.

W: I got a bit bored so I decided to get in touch with some old flames, see if they wanted to meet up, have a catch up, maybe reminisce about old times.

H: A trip down mammary lane?

W: No, it's not like that, honestly! I'M not like that anymore, not since the cancer. There'll be no funny business. I suppose I just want to leave them with some nice memories of me. A bit of a last hurrah. Thoughts?

H: Hmm. It's quite possibly the worst idea anyone in the history of mankind has ever come up with.

W: Now you get off that fence and tell me how you really feel.

H: There's something I don't get - you're telling me all of these women are still single?

W: No no. Look, I shouldn't have used the word 'date'. We're just meeting up. Some of them are married now, but that's okay.

H: Well, this all sounds incredibly unhealthy and dysfunctional. It's a plan riddled with so many possibilities for something to go wrong; you're inviting women back into your life who you chose to get rid of for whatever reason and I'll bet most of them still have an axe to grind. What the hell are you thinking? It's going to be disastrous. So of course, I'm all for it and will expect a phone call after each and every date, no matter what time that may be. Got it?

W: Got it.

H: Well I'd better let you get on with it! Good to see you, chick.

W: You too. Love ya.

H: Love ya too.

As you can see, the Cosmopolitan hustle bustle of a top international fashion magazine office had clearly done nothing to water down Helen's schoolboy brand of humour. Similarly untainted was her dye-in-the-wool Leeds accent, still as thick and flat as the day she stepped off the plane (though occasionally, when the 'a' made an 'ah' sound - as in 'bar' and 'Chicago' itself - the two accents intertwined effortlessly. She said those two words a lot).

Look, I know what you're thinking. You're thinking – *okay, Will, I see where this one's going. Your friendship with Helen is going to develop as this story unfolds and – whaddya know – the two of you are going to fall in love. Everyone lives happily ever after – although in your case, it's not a particularly long ever after. Right?* Right? Wrong. That's not what happens, and if that's the kind of ending you're hoping for, close the book now because you're going to be sorely disappointed. As I've already made clear, Helen and I are, were, and will always be, strictly good friends. It is, as far as she and I are concerned, as simple as that. She has been my rock and a constant source of good advice – let me tell you, having a female best friend is an excellent accessory to the budding womanizer. They really know their onions.

Indeed, I'm going to give Helen the honour of being the inspiration behind my first Top Tip.

Top Tip Number One: Have a female best friend.

No, ours is more like a brother / sister sort of relationship (even if, admittedly, my sister in this metaphor has an absolutely outstanding rack, but that's by the by).

Friday, 8th July, 2005

Three down, four to go. I updated my table, which was now in the following more streamlined state:

Name	Year(s)	Relationship length	Marks out of 10 for looks	Marks out of 10 for personality	Total
Suzie Dewhurst	2002	5 months	10	3	13
Kayleigh Law	1999	2 months	7.5	5	12.5
Donna Barton	2001	7 weeks	8	3	11
Rachael Rothstein	1989	1 month	6	6	12
Narinder Takkher	1989	2 months	8	7	15
Patty Bronson	1988-9	9 weeks	9	4	13
Samantha Biggins	1988	1 month	3	2	5
Elodie Dupont	1989	1 month	7	4	11

Yikes. My options really were running out, and so was my time. Was it time to contact Suzie? No. NO. I still had other avenues to explore – less interesting avenues, albeit. Kayleigh and Donna still lived fairly locally, as far as I knew, and had ranked highly on the list in terms of convenience as a result. I hadn't been in a rush to contact them thus far for the simple reason that neither had particularly set my world alight. I had found Donna to be a bit on the vacuous side – we had struggled to find common ground. A good looking girl, for sure, but a day with her would have been hard work. Kayleigh was just a bit bland. The age gap between us was greater than any other on the list – she was very young and perhaps still growing into the person she would one day become. Or perhaps she was just bland.

I had Kayleigh's phone number but not address and Donna's address but not phone number. Kayleigh ranked higher in terms of her total score on my table and was, theoretically, going to be the easiest to track down, so trying her first was a no-brainer.

I hadn't known Kayleigh's home address because she had always come to me. She was another one who still lived with her parents when we were together (though I was getting far too old still to be dating such girls by that point – at thirty years old I had a good decade on her). She never pressured me into meeting them (for which I was always grateful) and insisted on driving either to my place or to a meeting point when she saw me. Unlike with Donna, when Kayleigh and I went our separate ways, I saw no reason to delete her number, and for that I was feeling glad at that moment.

I knocked up a truncated version of the email – short enough to be a text message without losing too much meaning, information or sentiment. I arrived at this:

Hi K! It's Will. Sorry to text you but got some bad news. I'm dying of cancer. Just wanted to let you know.

Beep! Her response was amazingly swift – ah, the speedy thumb action of the young! *Hi. No way. Sorry. Y U tellin me?*

Would like to see you again to say goodbye. Please.

Beep! OK. When?

Can I get back to you in a few days' time? Just got a few things on at mo.

*Beep. **OK. TTFN. Sorry.***

And as simply, painlessly and inarticulately as that, I had my fourth date sorted in principle. Donna, however, was not going to prove such a straightforward catch.

Sometime after our final date, I had decided I really didn't want to cross paths with Donna again. Not that it had ended badly – not that it had officially ended at all. Our ill-matched overly-long fling had run its course – so I just stopped seeing her and stopped ringing or texting her. She did the same. It seemed to be a mutual arrangement. Perhaps she never noticed we had split up – she was a terribly self-obsessed woman. She was also not the sharpest tool in the shed – perhaps she thought we were still together or something! I never imagined for one minute I would ever have any to speak to her again (or any desire to do so for that matter), so eventually I deleted her number. Unusual behaviour for me – 'never say never' is my motto, and usually I found I couldn't rule out reuniting with an ex at some point. In this case – wrongly – I could.

So how to get in touch with someone whose address you have but to whom you don't actually want to speak? How about a good old-fashioned letter dropped through the letterbox? I clearly thought so little of Donna that I simply copied and pasted that trusty old email onto a Word document adding only her name and a sentence at the end reminding her what my phone number was. Yes, even handwriting a few simple sentences seemed like a chore. I'd say that I did it because I was against the clock – but then I had managed to find the time to watch the first five episodes of Season Two of my *24* box set before Helen had got in touch last night. I just couldn't be bothered – let's be honest.

It took about fifteen minutes to get to what was I presumed to be her house. So desperate was I not to get a face-to-face rejection from someone I really hadn't been that interested in when we were going out that I parked my car as far away from her house as I could whilst still being able to watch it for signs of life. It was a spot of casual stalking I suppose. I figured I would give it an hour – and if in that time none of the lights came on and no one came in or out of the house, I would go in for the kill. I'd hotfoot it to the door, post the letter and hotfoot it back to my car. In and out in less than a minute (and remind me never to use THAT sentence fragment in conversation with Helen).

I didn't want to drain the battery in my car, so I turned the engine off completely. This meant I didn't have the radio to keep me amused, and clearly I couldn't whip out a Sudoku or some such because blink and I could have missed a small sign of life in the house. This in turn gave me lots of thinking time. I decided that if I had a stamp in my wallet, I would stick it on the envelope and write her full address. I did, so I did. I tried my best to write without looking down at the envelope, meaning it ended up a bit wonky and harder to discern than even my usual standards. My thinking behind the stamp was that whilst snail mail had a kind of old-fashioned sincerity, it wouldn't seem like I'd made the effort of actually driving up to where she lived – I didn't want to seem desperate or anything, because I definitely wasn't, not while I still had a few exes to contact. All of which made me wonder to myself why I was even bothering to track her down in the first place. I held the envelope in my hand.

My next thought was – *what if her boyfriend is here?* What if, as I was midway through posting it and legging it back to the car, he opened the door? It's not that I would care one iota that she actually had a boyfriend, but how would I explain why someone who was very clearly not a postman was posting a stamped envelope through their door? How would I even explain that if Donna herself answered? Maybe the stamp thing wasn't such a good idea after all. I could still take it out of the envelope and post the folded sheet. I ate up a good five or ten minutes debating the stamp issue but decided eventually to stick with it. So to speak. Then I got to thinking about whether this was still actually Donna's house. I last saw her four years ago – so probably so, but maybe not. She could be living elsewhere and this whole thing could be an act of futility. Maybe the kindly new residents would forward it onto her new address? Maybe they wouldn't. I had to ask myself if I would really be bothered if she never read the letter and the honest answer was no. I was just filling up the numbers really.

The hour eventually elapsed, feeling much more like five when it eventually did so. I started my engine, got out of the car and posted the letter with as fine a balance of discretion and speediness as I could manage and returned to my car without Donna or her hypothetical boyfriend catching me. I drove away without my seatbelt on, buckling up only when I reached the stop sign at the end of Donna's street.

It was the middle of the afternoon when I got back home. I chucked my keys down on the table and before I even sat down I checked my phone to see if Donna had texted – she hadn't. I wasn't prepared to give her the same 48 hour deadline allotted to previous exes – this would be a strictly first-come-first-served situation from now on. So I decided to give bestdaysofyourlife.com another spin – try the uni girls this time. It might have meant travelling a bit further afield during The Week, but so be it. I didn't bother searching for Elodie's name for previously stated reasons. I typed in Narinder's name to start with (she being the highest ranking of the university bunch) – and a mouse click later, there she was! Her profile picture suggested that she still deserved that 8 for looks (presuming she hadn't gone for head shot rather than full body shot to focus on the former and hide the latter). I sent her the standard issue message. Patty was next in the rankings – there were four of them, but one was definitely her! Same message. A search for Rachael's name was fruitless. That just left Samantha. To call her a bit of an ugly duckling would be hugely unfair, both on her and on me – as if I would stoop so low! But in comparison to the other women on the list, she kind of was. Still – a long time had passed! Maybe that ugly duckling had turned into a beautiful swan! Maybe it was like one of those awful teen movies where the geeky girl in the glasses gets transformed into the prom queen! I did manage to find her on the site. Still a 3. Her profile picture was her and what looked like either her husband or boyfriend. I had to mull over whether I really wanted to meet up with her again, eventually deciding that it would be preferable to being one date short of reaching my full quota for The Week. Same message.

I checked my phone – a needless action since I had it right next to me and would have heard if I had a text or phonecall.

I checked the computer screen.

I checked my phone.

I checked the computer screen. Something happen, dammit!

When I eventually conceded that nothing was happening, I returned to the adrenalin-fuelled distractions provided by Mr Jack Bauer, finding myself nine hours into his second adventure when my phone beeped. I hit pause. It was a number rather than a name on my screen – this had to be Donna.

It was.

Hiya babes! Just got in from work and seen your letter. You poor thing. Text me and we'll meet up x

Erm...result? I wasn't exactly cartwheeling around my living room, but I did at least have another rendezvous sorted – I was up to five now! I felt inclined to check bestdaysofyourlife.com before I got back to *24* – but still no messages, and neither were there any when I eventually trundled off to bed, my eyes square and bloodshot. I'd spent altogether too much time staring at screens today, and I'd consumed episodes of *24* like a greedy kid gorging on his Easter chocolate, continuing long after he felt full.

Saturday, 9th July, 2005

So of course the first thing I did when I awoke was turn on my computer screen.

Samantha had messaged. I would have preferred to see Narinder or Patty's name on there, but beggars can't be choosers.

Hello there, stranger! Oh my God, what terrible news. I'm really sorry. I'd love to stay in touch with you – can we keep it to online messages? I live in Newquay now and it would be a heck of a journey for either of us to make, even if we met somewhere in the middle. The other thing is – I'm a lesbian!

Stop the press! What?!

I think when I was with you I sort of must have known deep down. After we split up, I started getting friendly with this girl from my Sociology class and – one thing led to another.

Into which I read – *I was teetering on the brink of lesbianism when I was with you but you finally unwittingly pushed me into it.*

My other half would be a bit funny about me meeting up with you, I know she would. So if I did meet up with you, I'm afraid she'd probably have to tag along!

I looked again at Samantha's profile picture. That wasn't her boyfriend or husband at all. If someone had told me one of my exes was going to tell me she was a lesbian and effectively offer to bring along her partner when we met up, I would have thought all my remaining Christmases had come at once. But looking at the picture in front of me – one of my least attractive exes and a burly spiky-haired woman who looked like she could kick the crap out of me if she so desired – it didn't seem that much of a turn on at all.

I hope we can be friends! Stay strong.

Sammy

Delete.

A couple of hours later, Narinder messaged. Now this was more like it. I had a good feeling about this one.

Hi Will. Lovely to hear from you. Listen, not sure if what you're telling me is genuine or not. God, if it is, I'm so, so sorry. But the thing is, I'm eight and a half months pregnant; really I'm due any time now. So I can't really meet up with you. In like six months time or something, yeah, maybe, if what you're saying is for real. Can you do that?

Narinder

Once again I hit delete - and yes, computer, I WAS sure. Stop asking me that.

My options were starting to run seriously low. The week I had pencilled in was fast approaching – I was supposed to be starting on Monday, for crying out loud - and I still only had five dates. I mean, it would still be a really nice experience – right? Meeting up with those five exes would be lovely – yes? It just wouldn't be the plan.

I couldn't throw in the towel. Should I do it? Should I sink that low? Scrape that barrel? Clearly I had no choice.

I was going to have to try Suzie.

I didn't have her email address but what I did have was her phone number, even though anyone with even an ounce of good sense and the tiniest morsel of good judgement would have deleted it. And changed phone numbers. And emigrated.

I considered dropping her the same text I had sent to Kayleigh, but instinct told me I needed to be a bit more tentative.

Hi Suzie! It's Will! Just texting to see if you still use this number. I have something to tell you.

I had a seriously bad feeling in my stomach. My hands were clammy and shaky. *Beep.* I got a text back about five minutes later, by which time I was a sweaty, quivering wreck. Her reply was this:

Will Gordon, Will Pickering or Will Jacobs?

There we go. Not the only Will that had passed in and (for good reason) out of her orbit. I was either top billing or bottom. I couldn't even claim she was alphabetising.

Will Jacobs.

Beep. Thought I'd heard the last of you. What do you want?

I have cancer. It's terminal. I wanted to meet up with you one last time.

Then - a long pause. A really long pause. At least five minutes. Seemed longer.

Beep. Oh God. Is this real? Is someone having me on here? Is this even Will?

Yes, no and yes.

*Beep. **In that case, I'm ringing you.***

My turn to take the Lord's name in vain. My phone did, indeed, start ringing. I wasn't ready for this just yet! All those memories - those awful, awful memories - came rushing back, memories of a woman I'd lamented meeting and worked hard to flush out of my life. I should just ignore it. Just throw the phone out of the window and run away.

'Hi Suzie!'

'Will. It IS you. God. I'm so, so sorry. How are you? No, no , no – silly Suzie. He's just told you he's dying.'

'Erm – don't worry. I'm fine at the moment.'

'Oh that's so good to hear! Yes, yes of course I'd like to meet up with you. When?'

I realised that, as Suzie was first in the queue, she'd get first pick of which of the seven days we'd meet up on. Now what did I want to do here? Build up to it and sway her towards the final day, the Sunday? Or get it over and done with - the first day, Monday? Think fast, fella!

'Are you free on Smunday?'

Idiot.

'I'm sorry?'

'I meant Monday.'

'I can't I'm afraid. I'm working 12 til 8. Got Tuesday off, though!'

It would have to do. 'Perfect! Do you want to come round to mine at say, ten in the morning?'

'Will - you should know I've got a boyfriend.'

A boyfriend! Hallelujah, praise The Lord! This was seriously good news. It meant there was no chance of her going all psycho on me, falling for me again and gate crashing back into my life.

'Oh no, it's honestly not like that! I just want to meet up as friends, say my goodbyes.'

'Fair enough, but I still feel a bit weird about meeting you in your flat. I think we need to meet on more neutral territory. It's not that I don't trust you; I just think I'd feel a bit more comfortable that way. How about we meet in town? Just by the library. Then maybe go for a Nando's or something and see how the day plays out.'

Why was she making ME seem like the nut job? This was rich. I did like Nando's, though.

'Right you are. Noon?'

'Okay. I'm so sorry, Will.'

'It's fine! Bye for now.'

Sweet Lord above, what had I done? I had nudged one date closer to a full week, but at what cost?

My train of thought was derailed by a knock. I opened the door and there they were, Daniel and Danielle, hand-in-hand and grinning the same inane grin - same as each other and same as always. Matching beige chunky knitted jumpers - how charming. My next door neighbours round for their usual semi-regular visit, uninvited but never unexpected.

Okay, so the above description was for illustrative purposes only - the only true bits are that they ARE my next door neighbours and they DO pop round quite a lot. I just wanted you to see them how I see them. Their names are in fact the distinctly non-alliterative Pete and Georgina. And yes, all right, they didn't turn up holding hands, but you do sometimes see them holding hands, or linking arms, or his arm around her shoulder, or hands on each other's knees, far too regularly for such an established couple. They do smile a lot, but admittedly not always at the same time. They don't wear the same clothes as each other, but they do both shop at Next and seemingly nowhere else ever. They're happily married - that's the adverb they use, anyway. I'd plump for smugly married. They are the model couple and boy don't they let us know it - childhood sweethearts who've stayed the course, who've either resisted temptations or never had them put their way. Never had so much as a squabble is what they'll have you believe - and if you met them, you WOULD believe it. They're sickeningly, annoyingly perfect together. They're devout Christians who, I believe, seem to feel it their godly duty to pop round my flat every now and then to check that I'm okay - their reward being that they get to flaunt their harmonious longevity, to rub it in my face that they've found true love and I haven't. They've been told to 'love thy neighbour' and they're flippin' well sticking to it. They upped the frequency of their visits when they found out about the cancer - before I was the loner, now I was the dying loner, so they got double Good Samaritan points.

Georgina, not for the first time, greeted me with head tilted and a sympathetic smile. She also had a cake tin in her hand, so I let it slide. 'How ya doin', Will? Ya doin' okay?'

I hadn't answered before Peter had thrust his hand into mine and started pumping it as we hadn't seen each other for years rather than six days.

'How ya doin', buddy? Ya doin' well?'

I didn't make up the near-identical greetings. That bit really happened. I didn't feel like seeing the two of them one bit, but I did have an eye on those cakes - Georgina's baking is as consistently and predictably perfect as her marriage, and it was worth a cup of tea's worth of inane chit-chat to have a sample.

'Oh you know...do you want to come in?'

They nodded, Georgina maintaining her sympathetic smile throughout. I'll wager that you're wondering if I've got, or have ever had, designs on Georgina. I think by now you've probably gleaned my fondness for Carroll diagrams, and I'm going to use one here to show how I have always perceived Georgina.

	Sexy	*Not sexy*
Attractive	Section 1	Section 3
Not attractive	Section 2	Section 4

Section 1 - attractive and sexy. Most women that are one are the other, and I'm happy to report that most of the women you have read or will be reading about in this story fall into this category.

Section 2 - not attractive, but sexy. It's rare, but it's possible. Occasionally I have met women who fall shy of my usual standards and yet there's just something about them. A certain confidence. Something about their personality - be it sense of humour, sense of mystery, SOMETHING - transcends their looks and I find myself intrinsically drawn to them.

Section 3 - not attractive, not sexy. Again, they usually go hand-in-hand. I've never been with anyone like this - and why would I?

Section 4 - and it's here you'll find my God-bothering friend from down the hall - attractive but not sexy. She's attractive in a sterile, anodyne sort of way. No physical flaws whatsoever and yet nothing about her ever set my pulse racing. Nothing about her suggested that behind her Good Girl Christian facade there was an uninhibited hellcat waiting to be unleashed. She was just...nice.

I told them all about my plan. They kept giving each other slightly worried looks – whether they were worried for me or for the women I was meeting I couldn't quite ascertain. However, they seemed to like the idea of me absolving my sins. I explained to them that, whilst I didn't wish to be rude (and now that I had eaten Georgina's cakes) I would have to continue with my quest, because my time was growing short. They said they'd pray for me – lucky really because with just Patty left to reply, Elodie most likely in another country and me having no clue how to contact Rachael, I was beginning to think I didn't have a prayer.

I walked around. I gazed out of the window. I drummed my fingers. I buried my head in my hands. Anything to stimulate the ideas process. Just how on Earth was I going to fill that one remaining space? Should I relax the rules a bit – try to dig out someone who didn't last the full month? I racked my brains, but the only ones I could think of were ones whose surnames I couldn't recall – so they were breaking two rules, and Lord only knows how I'd go about finding them.

Come on Patty! I'm on my knees here!

I was starting to feel like I had no choice - with The Week fast approaching, it was time to actually make some plans. I would have to keep hoping something – someone – would turn up during the week so that I could complete my challenge.

My first step was to email those women whose mobile numbers I did not have asking if I could have them and also offering them mine. It was set to be an action-packed week, and I might not always have time to be checking my emails, so from now on it was to be texts and phone calls all the way.

It dawned on me as I lay in bed that I had invested so much time and energy into locating these women, I hadn't actually thought about what I would do when I did meet up with them. Maybe they would have some ideas – if not I'd better get my thinking cap on. I was just drifting off into sweet slumber when the house phone awoke me. Most people would panic getting a phone call at this ungodly hour – not me. I knew it had to be Helen. I raced over to the phone.

H: *How's you?*

W: *Oh not too bad. How come you're up at silly o'clock? I presume Jeff's keeping you up again.*

H: *You presume correctly, old pal. He can't seem to keep his feet to himself tonight. Bloody Kicky Martin. The consequence of which is he's currently Livin' La Vida Sofa. I'm now wide awake and bored. Entertain me, bitch. Tell me about this wacky plan of yours. Have you found any more victims yet?*

W: *As a matter of fact, I've got all but one in the bag now!*

H: *Get in there my son! Back of the net! And all the other things your best friend would say to you if said best friend was in fact a bloke as per normal convention.*

W: *You do just fine, don't you worry about that.*

H: *Go on then, reel 'em off. Let's see which ones I can recall.*

W: Mandy.

H: Randy Mandy?

W: Bingo.

H: Randy Mandy, eh? Pray tell, young Mr Jacobs. What was it that drew you to this young siren? Her witty repartee? Her immaculate taste in classic literature? Randy Mandy. The clue's really in the nickname, isn't it? You're as deep as a puddle, Willy Wanker, and twice as mucky to boot. Who else?

W: Maria.

H: Five Beers Maria? Isn't that what you said you needed to find her attractive?

W: That's a different Maria. This one's Maria Jenkins. I went out with her about ten years ago. She's nice.

H: Hmm. Not ringing any bells. The nice ones are boring to me. Next.

W: Harriet.

H: Harriet...Harrison, was it?

W: Close. Harriet Hamilton. She came along before you did. Teenage romance.

H: Yeah, I remember you telling me about her when we first met. You told me your whole bloody life story that night. I seem to remember she was a good one. Keep going.

W: Kayleigh.

H: Drawing a blank here. Kayleigh, Kayleigh.

W: Yeah, she was definitely one of the more forgettable ones. I met her during my forays into speed dating. Then there's Donna.

H: Oh, you've got to be kidding? Not that brain-dead Barbie doll you were dating about four years ago?

W: The very same! You approve then, clearly. If you thought that was bad you'd better hang up now.

H: William Jacobs, you had better not be about to tell me what I think you're about to tell me. You didn't...

W: Yep.

H: ...get in touch with...

W: Yep.

H: SUZIE?!

W: Erm, yep.

H: Jesus H. Corbett. For a clever fella, you don't learn very fast. I'll make sure I've stocked up on popcorn that day, because boy you're gonna have some stories for me! So you're still on the hunt for the final piece of your jigsaw? The seventh one?

W: Yeah. I've not given up hope quite yet, but the dates are supposed to start on Monday. Wish me luck.

H: Good luck, love. Take care.

Sunday, 10th July, 2005

It was the eve of the Week. Much like Christmas Eve, there was a definite sense of excitement in my apartment.

By lunchtime, I had the complete set of mobile phone numbers. I knocked up another generic message: a rather long text, which, once again, I copied and pasted and personalised a little before sending it to each of my dates.

Hello again, x! Really looking forward to seeing you. So what do you fancy doing? If you like, you can leave it up to me (I've got lots of time on my hands to mull it over!). I've not got anything in mind yet, so if there's something you'd particularly like to do, you just name it. If you like, we can play it by ear and just decide on the day. And if you'd like to just come round to my flat and hang out, that sounds like a pretty good day to me. Let me know. Will x

The replies had all arrived within about six hours, which I'll present here not in the order they were sent, but rather the order I would be meeting up with the senders. On the whole the five remaining ladies were highly flexible and accommodating, and it was with much less fuss and hassle than I had expected that I managed to sort out the following:

MONDAY

How about you leave it to me, sweetie? I've had an idea. I think you'll like it. You just be ready on time as it's gonna be a busy day. See you then. Maria X

TUESDAY

That one was already sorted. Nando's. Noon. Suzie. Petrifying.

WEDNESDAY

Hi Will! Really, really looking forward to seeing you. You know, a day just hanging out at your place, chilling and chatting, sounds just perfect to me. See you Wednesday then! Harriet.

Harriet, as you'll soon find out, was a great big liar.

THURSDAY

Still up for grabs.

FRIDAY

I've got something AMAZING in mind! Gonna surprise you. Kayleigh x

SATURDAY

Oh, I'll think of something, chick. I'll come and pick you up, not too early - it's Saturday after all and a girl needs her beauty sleep at the weekends! BFN. Donna X

SUNDAY

Hiya Will. I'll come to your place. I'll aim for about half ten. I've moved to a place just outside Melton Mowbray, so I might be a bit late - I'll have a couple of bits and bobs to take care of as well. Don't ask. We'll go out for a coffee, have a walk in the park, catch up. Sound good? Mandy

And to all of these, I sent the generic reply: *Sounds great!*

My excitement was not to last. It was Sunday night. The Week was upon me, and I had to face facts - I'd failed. Failed to find a date for each of the days. Failed to find the Magnificent Seven. Yes, I could and would still meet up with the other six - but the incompleteness of it all would bug me, would leave me feeling somewhat unsatisfied. I checked my emails one final time, just in the off chance Patty had responded. Or maybe one of those women who had rejected me had had a sudden change of heart, a crisis of conscience, something like that. I held no real hope...and I was right to. There was no eleventh hour message from any of the potential dates. I shut the computer down and slumped in my chair.

Then it dawned on me. There was, of course, one other person who hadn't said no - she just hadn't said yes, that's all. It was Rhonda. That's who I would spend Thursday with. The day could be devoted to her memory. I wasn't sure exactly how or what I'd do, but I'd think of something. Sorted! I'd found my Magnificent Seven after all!

I opened a celebratory bottle of beer, the dual function of which was to make me sleepy, to stop the buzzing feeling I had. Part way through, that familiar beep I seemed to have heard a thousand times today let me know I had a text message. It was from Harriet, who was clearly suffering from some jitters.

Will, are you sure about all this? It's a bit weird lol. You're not gonna stand me up are you?

I texted back a reassuring message of confirmation and no sooner had I fired it off than I heard the beep again. This time, though, it was tomorrow's date, Maria, whose name was coming up on my phone. My first instinct was that she was cancelling on me, which would have been a less-than-perfect start to the week. Fortunately, she was merely confirming our plans:

C U at 10. Be ready! x

I mulled over the meaning (or otherwise) of the kiss at the end. I have long-since been fascinated by the notion of kisses at the end of letters, notes, text messages and emails: they're a funny old thing when you think about it. Imagine a world where, if you were speaking those messages out loud and face-to-face with the recipient, you ACTUALLY gave them a kiss.

'Gonna be a bit late for our dinner reservation later.' Kiss.

'Okay, no worries. What time do you think you'll be there?' Kiss.

'Eight at the latest.' Kiss.

How weird would that be? Answer - not as weird as if you were enacting messages that end with more than one kiss. Re-read the above conversation with three actual kisses at the end of each exchange.

It's not the only mystifying thing about message kisses - I would really like to know how come the letter x in particular has come to be the universally accepted shorthand for a kiss. If anything your lips are o-shaped when you kiss - why not that? Or maybe the letter k - k for kiss! This latter option does, admittedly, bring forth the problem of how you would represent three kisses - that particular trio of letters of course already being in use elsewhere. But why x, for Christ's sake? It's already the go-to choice for algebraic notation, as well as marking the spot! There has to be a more deserving letter?

Strange creatures though they are, text kisses can be a useful barometer, and over the years I have become quite the student of their implications. No kisses at all is, more often than not, a sign that she's not interested. Either that or she's going to make you work hard, going to play ultra-hard to get, and I personally have never felt inclined to do too much chasing. So a few no-kiss texts in a row and I usually throw in the towel. Of course, a no-kiss text could mean she's mad with you, in which case you've got a judgement call to make. Is what you've done bad enough to warrant this cold shoulder? If so, make amends. If not get the hell out of there - it doesn't bode well for the future now does it? Do you want to spend the rest of your life in and out of the dog house?

One kiss is the norm for brand new couples or potential couples. It's an amber light, a cautious declaration of interest. In most instances I've left it at one until she herself has upped it to two, because in those early days it's all about power struggles and who's got the upper hand - an often fatal error is to seem slightly keener than the other party. Women REALLY don't respond well to that. This might lead to a one-kiss stalemate if she's playing the same game, but so be it. Do not surrender your advantage. If you're a more established couple and you receive a one-kisser out of the blue, this might be a subtle hint that you're skating on thin ice and need to sort yourself out pronto, before a full-blown argument descends.

Two kisses is about the standard for a new relationship with a bit of potential. I like the two kiss phase. Things are still fresh and exciting, yet some of those early insecurities have started to drop off. I could very happily give and receive two kiss texts up to the twelve month mark. After that it's time to piss or get off the pot - either start three kiss messages or start looking at other avenues.

Three kisses and you're a keeper. It's love. You're the horse she's backing. Which is fine if the feeling is mutual. If it isn't, drop your own kisses down to two per text, and she'll soon reciprocate. When you're both established three kiss types, consistency is crucial - any less than three kisses on any message you ever send her and she's going to want answers.

Four kisses is just a bit too keen, isn't it? In my whole life I've never exceeded three kisses per text. Alarm bells would be ringing by this point in my head (and wedding bells in hers). Four kisses and I would feel smothered. It's not Game Over by any stretch, but you'd have to be worried.

Five kisses or more means she's clearly a bit crazy and / or one of those over-excitable types who WRITES LOTS OF THINGS IN CAPITALS AND ENDS SENTENCES WITH SEVERAL EXCLAMATION MARKS!!!! SUZIE USED TO DO THAT!!!! STAY AWAY!!!!

After much consideration, I took Maria's single kiss as a mark of friendliness – a symbol of respect for our former relationship and a sign that she still held some affection for me.

I slept lightly that night, finding myself in that strange place halfway between definitely being asleep and definitely being awake. My mind was racing with all the possibilities that lay ahead over the next seven days and nights. I explored every avenue, every possibility, treating it as a spectrum which went from this being the best idea I'd ever had to, as Helen prophesied, the worst. I imagined the best to start with - I imagined tearful, whispered goodbyes, which were redemptive even if that wasn't what I was looking for as such. *You've changed, Will*, they'd all tell me. Every day would be filled with sunshine, literal and metaphorical. *I'm so glad we did this*, they'd all say. We'd take glorious trips down memory lane. We'd create a kind of post-script to our relationships - a beautiful final memory for each of the six to remember me by. Then, eventually, I arrived at the opposite end of the spectrum. I imagined tearful goodbyes of a very different kind - tears of anger, screamed goodbyes. *You haven't changed, Will*, they'd tell me, and not affectionately. The days would be rainy and miserable. *I wish we'd never done this*, they'd all say. Memory Lane would be a menacing and hostile place, not safe to walk down. The post-scripts would be unfortunate ones, undoing any nice memories formed back in the day. They'd hate me. Each and every one of them.

These thoughts ended up being so alarming that at 2 am I was wide awake. To tire my eyes I thought I'd do a bit of net surfing. As I'm now preconditioned to do, I began by checking my emails. I wasn't expecting any correspondence relating to The Week - after all, I'd only looked four hours ago. Who else would still be up and emailing at this hour?

The good folks at bestdaysofyourlife.com, that's who. They were notifying me that I had received a message from Patty Bronson, my old university girlfriend. This was it:

Hiya Will! It's Patty. Thanks for getting in touch! Listen, I'm sorry about this late response. I've just got back from a holiday in the Canaries. Literally, like an hour ago. I switched my computer on and saw your message and basically just dropped everything. So - cancer. I don't know what to say. I'm sorry.

I'd love to meet you, for old times' sake. Yes, yes, yes. Let's do this ASAP, okay? I live in Bristol now, but I'd be more than happy to come up to you if you want.

All my love,

Patty

X

Bugger.

I'd gone from being a date short of the full week to a date too many. I had really, really wanted Patty to get in touch – and now that she had done so, I realised I would much prefer to spend a day with her rather than Donna or Kayleigh. So I could just blow one of them off, right? How would that text message go?

Sorry to break this to you, but I won't be needing to meet up with you anymore. What I neglected to tell you before was that you were in fact part of a sequence of women I was planning to see over the course of a week. Someone I like a bit more has got in touch, and now you're no longer one of the seven ex-girlfriends I would like to see. See you in the next life if such a thing exists. Will.

I could lie to one of them, of course. I could lie my arse off. Not like I haven't done it before. I could tell them I had an emergency doctor's appointment or something. But wouldn't that defeat the object of this whole exercise? I was supposed to be showing these women how much I'd changed and grown, how in my dying days I was gentler, more noble. I was supposed to be showing MYSELF that. I couldn't break what was essentially a promise. Of course, there was one woman I hadn't actually promised as such - Rhonda. Something just didn't sit right about cancelling that day, though. Rhonda was a good woman: she deserved more than that. I messed her about enough when she was alive. This left me only one viable option - ignore Patty's message, as well as any subsequent messages from her. Play dead, I suppose. Not exactly that honourable, but it was the best I could make of the situation. I slept well enough afterwards, put it that way.

Monday, 11th July, 2005

It was here! The week - The Week - had begun. I felt a little groggy from my truncated sleep, but a quick shower and shave and two slaps of Joop eau de toilette and I started to feel a little more presentable.

I opened my wardrobe and quickly realised I had a small task to tend to before I got started with The Week; my clothes. I would treat each day as a date, and dress accordingly smartly. It was set to be a frantic seven days, with - if all went to plan - little or no respite or down time. This meant I would have no time to do any washing or ironing. Not a problem in and of itself - I had lots of nice shirts, and with the abundance of free time I've got, I manage to keep right on top of my laundry. No, the issue was deciding which shirt to wear on which day. It wasn't like I could keep washing, drying and ironing my favourite one.

Job one, then, was to pick out my Top Seven going out shirts. My wardrobe was already organised into categories, so that saved a bit of time. I had a 'T-shirts' section. I had what I anachronistically still called my 'Work Shirts' section. I had my 'Wedding Shirts' section - an umbrella term covering more formal family-and-friends type occasions, like Christenings. And I had my 'Going Out Shirts' section, sub-divided into short sleeves and long-sleeves. Though it was summer, I was going to stick to the long sleeved options, which I felt were a little smarter on the whole. I took them all out and laid them across my bed, wondering why it hadn't crossed my mind before to organise each sub-section of the wardrobe by preference. After minimal deliberation, I managed to pick out my favourite shirt - who doesn't have one of those? Almost as quickly I managed to discard my least favourite. This struck me as a decent selection process, so I continued - next best, next worst, next best, next worst, until I had managed to find my seven best long-sleeved shirts.

That was the easy part - job two was to allocate one to each date. What this essentially forced me to do was rank the women involved from favourite to least favourite, just as I had with the shirts. Using the points system from my original table, that list was as follows:

1. Rhonda (17)
2. Maria (16) / Harriet (16)
3. Mandy (15.5)
4. Suzie (13)
5. Kayleigh (12.5)
6. Donna (11)

Well, you can see one problem right there. Maria and Harriet were tied. I was going to have to choose between them. Harriet had scored higher on looks – 8 against 7 – but Maria had scored higher on personality – 9 against 8. Maybe Harriet had the slight edge because it had been longer since I last saw her. Or maybe, for that reason, Maria had the slight edge – she was more likely to have held onto her looks and still be a 7. Maria or Harriet? Harriet or Maria? Maybe longevity was going to have to be a factor. I was with Maria for two months longer than I was with Harriet, so she won on that count. Aargh. Too many factors in play. I think Her Majesty was going to have to step in. Heads it was Harriet. Tails it was Maria.

Heads.

Just one quick adjustment to make before I compiled the final version of the list. I was going to bump Rhonda down from first to last. The harsh truth was that she was dead, and would be the least appreciative of a nice shirt. The list was now as follows:

1. Harriet
2. Maria
3. Mandy
4. Suzie
5. Kayleigh
6. Donna
7. Rhonda

And so - I threw on my second favourite shirt and a pair of jeans that went well with it and I was good to go.

Half an hour later, I was still good to go. Despite her 'Be ready!' warning, Maria was late and the thinking time had not been a good thing. My nerves had kicked in and then multiplied like germs. I felt more nervous now, I was sure, than I was before my real first date with Maria. More nervous than I felt before ANY date I could remember. That thought triggered off reminiscences of our relationship, which I pictured in my mind as a line graph. Specifically, this line graph:

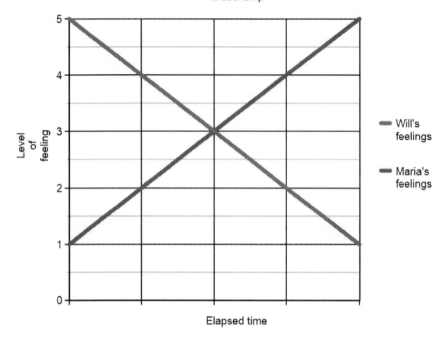

Graph showing the feelings of Will and Maria over the course of their relationship

- Will's feelings
- Maria's feelings

Level of feeling (y-axis)

Elapsed time (x-axis)

Clearly the graph is hugely over-simplified – there were good days in bad periods, bad days in good ones, little wobbles here and there – but it nicely represents the general trend of those four months. As you can see from the graph, when we first met – she was a Newly Qualified Teacher in the English Department at my school and I was the helpful, ever-so-slightly flirtatious colleague from the other side of the wing who soon managed to talk her out of her on-off boyfriend – I was smitten. Totally smitten. I asked her out. She, however, was a little sceptical at first, and I think she really just needed a friend. We'd have been good friends, I think. We had common ground and she was sweet-natured. But I wanted more than that: much, much more. With just the right measure of persistence, that's exactly what I got. We started dating. Just four months later – and if you look back at the graph, you'll see this – my feelings for her had all but dried up, and yet by this point she was hearing wedding bells. All I was hearing was tinnitus from the constant half-jokes *about* wedding bells.

By the end of our relationship, I was like one of Pavlov's Dogs; she would say 'I love you' and I'd say it right back immediately, perfectly conditioned. It was a pretty sorry state of affairs, really, although I imagine there are millions of couples living exactly like this. But look once more at the graph – look at where the two lines intersect. For a small period right there, I managed to find a small moment of mutual harmony. It was fleeting, but for a while we were just perfectly balanced; we loved each other seemingly equally. We seemed settled yet still a bit giddy.

So what went wrong? You know how when people break up with someone and get with someone more suited to them, they often say they didn't realise they were unhappy with their ex, but now they're much happier? Well, that's part of my trouble. Mathematically speaking, unless someone is 100% suited to me - in looks, interests, age, friends, geographical location, the whole shebang - then there's always potentially someone better out there. I've spent my adult life searching for my 100%-er. And I'm afraid that means I've discarded a few 90%-ers - women I should have been grateful to have found. I'm the sort of person who would throw away a perfectly good pair of shoes just because one of them needed a new insole. Happy, lifelong unions have probably been founded on less than what I've got rid of many times over. Falling into this category would definitely be Maria. I WAS happy with her. I DID fancy her. We DID have lots in common. Trouble was, I could never shake the niggly feeling that I could have been that bit happier with someone else; that I might fancy someone else that little bit more; that there might be someone out there with whom I shared even more common ground. That's when things started going downhill for me. I figured - *you only get one life* (and I didn't even realise how short that one life would be). So instead of ending my search, as any normal person would have, I split up with her and kept looking. She left the school at the first opportunity and that was the end of the story.

Five firm knocks, quick in succession and equidistant to each other, brought me back to 2005 with a jolt. It was a set of knocks that said 'I mean business'. And indeed she did.

'Maria! Wow, it's lovely to...'

'No time! Grab your stuff and let's go!'

Hmm. This wasn't the Maria I had remembered. The Maria I had remembered was a bit of an ambler. A bit laissez-faire.

'Go where?'

'The pub!'

'It's 10 a.m. on a Monday morning!'

'Exactly! If you've ever seen those old men who sit there all day in Wetherspoons, you'll know we've got some catching up to do! Or if you want to be a spoil sport, you could just have a coffee! Either way, I want you in,' she peered around her before finally spying her prey. '*That* pub in ten minutes! Not nine, not eleven. Ten minutes! Got it?'

I loved the mathematical precision! I smiled at her. 'Whoa! I'm dying, but not today, you know! I'm not in that much of a hurry! What's all this about?'

She placed her hands on my upper arms. It looked as much like she was shaking sense into me as comforting me. 'What this is all about is starting our relationship again, but this time doing it better. Doing it properly. Don't worry, I know you're not looking for anything like that, and we WILL split up at the end of it. You and I - we're going to have a Relationship in a Day. Just like a ship in a bottle - it's going to be a beautiful, miniature version of the real thing. That way, when I remember you, it will be with fondness. I won't think, Will Jacobs, what a wanker.'

Before I could respond, she had released her grip and disappeared towards the pub.

Obligingly, I followed precisely ten minutes after. This was my local pub, but not once had I set foot in it, and it was easy to see why. It was dark and dank and dated, with a dartboard in one corner and, as predicted by Maria, a group of pensioners in another corner, partway through their pints of Guinness. Sitting together but not actually interacting with one another. For a brief moment I felt thankful I wasn't going to make it to old age. Maria was perched on a bar stool. She had plumped for the coffee. I felt sure she must have heard me come in, but she hadn't acknowledged me. I knew the game we were about to play. And it wasn't dominoes.

The barman - saggy-faced and surly - nodded at me, which I could see was the closest I was going to get to friendly customer service.

'Cappuccino, please.'

He narrowed his eyes. 'Coffee it is.'

I tried to catch Maria's gaze. When I eventually did so, we shared a reciprocal smile, whereupon she raised her eyebrows and returned to her newspaper. She was playing hard to get. And I, as ever, was falling for it. The coffee arrived shortly after, without froth and with a tiny bit of what looked like lipstick still on the rim. I didn't complain. I didn't drink it either.

It was time for a well-chosen chat-up line.

Top Tip Number Two: Carry a bank of chat up lines. Could be a pocket-sized notebook. Could be a scrap of paper. Could be stored on your phone. The key is to have a good variety, as you will hopefully see in a second.

In the following matrix, I have charted, as best as I can remember, the success or otherwise of various chat up lines I have used in the past, dated and slightly sexist though some of them now seem. Each has been assigned a fairly simple and self-explanatory star-rating to illustrate its effectiveness (again, or otherwise). The chart clearly demonstrates that the ideal chat up line borrows from the fourth and fifth quintiles of humour and the third quintile of flattery. Why only third? Fourth quintile flattery comes across as rather too keen, and by the time you're in the realms of fifth quintile flattery, the girls just become embarrassed by your compliments. They think you're being insincere.

I have excluded the old classic in which the boy asks the girl if she's got 10p so she can call her mum because, let's face it, it's the mobile phone age. I'm pretty sure she's not going to be too keen if you can't even afford a mobile phone!

Humour rating (5 representing the highest degree of humour)

	1	2	3	4	5
5	Hi! I suffer from amnesia. Do I come here often? ^^^	You: Have I shown you my magic watch? It tells me that you're not wearing any underwear ... Her: Nice try, I am wearing underwear. You: Damn it... it must be an hour fast! ^^^^	You're so beautiful, I want you to have my children. In fact, you can have them right now; they're out in the car. (See Note 9) ^^^	Is your last name Gillette? Because you are the best a man can get! ***	Are you from Tennessee? Because you are the only ten I see! (See Note 16) ***
4	Hello! My surname is Jacobs and, yes, you're right, I'm a cracker? (See Note 1) ^^^	Hello! Is your surname Jacobs? Because I must say, you're an absolute cracker! (See Note 5) ^^^^	Excuse me, madam, I wonder if I could spare a few moments of your time. I'm from Williams and Jacobs Market Research and I'm doing a survey on beautiful women. You fit the bill perfectly. Do you mind if I ask you a few questions? Fantastic. Number one – are you single? Number two – what's your favourite alcoholic beverage? Number three – can I buy one for you right now? Number four – what's your phone number? And finally, number five, are you free on Friday night? (See Note 10) ^^^^^	Excuse me, but I think I dropped something. MY JAW! How unbelievably gorgeous are you? ***	Congratulations! You have just been officially voted the Most Beautiful Girl in This Room and the grand prize is – a night with me! ***
3	I know Jedi mind tricks. Go home with me tonight you will. (See Note 2) ^^	I hope you know CPR, because you take my breath away. (See Note 6) ***	Nice to meet you, I'm Will and you are...gorgeous! (See Note 11) ^^^^	So – what do you do for a living? Or is being indescribably gorgeous, a full-time job? (See Note 14) ^^^	Hi, I'm from the future, and our wedding was amazing. You looked absolutely stunning, but then, that's no great surprise, is it? ***
2	I'm a Maths teacher! Do you fancy going to my room, add the bed, subtract your clothes, divide your legs and multiply? (See Note 3) ^^	Hi! I just saw you looking at me and to answer your question, yes, I'm that interior decorator off the television. I couldn't help but notice your hair and my pillow are perfectly colour coordinated. (See Note 7) ^^	If I could rearrange the alphabet, I'd but U and I together. (See Note 12) ***	Excuse me – can I take your picture so that I can look at the girl of my dreams more than once, or will you go out with me tonight? **	You: Yeah, Nigel, it's definitely her! Sorry to bother you. I bet you get fed up of people asking for your autograph, so I'm just going to offer to buy you a drink instead, and then I'll go, I promise. Wow, a real-life supermodel, in this very bar! Her: Who do you think I am? (or some such) You: You're Tatiana Sorocco! And I must say, your English is impeccable! (See Note 17) ^^
1	Do you believe in love at first sight, or should I walk by again? (See Note 4) ^^	I bet you £10 you'll turn me down if I offer to buy you a drink. (See Note 8) ^^	My mum always used to tell me love at first sight was ridiculous. So would you mind walking out of the room and coming back in again, please? ^^	Louise, hi! It's me, Will! My God, I haven't seen you since school! Wow, you look absolutely amazing these days – what's your secret? (See Note 15) **	Wow. Listen, I honestly never approach women in bars, because I've got a girlfriend and I'm madly in love with her. But you might just be the most exquisitely beautiful woman I have ever laid my eyes on and I just think you deserve to know that. You're just...perfect. (See Note 18) ***
	1	2	3	4	5

Flattery rating (5 representing the highest degree of flattery)

Note 1 - Of course, this one works particularly well for me being as it's my actual surname, but I see no reason why you couldn't use it anyway. How's she to know?

Note 2 - I'm sure you're one step ahead of me when I say this, but please judge the kind of girl you are going to use this on carefully. If she's peroxide blonde, legs up to her armpits and head-to-toe in fake tan, you can be pretty certain she has not seen Star Wars.

Note 3 - Just as in (1,4), when I used to use this one, it was actually true – but you can still use it anyway, surely? For me, though, it had the bonus of me being able to rescue a sinking ship by adding something like: 'God, I'm sorry. That was awful. I really am a Maths teacher, though' – ergo, a conversation has now started.

Note 4 - Careful! A possible response is: 'Yeah, but this time don't stop!'

Note 5 - Yes, that's right, it's the chat-up line in (1,4) rehashed. Again, how's she to know?

Note 6 - Look, I never claimed I invented these! If they work, they work!

Note 7 - Play this one carefully. Leave a small pause after the word 'television'. That may be enough, if she believes you. If you're planning to go down that route, invest ten minutes concocting and rehearsing a mini-biography of your celebrity alter-ego before you go out.

Note 8 - If she spends any more than a few seconds pondering this one, then at best you should consider her a possible one night stand.

Note 9 - This one usually raises a small giggle, but of course the kids part can be off-putting. I realise it's ironic that most men with kids pretend not to have them when out on the pull, whereas I didn't have kids but was pretending to have them.

Note 10 - The beauty of this one is that if you're a bit scared of rejection – and I thought I'd trained myself to be desensitised to that many years ago, but those rejections I got when searching for the Magnificent Seven hurt pretty bad – then question one is a good way for the girl to say no to you without making you feel too bad. For added authenticity, you could even use a pen and a small pocket-sized notebook. I had one leather-bound and embossed with the words 'Williams and Jacobs Market Research', but this level of detail is a bonus and not a necessity.

Note 11 - It's simple, it's not too cheesy, it's nice and quick...it works!

Note 12 - Be careful. This old chestnut has done the rounds so many times that a few common responses have developed, one being: 'Oh really, because if I could rearrange the alphabet, I'd put F and U together'. A lesser-known variant is: 'Can beauty be spelt without U in it?' Just as with (2,1), if her eyes move skywards and she actually starts thinking about this one, she may not necessarily be the girl of your dreams. A cruder variant – which I've only tried once, unsuccessfully, but then it really wasn't my style – is: 'I have the F, the C and the K. All I need is U. Shall we?' You'd be better sticking with the same line, only using the word FUN as a substitute.

Note 13 - Yes, it's (1,1) with an added dose of flattery. Be aware that – as I will mention in a moment – some women prefer cockiness over flattery, so you might be better sticking with (1,1).

Note 14 - One woman once replied 'I'm a female impersonator. Good, aren't I?' She was either very quick-witted or an actual female impersonator. Either way, it shut me up, so full marks to him / her for that.

Note 15 - Of course, it's not Louise, and you knew that full well. But you have successfully broken the ice. You can take it from there, maybe by offering an apology and telling her that she really does have a doppelganger! An added bit of fun here is that Louise is such a common name that if you try this one often enough, you will stumble upon someone actually called Louise. Cue lots of hasty 'Will! Wow, long time no see!'-type interjections. It might just work! If you're really serious about using this latter strategy, Google a list of common UK girls' names. If you search hard enough, you will find archives rather than simply current popular names. Find your year of birth and pick the number one name! Alternatively – because remember you just told her she's looking young – use the list from a few years after you were born.

Note 16 - Yes, in the world of chat-ups, word play and puns feature surprisingly often. One would imagine Richard Whiteley would have been an excellent wingman.

Note 17 - This one works best if you have a partner-in-crime (more about mine later). That name, by the way, is a random mix of two real- life supermodel names. The devil is in the detail, as they say, and it sounds so authentic that she might just suspect you're for real.

Note 18 - At this point, you turn to walk away. Sometimes, she will then call you back. If she does, she will either have ignored the girlfriend part or else have seen it as a challenge.

Now, for each of the above chat-up lines, there are a potentially infinite number of possibilities in terms of how the conversation will flow – it's not merely a case of yes and no. However, each of the lines is sufficiently well-used by myself for me to have constructed a small branching diagram of common responses and counter-responses (which I have internalised, naturally, although I do usually carry a small notebook with me when I am on a night out, which contains the various branching diagrams. I might pop into a toilet cubicle and have a quick read before I make my move, in the way that an actor might have one last glance at his lines backstage just before his scene).

The example below illustrates the 'Magic Watch' chat-up line branching database of possibilities:

Me: Have I shown you my magic watch? It tells me that you're not wearing any underwear…

1.0 Her: Nice try, I am wearing underwear. Me: Damn it… It must be an hour fast! I'm Will by the way. Can I buy you a drink?

1.1 Her: Yes. Yes is used here as a generic term – possible alternatives are 'okay', 'ooh…go on then' and 'I suppose'. Even 'maybe' counts as 'yes', since it's not a 'no' – this also applies to a hesitant pause. In the latter case, one must act fast before it is followed by a 'no'. Time to engage in some well-versed nightclub banter and wait for the green light. Your next action depends upon what kind of woman she is and how much you like her and want to see her again:	1.2 Her: No. Again, a variety of possible responses fall under the 'no' umbrella, including shaking her head, turning her back, sticking two fingers up, sticking one finger up, and of course, that succinct old classic, 'fuck off'. This is to say nothing off the 'fuck off' family of responses, wherein 'fuck' may be substituted for 'sod' or 'piss' and 'off' is interchangeable with 'you' and 'this'. Each possible variant may be and often is supplemented with a short derogatory sign-off, such as 'loser', 'prick' or 'creep'. Two choices now present themselves:

1.1.1 You like her a bit but don't really want to see her again. Go in for the kiss. What have you got to lose? Of course, as with all chat up lines, there is a chance she is going along with it for a free drink, but this is a risk you must be prepared to take. Hence, if she pulls away at this point, go to 1.2.	1.1.2 You like her a lot and would like to see her again. Ask for her phone number. You can then proceed to either 1.1.1 or 1.2.1, the latter of which will most likely lead to 1.1.1 anyway, only you've made her work that bit harder for it.	1.2.1 Choice 1 – Walk away. Always resist the temptation to reciprocate her rejection with a pithy comment. After all, she might change her mind later in the night.	1.2.2 Choice 2 – repeat the whole process with a different woman just within view and / or earshot. At best, this will make your original target slightly jealous and thus reignite your chances. At worst, it shows her that she was nothing special to you in the first place and you've saved a bit of face.

2.0 Her: Your watch is right…I'm not. Me: Ah, splendid! You know, I'm wishing I'd splashed out a bit more and bought the Deluxe X-Ray Version now I know that. Now, it's fair to say at this point that you probably haven't met the woman of your dreams, but your chances for tonight are looking pretty good. Your next move depends on how she responds to the 'X-Ray' comment:

2.1 Giggles and / or turns her back. As long as she doesn't actually walk away, you're still onto a good thing – you just need to invest a bit more time / charm into the situation. Two choices:	2.2 Responds with a flirty comment. You might just have met your match! Stay sharp, stay focused – it's action time. Time for a game of flirty tennis. Follow every one of her comebacks with a counter-comeback, and match her like-for-like. If she's being smutty, you be smutty. If she's being witty, you be witty. One of two things will happen:

2.1.1 Offer to buy her a drink. Proceed to 1.0	2.1.2 Walk away. You've registered your interest. Her move now.	2.2.1 You win flirty tennis. Time to claim your trophy – her phone number. Of course, you need to gauge the situation. If you feel like more time is needed, or you're still unsure of your chances, proceed to 1.0.	2.2.2 You lose flirty tennis. No shame in this defeat – she's clearly a pro. As with 2.2.1, you need to use your instincts here. Maybe you were a bit of sport for her. Go to 1.2.1. Maybe your chances are still alive – go to 1.0.

I chose this one for illustrative purposes as it is structurally quite simplistic, branching out evenly as it does – some are quite complex and branch out in a multitude of different directions. Anyway, on this occasion (though of course it was all artificial – success was guaranteed, but I was enjoying myself enough to suspend my disbelief) I went for the trusted 'Market Research' chat-up line. I didn't have my special leather notebook with me, since I hadn't anticipated this situation arising, but I plodded on regardless.

'Excuse me, madam, I wonder if I could spare a few moments of your time. I'm from Williams and Jacobs Market Research and I'm doing a survey on beautiful women. You fit the bill perfectly. Do you mind if I ask you a few questions?'

'Oh, that's very flattering, but I'm afraid I don't respond to cold callers.'

Ooh - that one wasn't on my branching diagram. I was going to have to think on my feet. 'Madam, I can assure you, I'm a...hot...caller.' Crikey. I was clearly rusty! We cringed simultaneously. She giggled.

'Not sure about that, but you're definitely a smooth operator! Go on then - fire away.'

'Here goes. Number one – are you single?'

She made a fist and bit it mock dramatically. 'Why, yes! Yes I am! I'm all alone! I once dated this fella called Will. He broke my heart into so many pieces that I've never been able to love again!'

'Ah, a common response to that question. This Will must be quite the ladies' man. And dashingly handsome, I shouldn't wonder.'

'Oh, he was. He really was. He had these beautiful blue eyes that I could just get lost in and hair that I could just run my fingers through all day. Yummy, yummy, yummy.'

'So what happened?'

'The sod had a bit of a roaming eye, I think.'

'I bet he's really sorry about that. I bet he's changed. I bet if he could see you now, he'd tell you what lovely, fond memories he has of those days, and how he wishes now that he could have had more time with you.'

She smiled. It was a different smile to the playful one she'd been wearing so far - softer.

'What's the next question, Mister Market Researcher?'

'It's two questions in one. What's your favourite beverage and can I buy one for you right now?'

'Well, as you can see, I'm rather partial to coffee, and yes, you can.'

'I like coffee too. I wonder what else we've got in common?'

'I've got lots of coffee back at my place! Maybe you'd like to come back with me and we'll see what else we both like?'

'I bet you say that to all the Market Researchers!'

'Only the handsome ones. Did you have any more questions?'

My mind had gone completely blank. She was good at this flirting business. I was much more used to being the cool customer, being in control. I could feel myself getting a little turned on, which hadn't been my intention at all.

'Erm...phone...phone number. As in, what is your?' Great. I'd forgotten how to use the English language. I was tongue-tied, for God's sake! Maybe I should have asked for Irish coffee after all. Too late now. I recited Pi to ten decimal places in my mind to calm myself and regain control.

'Here, I'll write it on your hand.' Her touch was soft and warm. She wrote the number slowly, followed by her name, looking up at me every now and again and finally ending with an x. It suddenly seemed a very different x to the one on the end of her text message last night.

'Thank you madam. One final question - are you free on Friday night?'

Shit! Force of habit there. Of course, unbeknownst to Maria, I myself wasn't free on Friday night - I had a date with another one of the Magnificent Seven, Kayleigh!

'I'm not, as it happens.' Phew! 'I'm a very busy girl, you know. But this must be your lucky day, because I've actually got nothing on for the rest of today. And if you're really lucky, maybe I'll have NOTHING ON for the rest of today. Call me.'

She took one final sip of coffee and stroked my cheek as she left the pub. I didn't get up to follow, for two reasons: number one, I was playing it cool. Number two, I had a stonking bloody erection. Clearly, I'd forgotten to tell my manhood that this was all just make-believe. For a moment I contemplated necking a few pints for some enforced Brewer's Droop, before remembering that it was actually still the morning.

The barman grinned at me. 'Blimey, mate, you don't mess about, do you?'

Normally I would have left it for four or five days before calling. This time I left it for four or five minutes. It still seemed like an age. Now erection-free, I pushed my untouched coffee away from me and headed towards the door, pulling my mobile out of my pocket. I really didn't need to look at my hand as I had Maria's number plugged in, but I did it anyway, just for the sake of authenticity.

As I was about to leave the pub, a man sitting by the door slammed down the broadsheet paper covering his face, jumped to his feet and grabbed me by the collar.

'Who are you?'

I wanted to ask the same question, but was struggling to find my voice. All I could manage was a strained, high-pitched 'Will! Will Jacobs!' *Pleased to meet you, good sir! And who might you be, pray tell?*

'You shagging my missus?'

Ah, well that answered that question. 'No, no, it's not like that!' As he had yet to relinquish his grip, I presumed he needed further clarification. I considered explaining to him that, in my dying days, I had made it my mission to track down and make amends with seven of my ex-girlfriends, of whom his current partner happened to be one, spending a platonic day with them. I didn't. 'Maria and I are old friends. I haven't seen her for years.'

And still I found myself in his clutches.

'Pull the other one, mate! I saw the way you were looking at each other. I saw her touching you.'

I was praying he hadn't seen the bulge in my trousers, too (which now felt as if it had recoiled into my body in terror). Perhaps I needed to explain to him that he was quite mistaken - that in fact, Maria and I were about to embark on a fake relationship which was set to last until the end of the day. No, I doubted that would have helped matters.

'Right, come on then, me and you. Outside. Now.'

He at last let go of me and pushed me out of the door. Would it have helped to mention to the shaven-headed fellow about to kick the proverbial seven shades out of me that I was, in fact, a lover, not a fighter? Probably not. Fortunately for me, before a punch was thrown, his attention was diverted by Maria's voice screaming at him from the end of the street.

'Rob! ROB! No!' She was running towards us. And finally, a punch was landed: Maria thumped her boyfriend on the arm. 'Have you followed me here? You're spying on me now?'

'Yeah, I knew you were up to something. Acting all secretive. Shielding your phone when you got text messages. You're cheating on me - with him!' He pointed at me but kept an angry yet pleading gaze fixed in Maria. It seemed just as likely that he would break down in tears as it was that he would break my nose.

'No, you idiot. This is Will. Will and I USED to date, a long, long time ago. I haven't seen him since. Will is - well he's dying. Okay? He's got cancer. And I just wanted to see him one more time. I didn't tell you because - well, because of this, really. You and I don't have that level of trust yet. So if you want to beat up a dying man, go for it.'

Whoa, Maria! Don't give him an open invitation! Luckily, Rob simply eyeballed me, got into his car, slammed the door shut and with a screech of tyres, he was gone. I tried my hardest to conceal the fact that my ankles were shaking by shifting around. I just hadn't anticipated this sort of thing happening; didn't consider that I might be delving in people's lives. Borrowing men's wives and girlfriends. Causing friction. The week had barely begun and already I was creating problems.

'Well, that was shit scary.'

'I know! I'm so, so sorry.' She put her arms around me. I really didn't want her to. I glanced round uneasily and wriggled myself free.

'No, I'm sorry. This was a terrible idea. Please, go. Go and sort things out with your boyfriend.'

'No. No. I've been looking forward to seeing you and I'm not about to let Rob spoil that. Trust me, you won't be seeing him again. He'll have gone off to sulk. I'll sort things out, don't you worry. Now, weren't we having fun before he came along?'

We were. I couldn't deny that. I was intrigued by this 'Relationship in a Day' idea. I weighed up whether a day spent alone in the safety of my house would be preferable to a day spent with Maria, which carried with it the small but not inconsiderable chance of an arse kicking. Ah, what the hell. Like I said before - you only live once.

'Now, I'm going to stay here. You're going to go back into that pub and do exactly what you were going to do before Rob accosted you.' I was pushed back into the pub with almost the same ferocity with which I was pushed out. The barman gazed at me quizzically. I smiled and immediately made my exit. As promised, there she was. Right, come on Jacobs. Let's get this train back on the tracks.

'Maria! Hi! It's Will. Remember me? We met in the pub the other, erm, minute.'

'Will, Will. Will...nope, it's not ringing a bell. But then, I've had loads of men chat me up in the last seven minutes. Oh hang on, were you the chap who came out with that cheesy Market Researcher line?'

'That's right! I WAS the chap who came out with that awesome Market Researcher line! I mean, you're talking to me now, aren't you?'

'Hmm, you've got me there. So how have you been?'

'Oh, not bad! I've been thinking about you. I was wondering - would you let me take you out to lunch?'

'Well, you do owe me a coffee, so, yeah, why the hell not?'

I told her to sit tight – I knew exactly what my next move was going to be. I had a method, you see.

We greeted just a couple of minutes later with a hug.

'Wow, Maria, you look great! Did you get a haircut since the last time I saw you?'

'No, but thanks! Wow, and you got me flowers! Oh I've always loved lilies! Did you remember that, you big softie? I am impressed!'

I hadn't remembered at all. 'Guilty as charged!'

'Oh, and this is the Italian we went to on our - what was it? - third date?'

'It...is. Yes.'

Bloody hell, that was lucky. But, if I say so myself, that was some world-class bluffing on my part. I was really getting back in my stride.

'Well, I must say our 'Relationship in a Day' is going really well so far! Good work, babe! Your reward - our first kiss.'

She leaned over and gave me a peck on the lips. I craved something a bit more substantial, more lingering, but romance was not supposed to be part of the game plan this week. So a peck was good - right? We walked into the restaurant arm in arm.

'Good afternoon, Marco!'

'Mr Jacobs! It's been a long time! And who is your lovely lady this time?'

I giggled nervously. 'This time indeed! You make me sound like a right player, Marco!'

I widened my eyes in a bid to convey my panic to Marco. It was exactly this sort of thing that ruined my proper relationship with Maria. I didn't want her being reminded of my womanising ways. I desperately wanted to get it right this time.

'Just my little joke, miss! Let me show you to your table. We've got a nice romantic little spot over in the corner. Marco is good to you, eh, Mr Jacobs?'

I thanked Marco, who was clearly working his tip as per usual, although in actuality we were the only customers there, so he hadn't done us any particularly great favour.

'You might have noticed you and I have this whole place to ourselves! That's right, I booked the whole restaurant out for the date!'

'My goodness, Will Jacobs, you are so sweet! And so full of shit!'

We spent just over an hour and a half in the restaurant in total. The shifts in conversation seemed to coincide with the arrival of the different courses. As we ate the starter, we engaged mainly in some slightly stilted first date small talk, about the weather, about the television, and so on. At first I couldn't tell whether we were maintaining the facade of being a couple on an actual first date, with all the awkwardness and nervousness that first dates bring or we both did feel rather awkward and nervous. By the time the main course had arrived, however, we were in full swing, laughing and chatting about old times, and generally coming to the consensus that we were really rather rubbish at being a couple back then, that neither of us played it as well as we could have. It was funny - I don't remember enjoying her company this much when we were going out. Had I changed? Yes. Had she changed? Maybe. I couldn't help but think I might have made more of an effort if we'd had this level of chemistry back in the day. Finally, as we tucked into dessert, the topic we had both avoided so skilfully up to this point reared its ugly head.

'So...erm...how to put this...you haven't really mentioned...I mean you *seem* so...all right, look, mister, you're dying and you haven't uttered a word about it. Typical Will Jacobs. I mean, Jesus, you're allowed to talk about it you know!'

I laughed. 'Oh, I know. But thanks for the window anyway! Okay, it's like this - do you know about the five stages?'

'The what? No, I don't'.

Welcome, reader, to Terminal Illness 101. Today's class – the five stages, less colloquially known as the Kübler-Ross model. Not long after I found out the cancer had spread, my doctor basically told me that most terminally ill people go through a series of very distinct phases. The first is denial. And my denial was, looking back, undeniable. Me? Dying? Of testicular cancer? Those overpaid buffoons – didn't they know they'd made some sort of huge mistake? I was in my thirties! I still had too many ambitions to achieve to be dying – mainy sexual ones, admittedly, but they were still ambitions. No way was I dying before my libido did. So I simply buried my head in the sand and continued doing what I was doing.

When Stage One wore off, Stage Two kicked in immediately afterwards - anger. How was it fair? What had I done to deserve such a fate? How come there were rapists, paedophiles and murderers languishing about in prison (or not, in some even more unjust cases) - how come THEY got the right to a full life, when a harmless Maths teacher with a few wayward morals received a death sentence? I'm a lady killer, not an actual one! And what about those people who didn't even WANT to live? The suicides and the suicidal. What a mixed up world when they don't want to live and I don't want to die. Such an injustice - and it infuriated me. For a little while I started to hit the bottle pretty hard. I was horrid to everyone – even to Helen, I hate to say.

Then came Stage 3 - bargaining. It was a more positive, but more deluded phase. God, Allah, Buddha, fate, whoever it was pulling the strings - I implored them to get me out of this situation. Let me live and I'll live better. I'll settle down! I'll get married, have kids and do something noble with the forty or fifty bonus years I was getting. I'd help save the rainforests! I'd go to church! No, scrap that, I'd become a missionary and spread the good word in far flung corners of the globe. Anything! That stage lasted right up until my next visit to the specialist, when I found out that I probably wouldn't have as long to live as first expected.

Stage 4 was a definite bout of depression. I became reclusive; retreated into my shell. Didn't speak to a soul for a long time. I cried. A lot. I cried in the anger phase, too, but those were different tears, different emotions. It was at this point that I decided to throw in the towel where women were concerned. I'd retire from the relationships game, like a top-flight footballer stricken with injury.

Stage 5, where I am now and have been for a long time, is acceptance. Good old acceptance. I'm dying and there ain't a damn thing I can do about it, so why bother with the self-pitying? You may even envy me a little if you wish. If you live to the old age to which you're almost certain to live, then that's how those who survive you will remember you; old, wrinkly and past your prime. Perhaps, if you're really old and really unlucky, they'll remember you as the incontinent and senile codger you were at the end of your life. Not I. If I die any time soon, I'll die as handsome as I've ever been, with all my teeth and marbles. Like a lot of men, as I've drawn closer to middle age, I've perhaps become more attractive, or at least that's what I've been told. I'm not suggesting I'm Jim Morrison or Kurt Cobain checking into the 27 Club or anything. But I'm more pleasing on the eye than the average coffin-dodger. Death doesn't scare me anymore – it honestly doesn't. I've thought plenty about what Heaven is probably like, and I reckon it's like some sort of huge party. See, I do believe in Heaven, but I don't believe in reincarnation. I think when you get to Heaven, you stay there – so it's this really busy, vibrant place, inhabited by every decent or half-decent person that ever lived. Imagine that. Imagine a place where I can have a cup of tea with my mum in the afternoon, then go and see Jimi Hendrix play that night, then probably pick up a hot rock chick type while I'm there, all in the same blissful day?

Maria had listened to me talk with such a sympathetic expression on her face that her eyebrows were practically perpendicular. Her hands had inched ever closer to mine, and before long she was cupping them. After I had finished speaking, she kissed me on the cheek.

'I'm glad we got the chance to do this,' she whispered, her voice cracking slightly.

We walked out of the restaurant hand in hand, Maria still clutching the flowers with her free hand. She swung my arm as we chatted, half walking and half skipping.

'So - we've been fake dating for almost two-and-a-half hours. We're officially fake boyfriend and girlfriend now, surely?'

'I suppose so!'

'Right. I just need to make a phone call. Back in a mo. Don't go anywhere!'

She disappeared for a couple of minutes, returning with a sheepish grin. I thought nothing of it and we continued our afternoon stroll, our conversation becoming more and more relaxed with each passing minute. I knew we were only pretending. I knew we were. Nonetheless, I was finding myself increasingly enraptured by her company. This wasn't good, but it sure as shit *felt* good.

On Maria's suggestion, we made a brief stop off at a newsagent's, not to buy anything, but in fact to meet her friend, Izzy, who was working behind the counter. Maria had assured me that it was time to step things up, and that included meeting her friends. We were only there for a minute or two, but I liked the gesture. Liked it so much, in fact, that it inspired an idea of my own. Before we left, I bought a bag of Hula Hoops.

'Crisps? You can't possibly be hungry after that Italian feast! Will, I hate to say this, but I think the curse of comfort is kicking in! We've been together so long that you're starting to get a bit complacent! You're letting yourself go, man!'

'I'm not hungry actually.' I opened the bag, took out a single Hula Hoop and threw the rest of the bag in the bin outside the shop. I got down on one knee and took her hand.

'Maria, the three hours in which we have been together have been filled with happiness and joy. I feel like I must do the right think and make you my fake wife. Will you fake marry me?'

'This is all so sudden - literally! But yes, yes, I will fake marry you!'

The small group of passers-by who had stopped to see what was happening let out a small burst of applause, clearly oblivious to the joke. Maria tried to squeeze the Hula Hoop onto her wedding finger, but in the end had to settle for her little finger.

'If we're getting married, you'll need to have a stag do. There's a Hooters over on Bridge Street. Go and have a quick pint - and behave yourself! I'll meet you back here in half an hour. Then we've got some serious wedding planning to do, Mister!'

I did just that. I went to Hooters, which was only a few minutes' walk from our current location, where I was served a slightly overpriced beer by a girl caked in makeup. Despite her inevitably being buxom and squeezed into tiny shorts, I found myself not attracted to her in the slightest. I stared at my drink more than I stared at the staff, rather self-conscious of the fact that I was the only person here alone. In a funny sort of way, I found myself missing Maria in the thirty minutes we were apart; missing the momentum and spontaneity of the strange day we were having, which was infinitely more appealing than these underdressed waitresses.

When we met up again, she had a carrier bag in her hand.

'Did you have a good time, honey? I've been busy while you've been gone, getting ready for the wedding. We've already got the flowers, haven't we? I've got these little plastic rings from one of those kids' machines where you put a pound in and get an egg out. I bought a cupcake from Greggs and a Lego man and woman to put on top. That's obviously going to be our wedding cake. And, of course, some confetti from the card shop. Came to £7.50 altogether.

'Christ, this wedding's really spiralling! £7.50? And don't I get a say in any of it? It's my wedding too, you know! Have we even set a date?'

'I thought maybe, oh I don't know, today. Five o'clock. My house. In fact that's where we're headed now.'

'So this is how the marriage is going to be, is it? You're going to be this bossy all the time?'

'Yes. Get used to it. Hey - another milestone! Our first fight! Wow, we're really whizzing through this!'

We made our way to her car, again hand in hand. I had the audacity to slip my hands into the back pocket of her jeans at one point, but it was quickly guided back out.

Before we went into the house, Maria turned to face me.

'Will, listen. I've got a confession. Remember this afternoon when I disappeared to make a phone call? Well, it was to my mum and dad. They want to meet you...and they're here right now!'

I laughed. She didn't. 'Oh - you're not joking, are you?'

She shook her head. I hadn't met them when we were dating for real, as they lived abroad. They must have moved back to Britain or, just my luck, been visiting their daughter at that time. 'I haven't told them about the wedding. That's just a silly bit of fun. Look, just - just go along with it. Please.'

By this point, I felt totally confused. I hadn't been allowed a cheeky touch of her bum, but I was meeting her parents? And wasn't the whole day 'a silly bit of fun' - was it actually something more serious to her? Was this a fake relationship or not? It was one thing chatting to her friend in the newsagent's, but to actually meet her actual parents was quite another. I felt a twinge in my stomach. It had been a long, long time since I had had to employ the particular brand of charm I used to use to impress a girl's parents. Why the heck was I nervous, though? It was a fake date for Christ's sake! Maria wasn't really my girlfriend! Her parents weren't really my potential in-laws! For all the difference it made, I could have stripped naked and danced the fandango as an introduction! She guided me into the hallway.

'Right - just wait here for a second.'

She disappeared into the living room and shut the door behind her. First

- silence. Then, audible voices.

'Okay, mum, dad. He's here and he's dying to meet you.'

Then a man's voice, strangely muffled compared to Maria's.

'Ah, fantastic! Bring him in!'

I straightened my collar and smoothed my eyebrows with my clammy fingertips.

And there they weren't. Maria was there, smiling nervously and shifting her weight from one foot to the other as i had done after meeting her real boyfriend earlier, but no parents. Odd. Then - the man's voice again.

'Ah, you must be Will! I'd shake your hand, except I obviously can't! Sit down, dear boy, sit down.'

I followed the direction of the sound. Maria's parents were indeed there - on her computer screen. Maria tilted her head away from the PC. 'You did remember that my parents had emigrated to Oz, didn't you? Now be nice to them! They've stayed in especially to meet you!'

'Ooh, are those flowers for us? They're absolutely divine! Bring them closer to the camera.' She sniffed the air. I could see where Maria's quirky sense of humour had come from. 'And they smell gorgeous! I'm Diane, by the way. And this is Derek.'

'We'll do our best not to embarrass you, darling. I mean, we've got the naked baby photos, but that's just standard, isn't it?'

I grinned. 'Don't suppose you've got anything more recent, have you?'

Diane chuckled and waggled her finger at me. 'I can see we're going to have to watch this one, eh, Derek?'

Maria laughed too, sighed fondly and slipped her arm into mine, tilting her head onto my shoulder. She let it rest there. I let her let it.

As the half hour chat progressed, it occurred to me that, unlike Maria and I, Diane and Derek weren't playing make believe. As we said our goodbyes, they told me what a great couple we made, how happy their daughter seemed, and that they hoped we could talk again soon. After Maria logged off, I turned to her and frowned.

'What the hell was that?'

'Listen, you did me a big favour in there. Those two have been on my back for being in my thirties and still being single. They think just because they got married at twenty and lived happily ever after that it should happen that way for everyone. They might leave me alone now I've got a boyfriend. Well, you know what I mean. Now they THINK I've got one.'

'Erm, you DO have one! Remember? That meathead who wanted to kill me earlier on today?'

'I know. I...haven't told them about Rob yet. He...just wouldn't be their cup of tea. I knew they'd like you.'

I put my hands on her shoulders. 'Well, I mean, if you want me to be your pretend boyfriend again, I could! It's not like I haven't got some spare time on my hands!'

She leaned in and gave me a peck on the lips, just as she had done before we went into the restaurant at lunch. This time, we followed it immediately with a full-on kiss. I honestly couldn't tell you who initiated it, but it was she who drew back from it, maybe ten seconds in. We mumbled apologies to each other and Maria pointed to her watch. It was time to pretend again – this was all getting a bit too real.

'Hey – look at the time! It's quarter to five! What are we doing faffing around here? Time to get ready for what will surely be Wedding of the Afternoon! Get in that bathroom, go and make yourself presentable,'

'No offence taken...'

'And don't come out until exactly five o' clock! Got it?'

'Yes dear!'

'Hey, you're learning fast. That's a good sign.'

I went upstairs to the bathroom and sat on top of the toilet seat, smiling to myself at the randomness of the day. It was the sort of day which, even if I'd had the chance to live to old age, I would have remembered for the rest of my life. I could hear lots of clattering and hurried footsteps. As five o' clock drew near, I sauntered over to the bathroom mirror, checking for any stray eyebrow hairs or bits of food between my teeth. I didn't look too bad for a dying man! It was go time.

Maria had changed into a white vest top and white trousers and had managed to dig out an old Casio keyboard. She was attempting to knock out

'Here Comes the Bride.' To say it was an approximation would have been charitable.

'I'm going to be a bride and vicar rolled into one today. Vicar to start with. Ladies and gentleman, we are gathered here today to...blah, blah, blah...some religious nonsense...something about the tenderness of sexual union – and I can definitely remember feeling tender on the first time around, you big stud – and that's it! You may kiss the bride! Go on then, what are you waiting for?'

'I make it my habit not to kiss vicars if at all possible.'

'No, I'm the bride now, you fool.'

'Oh, in that case – don't mind if I do!'

Our third lip-kiss of the day – a more stilted, self-conscious attempt than its predecessor – was broken after a couple of seconds by Maria, who had a panicky look on her face. By now the line between reality and make-believe was becoming seriously blurred, so I wasn't sure whether it was genuine panic or not. 'You know what we've forgotten, don't you? We've forgotten to book a bloody wedding photographer. Right, let's not stress. There's a Post Office on the corner, with a photo booth in it. Come on, no time to waste!'

She picked up her keys and dragged me by the hand out of the door.

With the same giggling abandon as teenagers, we did that classic thing that teenagers used to do before every single one of them had a camera on their mobile phones – had four pictures taken in a photo booth. Marie barked out the orders before each snap.

'Face forward and smile for this one!' Snap! 'Cheek to cheek for this one!' Snap! 'Gaze into my eyes fondly for this one!' Snap! 'And now let's just pull a funny face for the heck of it!' Snap!

We exited the booth sporting sheepish grins and waited for our wedding snaps to be delivered to us. They were terrible, of course – there wasn't one in which all four of our eyes were open and one or the other of us was always too close to the camera. It didn't matter.

Maria planted her door key into my palm. 'Right – go back to my place! I trust you won't rob all my worldly possessions. I'll be back in about five minutes...my darling spouse!'

She returned, slightly out of breath, with a carrier bag in her hand, the contents of which were steaming. 'Of course - no wedding would be complete without a wedding meal. Fine cuisine. Something classy. To that end,' she dumped the contents of the bag onto the table. 'Enjoy your kebab and chips.'

We stuffed the food into our mouths, too caught up in the fun of it all to eat at a normal pace. We didn't really talk, just spat out occasional sentence fragments between fits of giggles.

'Okay, that's our gourmet feast over and done with. It's normally the speeches at this point.' She drummed her fingers against her lips and looked skywards for inspiration, which, in the spirit of the day, was quickly forthcoming. 'Okay, in a slight variation to normal wedding protocol...'

'Because everything else has been highly conventional thus far.'

'...I'm now doubling as both bride and best man. Give me a minute.'

'Okay, but are you still the vicar? Because this is starting to get a bit confusing now.'

She ignored me and shot over to her computer. After a flurry of key strokes and mouse clicks, she had arrived on a screen called 'Best Man Speeches'. Good old Google, eh? Can you imagine life without it now? Children born from now onwards will struggle to conceptualise a world without search engines. How the devil did people find things out, they'll wonder. It makes ME wonder what sorts of things the future world will offer up which turn out to be life-changing and indispensable - you'll find out but I won't.

'Right, I've got a decent generic best man's speech here. It's a bit of a multiple choice thing. Here goes. Ladies and gentlemen, I would like to thank *name of groom* - that's an easy start, Will - on behalf of the bridesmaids for his *brief/patronising/kind* words - shit, you haven't done your speech. Quick, do one now. You can go for brief, patronising or kind.'

I pondered my options. 'I'm going to go for all three. I'm honoured to be married to the most amazing woman in the world - or at very least, in this room. Imaginary bridesmaids, you all look beautiful. Cheers, everyone.'

'Touching stuff. I agree that the bridesmaids all look *lovely/drunk/sweet/taken aback*. Well, you plumped for beautiful, so I'd better choose lovely. I was *honoured/shocked/confused* when Will asked me to be his best man - well, technically I asked myself, so I think we can agree that a degree of confusion surrounds this whole thing. I had presumed everyone else had said no. So here I am, and where do I start? I first met Will when we were both *at school/reform school/pub, etc* - right, well, technically the answer to this is when we were dating, which would have to make this a pretty unique best man's speech. But we were both working as teachers, so let's go for 'school'. His nickname was *if none used, make one up* - right, well I'm spoilt for choice for nicknames you could have had while we were going out, depending upon which point in the relationship we're referring to. But I'll be nice. It's our Big Day after all. I'm going for 'The Stallion' - that okay?'

'That's more than okay, thanks! Does seem a strange thing for a best man to call a groom, though.'

'We immediately became great *friends/enemies*. Hmm, I wouldn't say we were either. And there doesn't appear to be an option for vociferous lovers, but it's that one I'm going for. We have been through many things together, including *puberty/drinking/partying* - well, I think we can cross the first thing off the list. Things didn't get much better when *years* - let's change that to a couple of hours - later he also *amusing anecdote*. Let's see - he was so stingy that he proposed to his future wife using a Hula Hoop instead of an engagement ring. And at last we come to the stag night. Let's just change that to stag afternoon. It all started off so sedately, but ended up in drunken debauchery - *story of stag night* - when Will ended up *naked/in jail/tied to a lampost/name of city, etc.* Right, did any of those things happen during your half hour in Hooters?'

'Well, no. I had a pint of Carling and contemplated ordering a burger but then decided against it.'

'Wow. Like I say, some serious debauchery. Meeting *name of bride*- that's easy enough, Maria – was the *best/worst/we'll come back to you* thing ever to happen to him. Oh, that has to be best, obviously.' She shot me an exaggerated wink to show that she was obviously joking, but for a brief moment I couldn't help but wonder whether I might have sabotaged what could actually have been the best thing ever to have happened to me, if I had let it. 'It was *love/lust* at first sight. Well, she was and is a stone cold hottie - is the best man allowed to say that? So I'll say lust. It took Will *number of days/months/years* to pluck up the courage to ask Maria to *go out on a date/go to bed*- about five minutes for the former who knows when for the latter - and the rest is history. I ask you all now to join me in a final toast to the future happiness of the bride and groom. To Mr and Mrs Jacobs; may their life together bring them much happiness and many children - hey, I'm just reading the script. To the bride and groom!'

'Don't suppose you've got any champagne or sparkling wine to mark this occasion, have you?'

'No, but I've got a bottle of supermarket brand vodka!' Without asking me, she poured a quantity of vodka slightly too large to be classed as a shot into a glass slightly too large to be classed as a shot glass for me, and one for herself. She necked hers so I felt duty bound to do the same. I couldn't help but wince - it tasted awful. Thankfully, again without asking, she followed it with a can of beer - the first of several.

'Onwards and upwards - it's time for our first dance. I served a dual role as vicar and bride earlier on today. Then I was bride and best man. Now I'm going to attempt to pull off a bride / DJ combo. I'll fetch my iPod.'

No doubt about it - this was turning out to be a weird and wonderful date. I only hoped the rest of the week would turn out to be quite this wacky. She returned with her iPod and plugged it into her speakers. I wondered what her next move would be.

'We didn't really have a special song, did we? There's loads of songs that remind me of when we started going out that you've perhaps never heard and I should imagine vice-versa. So what are we going to dance to?'

'We're going to leave it in the hands of the Gods - shuffle button, we're at your mercy. Whatever comes up, we dance to. Deal?'

'Deal.'

So what did the iPod have in store for us? Something suitably clichéd and smoochy? 'Three Times a Lady' perhaps? 'Your Song'? 'Truly Madly Deeply'?' More Than Words'? Nope, nope, nope and nope. The iPod chose Paul Simon's 'You Can Call Me Al'. Despite its jaunty rhythm and complete lack of romantic sentiment, we slow danced to it, embracing tightly as we circled round.

'Right, well, that was...weird.'

'Weirdly beautiful?'

'Just weird. Time to kick this party up a notch. Let's think about all those songs you've heard at every single wedding you've ever been to, I'll see if I've got them and add them to an on-the-go playlist.'

'Right, so we're talking...'Sweet Caroline'?'

'Yes, and you're in luck - I've got it.' Her thumb made rapid clockwise circles around the iPod control wheel as she located the song.

'Wow, and here's me thinking I couldn't get any luckier after fake marrying you. Okay, I mean, obviously 'Macerana' has got to be there.'

'Obviously. Except I haven't got it.'

'Damn!'

'I've got 'Agadoo'.'

'That'll have to do do do. 'Build Me Up Buttercup'?'

'Got it.'

''I'm Your Man'.'

'Yes. Yes you are. It's official. In a fake sort of way. Oh, you mean the Wham song? Got it.'

''Come On Eileen'?'

'Only if Eileen's okay with that. Anyway, haven't got it.'

''Tragedy'.'

'Chin up, babe - we'll find another record instead. Oh, you mean the song. Got it.'

'Bee Gees or Steps?'

'Steps.'

'Tragedy. Kool and the Gang, 'Celebrate'. That's a given.'

'It's in.'

'Then of course you've got to have your Motown section. 'Dancing in the Street'. 'Under the Boardwalk'. 'My Girl'?'

''My Guy'!'

''The Grease Megamix'. You're a chick. You're bound to have some Grease on there.'

'Will, that's very sexist and very presumptuous.'

'Have you?'

'Yes. And I suppose you automatically presume I've got the *Dirty Dancing* soundtrack?'

'I do.'

'I have. So let's finish up with 'I've Had the Time of My Life'. And there we have it! Every wedding disco you've ever been to in one handy playlist!'

She fired up the iPod and we partied. I don't know whether it was the alcohol or the nature of the day, but I felt totally unselfconscious as we danced. It didn't matter that I didn't particularly like most of the songs being played. In all honesty, I think I'd have danced to anything - I could have flicked on the radio and danced to the first thing that came on. Hell, I'd have danced to *The Archers* the mood I was in - I'd have danced to the bloody static.

After half an hour of sweaty, silly dancing, we collapsed onto the sofa. Maria blew the hair from her forehead.

'Heck of a shindig, hubby. You know what it's time for now?'

'A nice lie down?'

'Wrong! It's time for or honeymoon! Sun, sea, sand!'

'Anything else beginning with s on your list?'

'A slap if you keep that up. So - let's start with sun.'

She grabbed my hand and her keys and led me out the door.

A matter of minutes later, the two of us were stark naked...in a tanning booth a few streets away from Maria's house. Alas, she was in a different booth. When I saw her again, we were both ever-so-slightly browner. She grabbed my hand again and before I knew it we were back in her house.

'So - that's the sun part sorted. Let's see...sea...sea. I could take you to the swimming baths - except they'll be shut now.'

'Well, I mean, you do have a bath, don't you? I can live without the swimming bit.'

She sighed. 'Fine. But don't get any ideas. I'm going in with my costume on. And you're keeping your pants on.'

She ran the bath and went into her bedroom, coming out in a bikini. She looked amazing, though for some unfathomable reason she was giggly and coy, practically shrinking into herself. It took a huge conscious effort to keep my eyes north of her neckline.

'Right, mister. Your turn. Whip 'em off.'

I stripped down to my undies. Even I hadn't been sad enough to order my pants by quality as I had my shirts – not like anyone was supposed to be seeing them. Thank the Lord, then, that it so happened that I'd worn my best ones today. We stepped into the bathtub - an ordinary-sized affair, which did not comfortably fit two people. This meant our bodies were pressed together. I was sat behind her, with Maria squeezed in between my legs. We'd shared a bath before, with bubbles and candles and not a stitch of clothing between us. That time, my hands were all over her, and the memory of that was starting to - ahem - excite me a little. I focussed all my energy into squeezing those images out of my head, trying desperately to pretend I wasn't attached to a nearly-naked woman. I couldn't do it. I jimmied myself out of the bathtub and grabbed a towel to cover my shame. I could probably have HUNG the towel from the bloody thing if I'd tried.

'Yep! That was nice! Good! Sea! Next!'

'Oh, come on, Will! We've just got in. I was rather enjoying it. How about you come back in for a few more minutes?' Jesus. I don't think she was TRYING to sound sexy as she said that last sentence, but that was how I heard it, and it really wasn't helping matters down there.

'I'm just really excited about the sand part.'

She looked down at my towel. 'I can see that.'

I giggled the same coy giggle Maria had used ten minutes earlier and scurried out of the bathroom and into her room, grabbing my clothes *en route*. Her room where the lacy black underwear she must have been wearing earlier was strewn all over her bed. Give me a break! I patted myself dry, quickly but oh-so-carefully. As I was now without my pants, I would have to go commando. I zipped my jeans up after a certain amount of prodding and tucking. I buttoned my shirt and left her room without haste. We exchanged a slightly awkward smile as we passed on the landing, Maria this time wrapped in towels.

I was flicking through a magazine I cared nothing about when she returned, both of us now in a fully-clothed state.

She looked at me and smiled. 'We've done the sun. We've done the sea. Now for the sand.'

As the sand turned out to be a sandpit in the local park, it was probably for the best that this was the only one of the three parts of our 'holiday' which didn't involve us taking off any of our clothes. We sat in the sand, legs crossed.

'Well, thanks, wifey,' I said as I picked up a handful of sand and let it slip through my fingers. 'That was a most enjoyable honeymoon.'

We walked hand-in-hand back to her house. I imagined it was all part of the charade. Either way, I didn't argue, and I can't pretend it didn't feel nice.

We hadn't been back in her house for a full minute when she said to me: 'Listen, we've been married for two hours now, and I really think it's time we moved onto the next stage - Will, I want you to be the father of my children.'

'You're right. It's what society expects. Get your clothes off and we'll get down to business.'

'Right. Because getting my clothes off worked SO well last time! Anyway, no need!' She stuffed the nearest cushion up her jumper, rubbed it proudly for a moment or two, then ran into her bedroom and returned almost immediately, the cushion gone, carrying a baby doll. 'I've got one right here!'

'Okay, at the risk of breaking character or anything, may I ask why a fully-grown woman, presumably sane although I'm beginning to wonder, has a child's doll in her bedroom?'

She slapped my arm. 'My niece was here last week and she left it behind. Now let's crack on, shall we?'

'Right you are. Our baby is...beautiful. Really beautiful. Is it a boy or a girl? I can't really tell.'

'Hang on, I'll check. Well, things are awfully smooth down there, so I'm guessing girl. We'll call her...Wilhelmina.' She dipped her finger into a stray can of Strongbow and ran it down the doll's forehead.

'Fine. I just want to assure you that if you want to breast feed the baby, I'm more than fine with you popping your boob out at any point. Don't be shy.'

'Thanks. That's reassuring. I used to think you were selfish and sex-crazed, but just look what a great father you're becoming: so supportive.'

I sighed theatrically. 'Have you noticed that since little Wilhelmina came along, we just don't seem to have any 'us' time? Do you remember when we used to have long, leisurely baths together and take romantic walks on the beach?'

'Earlier today, you mean? Yeah. It all seems so long ago now. Look at us. Just sat here, wasting our lives in front of the,' she switched on the television. 'TV. You never tell me you love me anymore. We've drifted, Will.'

I nodded my head sadly. 'So what now?'

'I think we should go our separate ways. Let's try and be grown-ups about it all, for the baby's sake. You can see her on Saturdays and every second

Wednesday. You'll be fine. Knowing you you'll move onto someone else in no time.'

Hang on - was this actually happening? Was I actually leaving? My jacket was on and everything. I didn't want the night to end - and the clock suggested it hadn't. But it just felt like a natural end point - much though I didn't want to leave, I didn't want to spoil things either. I'd enjoyed it and the longer I stayed, the more opportunities I'd have to mess it all up. I wanted Maria to remember me this way. She, however, had other ideas.

'Whoa, tiger! You're not leaving, are you? Look, we've got one final thing we need to do. One more shot at goodbye. The first time we were together - well, you know what I mean, when we were actually together, for real - you just sort of phased yourself out. It was a pretty unsatisfying way to end things. Let's have another crack at it. We'll try out some different possibilities and see which one we like best.'

'Right. I think I'm on your wavelength. Something a bit more dramatic. How about the Hollywood soap opera goodbye?'

'Yes! Now we're talking!'

I put my hand on her shoulder. 'Maria, I'm leaving you. See, I've been having an affair with...your sister! We're in love!'

'Take your hands off me, you scoundrel! Go! Just go! Because see Wilhelmina over there! SHE'S NOT YOURS! That time you were in a coma? I had a night of unbridled passion with Doctor Cheekbones, the very man who was saving your life! Haven't you ever noticed the similarities?'

'Well, brace yourself, honey pie, because I've got a bombshell for you. I'm not even Will! I'm Will's evil twin brother, BILL Jacobs.' Maria gasped loudly.

'That's right! I kidnapped Will - and you'll never see him again! Mwah ha ha!' I did a flourish to signify the end of a well-acted scene. 'How was that?'

'I liked it. Subtle. Dignified. Right, my turn to choose. Let's try the emotional finale. Hankies at the ready.' She cleared her throat, looked down at the floor and then back up again with a sorrowful expression on her face. 'Will, I think we both knew this day was coming. The last twelve hours have been the best of my life, but we just can't carry on like this. There's someone out there for both of us, and I guess we've just got to keep searching.' She looked me right in the eyes. 'I'll always love you, Will. Goodbye my darling. Take care of yourself.'

We didn't speak for a few moments, and nor did we break eye contact. I eventually smiled and spoke. 'That was good. Powerful. A bit of closure there, eh? Now it's my turn to pick. This time we'll try the shouty goodbye. Do you want to be the shouter or do you want me to be the shouter?'

'Ooh me me me please!'

'Let's do it. Maria, I'm just going to come out and say this. We're not compatible and I don't love you. I'm leaving you.'

'WHAT? You're WHAT?! Fuck you, Will Jacobs! FUCK YOU! I HATE YOU! I NEVER WANT TO SEE YOU AGAIN YOU PIECE OF SHIT! AAAAAAAAARGH!' She slapped me round the face, with a little more force than I imagine she intended.

'Erm - ouch!'

'Sorry, sorry, sorry! I think I got a bit carried away there!'

'You reckon? I can see why you wanted to be the shouter! Anyway, your turn.'

'Right. I choose the goodbye where you say sorry.'

'Okay. Let me think. Here goes,' I cleared my throat. 'Maria - I'm sorry. I'm sorry for all the pain I've caused you. I'm sorry for messing you about. I'm sorry for all the lies and hurt and upset. I'm sorry for wasting your time. I'm...I'm sorry. I'm going to leave now. I truly hope you find happiness - you deserve so much better than me. Just know that I'll always love you.' I bowed. 'Right, it's my turn to pick.'

Maria smiled and shook her head. 'You know what? Let's not bother. I really liked that one. I think that's the perfect end to our Relationship in a Day! How was it for you?'

I smiled. 'Good. Fulfilling. Listen, I'm actually going to leave now.' She didn't argue, or seem surprised - we were clearly on the same page. 'Thanks for an amazing day.' I gave her one final kiss on the lips, just a peck this time, and one final embrace, just a squeeze this time.

'Goodbye, Will.' She smiled at me warmly but not sentimentally. Her eyes were dry.

As I returned to my flat I contemplated the fabulous irony that in my dying days I suddenly felt more alive, more exhilarated, than I had for a long, long time.

I rang Helen to let her know my date was over and ask her if she wanted to speak on the webcam.

W: Helen! Good to see you. You look like shit, by the way.

H: Aww, thanks, sweetie. It's called lack of sleep.

W: Jeff again?

H: Yep.

W: Taking up too much of the bed?

H: Nope.

W: Wriggling?

H: Nope. He did a gig last night with his new band and they celebrated the fact by getting smashed afterwards. So I got treated to his usual post-alcohol cacophony of noises. Tonight, Matthew, I'm going to be – Snorer Jones. Enough of my moans - tell me, tell me! I've been dying to find out - ooh, poor choice of words there! Sorry! How did Date Number One go?

W: Yeah, ok.

H: Steady on there Shakespeare.

W: Now you know perfectly well a gentleman doesn't kiss and tell.

H: Right, well you're exempt from that one. How did it go? Did you actually kiss her?

W: Yeah, we kissed. A few times actually.

H: Surprise surprise! So after all your big talk about how it's not really a date, how you just want to catch up, blah blah blah, you're sticking your tongue down the poor girl's throat. How long did you hold out? Five minutes? Ten?

W: About an hour. But that's not all. I met her parents. And we got married. And went on a honeymoon. And raised a child. And got divorced.

H: Excuse me?

W: Yeah, we did the whole thing in a day, the whole relationship shebang. Her idea. I made a much better job of it this time as well.

H: Hang on - you like this chick, don't you? I can hear it in your voice!

W: Nah. Does make me wonder what it would have been like to get married, though. You know - if I had found the perfect partner.

H: It's not about finding your perfect partner, you daft prat. It's about finding someone you can stand to be around every day. Jeff isn't perfect for me as such, but I can spend a whole day with him and not want to murder him. Usually. So do you think you'll see Maria again?

W: I really enjoyed being with her today; I can't deny that. But I like how it ended. I got some closure. Hopefully she did too. I've rewritten our ending to a happy one. I wouldn't want to jeopardise that by seeing her again - besides, I've got six more happy endings to work on! God, I REALLY hope they go as well as today's.

H: So who's the poor sap - I mean lucky lady - tomorrow?

W: Suzie.

H: Brilliant! It's going to be carnage. Didn't she tell you she'd kill you if she ever saw you again?

W: Yep.

H: So you might not need to worry about the cancer after all. Crazy Suzie, eh? Best of British, old boy! I think you'll need it this time.

W: I think I'll be alright, touch wood.

H: (sniggering) Touch wood! No one knows more about touching wood than you since you stepped out of the game.

W: Right, just to be clear here, we're doing masturbation jokes? That's our level.

H: Yes we are, and yes it is. And I've got loads left. Now sod off.

W: Love you too. Say hi to Jeff for me.

Tuesday, 12th July, 2005

The story of how I met Suzie – and I have lamented the fact that I did many times, so Lord knows why I bothered looking for her again – is a strange one. One, I think, that says a lot about my personality and my need to complete what I have started.

I was driving in my car in the spring of 2002 when a track called 'Song for Whoever' by The Beautiful South came on the radio. I'm quite sure you'll have heard of the band – I never was and am still not a great fan, but I am enamoured by the frankly gobsmacking statistic that 1 in 7 UK households apparently owned a copy of their Greatest Hits album, *Carry On Up The Charts*, back in the mid 1990s. As for the track itself, it's one of those songs, like 'Bohemian Rhapsody', which never mentions its title at any point, so although you may or may not recognise the title, you'll know it by its chorus. Released in 1989, it's the one that lists all the girls' names: 'Jennifer, Alison, Phillipa, Sue, Deborah, Annabel too'. I'd heard it before that point, of course – but I had never until that moment considered how many of those names were shared by girls and women I had met and at very least snogged: five of them to be exact. My rules for this one were much more relaxed than the ones which governed my Search for the Magnificent Seven – basically, I just had to have kissed them and still remember their first names – but I could tick off my list a Jennifer (not that I once called her that during our five-date run in 1991 – she was Jenny), a one-night stand called Alison (which, in fairness, could have been Allison or Alyson, since as you can surely appreciate, I never actually saw her name written down. Let's agree that it still counts), a Phillipa (which was definitely NOT to be shortened to Phil or Philly, as I found out during the two weeks we were together in 1988/9), a Deborah with whom I spent a mismatched blind date in my second year at university, out of whom I still managed to get a consolatory snog / grope combo, and a woman called Anne who I can seem to recall nothing about other than she wore glasses and we dated for about a month in 1990. I didn't think it too much of a stretch to now call her Annabel. There was only a Sue missing from my list.

At first I found myself mildly titillated by this – what a Casanova, eh? The song just wouldn't leave my cycle of thoughts, however, and after a couple of days I found myself less titillated than bugged. How agonising that I was one woman – one date, really, one *kiss* even – short of being able to say that I had gone out with all of the girls in the chorus of that song. I wasn't really sure what I would do with such a fact, were I to claim the full set – fun fact for conversation lulls maybe? Perhaps it was just a private sense of satisfaction I was seeking. Either way, I knew I wanted to make it happen. It called to mind an eager Bingo player with one number shy of a full house, willing for that elusive final number to be called; hence I christened it 'Song for Whoever Bingo'.

Now, admittedly, this game would have been considerably more fun had I been playing against someone else with a fair track record for dating lots of different women – but that did not quash my determination. I wanted – *needed* – to meet a Sue. I was quietly confident (what other kind of confident could I possibly be when no one else knew what I was doing?) After all, a lot of names fall under the Sue umbrella, and any one of them would have done the trick. Indeed, surely few first names could have as many possible combinations. Just look at the interchangeable s/z in the middle of Susan - I could find a Susan, Suzan, Suzanne, Susannah, Suzannah, Susie or Suzie. Let's not forget the plethora of hyphenated combinations out there (admittedly more common in North America - I have to wonder whether I would have gone so far as to jet off to the States if necessity had called for it, and I'm afraid I can't say I wouldn't have) – Sue-Anne, Sue-Ellen, etc. Furthermore, each of those could plausibly have the suffix Su rather than Sue. I would even have accepted a hyphenated name *ending* with Sue – Buddy Holly managed to find one! Foreign applicants would have been more than welcome – the Japanese names Suzu, Suzuki and Suzuko were not too tenuous to make the grade. All of this considered, it was a great surprise that I did not already have a Sue in my collection. The only kind of Sue I would definitely disregard is, as Johnny Cash encountered, A Boy Named Sue. A Tomboy Named Sue would have been acceptable.

Back to the Sue challenge, though. My first strategy was not actually a strategy at all – I would just wait until a Sue came into my orbit and somehow conspire to kiss her. I had to rethink this strategy when a Suzanne started teaching History at my school, a couple of months into the challenge (and believe me I had not forgotten about it in the interim – I was the proverbial dog with the bone, if you'll excuse the crudity of the analogy). Suzanne was perfectly nice – perfectly kissable – and I had managed to strike up a conversation or two with her. The only problem was that she was married. I will be honest with you and admit that it took a small amount of wrestling with my conscience before I decided that it was not acceptable to interfere in other people's marriages to win Song for Whoever Bingo. I would also take the high road with common law relationships – other relationships I would consider on a case-by-case basis, depending on the length and strength of the relationship and how desperately I wanted to win the game at that point. The incident did open up other questions, though, which also related to how much I wanted to win the game. What if Suzanne hadn't been married but also hadn't been kissable? Would I allow myself to be with someone I simply didn't fancy, just to complete the set? The answer was, of course, yes. Yes I would. I just needed one kiss, on the lips, for a period of five seconds (my new stipulation), and victory would be mine. Pretty soon I became tired of waiting – by the time the New Year had rolled around, my desire to win had not diminished, but my optimism had. Mathematically speaking, I had conceded that even with the multiple possible combinations, all the Sues put together were only a percentage of a percentage of all the girls' names out there. Non-mathematically speaking, Sue was the needle, and all the other names were the haystack. I needed to step it up.

I first tried the rather quirky ploy of placing an advert in the local paper saying 'Desperately Seeking Susan' accompanied by a deliberately vague explanation about needing to meet anybody with a name similar to Susan – unsurprisingly, no one responded. The word 'desperate' was probably the sealer. I could imagine people's thoughts as they read it – some people have a uniform fetish, some people have an S&M fetish, some people have a high heels fetish, but this weirdo's got a *Susan* fetish!

And so to something more practical. Something I had never tried before – not because I was morally opposed to it, or because I felt it carried with it a kind of stigma, or because I felt it was beneath me – I had just never needed to do it before. That something was to create a profile on an internet dating site. I had done speed dating, of course, and it didn't seem that different a concept. I chose soulmatesearch.co.uk, which I believe is now defunct. I would like to say I chose it randomly or because of a recommendation, but the truth is that I was drawn to the alliteration. Soulmate; search; *Susan.* Surely? It turned out to be a good choice (in some ways but not others – as you'll soon see) – but then, realistically speaking, I suppose any of the sites would have yielded a positive result. I really should have done it sooner. You've heard the old chestnut people say to those who have been dumped – there's plenty more fish in the sea. They're not wrong. To mix my fishy metaphors, it was also like shooting fish in a barrel. Even though the protocol is to use a handle rather than one's real name, it proved no challenge at all to find a Sue variant. More often than not, people would write their real first names in their profile description. So it was simply a case of scanning through the profiles, starting of course with the attractive ones - a Sue would have been great, but a hot Sue all the better! This created, in my mind, a Venn diagram:

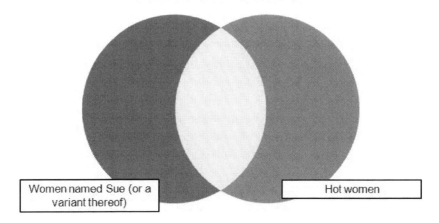

Venn Diagram to illustrate the use of an online dating site to find a woman named Sue.

Women named Sue (or a variant thereof)

Hot women

Clearly, the ideal scenario would be to find someone who fitted in the intersection, but I would not rule out women falling into the left section. Nor would I disregard anyone in the right section – what the hell, I was using a dating site, so why not get something else out of it, like a date with a hot non-Sue? I didn't actually get that far because of what happened next, but I did get to flex my flirting muscles, try out a few new techniques, so it was not a wasted endeavour by any means. What I would definitely disregard was anyone who fitted into the outer section diagram (and the majority, I'm afraid to say, did just that).

In some cases, there was an even easier way to find a Sue, as the name was incorporated within the alias itself – so for example, there was a suzzanesoapfan and a sexysuzie. Needless to say, of the two, it was the latter I chose first. It would be unfair to suggest her profile name was a misnomer – she was terribly and undeniably sexy. It just wasn't quite accurate enough. A much more apt choice would have been crazysexysuzie. In hindsight, I ought to have used my deduction skills a little more carefully. I had simply skimmed over the fact that she had been on the site for two and a half years – if she had been a decent catch (those fish metaphors again!), someone would surely have reeled her in by now. Those who had had clearly thrown her back in the water, as I later did (last fish metaphor, I promise). Suzie was extremely keen to meet up (most people seem to like to build up that online rapport first – not Suzie) – hence, I went for her and not the ditherers. I had seen several profile pictures, all of which highlighted her physical beauty. Even if she was dog dull, I would get that kiss then get the hell out of there and claim my victory. What was the worst that could happen? Little did I know that to catch this particular fish, I had just opened a whole can of worms (okay, I couldn't resist that one).

Suzie was essentially a very skilled, very measured relationship psychopath. If it was a career, she would have been a top-ranking professional. If it was a sport, she would have been an Olympian. With my experience of women – and a fair few nut jobs had come into the mix over the years – I ought to have spotted her type a mile off. Stamped on the flames before the fire raged out of control. But I didn't; I was simply too consumed with lust. To reverse those fishing analogies, she reeled me right in - got me hook, line and sinker. She hid the crazy pretty well on the first date, a standard restaurant date in which she turned up in a slinky black dress, blonde hair cascading down her shoulders. I guess it's a bit of a dating site cliché that when dates meet in the flesh, they don't look anything like as good as they did on their profile picture. Maybe the picture was taken from the neck up and failed to show the overweight torso beneath. Maybe the picture was taken ten years ago and failed to show the wrinkles and thinning hair of the present day. Neither of these was the case with Suzie, who somehow managed to look even more attractive in person than online. I hadn't really made that much of an effort – I'd put a nice shirt on, and worn my best jeans, but they were still jeans after all. Without meaning to sound conceited, there haven't been many occasions in my life when I've felt significantly physically inferior to the woman on my arm – but this was definitely one of them. Heads were turning – was it because we looked so mismatched, or were they simply looking at Suzie? All through the night, I kept catching glimpses of men sneaking a split second peek at her while their partners' gazes were averted. Hell, I even saw some *women* doing the same. I felt quite conscious at first, but this soon turned to a kind of smugness, and eventually both of those sensations disappeared, washed away by the champagne for which I found myself forking out. It was undoubtedly going well. She was chatty without being inane, and just the right level of flirty to make me think things were going well without thinking she was slutty. I see now that she had honed this skill well over the dozens of first dates she must have had over the last two-and-a-half years. We held hands as we left the restaurant, and kissed against a wall almost as soon as we were outside. I was either too drunk or too caught up in the moment to realise I had just won the game of Song for Whoever Bingo over which I'd been obsessing for the last nine months. Within an hour, we were tearing off each other's clothes and throwing one another around my bedroom.

There were none of the games that have accompanied the vast majority of my relationships. Neither of us was playing hard to get or playing it cool. Neither seemed bothered about being too keen or not keen enough. Rather, we just got on with it. We spoke on the phone the next evening and by the end of that night, we were once again in the throes of passion. It was nothing less than a whirlwind. This pattern continued, and by the end of the first week, my dick was doing all the thinking. Neither Suzie nor my inflamed sex drive were giving me any opportunity to stand back from it all and ask myself whether she was right for me, or whether we were moving too fast. She was absolutely insatiable, and I suppose I was too. She would text me dirty pictures of herself while I was at work, and on several occasions, I found myself spending my free periods not planning or marking, but in fact meeting her in the woods near the school for a quick fix.

The first time I told her I loved her, it was an accident, and I hadn't meant it anyway. We were only on our fourth date, and she was moaning about the clothes she was wearing, how they were making her look fat and frumpy - of course, she was angling for a compliment. I told her, clearly with the minimum of forethought, 'Don't be silly! I love you in those jeans!' I immediately covered my mouth, realising that sentence could be misconstrued, but she took the gesture to mean I actually did love her, that it had slipped out. What I really meant was that I loved the way she looked that day. I loved her jeans. Even, I loved her arse IN those jeans. I did not, however, love her, but by that point the wheels were in motion. 'Oh my God, Will!' She brought her own hands to her mouth, only her gesture seemed to convey her pleasant surprise at what she had just heard. 'I love you too! I'd have said it myself if I had had even the slightest feeling that you felt the same way! You dark horse, you!' She threw her arms around my neck and started crying. Then we had sex. Good sex (in all honesty, I've never had any other kind, with anybody. Even the worst sex is better than none, surely?)

Three weeks after the first date, as I sat alone in the staffroom absent-mindedly stirring the coffee upon which I was becoming increasingly dependent to juggle Suzie and my job, it dawned on me that she had spent every single night with me – that we'd had sex on each of them, and that she'd stayed over on each of them. No respite at all. The top of my drawers was covered with her cosmetics, and her toothbrush hadn't left my bathroom since it had first arrived. We were practically living together, yet I actually knew very little about her. It scared me a bit. When I tried to talk to her about it that night, she quickly changed the subject and before I knew it her hand was in my boxer shorts. We ended up spending that night together too.

I tried again the next night – only this time, I made sure I'd spent a few minutes being reacquainted with my right hand before we met up. This time, I found I (just about) had the resolve to persist with my conversation, even when she tried to use her distraction tactics. I told her that things were moving fast, that I really, really liked her, and still wanted to see her, but maybe we didn't need to see each other *every* night. Maybe if we saw each other every second night, we might appreciate each other even more – now that's a reasonable request, isn't it? Apparently not. She flipped, and for the first time, I saw Nutty Suzie. She started screaming about me using her for sex, about how men always do this. She started hurling objects at me – remote controls, shoes, even a footstool. She was like some terrifying love child of the Tasmanian Devil and the Incredible Hulk, whizzing manically around the apartment throwing my possessions about. I just sort of stood there, scared and slightly puzzled by it all. Like a forest fire, I just presumed I had to leave her to burn herself out. Instead, after a prolonged rage, she stormed out, practically slamming the door off its hinges and screeching off down the street in her car.

So, of course, the whole thing ended there, right? I would have been off my rocker to continue with that firebrand, yes? Much though I know that and *knew* that, she was back in my bed that night, sleeping soundly in my arms after a sobbed apology at my doorstep had ended with some absolutely amazing make-up sex (so that, ahem, moment of relief earlier had counted for nothing). That in turn was followed by her whispering she loved me in my ear, which I reciprocated. I didn't love her, so who knows why I said it – perhaps I was too scared to say anything else! I was, in every possible way, screwed. She had me in her grasp. I got little sleep that night, rehearsing in my head lots of different ways to get out of the relationship without causing too much damage either to her feelings or my apartment. I couldn't think of any, and in the end I resigned myself to the fact that whilst she may have been insane, she was at the very least insanely gorgeous to go with it. Yes, I would be dating a nutcase, but I would be getting wild nightly sex as part of the bargain. Things could be worse...couldn't they?

We spent a couple of days shy of five months together, on and off, engaged in a constant make-up-break-up-make-up-break-up cycle. And boy, were they five eventful months. It seemed like we were either perennially engaged in coitus or engaged in passionate arguments. We did none of the things a proper couple does, like meeting each other's friends and family. I was actually sort of glad I had no parents for her to meet – mum would have absolutely hated her.

Towards the end of the relationship, when even she could see that all hope was disappearing for us, she resorted to the old 'I think I'm pregnant' trick. It looked very well rehearsed – her skin was all pale and mascara was running down her cheeks. The truly scary thing is that I actually think she had even convinced herself; lied to herself so much that eventually even she believed it. Certainly, when the time came that she took the test, and it inevitably came out negative (one test I was delighted to fail), a look of grief spread across her face. Perhaps it was all part of her big plan - because, *quelle surprise*, I then found myself consoling her. Cuddles turned to kisses, kisses to sex, and sex to another shot at going out with each other.

On another occasion, during one of our 'off' periods, I was walking from my car to the school gates when I found myself being pounced on from behind – one arm locked around my neck and the other smacking the top of my head like a bongo. I thought I was being attacked by one of the kids – but no, it was Suzie, and she was seething after I had told her to 'piss off out of my life' earlier that morning. I wasn't hurt, but my pride was. I had to talk the Head of Humanities out of calling the police on my behalf, embarrassingly having to assure him that it was okay, she was in fact my girlfriend.

She was just so hard to break up with. I like to think I've mastered the fine art of the tablecloth breakup. You know - a bit like those people who can pull a tablecloth from under a load of cutlery and crockery and they somehow all remain standing. That's me. I can say all the right words, make all the right gestures, so that the woman I'm dumping doesn't make a scene or break down there and then. What happens when I'm gone - that's none of my business. I just like to get the Hell out of there while the going's good. I couldn't seem to do that, though. Every time I tried it ended up causing a huge spectacle, either privately or publically.

It eventually happened, though. The last time I saw her, she was sitting slumped at a lamppost near my apartment, penknife in her hand, sobbing and carving what I later found out were our initials into it. I should have gone down to confront her – but like I just said, she had a knife in her hands! I watched from behind my curtains as a kindly-looking old man bent down to speak to her. He put his arm around her and led her away. I don't know who it was and I don't know what he said. I just know it worked. I returned from work the next day to find an answer machine message from Suzie telling me I was a waste of space, that I was forbidden from ever seeing her again (oh yes!) and that if she ever did see me, she would actually kill me. There can't be a death threat in the history of death threats that has ever inspired so much joy – I danced around my living room, finally free from what had been a truly traumatic relationship.

All of this does, of course, make it rather incredulous that I should ever want to see her again. I was having major cold feet, but it was too late to back out now. As I waited on the bench near Nando's, I busied myself with one of my favourite time-fillers - my list of unsolved Countdown numbers games. I should explain. Every now and again - and it is a rarity indeed - Carol fails to get to the exact number target. Often she manages to get closer than the contestants, but still ends up falling short. Thus, we are to assume, its an impossibility; it's Carol, after all. Well, I refuse to believe it's impossible, and so I keep a record. Have done ever since I first started watching the show in the mid 80s. The thing is, I just hate leaving things up in the air, unresolved - so I try to find the solutions. Whenever I do manage to solve one, I send a letter (and it's still a letter, even nowadays) to the Countdown producers to let them know of my feat. As recently as nine months ago (a matter of weeks before the great Richard Whiteley's death - I'm hoping there's some kind of ethereal version of Countdown, with Richard back in the hot-seat. I'll perch on a cloud, studiously making notes of the unsolved numbers games), I sent a solution in informing them that the target of 801 with the numbers 75, 10, 9, 7, 6 and 4 was in fact achievable thusly:

$$(((75 \times 10) + (9 \times 6)) + 4) - 7$$

I reassured them that Carol was not to feel too crestfallen about this; that it was, indeed, a particularly tricky problem, which had taken me over three weeks to crack. I refrained from suggesting that the use of multiple brackets - or brackets within brackets - might improve Carol's success rate, as such advice had always fallen on deaf ears before.

The producers have usually been really nice, though sometimes they haven't bothered replying. Oftentimes I have received a letter back – most recently addressing me as 'Will' and not 'Mr Jacobs' - thanking me for my hard work and encouraging me to keep watching the show and finding solutions. One time they went one better and sent me a signed photo of Richard and Carol. Sometimes I have had gifts - everything from Countdown pencils to Countdown board games to Countdown mugs, all of which, needless to say, I've kept and cherished. Once, in 1998, after a particularly fruitful year in which I sent in half a dozen solutions, they sent me a Christmas card. My second-favourite reward was a Polaroid of Carol smiling at the letters board, which spelled the words 'THANKS

WJ'. Nothing, though, will ever beat getting an actual name check from Richard himself, who, on January 23rd, 1986, informed the nation that 'a very clever young man by the name of Will Jacobs has solved last Tuesday's numbers game, which even our very own Carol didn't manage to do. Looks like you might have a bit of competition there, Carol!' I still rank it as one of the top five experiences of my life. I've kept the video tape, though that part of it is jumpy and the audio a bit distorted from the hundreds and hundreds of times I've watched it, rewound it and watched it again. I keep meaning to get the tape transferred into a digital format to preserve what's left of it - in all honesty, though, there's probably not a great deal of point now. Who would see it? The grandchildren?

The great majority of the targets - 73% of them if we're being exact, and we're on my watch, so we are - are still works-in-progress. I haven't managed to solve them - but nor have I given up on them. I flit between them, hoping for my Eureka moment. Of course, this does, in theory, mean I could find a solution to a problem from, say, 1989, and I can imagine the producers being somewhat indifferent to that kind of news - I'm sure they care a good deal less than I do - but I'd send the letter anyway. You never know. I'd like to get the percentage down a bit before I do shuffle off this mortal coil - 50% would be nice.

I know what else you're probably thinking. You're having trouble squaring up the borderline-OCD Countdown obsessive with the man who has somehow managed to persuade six of his ex-girlfriends to go on a date with him. The truth is, I kept the two worlds apart when I was with any of them. Doesn't every one have secrets they keep from their partners? Don't you? Only mine weren't sordid or scandalous or pervy - just really, really geeky. My guilty secret involved Carol Vorderman. A fully-clothed one at that.

Anyway, mathematical inspiration was not particularly forthcoming early that afternoon - I was finding the prospect of my imminent date consuming more of my thoughts than the numbers, so my plan was clearly failing. Was I nervous? I certainly had a right to be after the way I had ended things with Suzie. And because, well, it was Suzie: crazysexysuzie.

My thoughts were interrupted by a distant voice. 'Will?'

The end of the Countdown clock music played in my head: bu-du-bu-du-bu-du-du-du. Bu! Time up. Time to start the date and, possibly, face the music.

As she came bounding into my eye line, I could see immediately that Suzie was in exactly the same state she was in the last time I saw her, three years ago – her eyes red and puffy and her cheekbones streaked with globs of mascara. She clasped her arms around my neck.

'Oh Will!'

Oh shit.

For the first couple of minutes, she spoke in a syllable-sob-syllable-sob pattern, like a small child in a state. *It's - sob - so - sob - good - sob - to - sob - see - sob - you - sob*, and so forth. A good deal of it was inaudible and high-pitched, but I did manage to pick out a couple of choice words which explained this emotional outburst: *can - sob - cer* and *tra - sob - gic*. Her breath was hot on my cheek and my shoulder was quickly sodden. I eventually managed to prize myself away from her grip.

'Hey, if anyone should be crying here, it's me! Come on now! I'm fine. Let's not start the day like this!'

She nodded, took a tissue from her rather over-sized handbag, wiped her tears away and blew her nose loudly. Amazingly, even at that very moment, I still found her unbelievably attractive. Therein lay the reason behind our relative longevity - no matter what she did, I still fancied the pants off her. She eventually forced a smile. I forced one back. And we stood there, exchanging strained smiles but no words. Say something, Will, for Christ's sake.

'I'm hoping there isn't a knife in that handbag!'

Say something better, Will, for Christ's sake.

'I'm sorry?' She peered down towards her handbag, rightfully slightly perplexed by my comment.

'It's just that, the last time you saw me, you know, on account of how we, well how I really and the things I, by which I mean the way it ended, you, in a nutshell,' come on, Hugh Grant, spit it out. 'Said you'd kill me if you ever saw me again.'

She stared at me for a while before bursting into a fit of laughter pitched in the middle of manic and awkward. The laughter not yet fully subsided, she started prodding me in the chest. 'That's because you were such a little git to me! But that's a long time ago now! Don't worry, I've got no intention of killing you. Life's too short, isn't it?'

'Well, for me it is, yes.'

She ignored me. 'So after a lot of soul-searching, I've come here today to forgive you.'

My teeth started to grind together. *You've come here to forgive me?* How about I forgive you for your behaviour, you nutty cow? I resisted the temptation to vent my spleen, on account of the fact that the date was a mere fives minutes old.

'That's...very...nice of you. Hey, listen, we've got some catching up to do, and I make it lunchtime. Shall we?'

We made the short journey to Nando's in a slightly uncomfortable silence, which was at least preferable to the wailing sound she was making a matter of minutes ago.

We sat down and proceded to squeeze as much small talk as we could out of our surroundings - how much we both liked Nando's, how overcast it was today, that type of mundanity - before a chirpy young waitress came to put us out of our misery by taking our order. We both ordered the same thing - flame-grilled butterfly chicken breast with rice. I really fancied the garlic bread, but for some reason unknown even to myself I resisted - it wasn't like I was planning to kiss her or anything. She suggested we share a side of onion rings, so I don't think she was planning to kiss me either. Maybe this day wasn't going to be so terrible after all! At least we'd managed to find a bit of common ground in terms of food preferences and no one was planning to kiss anyone. I ordered a beer to take the edge off my nerves, but she stuck to Coke.

Right - time to nudge the conversation up a gear.

'So, what have you been doing for the last few years?'

'Well, I imagine you picture me crying into my pillow for weeks on end after you chucked me.'

'No, I...'

'WRONG! When Suzie falls off the horse she gets straight back on it. That very night, I got back on soulmatesearch and kept looking.'

I wasn't sure whether the horse in this analogy was me, the website or love, but I nodded anyway.

'As soon as I un-suspended my profile, the offers just came flooding in. I must have had a different date every night for a month.'

The glint in her eye suggested she was trying to make me jealous.

'Then, I met my Prince Charming, Derek.'

Funny name for a Prince, charming or otherwise.

'Eric was so...dreamy! He was a fireman, you know. Big, rugged man's man.'

Subtext - unlike his scrawny Maths teacher predecessor.

'We had a whirlwind romance.'

I wondered if there was any other kind in Suzie's world.

'The kind of love you only ever see in Julia Roberts films.'

'I don't watch Julia Roberts films, so I guess I don't know the true meaning of love.'

She narrowed her eyes at me. 'I'm talking fresh flowers every day. Romantic walks in the park. The guy just swept me off my feet.'

I smiled. 'Good for you, Suzie. I'm glad it all worked out.'

'I haven't finished my story.'

'Oh, sorry.'

'Anyway, he said to me one day - 'Suzie, I love you more than anything in the world. But I think I've got a higher calling in life than just being a fireman. I'm going to Africa to help build an orphanage. I'll be gone for a long time. If it's meant to be, we'll pick up from where we left off when I get back, but I know it's totally unrealistic of me to expect you to wait'.'

Goodness - someone was telling porkies here, and I wasn't sure whether it was Derek or Suzie.

'Wow, what a story. And did you reunite when he got back?'

'No. I never saw him again. Probably still out there, doing his bit. That was just Derek - selfless. So eventually I decided to get back,'

'On the horse?'

'Into the dating game, I was going to say. I did the whole internet dating thing again.'

For the next part of the conversation, Suzie proceded to list her succession of dates, boyfriends and almost-boyfriends - there was John, Paul, George, Ringo, Mick, Keith, Gary, Mark, Howard, Jason, Robbie, Dave Dee, Dozy, Beaky, Mick and Titch and, of course, our pair of Wills. Okay, so (the pair of Wills notwithstanding) these may not have been the EXACT names, which I chose not to commit to memory. It was a pretty exhaustive list, one which easily out trumped Song for Whoever Bingo for magnitude.

'...and eventually I met my current boyfriend, Roger.'

'And you met him...'

'Last week.'

'Ah. Serious, then?'

'I'm detecting some sarcasm here, but if you must know, yes, it IS serious. Roger told me he loved me after our first date - how romantic is that?'

I guffawed. 'Oh God, Suzie. You must have realised he said that to get straight into your pants? I mean, love after one date? Surely you of all people can't be that naive?'

She glared at me. 'Me of all people? And just what is that supposed to mean?'

I recoiled a little, but there was no turning back now. 'Well, clearly you've been around the block a bit! I would have thought you'd have known a bit about how men's minds work by now?'

She inhaled audibly to express her shock and disgust. '*I've* been around the block? *I* have?! You're hardly a Trappist monk yourself, Will!'

She slammed her cutlery down onto the table and crossed her arms, causing a number of other diners to look in our direction.

I spoke in a tone louder than a whisper but quieter than my normal speaking voice in an attempt to persuade her to reduce her own volume. 'Look, I'm sorry. It came out wrong. I'm sorry. Let's carry on, shall we? Let's change the subject.'

We continued to eat in silence. I couldn't think of anything to say. Either she was in the same predicament or she was still pissed off at me. She watched me eat, gazing at me slightly quizzically throughout. Eventually I could take it no more.

'Are you okay, Suzie?'

'What? Oh, yeah, yeah, fine. So you still eat like that, do you?'

I knew exactly what she meant by 'like that'. She was referring to my food hierarchy. In a nutshell, I eat in reverse order of preference - worst to best. So let me give you an example. Fish, chips and peas would go peas first, then chips, then fish. A more complex example - a roast dinner. That would go brussels, parsnips, peas, potatoes, Yorkshire pudding, chicken. The rationale is quite simple - I like to save the best til last, to work up to the finest part of the meal. Of course, some meals present more of a challenge than others - a stew, for example, is a nightmare for an organised eater like myself, as everything is all mixed up. I still endeavour to compartmentalise it - pick out the vegetables and eat them first, then the meat, then the dumplings. I tend not to make stews for myself for this reason - who wants to go to all that effort? Another example - if I'm at an Indian restaurant, I insist on arranging the food on my plate myself - I realise a lot of people make a rice bed then pour the meat and sauce over the top of it. Not I. I like them side by side, not even touching. That way it's easy to eat the rice first and the meat second. I appreciate that all of this raises more questions than it answers. What if, you're doubtless wondering, I get full before I reach the end of the meal? Then I've wasted the best bit. It's for this reason that I accept that the opposite system to mine - eating in order of preference, best to worst - is a very viable way of eating, just as good as mine. However, my system works for two reasons:

(a) You wouldn't know it to look at me, but I can put away a lot of food. It's all about maintaining a steady, comfortable pace;

(b) I'm a good judge of how much of each food I'll need. If I think the whole thing looks beyond my reach, I'll do a quick estimate of what percentage I DO think I'll manage, then eat that percentage of each kind of food I've got on my plate. That's not a hard and fast rule, though. If something's particularly carb-heavy, I might reduce the percentage of that food and adjust the percentage of the best food on the plate accordingly.

Look, this isn't as strange as it sounds; we've all got our little systems, our strange routines. Haven't we? I've probably got more than most, admittedly. Even as a small child, on my birthday I would separate my things into two piles - a pile for cards, a pile for presents. Cards were opened first, obviously, then presents - I mean, who doesn't prefer presents? The presents themselves I would tackle in order - smallest to biggest is an obvious temptation, but as we all know, bigger doesn't always mean better. Ahem. So I'd use my second-guessing skills, drawing on past birthdays and the typical quality of present given therein to figure out what was likely to be the worst present (the one from mad old Auntie Beryl) and work my way up to the one likely to be the best (always mum's). It's a system I have never abandoned, even as the number of presents given has dwindled and the present givers have changed - there's no mum any more of course, but there is Helen, and it's always the present she has sent over that I save until last and will continue to do so for however many birthdays I have left.

But back to the conversation. Just to refresh your memory a sulking Suzie was having a go at me for how I eat.

'It just used to aggravate me a bit, that's all. Still does!'

'Okay...'

'I mean, you have to admit, it's just a tiny bit...weird?'

She inflected on the end of her sentence to make it sound like a question, but we both knew full well it was a statement. Weird was exactly what she meant. Great. Crazysexysuzie herself was implying my behaviour might be viewed as a bit - well - crazy. Weird it was not. Systematic, yes; logical, yes; weird, no. I couldn't be bothered wasting my breath justifying myself, though. I didn't care. I'd already gone past the point where I wanted to salvage something from this date. It was a mistake meeting up, and this tetchy excuse for a rendezvous was proof of that. I was clock watching (not something of which a dying man does a lot) - just waiting for the day to end. I was already thinking about tomorrow's date with Harriet, which was sure to go better than this fiasco. I shrugged and continued to eat my food, no longer straining for conversation topics. She cocked her head upwards and scraped her hair back with her hands, looking slightly exasperated.

'Look, Will, I'm sorry. This isn't going well, is it? The truth is, I'm really nervous. You meant the world to me and I didn't want to split up. When I found out about the cancer, I freaked out a bit. I mean, I was okay with never seeing you again, but I didn't want you to die! I wanted today to be really nice, for us to make amends.'

'And that's all I wanted!'

'But I suppose I'm still a bit angry with you, and that's why I'm acting a bit off.' She grabbed my hands just as I was about to go in for another round of food and looked at me pleadingly, her eyes soft and glistening now. 'Will you give me another chance?'

I nodded. 'Of course. Hey, we were always a bit fiery together, weren't we? It's just like old times!'

'Yeah, except in old times we'd be naked within the next five minutes!'

Don't respond, Will. Don't get drawn in! Don't, whatever you do, flirt with this woman. It wasn't like yesterday. She wasn't Maria. Engaging with her in that way could have dire consequences. I let out a fake giggle.

'Listen, Will, I've got something to show you.'

She leaned over and fished around in her handbag. I still hadn't quite managed to convince myself that there wasn't a murderous weapon in there. Suzie Dewhurst. In Nando's. With a candlestick. She produced a thick, heavy-looking hardback book. I weighed up the damage it could do were she to use it to bludgeon me with, and decided that at worst it could give me a rather nasty headache but wouldn't kill me. I was safe: for now. I looked at the cover. It said 'Will Jacobs, 2002', the font all maudlin, like the cover was some sort of headstone for our dead relationship. I opened the book (with no little trepidation, though I did my best to mask this) and could see straight away that it was a scrapbook cataloguing / commemorating our time together. The pages were annotated with some quite lovely-looking calligraphy - it had undoubtedly taken time, care and effort. I looked up at her and smiled. The first artefact was a restaurant receipt. The handwritten note next to it explained that it was from our first date. What it did not explain was WHY it was there. Keeping a record of what exactly we ate and drank during our first meal together was on a level of anal retentiveness beyond which even I could comprehend.

'I see that I had steak and chips that night. Hmm.'

Chips and steak, really. Either way, it was a dull snippet of information. Matching the receipt for banality on the same page was a ticket for the train journey we took back to my home that night.

'Don't you just feel like we're right back there when you look at these old treasures?'

'Hmm-mmm!'

I turned the page, expecting yet another example of tedium. How wrong I was.

'Erm, Suzie...what exactly is this?'

It appeared to be a clump of human hair Sellotaped to the page. It WAS a clump of human hair Sellotaped to the page. Specifically, it was a clump of MY hair Sellotaped to the page. This was getting a bit weird. Not eating-your-food-in-reverse-order-of-preference weird. Just weird-weird.

'I thought you might recognise your own hair! It's a shade darker than yours is now, no offence - but, yep, it's yours!'

Okay, so many questions here. Where to begin? 'So how did you come by this? Did you cut it off while I was sleeping?'

I was trying my hardest not to sound alarmed or accusing, even though I was both. My voice seemed to be pitched a little higher than usual. Suzie giggled into her hands.

'No, no, no! What, do you think I just sat there in bed with a pair of scissors while you were asleep next to me?'

Yes.

'No!'

'This was that trip to the hairdresser's we took together. Look, it's all there in the notes. When we got home, I noticed there was still some of your hair in the hood of your jumper, so I thought I'd have it as a keepsake!'

Good Lord. What exactly did she intend to do with a clump of my hair? Was she planning to clone me or something? When I was dead and gone, would there be a Will Jacobs version 2.0 roaming the Earth, bedding scores of future ladies? Actually, I quite liked that idea! The theory was backed up when, a little later in the scrapbook, I found something even stranger / more disgusting - a set of nail clippings. I kid you not. It's just the thing to round off a nice meal, isn't it? Seeing a three year old collection of your own fingernail clippings. I tried to gloss over it.

'So do you...carry this thing around with you?'

'What? No! That would be crazy!'

Right, Suzie. THAT would be crazy.

'No - I brought it along today specially. I thought you'd like it. You do like it, don't you?'

Lie through your teeth, boy. 'Are you kidding? I love it! It's like stepping into a time machine!'

I continued flicking through the scrapbook, unsure as I turned each page whether I would be bored or terrified by what I saw. Generally, it was the former - there was a cinema ticket from the first film we saw together (the Tom Hanks / Leonardo di Caprio film *Catch Me If You Can*), a short shopping list she must have found from the first time I cooked for her, a ripped section from the wine label from that same evening, a nightclub flyer from the first time we hit the town and so on. Of course, there was the standard scrapbook fare - lots of photos from our time together (which I have to admit I did enjoy looking at, and my unforced smiles on those photos were proof that there were plenty of good times, that there was in fact more depth to our relationship than the bonking and the bickering). Some of the photos were a little more bizarre, though, and were clearly taken without my knowledge or consent - one of me getting into my car to go to work and one of me fast asleep, which seemed rather creepy. Then - hello! - a Polaroid of my manhood. I couldn't just skip by that one. I blushed.

'Suzie, why - I mean when - which is to say how...'

She grinned at me sheepishly. 'What? You don't mind, do you? It's there to remind me of some very,' she walked her long fingernails across the table, across the page and up my chest. 'VERY good times. I mean, I can take it out if you want?'

I cleared my throat and shuffled around on my chair. I reminded myself again that I was not, under any circumstances, to get drawn into any situations that could be construed as flirting. 'No, no, that's okay. You keep it.' Change the subject, change the subject, change the subject. 'So all those fellas you mentioned before - have you got a scrapbook for each of them, too?'

I envisaged a big bookshelf full of these things, each one labelled with different boyfriends' names. When I pictured it, I pictured them first in chronological order. Then I pictured them in alphabetical order. Then I pictured them in order of thinnest to thickest, the thicker the scrapbook theoretically denoting the longer the relationship. I snapped out of it, realising I was getting sidetracked and not listening to Suzie's response to my question. I jumped back onto the moving train, catching her mid-sentence.

'....important to me as you were. I kept this one because I think that what we had was really special and I wanted to preserve you. Preserve it. Whatever.'

'I see. Well...thanks!'

I closed the book and slid it back over the table to her.

She bit her lip. 'Would you mind if I took a little something from today? A souvenir of our last-ever date together, just to finish the collection?'

I shook my head. 'Go for your life!'

Perhaps she'd like me to sign my name in earwax or some such. Instead, she took a napkin, scribbled the date on it and stuffed it into the scrapbook, which she closed and returned to her handbag. 'Shall we get out of here?'

We paid up (she actually insisted on paying, surprisingly) and stood outside Nando's, looking at each other. If this had been a real date, we'd be at the point where we either kissed or went our separate ways. In some ways this situation didn't feel that dissimilar. This was a pivotal moment, a juncture. This was my opportunity to cut my losses and write off what had been a less-than-successful reunion. I could say my goodbyes and go home, or we could plough on. If we did the latter, the day was as likely to get much better as it was to get much worse - continuing with the date was a gamble for sure.

'So...'

'So.'

'Thanks for treating me to a nice lunch.'

'You're welcome.'

More silence. Jesus, this was awkward. I couldn't take it anymore. I buckled. 'So what do you want to do now? I mean, presuming you want to do something else.'

Please say you don't, please say you don't.

'Oh, I do! I really do.'

Damn.

'Any suggestions?'

More silence. Eventually, I threw my hands up in the air.

'Do you know what I'd really like to do? Something we never really seemed to do when we were together: nothing. Just hang out together. Enjoy each other's company. Back then, we were always either at each other's throats or tangled up in bed sheets. Weren't we? There was never a dull moment, but I think that was part of the problem. We never did 'normal' boyfriend and girlfriend stuff.'

'You're probably right. So what are you saying, you want to go back to your place?'

No. God no. No way José. Definitely not. Bad idea.

'Yeah, okay.'

Damn again!

So before I knew it, there she was, back in my flat - a site I was sure I'd never see again. It felt wrong. Not wrong in a sexy, illicit way - just wrong. Dangerous. Not dangerous in a taboo sort of way, either - just dangerous. Alarm bells were ringing - what the hell was I doing?

I made us both a cup of tea, using the time it took the kettle to boil to ponder all the possibilities that lay ahead, and almost all of them were terrifying. I still hadn't quite ruled out the possibility of her making good on her promise to kill me - and in my own home! It would be so easy to make it look like an accident, like I'd slipped and banged my head or something! Or maybe she'd coerce me into having sex with her - the woman was still drop dead gorgeous. Then she'd be back in my life. I'd probably have to go out with her again. I think I preferred the murder thing! She was so volatile and unpredictable that maybe I'd say something to upset her and she'd start hitting me or something. Most likely of all, though, was the possibility - probability - of the two of us having a blazing row and this whole day turning out to be a wasted endeavour. The kettle was boiled. Time to give her an opt-out clause.

'Are you sure your boyfriend won't mind any of this? Roger, wasn't it?'

'Relax, Will. I've told him exactly what I'm doing today - I'm spending the day with an ex-boyfriend who's dying of cancer so I can say goodbye to him. He's okay with that, believe me. There's not going to be any funny business. You're not expecting any, are you?'

'No! God no. So - fancy watching a film?'

'Sure!'

Watching a DVD seemed a great idea. It would be a nice, 'normal' thing to do and, best of all, we wouldn't have to talk to each other. Because if one thing was getting in the way of us having a nice day together, it was definitely the talking to each other bit. But what to pick from my collection? It's alphabetised, unlike my record collection, although I was now wishing it was organised in that same way - being able to go straight to a particular genre would have been helpful. Instead, I closed my eyes and pointed to a random choice. *Schindler's List*. Nice and long and would have eaten up the hours, but it would have been a pretty depressing choice. I tried again. *Psycho*. No, really. Very exciting, but I really didn't want to put any ideas into her head. I tried again. *The Ring*. A gripping flick, but I envisaged her clinging to my arm when it got scary. I tried again. *Four Weddings and a Funeral* (left over from a previous relationship, honest guv'nor). Suitably girl-friendly, but I really didn't want to get her into a slushy, romantic mood. I tried again. *Goldfinger*. Too boy-friendly for her tastes, surely - I had to keep her interested, to keep her fixated on the film and not my shortcomings. I tried again and arrived at what had to be the most neutral film in my collection - *The Wizard of Oz*. Who doesn't love that? Suzie whooped her approval.

'Are you coming to sit with me, then? I don't bite!'

'Erm, excuse me, Madame, if I remember rightly, you DO bite! In a good way, mind you!'

She laughed, reached over and slapped my arm. 'Cheeky!'

What was I doing? Suzie - *Suzie* - was in my flat. We were about to watch a film together. And I was flirting with her. Cool it, fella. I trudged over to the sofa, but sat as far away from her as possible and pressed play.

The plan was working, insofar as we weren't talking to each other. Nobody was doing or saying anything crazy or hurtful and there was no flirting, nothing suggestive. We weren't arguing and we weren't having sex - it was fantastic! We were just having a nice time, watching a nice film, like a nice, normal couple. She'd occasionally interject with a comment about how much she loved the film as a little girl, how she'd put her hair in pigtails and walk around in her mother's red high heels pretending to be Dorothy. I (half-)jokingly told her the Wicked Witch of the West might have been a more appropriate figure to aspire to, that I was tempted to pour a little bit of water on her to check. She responded by telling me that if I was any character in the film it would be the Tin Man on account of my heartlessness. I actually think the Lion might have been a bit closer to the mark, on account of the fact that I really should have had the courage to go home on my own after the meal at Nando's. Still, we were here now and, touch wood, it was actually going pretty well.

Then, apropos of nothing, halfway through the film she grabbed the remote and turned the television off, which I thought was a bit of an audacious thing to do in someone else's home. She was obviously more interested in getting something off her chest than seeing Dorothy return to Kansas.

'So go on, then - what's all this about?'

'What's what about?'

'Getting in touch with me. Why did you do it? What did you want to get out of it?'

'I told you! I just wanted to end things on a nice note between us, have one last nice memory of you to take to the grave.'

'And it's just me you're seeing, is it? I'm the lucky one?'

I could tell by the way she was phrasing the questions that she wasn't buying it. I figured I had nothing to lose by telling her the truth. 'Well, if I'm being honest, it's not just you. There are seven of you. I'm meeting up with a different ex every day for a week.'

She huffed. 'I knew it. Lovely. Just lovely. And here I was thinking I was special. I'm just one of seven.'

'No, no, you're definitely special!' I pressed on before she had the chance to dwell on the ambiguity of that adjective. 'If it's any kind of consolation, you were the first one I got in touch with.' Technically true, though if you recall, it was by accident and not design. I made a mental note not to tell any of my remaining dates the exact ins and outs of my plan.

'You know what? I think I'm going to leave.'

'Leave? Why? I thought we were having a nice time?' Hard to believe I was pleading with her to stay – but apparently I was!

'I just don't want any more of your false pretences, your lies. You're a liar, Will. I'm going home to see Roger.'

My blood boiled. I knew that the right thing to do would be let it wash over me, let her leave. But I couldn't resist a cheap potshot: I had to retaliate.

'I'm a liar. Nice. And what are you? Tell me, all these boyfriends you've had that you've been boasting about - does it not tell you something that none of them wanted to stick with you?'

'Oh. My. God. Can you hear yourself? The great Will Jacobs, Mr Ladies' Man, Cassanova himself, the man who sees women as disposable and dispensable, has the cheek to call me out on the number of boyfriends I've had. Talk about the pot calling the kettle black.'

'No no no. Let's get this straight. The pot is in fact calling the kettle a borderline psychopath.'

'Aargh! If you weren't dying, I'd kill you, you tosspot! You're a self-centred, arrogant wanker. You're going to die alone, and you deserve to.'

She wept loudly into her hands, her shoulders rocking up and down in grand, rhythmic movements. Shit. What to do here? I suppose consoling her would have been quite a gentlemanly thing to do – but then after what she had just said it should rightly have been *me* she was consoling, surely? I gave her a very gentle pat on the back and retreated back to a safe distance away from her. Still the crying continued. I twiddled my thumbs, desperate to think up a way to get her out of my apartment in a manner that was quick and efficient whilst also guaranteeing my safety.

More thumb twiddling.

I decided the best way, though it was to prove neither quick nor efficient, was to leave her until she was all cried out. I mulled over turning the film back on, but sensed this would anger her. I mulled over sneaking out of the room to make a cup of tea, but figured any movements might awake her from her teary trance and she'd have another go at me. So I just sat there, a prisoner to this massively awkward scenario.

Eventually, the crying began to subside – the shoulder movements were less pronounced, the sobbing quieter and less alarming until eventually it had stopped altogether. Head still in one hand, she used the other to fish for a tissue in her handbag. She mopped her face, smeared once again in mascara as it had been when we met up earlier that day, and fixed her red glassy eyes on me. It was a different look, though.

'Listen, I'm really sorry about how things turned out between us. I mean, I know you dumped me – but I also know I can be a little crazy. I really, really didn't want today to turn out like this. So,' she looked at me intently, intensely, 'I'm sorry,' And what a lovely moment that would have been, should have been, if only her apology had ended there – if not for the next three words. 'It's just that...'

Yes, those three words that should never feature in an apology but so often seem to. Three words that mean – *brace yourself. I've still got beef with you.* Three words that mean – *I am sorry...sort of. But you should be sorry, too, and here's why...*It's just that – what? You made me angry? You just weren't committed enough? I didn't trust you? Place your bets.

'...I think there was someone else. Someone...else.'

Well I didn't see that one coming. I racked my brains, desperate to locate the source of her confusion.

'No, honestly, there wasn't. Look, I've got nothing to lose here. I might as well be honest and I am being. There was nobody else.'

'Yes there was, Will. I just don't think you realised. If I was crazy, it's because you drove me crazy. The *situation* drove me crazy.'

I looked at her quizzically.

'It was every time the phone rang. Every time you heard her voice.'

Ah. I knew exactly who 'she' was.

'Your whole face would just light up. You sort of - I don't know - came to life or something. And you'd twist that telephone cord around your finger like some love struck teenage girl while you were talking. You'd have this look in your eyes, this look of pure and utter contentment, enchantment. And you'd make your little private jokes and laugh like you were going to explode. Then you'd put down the phone and for a while be so fizzy that you could barely sit still and she'd be all you wanted to talk about. Helen this, Helen that, Helen the other. To be honest, I couldn't have given two hoots what she was doing in her glamorous Stateside life, and I didn't try to hide the fact, but you were oblivious, too enraptured in her to see what was going on with your actual girlfriend. Then when you eventually came down from Planet Helen, you just didn't seem that bothered about me. Not once did you ever laugh with me the way you did with her. How do you think that made me feel, Will?'

I didn't know what to say. 'Sorry' didn't seem like the right choice, though it was clearly what she wanted - I had nothing to be sorry for. She was wrong. Helen was married. She knew that.

She stood up, slung her giant handbag over her shoulder and kissed me on the cheek. 'So now you know. I'm so sorry about your illness. I'm sorry about what I said before about you dying alone. I truly hope you've still got a good long run left. And I'm sorry I can't finish the date. I just can't. Goodbye, Will.'

She glided out the door and started her car. She was gone. I was safe! I think you'll agree with me that that was quite a result, all things considered. I rang Helen almost straight away - this one would tickle her!

W: Evening Helen!

H: Juan!

W: Juan. Let's see - oh I get it. Juan as in Don Juan. Because of all the dates.

H: Nope. Juan as in Juan Kerr. Get it?

W: Ah, the debonaire musings of a glamorous Chicago fashion writer. Very mature!

I laughed, but stopped myself as I realised how hearty the laugh was.

H: So – you survived! Congratulations. Any stories?

W: Well, you know that expression 'a fate worse than death'? I think I would put Suzie in that category. Dying doesn't scare me as much as she does. The woman's as mad as a box of frogs, so no change there then. Called me a selfish wanker at the end of the night – ouch! I dodged a bullet there.

H: A literal one or a metaphorical one?

W: A metaphorical one. But a literal one would honestly not have been that out of character for Suzie today. She did let me know how much she wanted to kill me again!

H: Beautiful!

W: And she had this weird scrapbook, with my hair and fingernails and a picture of my nob!

H: You're shitting me? Hey, maybe we should put the picture on your gravestone – clearly that's what a lot of women think you are! Not me, though. I think you're all right. Listen, I'm absolutely knackered, so unless you've got any more particularly juicy stories about psychotic exes, I'm going to hang up now. She didn't say anything else that was really crazy?

I pondered over whether to tell her about how the date actually ended.

W: Nah. That's about it.

H: Okay. Goodnight, then. Oh, Jeff and I are fine, by the way. Thanks for asking. Selfish wanker.

W: Good to know! Love ya.

H: Love ya too.

Wednesday, 13th July, 2005

Wednesday morning's knock was the quickest of the week - a rapid, hurried quartet of knocks, equidistant to one another.

The strange thing was, when I opened the door, there was no one there. Just a tatty old briefcase, and on top of it, a metallic DVD gift box. The case inside was black and blank, and inside it was a disc, labelled by what looked like one of those old Dynamo machines. The label read 'Play me'. I was intrigued and wasted no time doing so.

I instantly recognised the face that appeared on my screen as that of Harriet. It seems a funny to thing to say of someone disguised by a comedy handlebar moustache and Sherlock Holmes-style hat, but she hadn't changed that much. I could still tell it was her, eighteen years – half our lifetimes – later. Her voice, too, was recognisable, yet disguised by a hammy, plummy old-fashioned male accent. I belly laughed and shook my head. What the heck was she up to?

'Mr Jacobs, we have grave news. Your former female companion, Ms. Harriet Hamilton, has been kidnapped! The kidnappers have requested no ransom of any sort, preferring instead to leave a complex trail of clues, the solving of which will lead to her whereabouts. Alas, the finest minds in all of Scotland Yard find themselves utterly bamboozled, and so we turn to you, Mr Jacobs. Locating Ms. Hamilton will require a combination of mathematical prowess and an excellent long-term memory, both of which we are assured you possess. The kidnappers have informed us that the clue to your first location is inside the briefcase. To open this, you will need to unlock the combination lock. The combination has been set to Harriet's date of birth. God speed.'

I liked this already. I was quite sure a quick jimmying with a screwdriver would unlock the frail and battered old case before me, but in the spirit of the activity, I racked my brains. I could recall plenty of ex-girlfriend birthdays, but for some reason not this one. It had been a long time since I had needed to know it. It had to end either 68 or 69, since she was in my school year although not my school. I remember being with her as she celebrated her 18th birthday, so I could narrow the month part down to between September and March. It was a four-digit combination, so it couldn't have been October, November or December. It had to be the 1st to the 9th of September, the 1st to the 9th of January, the 1st to the 9th of February, or the 1st to the 9th of March. That left only 36 possible combinations. I figured I would have remembered if her birthday had been on the 1st of any month, so I ruled those out, reducing the possibilities to 32. Time to get down to business! I started with 2968 – nothing. Then 3968 – nothing. 4968, 5968, 6968, 7968, 8968, 9968 – nothing. So she definitely wasn't born in 1968. 2169 – nothing. 3169 – nothing. Truly a man on a mission, I worked frenetically, carrying on in this fashion until I got to 8369 – bingo! The case popped open. Inside was a piece of paper, ripped out of a spiral pad, which read:

'Well done, Mr Jacobs. You have cracked the first code. Harriet is safe and well – for now. We have attached the next clue to the place where you and

Harriet shared your first kiss. Be careful not to bark up the wrong tree. Hurry now; time is of the essence. Signed, The Kidnappers.'

Well that was an easy one! Even without the clue / awful pun Harriet had managed to shoehorn in there, I knew exactly where I was going. I grabbed my car keys and headed to Brackenfield Country Park, a popular local beauty spot both for people generally and me specifically - it had proved a more than suitable place to romance the many and various girls and women who had entered my orbit. It was a quick journey, only a couple of miles from my house. For a brief moment I felt a little peeved about having to pay £4 to park my car for what I could only imagine would be a matter of minutes, but on the grand scheme of things I supposed it didn't really matter that much.

I made a beeline for the tree they nicknamed 'The Major', presumably in reference the Major Oak at Sherwood Forest - a tall, broad and imposing tree which stands alone at Brackenfield and which bore the carved initials of countless young lovers - HH + WJ (in that order) was once among them, but I could only presume the letters had been obscured over time.

Harriet and I met in that strange overlapping period whereby you're legally becoming an adult and yet you don't quite feel like you've shaken your childhood off. We were teenagers still, just, and looking back our relationship seems like a strange hotchpotch of youth and adulthood – and so it was as I recalled the two of us beneath the tree. I stood and stared at the ghosts around me - a younger me with Harriet, our legs intertwined as we lay together, sipping lake-cooled white wine from plastic glasses in between nibbling each other's earlobes. So full of promise and lust and joy. I smiled - a different smile to Ghost Will, the randy bugger. A remorseful one I suppose, if such a thing can exist. I resisted the temptation to see what the other Ghost Wills, differently aged and accompanied by different dates, were up to at other points around the park - what they were doing and, in some cases, who they were doing. I figured Harriet deserved better than that on her day, especially after all the effort to which she had clearly gone.

Even with the size of the tree, it was not difficult to spot a Manila envelope dangling from a branch. I endeavoured not to disturb the teenage couple with near identical hairdos sucking each other's faces off on the still dewy grass beneath The Major as I reached for the envelope, but failed - they gawped at me, fixing their collective gaze. I decided therefore to move away from The Major to open the envelope.

'The kidnappers here again. Congratulations on making it this far - your powers are clearly not to be underestimated. We're going to have to step up the level of challenge. Enclosed is a sheet containing seven rows of boxes. You will notice that one box from each row is shaded grey. When the clues are solved, the grey letters will spell out your next destination. A pen is enclosed in case you do not have one about your person. Be quick.'

I had to admit to feeling a tinge of genuine excitement - I had become properly engrossed in the fake mission. I threw myself into this mini-challenge with a giddy, almost childlike aplomb, dashing towards a nearby tree stump to lean on.

Row 1 - Harriet's favourite alcoholic beverage, both then and now.

Hmm. Ten letters. Would it be quicker to cast my mind back and try to envisage Harriet with a drink in her hands or to think of as many ten letter alcoholic drinks as I could? I plumped for the former - after all, it was a matter of mere moments ago that I was picturing the two of us drinking wine underneath The Major...white wine I was sure of it...but was that her favourite drink or just my choice? Time to think of some white wines and hope at least one of them contained ten letters (or better still that ONLY one of them did). Colombard? I counted the letters as I recited them in a whisper - a letter / finger too few! Pinot Grigio? A letter / finger too many! Although it did raise the issue of whether she was leaving a space between words, and if so that one would have required twelve squares. Pondering this caused a derailment of my train of thought, and suddenly I could think of no more white wine varieties. Clearly, this was not my Chosen Specialised Subject and, to mix my game shows, I could have really used a lifeline - perhaps I'd Phone a Friend. Helen was a massive wino (or 'connaiseur' as I believe they prefer to be called) - she would be able to reel off a list of wines, but as it was about four in the morning in Chicago, I figured it would not be with a great deal of zest. I could always Ask the Audience - maybe I'd go back and plead with the love struck teens for some inspiration. Come on, Will - think, think, think. The word 'Semillon' popped into my head from nowhere - I debated whether it had two 'l's as per my first instinct, or just one as per my nagging doubt, before realising that either way it was short of the target. Hang on, what about Chardonnay? Too obvious, surely? But it did fit. I wrote the word in half-sized letters in case it was wrong and I needed to write the correct answer above it. As things stood, my next destination started with 'R'

Row 2 - Harriet's greatest fear.

Seven letters this time. The grey square was the fifth one and I figured that as the answer wasn't immediately rushing to the front of my mind, I'd narrow it down a bit. Realistically speaking, that square would have to contain one of the vowels, the wannabe vowel ('y', of course) or, at a push, an 'h'. I was sure no other letter could follow 'r'. So my next move was to think of some common fears and see if first of all they fitted in terms of length, then in terms of whether their fifth letter was one of the seven possibilities. This process of elimination rules out commitment (and, yes, my mind went there first), vampires (although if she was going to express that - grammatically incorrectly - in the singular, it could go on the possibilities list), dying (and I decided not to waste any time thinking of synonyms for dying, since she surely wouldn't have been that insensitive anyway), drowning, ghosts, flying and snakes, but left heights and spiders. Then my mind went blank. As I weighed up the two possibilities, both perfectly and equally plausible, I was struck by a flashback of using a glass and a piece of cardboard to trap a spider in the bath at her parents' house when they were away one weekend, an act of heroism which was met with Harriet's arms draped around my neck and my cheek being kissed vigorously, so I figured I could confidently write the word 'spiders' in full-size letters.

So - RE_ _ _ _ _. I was really hoping I didn't have to travel to Reading for the next clue.

Row 3 - my favourite singer (and she still is!)

This one didn't take much pondering. At seven letters, it simply had to be Madonna. Few musical artists occupied the intersection of our musical Venn diagram, and Madonna certainly wasn't one of them (though one of my more successful relationships, I would never have said Harriet and I were blessed with plenty of common ground). Madonna's career was in full swing (yet it turns out still in its infancy) as we started out, and she would play her albums over and over on her tinny portable cassette player - hence the reason I know all of the words to songs like 'Borderline', 'Holiday' and 'Crazy For You', despite not particularly liking them. Harriet idolised her and as such she came along as part of the package, like a mildly annoying child from a previous marriage. I suppose looking back, those songs have a kind of period charm, irrevocably intertwined with my memories of that time. Kudos to the old bird in the leotard by the way - both she and her career are going to outlive me.

The grey square was the third one. Even without its determiner 'The' and the space in the middle of the other two words (guess that answered my earlier question), it was not difficult to work out that my next destination was The Red Lion, but I played the game anyway. It's a good job I wasn't relying on the fourth grey letter as I could have sat there all day racking my brains in a vain effort to come up with her father's first name (with an 'I' as the fifth letter of seven I'm going to guess Charles or Charlie, but it's immaterial now). I seem to have a much better propensity for remembering mothers' names (Harriet's being Brenda). However, I was quickly able to recall she had shown some early promise at tennis, that her parents took her on holiday to Florida during our first month together and that she had a wholly inappropriate crush on Larry Hagman - and not even 'I Dream of Jeannie'-era Hagman (a bad boy thing? A daddy issues thing? A cowboy hat thing? I made a mental note to ask her when I eventually found her but it never came up).

So that was that puzzle solved. To The Red Lion!

For the sake of my petrol and the limited time we had at our disposal, I was glad Harriet had chosen to order the locations geographically, as opposed to chronologically - if that had been the case, The Red Lion would have been the final location. I remember it as being the setting of what was effectively our swan song - our relationship was rapidly running out of fizz by this point and we went there for a bit of a change of scene, hoping the always effervescent atmosphere would rub off on us. It didn't. We barely spoke; barely looked at each other. A better man than I would have been trying to think of ways to salvage something that had once been so special - instead, I was looking around to see if any of the other patrons at The Red Lion might possibly be my next girlfriend. That's always been my trouble - there have always been so many other possibilities. We'd laugh at how the first time we met I was there with another girl - for that was what

Harriet had already become to me. Recollections of this final date could have become a downer.

However, on the short journey there (five miles from my house and three from Brackenfield Country Park), I found myself having to curb my speed on more than one occasion - I don't know whether I was caught up in the excitement of the mission or couldn't wait to see Harriet, but either way it would have been a strange thing to have to explain to a police officer, so I decided to play it safe and stick to the limit.

There are, of course, a thousand Red Lions in Britain (well, 759 to be exact, and you know how I like to be exact. Thank you once again Google), but few can be as lovely as this particular Red Lion, set as it is at the foot of rolling hills and with a beer garden that spills out onto a cricket pitch and woodland. Had it not been a Wednesday, and had it been a few hours later, on a sunny day like this the place would undoubtedly have been heaving. As it was, I was glad of the solitude, because what I was about to do would have seemed strange to the uninformed.

Finding the next envelope would prove the hardest part of the entire challenge - 'needle in a haystack' would have been stretching it but, as I said, it was a big place. At least I could rule out the inside of the pub, which was shut. Beyond that it was anyone's guess. My best strategy was to check the immediate perimeter of the building and work gradually outwards - I was hoping it wasn't as far out as the trees, but if need be I would check them as a last resort. So I walked around, looking up and down, side to side, for the elusive envelope, focusing particularly on objects to which it could be taped or tied - drainpipes, plant pots and so on. No joy. I widened my search, all the time dividing my attention between looking for the envelope and checking for onlookers - the longer the search went on, the more self-conscious I seemed to feel. I was just in the middle of checking to see if she had taped the letter to the underside of a bench when my concentration was broken by a loud and stern 'Excuse me!'

A tall, stocky chap in a black shirt and black tie was advancing towards me. The manager of The Red Lion, I wagered. No doubt in need of answers as to why someone was scouring the beer garden of his pub at eleven in the morning. The truth would have been stranger than fiction, but I failed to rustle up any fiction in the time it took him to go from the pub entrance to my personal space.

'Everything okay, sir?'

'Yep! Yep. I...'

'Do you mind if I ask your name?'

'It's Will.'

'Will Jacobs?'

I scrutinised his face but was sure I had never seen him before. 'Erm...yes?' I wasn't quite sure why I'd felt the need to inflect at the end - I was definitely Will Jacobs.

He smiled and produced an envelope from his pocket.

'You'll be needing this then. Harriet's an old family friend. She gave me strict instructions to leave you to sweat for a little bit. Good luck, mate.'

With that, he turned back around and disappeared into the pub. I parked myself on the same bench I had been investigating and opened the envelope.

'Mr Jacobs, you are proving a more than worthy foe! You have now passed the halfway point of the mission. To advance to the next checkpoint you will need to unscramble some names, words and phrases pertinent to your time with Harriet - specifically, these were some of her favourite things, so it is a test of your memory and your listening skills as a younger man. Once again you will notice that each letter in the answer is a square and that one of the squares is shaded grey. This time you must change the grey letters for their numerical value - A = 0, B = 1, C = 2 and so on and so forth up to J = 9. This will give you a mobile phone number. Ring it post haste. Goodbye for now.'

Great - anagrams! The part of Countdown I always fast forward. With only the bare minimum in terms of clues, I could have been there for quite some time. Either Harriet or the establishment manager must have realised this, as about five minutes later he returned with a cup of coffee. I effused my thanks and knuckled down.

I didn't really need to unscramble the first two anagrams - this being a mobile number, the first two digits had to be 0 and 7, so the letters had to be A and G - but did it anyway. It dawned on me that this was probably her own mobile number, which I had in my phone - however, after solving the third anagram I realised this was not the case - what I expected to be a 6 / G was actually a 5 /F. She clearly wasn't going to make this too easy for me - payback, perhaps?

I'm going to present the results of my endeavours as a table, though it will give the false impression that it was a simplistic process. In fact it was a long and often very frustrating pursuit which consumed the best part of an hour, during which time I went down many blind alleys. It was a much more taxing challenge than the previous one, wherein once I'd got a few letters I could easily work out the rest - I had to reveal each and every one of the eleven digits - and, as you will see, I in fact failed to accomplish that.

Feel free to play along with the ones you can, by the way. If you're that way inclined...

Clue given	Jumbled version	Eventual answer	Commentary	Highlighted letter	Numerical value
FILM.	A beatnik's taffy farts.	Breakfast at Tiffany's.	Her favourite film. She had a poster of Audrey Hepburn in her bedroom - you know the one. Looking timelessly glamorous in a black dress, swan-necked and long cigarette in hand, tiara on head.	A.	0.
DOG.	Big Dy.	Digby.	Digby the Dachshund. Her childhood pet. Died a few weeks before our relationship did. She was mortified. My timing might not have been particularly great.	G.	7.
CITY.	Clone ref.	Florence.	I initially struggled on this one, being drawn to thinking of British cities - but then I remembered her obsession with visiting Florence, where she had a pen pal she had met as a child while visiting the South of France (clearly Brenda and Charles / Charlie were not short of a bob or two as they raised their kids). I made another mental note to ask Harriet if she ever realised her dream, and if so if it was as romanticised as the Florence in her head, but again I forgot. Mental note - actual notes are better than mental notes).	F.	5.
CAR.	I'm in!	Mini.	Not really much you can do with four letters, is there? So this was a cinch. She had the car - a 1976 model – as a present on her 18th birthday, loving it and caring for it in a way I have done with very few human beings.	I.	8
ICE CREAM.	Ill in one go.	Gino Ginelli.	That quintessentially 80s ice cream, she practically ate the stuff by the bucketload (Tutti Fruity specifically), whilst fortunately retaining the metabolism levels of a pre-teen. If you ever saw the advert, I'm quite sure you're singing the jingle in your head right now – *Take a Gino home with you!*	C.	2.
COLOUR.	Quite sour.	Turquoise.	Not too tricky to figure out with that Q sticking out like a sore thumb, but in fairness to myself I had remembered anyway - it was a colour she wore often (and whether for the sake of consistency or the sake of old times, it was a colour I was to see	E.	4.

FRIEND.	Male liar.	Mariella.	I didn't actually know this one - and I really hoped it wasn't that Italian pen friend of hers, otherwise I'd have been there til Doomsday. It wasn't, but boy did it take me ages to get the answer, pushing the letters around until they formed a girl's name (and I presumed it was a girl despite the fact that my own best friend is of the opposite gender, which I concede is unusual). So many girlfriends, so many friends of girlfriends - how am I supposed to remember them all? I'll wager that Mariella doesn't remember me either, and I'm okay with that.	E.	4.
AUTHOR.	Award me a grotto.	????	I still have no idea what the answer to this one was. Harriet was quite the bookworm, and we'd wile away many hours cuddling, my hand on her spine, hers on the spine of a book. She no doubt talked to me about what she was reading - no doubt enthused - but as I wasn't really into books, I probably gave the impression I was listening when I wasn't.	The best I could do here was narrow it down to the digits corresponding to the letters in the anagram which fell between A and J inclusive - those being A, D and E.	So the digit had to be 0, 3 or 4.
PROGRAMME.	Had spy pay.	Happy Days.	I had to figure this one out, and again it slowed me down. I have no memories whatsoever of us watching TV together, so I can't say what it was that so appealed to her about the programme, but it really was the only thing I could find to fit.	A.	0.

SUBJECT AT SCHOOL.	Ooh, Science mom.	Home economics.	Despite the red herring in the jumbled version, this was a little easier - there were only so many possibilities, which was a relief as my instinct of English (the bookworm link) was clearly incorrect. So apparently she liked sewing and baking and so forth. I would have remembered if it had been Maths to which she had been drawn - but I was quite surprised at the answer.	H.	7.
PLAY.	Demarcate as dense trier.	A Streetcar Named Desire.	A gentle saunter to the finish line there - I knew it straight away. For one of our first dates, she took me along to see an amateur production of the play, in which one of her friends had a part (was it Mariella? Who knows), Okay, dragged me along. We didn't see any other plays after that.	I.	8.

This gave four possible phone numbers - and my only option was to ring them all.

I started with 07582440078. I felt genuine butterflies in my stomach, unsure of whether it was nerves or excitement making me feel that way. I hesitated a little before I hit the green call button, but this only served to exacerbate the situation. After a small delay, I was greeted with a trio of beeps escalating in pitch, followed by that familiar female voice (who IS she?) informing me the number had not been recognised.

So I tried 07582443078, this time not thinking about what I was doing and not hesitating. Which was all well and good until I heard a dialling tone, at which point my nerves returned. After no more than half a dozen rings, I was greeted with a female voice - not the clipped tones of the previous phonecall and not, as far as I could remember, the voice of Harriet. But then we were talking about someone who had pretended to be a Scotland Yard detective, so it could easily have been another hoax.

'Hello?' She began.

'Hello?' I responded, framing my greeting as a question as she had.

'Who is this, please?'

'Erm, who is THIS please?' This had started to feel like that game you play as a kid, copying someone to annoy them. And annoyed she indeed was becoming.

'It doesn't work like that! You rang me! I'll ask you again - who is this, please?'

'Harriet?'

'Pull the other one. I can tell you're a man.'

'No, I mean - are you Harriet?'

'No.'

'Really?'

Click. I don't think it was Harriet. That left one number. Unless I had messed up on one or more of the anagrams, of course - which suddenly seemed a very real possibility. I dialled 07582444078. Again, it rang. And it rang. And it rang. Eventually, it went to voicemail. The sound on the recorded message was a man's voice.

Or rather a woman doing a man's voice.

Specifically a woman doing a catch-all Eastern European accent, in a man's voice. I think she was going for a Bond villain effect.

'Bravo, Mr Jacobs. You are closing in on your target. We have released Harriet and she awaits you at your final location, although we are not at liberty to specify exactly where that is. We are sending you a picture of said location. It is a place you spent many happy summer days – sort of. Farewell.'

Sort of? Sort of what? Sort of happy? Sort of summer? When the picture message eventually came through, my confusion grew. The picture was of a new housing estate, too modern-looking to have been a backdrop to our relationship. So how can we have spent many happy summer days there? Maybe it was time to order another coffee. I racked my brains trying to think of a special place I had not visited today, somewhere we would visit in the summertime, but the only one I could come up with was Adventureworld, the rather generically and ambiguously named theme park which used to be situated in the next village along from us. It couldn't be that, though, because it was demolished in the mid-to-late 1990s as its popularity waned. Demolished and replaced by…a new housing estate! Aha! I waved at the kindly bar manager through the window as I got back in my car. He stuck his thumb up – perhaps an act of congratulations, perhaps to wish me luck, perhaps both.

I remembered Adventureworld as I drove towards its former location; remembered what an odd little place it was – like so many 'theme' parks, the theme was a loose one, the different rides and attractions all supposedly representing different parts of the world. So there were dodgems painted yellow to look like New York City taxi cabs and pyramid-shaped food huts. They weren't even grouped into continents – the Ganges Rapids sat happily in between the CN Tower vertical drop ride and the Niagara Drop log flume. I remembered the time

Bros played an open-air concert there but stormed offstage after about ten minutes after being pelted with hot dogs and drinks cups. I remembered long, hot afternoons queuing up for the Pyrenees rollercoaster, Adventureworld's star attraction, not minding one bit about the waiting because it gave me more time to snog Harriet; in fact, sometimes I was disappointed to get to the front of the line. The thrill of her company – and the thrill of a sneakily-groped boob in between the attractions – more than matched the thrill of the white knuckle rides. The park itself was shoddy – it's a wonder it lasted as long as it did with Alton Towers just three quarters of an hour drive away. But for the carless locals like myself and Harriet it more than did the job, and as I recalled the place, it was with a small but definite pang.

I parked my car in the vicinity of where I imagined the Pyrenees was located – it seemed as good a starting point as any. Finding her was going to be a challenge, and initially the only thing I had to fall back on was sheer dumb luck. So I picked a direction and followed it. On the way I passed a little park which, to my great nostalgic delight, contained a ride in which the front carriage of the Pyrenees ride had been attached to four huge springs fixed to the ground. I couldn't resist delaying my search by a minute as I got in it and rocked about. A single, childless man in his thirties isn't best advised to be lingering too long on children's parks, though, so I quickly moved on and back into the suburban maze. It was a big old theme park and, as such, a big old housing estate. She could have been anywhere.

I checked my phone, praying she had thrown me a lifeline by texting me another clue. No such luck. I opened the picture message up again, scrutinising it for any clue as to where she could be in this sea of identikit housing. I noticed that in the background there was a luminous red sign. A shop maybe? I kept walking until I found a passer-by, an older but sprightly-looking gentleman in a track suit. He pointed me in the direction of a little strip of shops on the outskirts of the estate. Still no sighting of Harriet, though. This could have been the world's most elaborate and long-delayed act of revenge.

Beep. I had a text message. It was from Harriet's real phone. *I see you. You're getting warmer.*

I looked around me. I couldn't see her. I started wandering around. *Beep. Colder.*

I walked back the other way. *Beep. Warmer again.*

I kept a straight line this time and quickened my pace a little. *Beep. Warmer still.*

And that's when I finally lay eyes on her again. She looked amazing. Beep. *You found me.*

'Harriet Hamilton!'

'Will Jacobs! Come here, you, and give me a great big hug!'

A great big hug it indeed was – probably about ten seconds, which is seven more than a regular hug is allowed to be. I didn't have the heart to break off, though, not after the mammoth efforts to which she had gone so far – and there was more to come it turned out. She eventually released me and took a step back, looking me up and down.

'Bloody hell – after all these years here you are! You're looking surprisingly well!' Considering my age? Considering the cancer? I decided not to ask. 'Anyway - well done on finding me and defeating those kidnappers!'

'I'm just disappointed you're not tied up.'

'Cheeky!'

'Jesus Christ, I can't believe you went to all this effort.'

'Well, it was like you said - we had another shot. One last day together. I wanted to make it the best one of all.'

I'm still not entirely sure what she meant by that - better than the other six dates I was due to have this week? Had she cottoned on? Or better than all the other days we had spent together all those years ago?

'It certainly is something else,' I replied, ambiguously. 'I just don't understand how you did it!'

'Well to be honest, it's something I've been working on ever since you got in touch. It started off quite small-scale - I just had the idea to post a note through your door telling you to meet me at the place we had our first kiss, just to see if you'd remembered. My plan was to spend the day there. Then it just started snowballing or spiralling or something. Ideas kept popping into my head, so I kept returning to eBay to order something new, a fake moustache or a suitcase lock or an old mobile phone. Then, as late as I could manage last night, I got in my car and drove round, following the trail I had planned, spreading the clues. It's a really good job no one saw me planting the envelope underneath the pub bench - they'd have thought I was some kind of terrorist or something!'

I shook my head and grinned. 'Well, that's the thing I don't get! So much could have gone wrong! There could have been a rainstorm overnight, or strong winds could have blown the clues away, or an eagle-eyed passer-by could have seen one of the bits of paper and taken it down. And that only needed to happen once, in one of the places, for the whole chain to be broken!'

'The thing was, Will, I didn't over think it. You should try it someday.'

'Ooh! Is that a little dig?'

'Take it that way if you want.'

'Well either way - thank you. It was an amazing gesture. So much fun.'

'You're welcome. But maybe it wasn't total altruism. Not that I wanted to spite you or anything, but maybe I wanted you to see you let a good one go. And you really did.'

I really did.

'And I guess I wanted to see if you still remembered all the little details, like I do. To see if you still cared about our time together, like I do. And you obviously do. So thank you. To be honest I was kind of picturing me still sat here waiting at midnight - I underestimated you, mister!'

'And would you have done that? Waited, I mean?'

'Well, I dunno. Maybe. You had my real mobile number after all. Would you have persisted or just given up after a while?'

'I'm not the quitter you've got me down as. Not nowadays.'

We both let out a slightly awkward giggle. 'Are we still talking about the mission or something else?'

'I'm not sure to be honest! Let's move on, shall we? What's in the bag? Looks ominous!'

'Oh right, the bag! Well, I bought you a little something to make today even more special. Go on, three guesses'.

'Hmm, well, it looks pretty heavy. Is it – ooh, it's not my very own urn, is it? Because if it is – thanks, and I'll save it for later'.

'It's...a big plastic bottle of cheap cider. Just like you used to drink in the old days before we turned eighteen! I know you're driving, but I thought you could have a few swigs.'

'Oh, wow! Or – now let me think, what would I have said in 1987? Wicked!'

'Dude, you were never cool enough to pull off 'wicked' all those years ago, so what makes you think it's acceptable now?'

'Oh, and you reckon 'dude' sounds right coming from a 36 year old, erm – what exactly is it that you do?'

'Chartered accountant.'

'Chartered accountant! Fantastic. Anyway, thanks for the booze. I really appreciate it. So were they out of paint thinner down at the corner shop?'

'Ungrateful sod! Just for that, I'm not giving you your other pressie'.

'You got me something else?'

Before she could give me the second present, a couple of likely lads in their late teens approached us.

'Fuckin' hell, Doddsy! It IS him. All right, Mr Jacobs?'

'Drew. Michael.' Michael Waterstone and Drew Dodds were, as you might have deduced, former students of mine. I didn't particularly take a shine to many of the kids I taught, but these two little toads were the bane of my life for a while. My Maths lessons were a great inconvenience to them, getting in the way of smoking, girls and petty vandalism, and boy they let me know about it. Michael was eyeing me, and Harriet, up and down, smirking the same smirk I'd yearned to wipe off his face a few years ago.

'How come you left school, sir? I heard you got sacked for touching up a couple of Year 7 boys behind the Sixth Form block. That true, paedo?'

'Nah, Mickey, that ain't it, that ain't it. I heard he got into smack big time and now he's a proper full on druggie. That's why him and his skanky girlfriend here are drinking cider. He's got no home now. He sleeps in a box on this park. Ain't that right, loser?'

Harriet looked lost for words, and more than a little intimidated. I don't know if I felt some slightly immature need to impress her, to match Michael and Drew's bravado, or if it was years of oppressed frustration at brain-dead time-wasters like these two coming to the fore, but I suddenly felt a surge of adrenalin, of fearlessness.

'Close, you degenerate little shits, but no cigar. I'm terminally ill. I've got testicular cancer. Let me put it as simply as I can so you morons can understand: *I'm dying.*' They gave each other a quizzical look, clearly mulling over whether I was telling them the truth or not. 'What this means for you is this: I've got nothing to lose. I don't have a job and I'll be dead soon, so I can't think of a single reason why I shouldn't pick up that broken bottle over there and stick it right in your ugly little faces. There isn't a court in the land would convict a dying man for defending himself from a couple of chavvy little oiks like you. So what do you say? You fancy it?'

The boys started walking slowly backwards, sneering and glaring at me as they retreated. 'Fuck you, you crazy freak,' shouted Drew. 'Come on, Mick, let's leave 'em to it. Nob heads.'

And with that, they were gone.

Harriet put her arms round my neck. 'My hero,' she said with an American accent – the fourth one I had heard from her today, if you include her natural one.

'Well, you know...' I responded with fake humility.

'Right, you've definitely earned this now.' She smiled mischievously and handed me a key.

'A key? Oh my God, you want me to move in with you, don't you? Well, this is all so sudden! I mean, I didn't even know we were officially boyfriend and girlfriend again...'

'Oh, you are such a...now, give me a moment to find the *mot juste* here...div!'

'Div, eh? Wow, I'm impressed! You're really going the whole hog on this 1987 thing, aren't you? So it's not your door key?'

''Fraid not, Romeo. Here, let me show you'.

She led me by the hand and sort of skipped around the corner – and there it was. An Mk 2 Raleigh Chopper, chained to a lamppost, caked in mud and rust, its original colour as such indiscernible but no less of a wonder to behold for all of that. A proper blast from the past. She could drive but at the start of our relationship had no car, whilst I could do neither, so it was my preferred mode of transport, as it had been for several years by that point. Harriet would sit behind me, clutching me tightly. I looked at her with great excitement, gratitude and fondness. She looked at me, her smile turning her eyes into little moon crescents. We held the stare for at least five seconds without saying a word. I suddenly wanted to kiss her, wanted it more than anything in the world. My stomach filled with butterflies. Blood filled both my cheeks and my nether regions. It really was 1987 again.

'Now, I don't wish to appear rude or anything here and – well, how can I put this delicately and tactfully? I think your bum might have expanded a bit since you were 17. I doubt we'll both fit'

'Oi! It's a good job you're not trying to get me into bed this time around, because you would have definitely blown it with that comment. Now come on, positive thinking. You get on first, budge forward and I'll squeeze my enormous backside in behind you'.

I was about to tell her that her backside wasn't really that big, and that in fact it was even more pleasing to the eye than it was when she was a teenager, but thought better of it (good instincts that were not to last).

'So where did you get this mean machine from anyhow?'

'eBay. Bought it for my son for when he turns thirteen in a couple of months. He loves all the retro stuff. Him and his dad are gonna do it up together.'

'Oh. Right. Your – son.'

'Yeah, my – son! I'm - married! I've got three kids as it happens – another son who's six and a daughter who's four.'

'Why didn't you mention this in your emails?'

'Would it have changed anything?'

'No, but still...and what about your name? It's still Hamilton!'

'I just wanted to keep my maiden name, that's all. You're allowed to do that, you know.'

And just like that, the illusion was shattered. It wasn't 1987 anymore. I wasn't 17 or 18. I was 36 and I had terminal testicular cancer. Suddenly everything seemed so...silly. Just what was I doing? What was *she* doing for that matter? My anger swelled.

'So, what – you go to all this effort and then I find out you're married? Brilliant. Thanks a lot. How come you didn't tell me any of this before?'

'How come you're getting so upset, more to the point? This was never supposed to lead to anything. You knew that. *You* told *me* that, in your email. I just wanted to do something nice for you. Don't have a go at me.'

I took a deep breath, closed my eyes, considered the huge acts of kindness which had been bestowed upon me today, opened my eyes and exhaled.

'I'm sorry. I guess seeing you has stirred up some old feelings or something.'

Not strictly true – it would have been closer to the mark to say it had stirred up new feelings. Feelings of remorse and regret – the niggling sense that I had given up on something that could have been really good. No – it already had been really good. Something that could have gone on forever, and should have. The new feeling was that I had undervalued Harriet, underappreciated her – the truth was that the kindness displayed today did not represent a change in personality. She was always so good to me, so supportive – hers was a shoulder to cry on at a time when I was terribly emotionally battered from mum's passing just months earlier. I just must have blocked all of that out. I should have thanked my lucky stars Harriet ever walked into my life, instead of ushering her out of it.

'I'm sorry,' I repeated.

'You don't have to apologise. I can't imagine what you must be going through – your head must be all over the place. Do you want to talk about the…you know…the cancer?'

I shook my head. I figured I had relied on her enough in the past. 'Thanks, though. What I'd really like to talk about is us. I want to reminisce. They were good times, weren't they?'

We sat down on the grass next to the bike, still chained up as it would remain for the rest of our date.

'Definitely. We were just kids, though, weren't we? God, when I think back, some of the things I did make me cringe. Like before our first date, you'd asked me to ring you, but I fancied you so much and was so nervous about our conversation drying up that I made a list of possible topics to talk about on a piece of paper, then took it to a phone box so no one would laugh at me if they saw me or overheard me. How sad is that?'

'I don't think that's sad at all! I think that's quite organised and practical!'

She laughed. 'If I'd known you were this much of a geek back then I don't think I'd have been half as nervous!'

'So where do you think we'd be sitting right now if this was still Adventureworld?'

'I'm going to guess we'd be smack bang in the middle of the car park, but let's suspend our disbelief for a second. Maybe we'd be on the Congo – you know, that lazy river ride. I used to love that. Just cruising along, cuddling, me and you with no one else around. And every time we went through that dark tunnel bit, you'd pounce on me and stick your tongue down my throat.'

'Well, how could I resist? I mean, Jesus Christ – look at you!'

Ooh, that was a bit forward, wasn't it? It was funny how quickly I was slipping back into wooing mode. She blushed.

'Pack it in, you berk.'

'Wow - berk! No one has called anyone a berk since the 31st of December, 1989.'

Had I not vowed to keep my celibacy in tact, I think I'd have asked her, right there and then, if she fancied a bonk. Were we – you know – *flirting* here? She punched me playfully on the arm, jumped to her feet and ran off, zigzagging and dashing around the estate, leaving me in her trail. There we were, two people in our late thirties, chasing around like kids. And I loved it. Joggers and ladies with buggies stopped to stare at us.

'Slow down, you mad woman!'

'Speed up, you old fart!'

She simply wasn't tiring. I, however, was. Lest we forget, I was terminally ill. Okay, and a bit lazy too. Between her nifty footwork and her boundless energy, she was soon out of my eyeshot. I kept running, panting her name as I went.

Before I knew it I found myself in the cemetery adjacent to the estate. My breathless giddiness quickly subsided. I looked around at the gravestones. I looked at their names. I looked at their ages. Shit. I wasn't ready for this; wasn't ready to give up the life I was leading, the fun I was having. I wasn't ready to die. Not even a little bit. The near silence of the graveyard engulfed me.

I looked up to see Harriet coming towards me. This time she was walking, and her beaming, girlish grin had turned into a sympathetic smile. She put her hand on my shoulder.

'Found you.'

I placed my palm over her hand, partly to acknowledge it and partly to secure it.

'Look at these people, Harriet. They're not like me. Look at Donald Littlewood over there. 78 when he popped his clogs. Look at Elizabeth Bainbridge. 80. Look at George Hockley down there. 97 years old, for God's sake. They all had their lives. They all got to either achieve their ambitions, or at least live a long time trying and failing.' I scanned around me, desperate to find anyone under seventy. 'Look here. Even Emily Sawford got 62 years out of it all. She must have at least considered herself to be approaching old age. Why do I have to lie with this lot for the rest of time? I'm too young, Harriet. I'm too bloody young to die.'

I lifted my hand from hers and slumped onto the bench behind me. She followed me and slipped her hand back into mine.

'You're not dead yet mister.' She guided my hand up her blouse and lifted her bra. As if in no mood for my self-pitying histrionics, my hand got straight into action, caressing her breasts. Harriet started to kiss me. She broke off and looked down at my crotch area with a smirk. 'And neither's he by the look of things.'

And lo, there was indeed another stiff in the graveyard. My horniness was completely trumping my wallowing. Harriet was right. I WAS still alive. My heart was still beating (quite quickly as it happens.) Blood was still flowing around my body (seemingly all of it towards my genitals). I still had my libido, that much was clear, and if I still had that, I still had lots of other things too.

'Now that, Mr Jacobs - that's got to stay our little secret. I'm married after all. You have to promise not to tell anyone what just happened.'

I looked at her and smiled. 'I'll take it to my grave.'

We sat, side by side, gazing out into the distance. I couldn't quite shake off the smile that had appeared on the corners of my lips.

'Hey, that Joanna chick over there was only 29. I KNOW you'll be banging her within about six hours of arriving at the Pearly Gates.'

I laughed. We sat in silence once again. It was a different silence to the one I first heard as I entered the cemetery. Pleasant somehow.

'So have you got a funeral photo?'

'Have I got a what what?'

'A funeral photo! I've seen it on the telly. You know - at the funeral, there's always an enlarged photo on canvas next to the coffin, for people to gaze at wistfully. It's usually got candles around it and stuff. Have you got a photo that would make people look all sad and wistful?'

'Erm - I don't really know! I mean, I've got shedloads of photos at home. I'll have a look tonight.'

'No you won't. You'll have a look now. Let's go back to yours and I'll give you my opinions. We'll choose a photo together.'

And so it was that I took the married woman who had snogged me back to my apartment. Which I agree is not the best of ideas on paper.

I realise in these days of digital cameras, most people store photos on their computers and only a small percentage ever get printed off, but to me there's a certain romance in holding a photograph. I suppose it's much the same as my preference for vinyl records over MP3s. I've also never been able to let go of my fixation on Polaroid cameras, hence the reason that Polaroids make up a large percentage of my collection. So it was to my bedroom and not my laptop that I turned in search of that elusive funeral photo. I suppose in hindsight I might have been a little vague with my suggestion - I had meant for me to bring the photos downstairs to her, but she had followed me up to the bedroom and was sprawled across my bed waiting, smiling. Not an image I was anticipating at the start of the day.

I doubt it will surprise you to discover that my photos are not stuffed randomly into boxes but are in fact organised in a way that would put the Dewey System to shame. You might expect me to have arranged them chronologically, and you'd be half right. More specifically, they are arranged thematically, and then within the themes, chronologically. The themes themselves are obviously alphabetised. So we start with 'Academics', a section containing all photos taken during my days at nursery school, primary school, secondary school, sixth form college and university. I don't store photos in boxes, but rather upright, much like an actual library, for ease of access, in a wardrobe. Large dividers (labelled using my special label maker, also kept in the wardrobe and used only for that purpose) separate the different phases of my education and smaller ones the different years within each phase (naturally I had wrestled with whether to separate these into academic years - which made logical sense - or calendar ones - which would have been in-keeping with other sections of the library. I opted for the latter). Smaller dividers still would denote clusters of photos within each year - so let's say there was a school trip or something. Tiny stickers, a bit like Post-it notes, are attached to the side of my absolute favourite photos so I can locate them easily, no more or no less than ten per year within each theme. The sections are as follows: Academics, Career, Helen, Holidays, Misc, Mum, Nights Out, Parties, Romances. I hate putting photos into the Miscellaneous section, but some just don't warrant having their own dedicated section. I appreciate that 'Nights Out' and 'Parties' sound like one and the same, but the former is for pubs and clubs while the latter is for parties of any description – from birthday parties I attended as a child to raucous university house parties.

I can probably read your mind now - I'll bet you're wondering how I decide what category to put a photo in if it falls into multiple categories. What if, say, it's a picture taken at a party on holiday with a girlfriend? Simple - I have a trump system. Basically, romances trump all, which is one of the reasons that's the largest section. So in the example given, that photo would go in the romance section, in the sub-section of whatever girlfriend it was, in the sub-sub-section of that holiday. It's really not rocket science.

Harriet had never seen my photo library before, so as I explained it to her, I expected her to be suitably impressed.

'Oh my God, you weirdo!' Maybe not. 'So go on then, let's have a look at the photos of you and me!'

I walked my fingers to the 'Romance' section, which didn't actually start in 1987 as you might imagine- there were a few proto romances starting as recently as 1983 – forgettable mid-teen flings lasting a week or two for which photographic evidence still exists. We spent a good fifteen minutes giggling and reminiscing as we pored over the photos of the two of us. I was especially intrigued by some of the later pictures. The camera never lies, they say, and that's true enough - but perhaps we are guilty on occasion of lying to the camera. Looking at those pictures, anyone would have thought us the perfect young couple, happy and carefree. And yet the end was nigh.

Harriet was blushing. 'God, some of these photos are awful. I wouldn't want to be back there.'

'You wouldn't?'

'Nah. I think I make a much better 36 year old than I ever did an 18 year old.'

'How do you mean?'

'I was so ill-at-ease at 18, and I can really see it looking at these photos. Not unhappy as such but never quite comfortable in my skin, never that secure with myself. But I sort of grew into that skin as the years went by. Spending a sunny afternoon at the park with my kids, watching them play with their dad, I feel a contentment I never felt doing what 18 year old girls do, getting pissed at nightclubs every weekend, snogging strangers while they're at it and breaking hearts or getting their hearts broken. That stuff was never really for me, but being a wife and mother really, really is. Having a nice house and a nice car and a job I like - it's all I've ever really wanted. No offence, but...'

Ahh, 'no offence'. The pre-cursor phrase to something guaranteed to offend. Let's see what we've got in store this time, shall we?

'...I think you probably made a better 18 year old than a 36 year old.'

Yep - offence taken.

'You're not married and I presume you haven't got any kids judging by the way you went off at me before. This footloose-and-fancy-free bachelor lifestyle you must lead - don't you think you should have outgrown it by now?'

Offence definitely taken.

'I think that's a bit harsh.'

'But accurate?'

'Well, I suppose. But so what if I'm not ready for that yet? Who's to say I wouldn't have wanted all that a bit later in life, if fate had given me that chance? Maybe I'd have made a better 50 year old than I did 36 year old or 18 year old. Maybe those would have been my halcyon days.'

'Maybe. I'm sorry – I feel like I'm having a go at you now. I'm honestly not.'

'It's okay. It's probably no less than I deserve. Shall we get on with the task in hand? I believe we were trying to find a funeral photo.'

'Oh yeah! I forgot. Let's do it.'

I suggested we find something from the latter days of the 'Academics' section - perhaps a graduation photo? This suggestion was shot down by Suzie, on account of those photos being too old. The 'Career' section seemed to offer good potential - I'd kept all of my staff photos. She didn't like any of them.

'Look - it's no good. We're just gonna have to take one now. I think I might have my digital camera in my bag. Back in a mo.'

She returned, as promised, with a camera - and a determined look on her face. She was doing that thing with her hands that photographers do, making right angles with her thumb and forefinger and squinting through them at me. Not entirely sure how it was helping her.

'Right, let's do this. We'll start with location. We don't just want one of you on the bed. Look at that beautiful evening sunshine. That'll look great - it will really bring out the colour of your hair and eyes. So I need you to grab a chair and sit just by the window, where the sun's coming in. Right, sit up straight and look at the camera.' Click. She looked at the screen and pulled her face. 'Nah, it's a bit moody. Let's try a smile.' Click. Again she looked at the screen. Again, she wasn't happy. 'Too jolly.' She drummed her chin with her fingers. 'How about you go for a sort of Mona Lisa look? A slight, melancholy sort of smile.' I tried it. 'Bit smilier. Bit smilier still. No, less smiley. Go for halfway between your last two smiles. Yes! Yes that's it! Fix that smile, because now we're working on your eyes. Let's get the best out of those beautiful baby blues. I want your eyes to smile, just a little more than your actual smile.' Click. 'Nah, that's not it. Okay, different tact. Let's go for a thousand-yard-stare approach. Ooh, I like it!' Click. 'Nearly there, I reckon. Hold that smile, hold that stare - we just need to work on your angle. Let's try you facing slightly away from the camera.' I felt like imploring her to be a little more mathematically precise. What angle? 25 degrees? 45? Clockwise or anti-clockwise? I resisted and tilted myself randomly. 'Looking up a bit. Bit more. Down a bit. Perfect!' Click. She showed me her creation.

'Wow! Funereal! Nice work, Ms. Hamilton!'

We gazed at the photo in silence, both smiling Mona Lisa smiles now. She put her arm round my shoulder.

'I'm so, so sorry. It shouldn't happen to anyone. Especially not our age. Especially not you. I hope I don't see this picture again for a long, long time.'

I nodded.

'I'm going to go now. I told the hubby a little white lie; said I needed to stay late at work. I don't want to take the Mick, though. And I'd better go and pick up that bloody bike, if it's still there. Listen, today has been amazing. It's been so good to see you and, well I have to say, you've improved with age; I think I'll always remember you this way. Anyway, I'm babbling. Goodbye, Will.' Her voiced cracked a little. 'Thank you and goodbye.'

She blew me a kiss before walking out of my bedroom door.

'Harriet, wait! Before you go- will you do me one last favour?'

She obliged. After she left, I had to label another divider with 2005 on it, to house a brand new Polaroid of the two of us, taken by her at arm's length, lying on my bed. It's got a Post-it on.

H: Alright loverboy?

W: Oh not so bad!

H: Right then, son, you're nearly halfway there. Let's have a bit of half time match analysis.

W: Well, it's a game of two halves, Ron. I was over the moon at first but then I was sick as a parrot. But there's everything to play for.

H: Yeah, you don't really make a very convincing bloke. Anyway, how did today go? Anything juicy to report?

I paused for a few seconds.

W: Nah not really.

H: Which means yes.

W: My lips are sealed.

H: I know, but were hers?

W: Disgusting. Anyway, I told you before, a gentleman doesn't kiss and tell!

H: And I told you you're hardly a gentleman. And you bloody do tell. You kiss and tell. You shag and tell. And all the bits in between. You're a gobshite. Now spill the beans.

W: Well, there may have been...another snog. There's your juicy bit.

H: Unbelievable. In a, you know, totally believable way which is perfectly in keeping with your general character. So really not unbelievable at all.

W: We did do other things! She set up this elaborate hostage scenario, and I had to drive around solving clues to track her down. It was really exciting!

H: Wow! This chick went to some serious effort! Tomorrow's date better pull it out the bag now!

W: Ah, yes, well, you see the thing is...

H: Hold that thought, flower, Jeff's tapping his watch. I'm already ten minutes late for our dinner date. We'll have a good gab tomorrow. Kisses.

W: Okay, enjoy your evening. Bye.

Thursday, 14th July, 2005

I hadn't set an alarm that morning, figuring that while it was a relatively hefty drive (at just under twenty miles, Rhonda lived further away from me than most, meaning there were often a good few days between our meetings), I could be a little more flexible with my timings. I started the day with an undeniable knot in my stomach, sensing it was going to be a tough one. However, it was a lovely, warm and sunny morning and large parts of the drive were quite scenic – so although I kept telling myself I ought to feel respectfully subdued and reflective, I actually found I was rather enjoying the journey. I was listening to one of my themed mix CDs – a while back, I had made a CD of my personal favourite tracks from each year from 1960 to the present day. I keep my iTunes collection sorted by the star rating I have given each track - and so, each CD comprised the five star tracks from each given year, sorted alphabetically by track name, of course, with any remaining space on the CD taken up by a cherry-picked selection of four star tracks, themselves sorted alphabetically. Inevitably, my choice of year for this particular journey was 1991. So it was a 1991-themed mix, not a Rhonda mix, which meant plenty of tracks released pre-'91 which evoked our time together were absent and plenty released during our timespan which did not remind me of her were present. There was, however, definitely a good degree of overlap, and it was to those that I found myself most drawn, those songs in which I found myself most immersed, those songs that really made my spine tingle. We both loved REM's album *Out of Time* which was released in March of that year, the month we started dating, and it was represented by two tracks – the evergreen 'Losing My Religion' and the more forgotten 'Near Wild Heaven'. The former came first, since I had rated it with five stars, and the latter second, since I had rated it with four stars. However, it was 'Near Wild Heaven' I seemed to enjoy more, perhaps because I'd heard 'Losing My Religion' a thousand times since, both by choice and on the radio – it didn't seem to 'belong' to 1991 anymore, but 'Near Wild Heaven' still did (I decided to bump it up to five stars when I got home). Sunglasses on, windows rolled down and this selection of musical gems blasting out, it was proving impossible to feel melancholy. Indeed, perhaps somewhat ironically, I felt truly alive at that moment, not for the first time this week and, as it would transpire, not for the last.

The feeling was, alas, not to last, as I soon got to thinking more deeply about music and my mortality. These were my thoughts:

I imagine that if you've lived to a good ripe age, you become somewhat disconnected with popular culture. You've probably lost interest in what today holds, let alone what tomorrow will bring. Well not me. Despite the age of the tracks on my mix CD, I'm not a prisoner to nostalgia. I'm still interested in modern day music (albeit not to quite to the extent I was when I was a teenager or in my early twenties). I still buy newly-released albums now and again. Whilst I would never for one moment suggest that this is any kind of golden period for music, I keep finding the occasional gem which makes its way into my 'All Time Top 100 Albums' list. I'm sure that by now you won't be too surprised to find out that such a list actually does exist, which is reviewed bi-annually. The list excludes Greatest Hits and live albums, and to be considered for inclusion, an album must have been part of my collection for at least six months. You HAVE to have boundaries and rules, don't you? I keep the list on a database on my computer and include fields for the year of release and the genre – that way, it can be easily sorted by date if I want to examine the list for trends (there are definite 'clusters' of years which feature prominently – the late sixties features heavily, which I'm sure most would agree was a halcyon period for popular music, as does the mid-to-late eighties, mirroring my own teenage years, when my music consumption was both in its infancy and at its peak, the time representing a personal halcyon period. Likewise, I could view the list by type (maybe I want to listen to my all-time favourite Scandinavian electro-goth albums in order of preference. I jest of course). Finally, and most practically, I suppose, the database can also by sorted alphabetically, either by artist or album, making it a cinch to locate the albums in my collection. My point being, it cuts me up to think about the albums I'll be missing out on after I've passed away. There could be a masterpiece just around the corner which critics mention in the same breath as, say, *Pet Sounds* or *Sgt Pepper* and – damn it – I won't be around to hear it. Or – as is the case with at least 80% of my list – it could be an album not part of the critical canon, but one which *I* consider a gem, which won't be released in my lifetime but which *should have been*, if only I hadn't been cursed with such God-awful bad luck. My would-be all-time-favourite album could be released the week after I die, for all I'll ever know. The same thing with films: what if the greatest film ever to be made - something every critic in the world will concur is greater than *Ben-Hur* and *Gone with the Wind* and *Police Academy 4: Citizens on Patrol* combined - is ten years away? And people who knew me will say - if only Will had lived to see this. He'd have loved it!

Do you think elderly folk have these thoughts? I doubt it.

My thoughts didn't stop there, continuing to gush out of me like a sudden nosebleed. It's the same with technology. I'm a real gadget addict; an addiction fed by my ever disposable income (much like my music fixation). Do you ever see pensioners sporting the latest iPod? Of course not. They don't care. They cling to the technology of their past – how many octogenarians have an email address? Me – I'm deeply fascinated by our ever-changing world, by the amazing and constant developments in technology. And I embrace that change. I crave the latest pieces of hardware and software. I couldn't help but speculate on that car journey about what the world would be like when I was dead. What new technology would there be a year after my death? What gadgets would exist which I would have loved and upon which I would have quickly become dependent? What about ten years after my death? By then, I wouldn't even recognise the world around me. What about forty years down the line? Maybe by that point I wouldn't even care about technology. Either way, I was supposed to be around. Me dying young and missing out should never have been part of the plan.

I arrived at Mrs Patterson's house just before noon, in the middle of the somewhere-between-eleven-and-one timescale I had given her. I knocked just twice, neither so quietly that it would have seemed as if I was drawing attention to the delicate nature of the situation, nor so loudly that it would have seemed as if I was ignoring it.

When we'd spoken on the telephone, Mrs Patterson hadn't told me the reason she wanted me to come to her house, and I'd felt it a little impudent to ask – besides, I liked the sense of intrigue. All she'd given me was her address. I'd contacted her on Sunday, as soon as I'd got the other six dates sorted, and fortunately she was free on the one remaining day, the Thursday. She greeted me with a weak smile.

'Hello again, Will. Do come in, my dear.'

I saw in Mrs Patterson's eyes the very same look I saw in my own eyes every time I stared at my reflection – a sense of pain and sadness that no outward smiles and no amount of time could suppress. I just knew, even without asking, that she thought about Rhonda every single day and still – still – missed her like crazy, *every single day*. I just knew. She seemed older than I had remembered. Of course she seemed older – she was fourteen years older – but I mean she seemed *older*. I suppose that's what grief does to you.

I accepted her offer of a cup of tea and figured the biscuit selection accompanying it would tide me over until my late lunch. The room was quiet. Really quiet. Other than the sound of a ticking grandfather clock and the slurping of tea, there were no sounds. I looked at Mrs Patterson and smiled politely. She did the same. I looked down into my cup. What the blinking heck was the protocol in this situation? Who was supposed to get this particular ball rolling? Should I start things off with a bit of small talk about the weather? Too trivial?

'How was your journey, Will?'

Oh, thank God!

'It was fine, thanks!' Let's see - I sang loudly, drummed on my steering wheel like a man possessed and had a great big smile on my face. You know, as you do when you're about to visit your dead ex-girlfriend's mother. Then I became mildly depressed as I contemplated my own mortality. 'Not too much traffic.'

'That's good.'

Tick-tock-tick-tock. Slurp. Tick-tock-tick-tock. Slurp. I guessed it was my turn.

'Erm...this place is pretty much just like I remember it!'

A lie. I had been in many houses since the start of my love life, some belonging to the girlfriend, some to her parents, and with a few exceptions, they had sort of morphed into one in my memory. I didn't really remember this house and there was a reason for that.

'Oh. We only moved here five years ago. We used to live a few streets closer to town.'

Oh God. My voice got a little higher as I attempted to worm out of my gaff. 'Oh! You did? Really? How strange.' These little sentence fragments were designed to buy me a little thinking time. 'This one seems really similar to your other house! Must be the furniture or something.'

She let out a small one-note laugh through her nose without smiling and sipped her tea again. I couldn't work out whether my second lie had passed muster or whether she was just letting me off the hook. I stuffed a Jammie Dodger into my mouth to prevent me from saying anything else stupid. I looked around the room as I munched. Where was Mr Patterson, I wondered? There was definitely a Mr Patterson before. Dead? Divorced? At work? At the shops? I could see no pictures of him anywhere, so my guess was divorced. I decided not to pry, but talking about the photos of Rhonda seemed like an appropriately respectful activity.

'There are some lovely pictures of Rhonda on the wall.'

It was practically a shrine, a whole wall covered with photos of Rhonda spanning her whole life. There were baby photos, school photos, photos with Rhonda looking about as old as the version in my memory and photos of her looking older than that. I had to observe to myself that they seemed to be in no particular order on the wall, and that I would have put them in time order or, like my photo collection, in themed clusters. They really were nice, though. None looked like a woman who was going to end up taking her own life.

'Thank you. Wasn't she gorgeous? Those lovely little pigtails and big eyes when she was a toddler – so sweet. And just look at her in her graduation cap and gown – I still feel so proud when I look at it. This one here was taken on her first holiday, in Devon. She always loved the English Riviera. We took a trip there the summer before she died. She was on her pills by that point – she was really struggling. We thought it would cheer her up. It did, briefly, so I can be thankful we had one final family holiday together.'

Pills? What on Earth happened to her? I had to know. It was probably going to be a huge *faux pas*, but I had to ask.

'Please tell me to mind my own business if you feel like I'm being rude, but can I ask what happened? The Rhonda I remembered had such a sunny disposition.'

'I'm glad you remember her that way. She used to be like that. Life changed her.'

'Was it...was it me?'

She laughed. 'Goodness me, no! Is that what you think? That when you broke up with her she went into a downward spiral?'

'No, I just...'

'It wasn't you. She had some good years after you. Met a lovely boy who she was with for a couple of years, but that didn't work out in the end. She had a couple more boyfriends after that but she never seemed to settle on anyone. She was still thirty years old and living with us and I think she felt in a bit of a rut. So I suggested she move away, have a fresh start. I honestly thought that would be for the best. She had a friend just near Birmingham and she moved in with her, took on a series of different jobs to pay her way while she looked for something a bit more befitting of her degree — she was a waitress for a bit, worked in a library for a bit, was a cleaner in an office block for a bit, but nothing was happening. I think she started to feel very lonely, very low. She ended up going to the doctor and he put her on anti-depressants. That seemed to make things worse, not better. She quit her cleaning job and her father and I ended up paying her rent and her bills. We'd visit her, take her food and new clothes, beg her to come home, but she just didn't want to. Every time we saw her she seemed a little different; a little gaunter, a little nervier, a little bit more withdrawn and seemingly each time with a new bloody tattoo on one of her arms. She only slept in her own bed in our house a couple of times after moving to the West Midlands and as I said before we did manage to talk her into coming on holiday with us.

But, yes, she was a different person by then – it really broke my heart. When the policeman came round to visit, carrying his hat in his hands – well, I can't tell you it was the biggest surprise in the world. I think I knew it was going to happen. It was history repeating itself for me. My sister took an overdose when she wasn't much older than Rhonda. Maybe it's genetic or something.' She returned her gaze from the middle distance to my eyeline. 'Anyway, that's the story, more or less! There are probably lots of things I don't know about the last months of her life, but that's for the best, I'm sure. It wouldn't change anything anyway.'

'Oh God, I'm – '

'Sorry? Yes I know.'

We sat in near-silence again. Just tick-tock-tick-tock this time. No slurps. I felt like the most courteous thing I could do would be to wait for her to speak again, which she eventually did.

'A mother should never have to bury her own child, Will.'

I nodded. For the first time I almost felt quite glad I had outlived mum – at least she didn't have to see me die. At least I didn't have to do to her what Rhonda had done to this shell of a woman.

'I'll love my daughter with all my heart until my last breath, but what she did was selfish. The pain she chose to put me through was – is – unbearable. My world fell apart and I haven't been able to put it back together. My marriage didn't last much longer either.'

Ah – that answered that question.

'Rhonda's passing was a big strain on her father and I. We didn't have any other kids and without her we didn't seem to have much in common any more. He would go on these long walks every day, sometimes for hours on end. I never asked him where he was going and he never told me. I wasn't much better, really – we'd sit through meals together in silence and I'd have no more intention of talking to him than he did of talking to me. It got to the point where I couldn't even look at him, because all I could see was Rhonda's eyes, Rhonda's jawline – and I wanted her, not him. We managed about a year together before we decided to give up. So we sold the house and I moved in here. We're not divorced – seems a bit pointless to me. I've got no intention of remarrying. Not at my age. If he wants to do it, he can, and I'll gladly divorce him then. Anyway, you've not come to listen to my moans, have you? Let me go and fetch the box.'

Though I imagined the chat must have been a therapeutic bonus, the box must have been why she wanted me to visit. When she returned, she was carrying a sturdy brown box with handles, the sort you would find in an office or something. In marker pen was scrawled the word Will and the number 91.

'I presume you must be the Will in question.' She set the box down in front of me. 'I found it in her bedroom when we were clearing out the stuff in the old house. I hope it won't bruise your ego too much if I tell you there were a couple of other boxes with different boys' names on.'

'What is it?'

'Well, I didn't think it my place to pry too much, but from what I can work out it's a Memory Box. You don't have to look at the things now. You can take the box home if you want.'

'What – and bring it back when I've done?'

'No. Keep it. It's yours now.'

'Are you sure that's a good idea? I'll be popping my own clogs soon, so I won't have much need for them.' Yikes. That was insensitive of me. I grimaced a little, but thankfully the sentence appeared to have fallen on deaf ears.

'I want you to have them. That stuff is of no use to me, really. I've got to move on, as much as I possibly can. Besides, I've got my memories of her – this is nothing to do with me. These memories belong to you. Just take the box. Please.'

I smiled and accepted.

'Do you still want to see Rhonda? I'm going to visit her grave today, take some fresh flowers. You can follow me in your car. That way you can head straight back home after if you want.'

I was glad she'd asked. That was part of my plan today – the main part really – but I hadn't quite known how to bring the subject up.

'Thank you, Mrs Patterson. That would be lovely.'

Lovely it certainly was not. After she had taken away the dead flowers and removed a crisp packet which had blown onto the headstone, Mrs Patterson gently laid down the new flowers and proceeded to cry, her palm pressed against the stone. It was a very uncomfortable situation; I felt like a kind of voyeur, except that would imply I was taking some sort of pleasure out of the situation, which was so far from the truth. I didn't want to witness it at all. It seemed somehow both slightly unbelievable and totally understandable that though she had probably visited Rhonda's grave dozens of times, the sight of it could still induce such a powerful emotional torrent. I fixated on the headstone, still a strikingly shiny black, heart-shaped and embossed with gold writing. The inscription read : 'Precious memories of Rhonda Patterson. 11th October, 1970 – 19th December, 2003. At peace now and forever in our hearts'.

Mrs Patterson eventually dried her eyes, blew a kiss into the ether and stood up.

'I'm going to leave you to it now, Will. You've come all this way. You deserve a private moment with Rhonda.'

I hugged her and she reciprocated. It felt nice. 'Goodbye, Mrs Patterson. And thank you.'

If my life were a movie, or if there was a kind of poetic congruence to it, it would have been raining at that moment – instead, the glorious early afternoon sunshine continued to illuminate the graveyard. I crouched down. I felt like I ought to say hello, though I wasn't sure whether to aim my greetings towards the sky, the headstone or the ground beneath which her bones lay. I opted for the headstone, specifically the small oval picture of her pretty face, clearly taken before the dark days had kicked in.

It took a few moments before my voice would come, and when it did, it was low and punctuated by occasional throat clearing.

'Hi Rhonda. It's Will. Will Jacobs.'

Jesus, this was silly. I looked around me, suddenly feeling very self-conscious. There was no one else around. I tried again.

'I've just been to see your mum. She told me all about what happened. Life's a proper bitch sometimes, isn't it? Things haven't turned out that well for me, either. I never managed to settle down with anyone and, worse still, I've got cancer. I'll be dead soon – who'd have thought it, eh? Both of us dead and gone before we've even turned forty, probably. Your mum was nice to me. She misses you so much, you know. I mean, I know you must have had your reasons for doing what you did, but...but hey ho. It sounds like I'm having a go at you now and I'm not. It's none of my business. Anyway, I'm going to be honest with you and tell you what I'm doing. I'm meeting up with seven different exes over the course of a week – how bonkers is that? You're number four in the sequence. I've got to tell you that you came number one in the rankings, though! 17 out of 20 for looks and personality combined. God only knows why I'm doing this, but it feels the right thing to do. I suppose I wanted to make amends with people, and you're no exception. I know this sounds like a rich thing to say to someone who you dumped, but I loved going out with you. You were so beautiful. Like, 9 out of 10 beautiful. And you weren't just beautiful. You were fun and you were sweet and you were classy and you were everything most blokes would give their right arms for. I'm an idiot. I'm not right in the head. No, seriously – I think I've got real problems. That's the only way I can explain letting go of someone like you. Listen, I'm sorry I haven't brought you any flowers. I didn't think, to be honest – but I'll bet you're fed up of flowers now anyway. I've rambled on a bit, haven't I? You haven't been able to get a word in edgeways, have you? I'll leave you in peace now. Take care.'

So that was that. For the second day in a row, I had found myself in a cemetery. Excellent job on taking your mind off things, Will. I returned to my car and headed home, the Memory Box in tow. There was a fair bit of traffic on the way back, meaning I came to the end of the 1991 mix CD, but when I did so, I played it again from the start, desperate not to break the spell the music was creating. I made a brief stop halfway for sandwiches, which I ate in the car, and wine, which you'll be pleased to hear was for later.

When I got home, I didn't even kick off my shoes – just went straight to the coffee table and placed the box carefully, squarely, on top of it. I removed the lid.

First up was a cassette tape, which simply said: 'Will mix'. No inlay – just the cassette. So to find out what was on it I would need a cassette player – something I hadn't owned for several years by that point. Maybe Pete and Georgina would have one. I abandoned the box and popped next door. No answer. I banged on their window: no answer. Almost as if they had normal lives and were at work or something. I wondered if they would mind if I *smashed* the window and went in to have a rummage round. I conceded that might be pushing the limits of their Christian sense of understanding and forgiveness. I glanced at my watch – 4.30. Time enough for a madcap dash to Argos?

There was. I parked in town and, taking a slight detour to ensure I went nowhere near Black Coffee, I sprinted to my destination and claimed my prize of a cheap tape player.

My journey back to my car was a little more leisurely, although certainly still faster than a walking pace – I was excited to find out what would be on the tape. Back at home, I ham-handedly tore the machine from its packaging and stuffed the tape into the deck, enjoying the satisfying click as the play button locked into place.

I wondered what musical nuggets awaited me and what kind of overlap there might be – would I be hearing 'Near Wild Heaven' once again? To my surprise, the first sound I heard was not actually music at all, although it was sweeter than any of the songs that followed – Rhonda's voice. She was with me, here, in my apartment, in 2005. A voice from beyond the grave. A voice filled with joy and optimism and love. Not the voice of someone who sounded like she would one day take her own life, tired of the world with which she was once so clearly enamoured.

'Hello, and welcome to RPFM, home of the best music of '91. I'm joined today by my very handsome co-host, the incomparable Mr Will Jacobs! Wooh! Say hello, Will!'

'Hello, Will!' Original stuff there, 1991 me.

'We've got a great show coming up today, including tracks by My Bloody Valentine, Crowded House and Morrissey. Plus we'll be hearing Will's thoughts on a variety of topics, including how much he loves his amazing girlfriend! Stick around, folks! We'll kick things off with this little gem from St Etienne. This is 'Only Love Can Break Your Heart'!'

The sound quality when the songs played was appalling – practically unlistenable. We must have held the microphone of the tape recorder to a set of speakers from a different hi-fi. It didn't matter. I let the rest of the tape be the background soundtrack of my journey through the rest of the box, stopping what I was doing when the songs finished to hear Rhonda's voice, squirming a little when I heard my own. Sometimes I would rewind the little spoken interludes, either because I hadn't quite been able to work out what one of us had said or simply because I wanted to listen again. I wanted to prolong the experience as much as possible.

The banter was nonsense, really. I don't think we would have lasted very long if it had been a real radio station. It was just a couple of young adults, still with the exuberance of children, mucking about together on tape, cracking corny and often private jokes and talking about the music they loved. What came across loud and clear was that here were two people totally smitten with one another. We were friends as well as lovers.

Much of the contents of the box were standard relationship relics like corny old love letters and a pile of photographs. Clearly Rhonda's was a different mindset to my own, as the pictures were just sort of stuffed inside a Click photo wallet, not in any kind of chronological order or grouped into themes. I unplugged the tape player and plugged it back in in my bedroom, taking the photos with me. I figured that as they were mine now, I might as well amalgamate them with my own collection. I spread them out across my bed and did the same thing with the photos I already had, taking care not to mess up the chronology of my existing photos. I put the ten photos with Post-its on to one side. Some of the photos were duplicates, so clearly we'd have two sets of the pictures from at least one film. Cold though it seemed, I threw the duplicates away. The synergy of hearing Rhonda's voice and gazing at the pictures of our time together, all the while with this wonderful collection of old and often forgotten songs playing, was spine-tingling and at times I was fighting back the tears. I swapped three of the Post-it notes to new additions to the collection – a picture of us huddled together under an umbrella in which we were pulling pretend unhappy faces which completely failed to disguise the joy of the moment, a picture of Rhonda on a trip we took to Paris, which I engineered to look as if she was wearing the Eiffel Tower as a hat, and a picture of us holding hands, facing away from the camera towards a sunset. I don't know who took it, whether we'd given them our camera or whether someone we were with had taken it with their own camera and given Rhonda a copy. Either way, it was a natural shot, and it seemed to show just how at ease we felt in each other's company. I ordered the photos on my bed, doing my best to cast my mind back if, as was often but not always the case, some of the photos I had inherited didn't have a date on the back. I went back downstairs.

Next out of the box was a newspaper, from the 21st March, 1991 – which I had successfully remembered to be the exact date we started going out. Usually people buy and keep newspapers when their children are born, so it might have seemed a strange thing to keep – but then just a couple of days earlier I'd been presented with my own toenail clippings, so my perspective had been altered somewhat. The headline was 'Major U-turn', a dreadfully mundane article about John Major and the Gulf War. I skimmed through the paper, which wasn't exactly filling me with nostalgia. Nothing of any great interest at all, really – until I got to the horoscopes page. She had crossed out the Taurus bit – something about mysterious news from a long-lost relative – and in the blank margin at the side of the page written: *You will meet the man of your dreams.*

The next item was an envelope. I opened it and removed the contents – a couple of sheets of lined paper, which I handled with such delicacy I might as well have been opening the Magna Carter. I instantly recognised my own scrawl on one of the sheets, while the other contained the kind of neat, bubbly handwriting which could have belonged to practically any of my exes – it was that generic brand of cursive which could only possibly have come from the hand of a girl. Both sheets contained that most simplistic of poetic forms – the acrostic. I'm not a great fan of poetry and wasn't then, but I am fond of Haikus - the ancient Japanese form which involves a three line poem - five syllables on the first line, seven on the second and five on the third. I like the symmetry of it; the rules.

In her handwriting was my name and in mine was hers. I sensed mine wasn't going to be very good. I started with the one she had created:

W is for the wishes that all came true when I found you.

I is for integrity – a heart so pure and true.

L is for the love that fills my heart when I see your smile.

L is for lasting and I hope our love lasts for the longest while.

J is for the joy you bring to my life every single day.

A is for absolute perfection in every possible way.

C is for your company and how I get lost in it.

O is for our time together, and I'm loving every minute.

B is for your beautiful eyes, blue and bright and beaming.

S is for the sweetness you bring – sometimes I think I'm dreaming.

Okay, a teeny bit corny at times, but the sentiments were nice. Now, I clearly had the harder job, having five more words to think of. Perhaps that was the reason mine was clearly inferior. Perhaps I was just crap at that sort of thing. You shouldn't ask a mathematician to write a poem any more than you should employ William Wordsworth as a code breaker.

R is for Rhonda *(imaginative start there, young man)*

H is for horny

O is for orgasm

N is for nice boobs

D is for drop dead gorgeous

A is for all the sex

P is for Patterson *(and the 1991 Nobel Prize for literature goes to...)*

A is for absolute beaut

T is for terrific kisser

T is for total babe

E is for everything about you

R is for really hot

S is for sexy

O is for orgasm *(multiple ones, clearly)*

N is for nice legs

Hmm. I could remember doing this. It was one rainy afternoon and we couldn't think of anything else to do. It was Rhonda's idea to write the poems and she gave us half an hour to do so. It was a competition to see who could come up with the best one. As I think you can probably gather, my thoughts were elsewhere. Maybe I was letting her win. Maybe I was trying to be funny. I can't remember her reaction, which is probably for the best. I can only imagine she was more insulted than flattered – there was so much more to Rhonda than her undoubted good looks.

I felt a bit ashamed that I'd been so shallow. There was only one thing for it – I was going to have another go. I timed myself – half an hour. No more, no less. This was what I came up with.

R is for rare. When I met you, I found a rare and beautiful creature and I shouldn't have let you go.

H is for the hope I've got that you've found happiness wherever you are.

O is for open – what I should have been with you towards the end. Maybe we could have worked something out.

N is for the nostalgia I'm feeling as I relive all these cherished memories.

D is for the days we spent together; I cherish every single one of them.

A is for always. I'll always remember you; always hold your memory dear.

P is for the pleasure you brought me.

A is for angel; what you were and what you are.

T is for talking until four in the morning, like we used to in the early days.

T is for true love – I wish I could have given it to you.

E is still for everything about you. Not just how gorgeous you were.

R is for the regrets I feel when I think back to how I treated you.

S is for sorry. Sorry I wasn't the one you were looking for. Sorry your life turned out the way it did.

O is for the optimism I took away from you as our months passed.

N is for nice. You were a nice person – that's all there is to it. You deserved none of what happened to you.

I screwed up the original and replaced it with the new version.

The next item in the box was a yellowing, slightly crumpled A4 sheet of paper divided into six boxes - sort of like a comic strip. Each box contained stick figure drawings of the two of us. Rudimentary to say the least, the drawings of me had a little scribble to represent my hair (I call it tousled, some might say messy) and the drawings of her had an arch representing her hair and some generously proportioned circular boobs in case there was any doubt who was who. The six boxes clearly represented either plans or dreams and contained nothing other than a date to represent the time she imagined each thing would happen. The first one said '1992' and showed us with sunglasses on, lying next to some waves under a smiling cartoon sunshine. Whether we were in Barbados or Bognor Regis was unclear. The second said '1993' and showed a picture of a house, her face peeking out of a window, with mine peeking out of another one. The third said '1995' and showed me down on one knee opening a small box, Rhonda sporting a shocked look. The fourth said '1996' and showed me in a top hat, her in a veil (and still no clothing below the neckline). We were next to a church. The fifth said '1999' and showed two identical-looking babies, one under my arm, one under hers. I had a look of comic exasperation on my face. The sixth and final picture said '2050' and showed the same two stick figures sitting on rocking chairs, holding hands. My squiggly hairdo was completely gone, whilst hers was tied into a kind of bun. Gravity had been exceptionally kind to cartoon Rhonda, whose boobs were still perfect circles and exactly as high up as they were before. We were both wearing glasses and feint pen strokes on our faces gave the impression of wrinkles. We were still sporting those same smiles we had on the beach on the first picture.

I didn't recall ever seeing those drawings before. Perhaps I had and had forgotten. I suspect I hadn't – I suspect Rhonda had had the good sense not to let me in on her long-terms plans for us in case it scared me off, as it almost certainly would have. Now it just made me smile – perhaps not the same beaming smile being worn by stick figure Will, but a smile nonetheless. I picked up a black Biro and to the final picture added two clouds – one under each rocking chair – and my best approximation of a little cherubic angel floating above us. In truth I was no better an illustrator than Rhonda was. To the very bottom of the picture I wrote the word 'Maybe?'

Last out was a scrolled up map of the world and, inside that, a map of the United Kingdom. I remembered these. Both contained coloured dots, and a key on the back of the world map showed that the pink dots represented the places Rhonda had been, the blue ones the places I had been, the purple ones – of which there were several on the UK map but only a couple on the world one – showed the places we had been together and the grey pencilled dots the places we dreamed of travelling together. I only hoped she got to visit some of those places, perhaps with another boyfriend, perhaps with a friend or family member, or even alone. I hated the thought that it was yet another dream that died with her.

I packed the souvenirs delicately and neatly back into the box.

I poured myself a glass of wine, from the £2.69 bottle of Liebfraumilch that I'd bought from the petrol station on the way home. Seeing it had jogged my memory – I remembered it was what Rhonda liked, and I hadn't touched a drop of the stuff since the last time I saw her. It tasted cheap – something Rhonda never, ever was – and sweet – something Rhonda always, always was.

I felt as if Rhonda would have approved of a cuddly night on the sofa drinking wine and listening to music. I intended to locate *Out of Time*, which was located somewhat disputably in the 'Rock' section of my collection (the album is actually a bit rock, a bit folk, a bit country, even a bit pop, but having a rock-folk-country-pop section would be convoluted even by my standards – so I went for what I considered to be a best fit). However, as my fingers walked through the middle letters of the alphabet, I came across Nirvana's *Nevermind* – also released that year (as I would imagine most people who know a bit about music already know) and also an album we both liked. Since I'd heard 'Losing My Religion' and 'Near Wild Heaven' a fair few times already that day, I decided a change wouldn't be such a bad thing. I took the record out of its jacket and placed the needle on its groove. I paused for just a second to speculate just how old the naked swimming baby on the album's iconic cover would now be, but stopped when I realised my calculations were spoiling the illusion of being back in time somewhat.

By the time the needle had returned to its starting position, I had drunk half of the bottle and was starting to feel light-headed. I stumbled over to my DVD collection, located *The Commitments* and stuck it into my DVD player in honour of my first date with Rhonda, when we saw it at the cinema.

As it was loading up, I got on the phone and ordered what I had still remembered to be Rhonda's favourite pizza – a Hawaiian with extra cheese. I ordered the 14 inch pizza, even though I knew full well I wouldn't eat it all. It was all so 1991 that it would have been no great surprise if Timmy Mallett himself had delivered the pizza. Wearing a pair of parachute pants. Singing that Bryan Adams song that was number one for half the year (and which I assure you did not feature on my mix CD). Much like the wine, which I drank more as a tribute to Rhonda than because I enjoyed it, I grazed on the pizza even though it would never have been something I would normally have eaten.

I don't know if the hectic nature of the last couple of weeks had caught up on me or if it was the film, which wasn't half as good as I had remembered it to be, but I was struggling to keep my eyes open. I soldiered on, cuddling the cushion as I tried my best to follow the plot. It was a futile battle.

When I awoke, the TV screen was blank. I looked down at my glass and the bottle and saw no more than dregs in either. An absolute silence surrounded me – a ghostly one, I suppose you'd call it. I got up and threw the remaining half of the pizza in the bin. I then uttered the words, 'See you, Rhonda' and spent the next hour or so in tears.

You want to know something funny? Well, I say 'funny' – really I mean painfully prophetic and ironic beyond belief. The final ten seconds of our final conversation together went as follows:

'Rhonda, let's not end things this way! I'd still like to you again – you know, as friends.'

'Ha! See me again? *Friends*? Over my dead body, Will Jacobs!'

But so it was that, in my mind at least, Rhonda and I had become friends again.

W: Helen...

H: Hello, wanker. Ha! I've been chuckling about that one all day. I've decided that your new nickname shall henceforth be – wait for it - Willy Wanker. Like it?

W: Hi...

H: Woah, okay. Clearly NOT in the mood for childish banter tonight! What happened, princess? Did your date with Rhonda not go too well?

W: No, it went well. I got a lot of things off my chest. Relived lots of nice memories. It's just that – well, there's something I haven't told you. Rhonda's...dead.

H: What? She died on your date? Holy shit – but, I mean...how did...what did you...

W: No, no, she's been dead for years now – I just didn't know anything about it.

H: Oh, God, I'm so sorry. (Long, protracted silence) *Wait – how do you have a date with a dead chick? I'm picturing some sort of twisted* Weekend at Bernie's *scenario here.*

W: We didn't. I did. I visited her mum and she gave me a box of souvenirs. I spent the evening looking through old photographs, reading letters, playing records she liked, that sort of thing. Was pretty brutal, actually.

H: Oh, mate. I'm sending you a big transatlantic hug. Did you get it?

W: Got it. Yeah, I think we could have had something really special. We already did. Anyway, onwards and upwards.

H: That's the spirit. Who's up next?

W: Kayleigh. You said you didn't remember her before. I dated her right at the end of the 90s.

H: So tonight you're going to party like it's - well - 1999, I suppose.

W: Tomorrow night technically. Sorry to spoil your joke.

H: I'm bored with you now. Bog off.

W: Ah, the epitome of elegance and ladylike charm as always. Love you, missus.

H: Love you, mister.

I looked around my apartment. It was perfectly silent, perfectly still. Perfectly boring. I needed to do something. I turned on the television and flicked through several dozen channels of crap. I turned it back off again. Even the thought of another mini-marathon of *24* wasn't floating my boat. It was human company I needed. I mulled over whether or not to knock on Pete and Georgina's door. Was I that bored? That desperate? That bereft of companionship?

'Will! Great to see you mate! Come in, come in. Georgina - look who's here!'

Yes. Yes I was.

'Will! Great to see you honey!' She wrapped her arms around me and squeezed. They did remember seeing me a few days ago, right? 'And to what do we owe this pleasure?'

Let's see. After three frankly surreal dates, in which I pretended to get married, relinquished my ties with a nut job and went on a treasure trail trip through time which included me kissing a married woman, I spent today on a date with a dead girl and now I'm feeling emotionally bruised, so I'm craving some company.

'Oh, you know - just a bit bored.'

That's right - I'm so bored that spending time with the two most boring people I know and have perhaps ever known will somehow make me less bored.

'Oh, well, you're in luck - Thursday night is Games Night here at Chateau Hepworth! Fancy a game of Chess?'

I did, actually. That was exactly what I fancied. The week had got a little bit bonkers, and Chess - with its rules and its strategies and its mathematics - would help me to feel more in control again. It would calm things down a bit. 'Yeah, why not? Who am I playing first?'

Pete and Georgina looked at each other and smiled, before chorusing, 'Both of us!'

They had to be joking, right?

'Georgina and I make an excellent team, don't we sweetheart? We've played this before, against other couples. It's great fun. We'll just take it in turns - you'll play, then Georgina will take a turn, then you'll play again, then I'll take a turn, and so on and so on. And we're not allowed to confer or anything, so we've got to try and be a bit telepathic with each other!'

Georgina clapped her hands together excitedly. Good God. Were they really going to do this? Not content with showing the world just how perfect they were together with their outward displays of affection, they were now going to show me that they were subconsciously compatible too? That they could read each other's minds? It just made me more determined to win.

It was a good game. They were the first to take a piece (just a pawn, a tiny victory they celebrated with a high five and a kiss on the lips, a nauseating routine they repeated with every piece they captured). However, on the whole, it was a pretty evenly-fought battle, which went right down to both sides having just two pieces left - a king, of course, a knight for them and a queen for me. The knight, with its limited L-shaped manoeuvres, is inferior to the queen, with its freedom to move any number of straight lines in any direction, so it only took me a few moves to capture the knight and claim my well-earned checkmate. I had to hand it them (begrudgingly) - they actually were on each other's wavelengths, playing what appeared to be a cohesive and strategic game.

Georgina yawned. 'Well, that was fun - but look at the time! Time to go up the wooden hill to Bedfordshire and all that!'

Pete did a rather hammy double take at the clock.

'Gosh! Nine o' clock! Time really has run away from us!'

I wanted to think that they were shoving me out of the door because they were desperate to tear off each other's clothes and have animalistic sex - because, after all, IT WAS NINE O' CLOCK, for, erm, Pete's sake. But I just knew that within five minutes they'd be in their his'n'hers pyjamas tucked up with a good book (literally, one good book, which they loved equally and which they'd be reading at the same time, her holding one side and him the other, turning the page at the exact point when both of them knew the other would be finished. That was what I was guessing anyway).

'Fancy coming round next Thursday for a rematch, mate?'

'Yeah, sure. I'll see ya.'

I suppose if you can't beat 'em, join 'em. I could think of nothing more exciting to do than retire, so that's what I did. I was pretty beat anyway - it had been, on the whole, a quite action-packed few days. And anyone who's cried their eyes out - which is everyone, surely - will tell you how exhausting it is to do so. I was over halfway, so perhaps it wouldn't be a bad thing to recharge those batteries before the second half. Considering Friday's events, in hindsight it was a wise move.

Friday, 15th July, 2005

I'd like to share with you a little idea, which would, I feel, benefit the needlessly tricky world of romantic wooing. Now, I realise this may sound a little silly, but here's my proposal: after you ask someone out, and they say yes, a questionnaire should be administered. Or rather, two questionnaires – one for the man, one for the woman. It would contain a wealth of key information, giving the relationship more of a fighting chance. It would be a godsend in the busy modern world, in which so many people don't have the time to waste on getting to know someone who simply might not be right for them. No guesswork for either party; no long term disappointment either.

I haven't thought as far as the questionnaire the man would fill in, but the woman's version looks something like this:

1. Which type of flowers are your favourite:
(a) Lilies; (b) Roses; (c) Sunflowers; (d) Lilacs; (e) Tulips; (f) Orchids; (g) other (please state). (h) I don't like flowers.

2. What type of restaurant do you like best?
(a) Chinese; (b) Indian; (c) Italian; (d) Thai; (e) Japanese; (f) other (please state); (g) I prefer to eat in.

3. On a scale of 1-10 (10 being the happiest), how would you feel if a man offered to pay for your meal on the first date?

4. On a scale of 1 - 10, 1 being not likely and 10 being highly likely, how likely are you to kiss at the end of a successful first date?

5. Based on previous experience, after how many dates are you likely to want to have sex?

6. In terms of facial hair, what is your preference?
(a) Clean shaven; (b) Stubbly; (c) Moustache only (please indicate preferred style); (d) Beard only (please indicate preferred style); (e) Moustache and beard combination (please indicate preferred styles).

7. Please tick up to five of the following adjectives to show what you would consider to be your ideal boyfriend:
Confident ( ) Family-orientated ( ) Fun-loving ( ) Funny ( ) Generous ( )
Impulsive ( ) Independent ( ) Intelligent ( ) Old-fashioned ( ) Patient ( ) Practical ( ) Protective ( ) Romantic ( ) Shy ( ) Sporty ( ) Sweet ( )

7. Please describe your ideal first date.

It's frank, it's direct, it eschews all of the old-fashioned conventions of snail's pace romantic etiquette and decency – in short, it's everything the world of modern love needs. Why the hell shouldn't you be able to ask how soon you're likely to have sex? It's what every lasting relationship eventually leads to – if you'll excuse the expression, let's cut out the pussyfooting!

The great advantage of the questionnaire system for the relationship hoppers of the world like me is that it becomes a kind of market research. You could collate the responses you've had over the years to build up a kind of picture of your target market. Oh look - 68% of the women I've dated prefer lilies to other flowers. That's a definite trend. A significant proportion of them - 3 in 4 - like Italian restaurants more than other kinds (and you may remember these being factors in one of my dates earlier in the week, so clearly I have done a rudimentary version of this in my head). 7/8 of them prefer a clean-shaven man to a stubbly or full-bearded one. And the top three most desirable personality traits are funny, generous and sweet. Ergo – if you are not able to administer the questionnaire for whatever reason, then on a first date, why not turn up freshly-shaven, carrying a bunch of lilies and take her to Luigi's? Presuming Luigi's serves fine cuisine and is not your local takeaway pizzeria. When you're there, crack a couple of jokes, pay for a bottle of the most over-priced champagne and tell her just how beautiful she looks. Chances are she'll be impressed! You've got the statistics to prove that! That element of surprise you're offering her is, in fact, based on fairly sound mathematical hypothesis.

You might think my idea a little far-fetched, and that's fair enough, because it is – but let's agree that at the heart of it is a concept worthy of being my next Top Tip:

Top Tip Number Three: Keep track of the commonalities in the people you date. Use what you have learned about the type of person you are attracting to help you prepare for the next one.

So, yes, it's somewhat unconventional to issue a potential suitor with a questionnaire. I understand and accept that. But I have found a way to gather the same type of data quickly - speed dating! The reason I am telling you all of this at this juncture is that it segues nicely into telling you how I met Kayleigh.

I had attended about ten speed dating sessions on the evening I met her and not once had I had the intention of finding an actual date. Most people there need to go down those avenues - I didn't. I'm not saying for one moment that all speed daters are desperate - but I am saying that plenty of them are. ENOUGH of them are to make me steer clear of using it as an actual dating platform. I would disregard the data of those women who didn't interest me, but make a mental note of the responses of those women who would have been of interest to me, under different circumstances. The great beauty of speed dating - and I wish you could say this about actual dating, which involves so much of that protocol I was talking about earlier - is that you CAN be direct. Indeed, you HAVE to be direct, due to the strict time limits. So it doesn't seem at all unusual or random if, appropros to nothing, someone asks you how shaven you like a man to be or your floral preferences. For all of these reasons, I'm making it my next Top Tip.

Top Tip Number Four: Go speed dating. You'll never meet so many potential lays in such a short space of time, and many of them are just as lacking in moral fibre as me – everyone is on the same page. It's very refreshing.

So why Kayleigh? What was it about her that made me break with convention? Was there something I particularly liked about her? No – in fact it was that there was nothing I particularly disliked about her. Nothing that annoyed me, nothing that was off-putting, nothing that made alarm bells ring. When I saw at the end that she had registered an interest in me, I could find no compelling reason not to follow up on it. I figured I would take a little break from the speed dating game, see how it all went with Kayleigh and return to speed dating when it all went belly up. It did go belly up, but I never ended up going back.

It would have been easy enough to keep a relationship with someone like Kayleigh going forever – certainly for many months longer than the two we managed. She was exceptionally low maintenance – she waited for me to tell her when the next date would be, and didn't nag or pester me if that turned out to be quite a long time. She would be perfectly happy doing whatever I wanted to do, never once suggesting we do something she wanted to do. Maybe it had something to do with the age gap – she seemed to want me to take control. She was passive, which got a little annoying after a while and was the main reason why I ended it. I needed just a bit more spice, a little more fire. Be careful what you wish for though, eh – my last relationship was with Suzie, who was nothing if not spicy and fiery!

Kayleigh's knock was loud and quick almost to the point of being impatient.

I didn't recognise the face that greeted me. Or the hair. Or the body. The Kayleigh I remembered had an auburn bob and was still carrying a little puppy fat. This Kayleigh had bright red spiky hair and a nose stud. She was slim and athletic looking and I can't say I fancied her one bit. Which was a good thing - right?

'Will! Good to see you man!' I leaned over to give her a hug and at the same time she leaned towards me with her hand held out, obviously expecting a handshake instead. This caused her to jab me in the stomach slightly. We tried again. Realising now that she thought a handshake would be more appropriate, I stuck out my hand - and clearly realising I had considered a hug the best way to say hello, she leaned in for an embrace, cause me to jab her in the stomach slightly. Ooh. Awkward start. She declined my offer of coming in, as she had left the car running and was eager to start the day.

Her car smelled of cigarettes. And when she turned to talk to me – for despite the fact that she was driving, that's what she would do, snapping her gaze in my direction every now and again - her breath had that richly pungent old cigarette smell. Did she smoke when we were going out? I didn't think so; I've always found it really off-putting and would probably have ended the relationship sooner than I did. I resisted bringing the subject up for fear of it sounding like a criticism. A better conversation starter, I figured, would be exactly what we were doing that day.

'So - I'm intrigued! Where are you taking me?'

'Oh, you'll see! Somewhere I'll bet you've never been before.'

'Can you give me a hint?'

'No.'

Well, that was that conversation exhausted. And less than one minute into the journey. Time to throw out the usual generic catch-up questions I'd been using all week. *So - do you still see x? Are you still working at y? Are you still into z?* I've refrained from transcribing these parts of the conversation, as I'm as disinterested as you would be, and was even as I was asking the questions. They were useful time killers or conversation patches. But one topic I was always keen to bring up was current relationship status and what has been happening in that department since I went off the scene.

'Yeah, I'm single. Had, like, shitloads of boyfriends, but I can't seem to settle on the right one. You know?'

I did know.

'Anyway, I'm ALWAYS busy, always trying new things, meeting new people, travelling to new places - I think a proper boyfriend would just get in the way. I get bored too easily.'

I struggled and strained through a largely one-sided conversation for just over half an hour, during which time she didn't once ask about my x's, y's and z's. But then nor did she ask about the cancer, or pry about my reasons for meeting up and whether I was meeting up with any other exes - and those were two conversation topics I was glad to dodge. Not that she seemed selfish or narcissistic - she didn't really seem to want to talk about herself for that matter. She was just sort of distant. Hard work. A bit edgy.

The drive took us way out into the countryside, where our destination awaited: *Thrillseeker's Paradise*. You've probably heard of it. It's becoming quite a popular chain, with several venues around the country. It's that place where they've got lots of high octane activities to choose from, from indoor karting to parachuting from a plane. Kayleigh explained to me that as she pretty much lived at the place, she had treated herself to a platinum membership card, allowing her unlimited access to any of the centre's activities and a limited number of guest pass activities, some of which she wanted me to use today. I can't exactly say the prospect filled my heart with joy, but Kayleigh was beaming, practically jumping up and down with excitement.

'Right, let's start off with something gentle.'

The something gentle turned out to be an indoor climbing wall. I watched Kayleigh go first. She didn't mess about. She put her left hand in a little brightly coloured plastic pothole and her right hand in one slightly higher up. She repeated this with her feet, which she used to push herself higher. She made it look so simple. Hand, hand, foot, foot, hand, hand, foot, foot. Before I knew it, she was ringing the bell at the top and waving at me. She abseiled back down.

Okay, I could do this. After being geared up and buckled to the safety harness, I grabbed the potholes and attempted to get some footing. My size eleven feet (you know what they say - big feet, big misconceptions) were not the ideal tools to use for this task. They just kept slipping off the potholes. I tried a different strategy, which was to position my feet sideways - this worked a little better, but I was struggling to gain any height. Kayleigh reminded me to push with my feet, not pull with my hands. It worked. I soon managed to get halfway up the wall, at which point I found my ankles were shaking uncontrollably. I didn't know if it was the exertion or the nerves - it seemed much higher up looking downwards than it had looking upwards. Kayleigh pumped her fist to motivate me. I resolved not to look downwards again - I would remain fixated on my goal.

No looking back. What seemed to be helping (apart from my newfound momentum) was that I had inadvertently memorised Kayleigh's route to the top, which I presume had been honed over dozens of attempts. I simply copied her - put my hands and feet in the same potholes as her, in the same order. It had taken me much, much longer than Kayleigh, but I finally had the bell in my grasp. I rang it joyously, victoriously, and abseiled to the bottom to receive my acclaim, adrenalin racing through my veins.

The climbing wall was more the appetiser than the main course.

'Right, I think you're ready to take it up a notch. Come with me – we're going bungee jumping.'

Oh Christ. Not bungee jumping. It was not something I had ever fancied doing – and especially not after yesterday. In my mind the only difference between how Rhonda died and bungee jumping was a bloody great piece of elastic. I tried protesting, tried stalling, tried suggesting we do a different activity first, but she was having none of it, at times literally dragging me by the hand to the bungee jumping station. We geared up and listened to the instructions. Or rather I tried to – Kayleigh (who had evidently done this many times before) had other things on her mind. She started whispering to me as the instructor was speaking.

'You know what would make this experience even wilder?'

Oh God. Because I was just thinking - *this all seems a trifle tame. How can we spice things up a bit?* She dug into her trouser pocket and dug out some tin foil, which she unwrapped in her palm to reveal two pills.

'What are those?'

'Speed! One for me and one for you. I swear by the stuff. Honestly, it's so good - it makes you feel so alive.'

Of course. It all added up now. The surplus of kinetic energy. The weight loss. The high excitement levels. It gave a whole new meaning to the phrase 'speed dating'.

'Go on - give it a go. No offence here, but what have YOU got to lose?' You're...'

'Dying anyway?'

'No, I don't mean that - I just mean...'

'No, it's fine. And I take your point. It's just - it's just not for me that's all. Thanks though.'

She shrugged. 'Suit yourself, mate. Double the fun for me.' She brought her palm to her mouth and knocked back both tablets. It didn't take long for them to kick in - her legs were twitching and she was fidgety. Her eyes seemed a little wider and she became uncontrollably chatty - she yacked on about anything and nothing at breakneck speed, the only respite often being the length of time it took for her to take a drag on her cigarette, which she did often. I couldn't quite believe she was smoking a cigarette – a 'cancer stick' as my mum used to call it – in front of someone who was dying of cancer. Not that it was going to make me any more terminally ill, I suppose. She made for pretty uncomfortable company - jittery and edgy.

As I awaited our turn, I reflected on the fact that of the women I had met up so far in The Week (and it would remain that way even after The Week had ended), it was Kayleigh who had changed most, to the point of being unrecognisable. If she veered slightly towards being bland when I first knew her, I see now that she was simply a blank canvas, ready to be painted on. Just as I feel that all of the girlfriends I have had have changed me to some greater or lesser extent, so too had Kayleigh been changed by her succession of boyfriends. She was young - much younger than me, not too far out of her teens - and I realise now that she was still in a transitional phase, still deciding what or who she was going to be. She might still have been in that transitional phase I suppose; it was hard to picture her carrying this persona into her middle age. Somewhere along the way she'd picked up a penchant for adrenalin and a taste for nicotine and Class B amphetamines.

We climbed the metal spiral stairs to the high platform from which we would be descending. What was I doing? I had never so much as jumped from a high diving board into a swimming pool, so what made me think I'd be cut out for this kind of insanity?

I stood on the platform and got clipped to the bungee cord. Looked up. Looked outwards. Looked around. Looked down. Once again, it seemed so much further from top to bottom than from bottom to top. My legs seemed rooted to the spot. My heart was absolutely thumping against my chest. My palms were dripping. I felt a little dizzy. Should I back out? COULD I back out? I don't mean could I live with myself and the shame and regret of chickening out, because I definitely could. I wouldn't have to live with myself for much longer after all. I mean was it possible? Who would I ask? What procedures would there be? Who could unclip me? I turned back to look at Kayleigh, who was almost scarily excited and giving me a look which suggested that whilst she was full of encouragement for me, if I didn't jump soon she would shove me herself.

'I'm sorry, Kay. I just - I just can't do it.'

She cocked her head skywards and laughed. She was practically twitching with adrenalin and excitement.

'What? Why not? What's the worst that can happen? You might DIE or something? News flash, Cancer Boy!'

I smiled at her. It was something Helen might have said, and that reassured me immediately. She was right, too! The realisation hit me that being terminally ill gave me something akin to invincibility. Okay, I wasn't literally invincible or infallible, but the fact that I was going to die soon anyway gave me a power most people don't have. I could do absolutely anything I wanted to do! If it was dangerous, so what? If doing it put my life at risk, who cared? Not like I had a wife or girlfriend or kids to worry about. It didn't just have to apply to high octane pursuits, either. Theoretically, could I not do, try or say absolutely anything I wanted? Take chances I wouldn't ordinarily have taken? Like Kayleigh said - what's the worst that can happen? Is it worse than DEATH? Of course not. Suddenly my illness felt...refreshing. Liberating, somehow.

This was it.

I chose to look straight ahead. So much less scary than looking down. The birds swooping around at my eye level seemed somehow comforting.

I closed my eyes. Tight.

And I jumped.

I've no idea why Kayleigh felt the need to enhance the experience with amphetamines, because the adrenalin / endorphin rush was unspeakably amazing. It must only have been three seconds from my feet leaving the platform to the bottom of the plummet, but they were the most giddily intense and thrilling three seconds I'll ever know. The cord pulled me back up a little, then gravity pulled me back down and this back and forth continued until all that remained was my upside down body dangling, rotating gently this way and that. I was laughing like a madman as a helmeted young gentleman with a goatee beard removed me from my harness and supported me as my feet returned to solid ground. I looked up to see Kayleigh whooping and hollering her approval before taking an unhesitant running jump off the platform. It didn't look half as impressive from this angle as it felt actually doing that, but I wasn't going to let that diminish my sense of achievement. Her scream was a very different one to mine, an undiluted expression of joy as opposed to my cocktail of excitement and primal fear.

When she was finally unclipped, I ran towards her and gave her a huge hug.

'Thanks, Kayleigh.'

And so, in my dying days, I finally took the plunge with a girl. Bu-dum-bum-chish.

After all that excitement, I was glad to round off the day with a bit of go-karting, which seemed positively tame compared with the previous activity.

It had been an amazing day, no doubt about that. I would have been perfectly happy to end it there; indeed, I thought that was what was happening. Kayleigh wasn't done with me yet, though.

'Listen, I want you to come back to my flat. Just for half an hour. I just need to grab a quick shower and change, then I'll ring for a taxi and we'll head off into town. Have a bit of grub while we're there and have some fun.' She spoke quickly and insistently - none of it seemed like I had a say in it or an option. So I just went along with it.

After a couple of drinks in her flat and a scoffed down kebab in a takeaway restaurant (most of which Kayleigh left, though I ate all of mine) I found myself in a dingy little pit of a club called The Crow's Nest, watching a charmingly named punk rock band called Shitstorm, drinking lukewarm cider out of a plastic pint glass. This was what she had meant by having some fun. My feet were sticking to the floor and every few seconds I seemed to find myself being splashed with the sweat of some heavily pierced / tattooed young man / woman

/ not sure. The music was ear-bleedingly terrible - you wouldn't catch a milkman whistling any of these particular ditties - and whether you measured the average age by mean, median or mode, I had to be getting on for double the years of the rest of The Crow's Nest's clientele. Kayleigh was younger than me, of course, but still older than almost anyone present. Yet with her unabashed energy, darker clothes, brighter hair and stick-thin frame, no one would have batted an eyelid. I looked like I belonged at a Level 42 concert, not here.

'So what do you reckon?' Kayleigh yelled into my ear.

'I love it!' And it actually wasn't a lie. I WAS enjoying myself, in spite of everything. It was so different to anything I had experienced before. In the last years of my life - last YEAR for all I knew - I was trying new and different things. I wasn't laying down and dying - far from it. I also liked the sense of community - this was a group of people who may or may not have known each other, but they were united, all facing towards the band they clearly worshipped, all having a great time (though admittedly, some expressed this through well-practised punk-rock scowls and pouts). Nobody was fighting or causing trouble (and how many times had I seen THAT sort of behaviour on a Saturday night in a club full of people who would have considered themselves normal and these people freaks?). I didn't feel intimidated. I'm more Johnny Ball than Johnny Rotten, but it mattered not a jot in this hot, adrenalin-fuelled cavern. Not that I felt engaged or interested all the time – it wasn't just bad music, it was samey. I found my mind wandering a lot. To amuse myself, I toyed around with different names I would call a punk band if I started one.

I chose ten suitable adjectives, each of them with an unpleasant or negative connotation – rancid, repugnant, sanctimonious, heathen, tone-deaf, shell-shocked, anorexic, selfish, arrogant (yes, I had been called those last two just this week) and – just for the hell of it - terminal. I then chose ten suitable pluralised nouns – monkeys, idols, virgins, bishops, corpses, infants, scabs, clowns, timebombs and victims. My choices fixed in my mind, I worked through every possible combination, all one hundred of them, starting with the ten 'rancid' possibilities and adding 'the' to the start of each. This gave me The Rancid Monkeys, The Rancid Idols, The Rancid Bishops, The Rancid Corpses, The Rancid Infants, The Rancid Scabs, The Rancid Clowns, The Rancid Timebombs, and The Rancid Victims. I chose my favourite one of the ten to add to my eventual shortlist – the first on the list, The Rancid Monkeys. I repeated this process with each of the remaining nine adjectives, adding the following to the shortlist: The Repugnant Clowns, The Sanctimonious Corpses, The Heathen Infants, The Tone-Deaf Virgins, The Shell-Shocked Idols, The Anorexic Bishops, The Selfish Monkeys, The Arrogant Scabs and The Terminal Virgins. After a not inconsiderable amount of deliberation, I plumped for The Heathen Infants as the name for my would-be punk outfit. Do you think the Sex Pistols went to all this effort?

About halfway through the gig, Kayleigh put her arm around my shoulder - not in a romantic or flirty way (there simply hadn't been that element to the day), but rather in a matey sort of way. I reciprocated. She started to pogo, taking me along with her. *Why the hell not?* I thought. So there I was, jumping up and down on the spot (a surprisingly knackering activity for a fella who hasn't seen the inside of a gym for years - how many terminally ill people do you imagine go to the gym? I was soon out of breath, but I wasn't about to stop – then I would have to admit I was too old for all of this). Did I dare do it? Did I dare take my free hand and turn it into a set of devil horns, even though I knew I was not nearly young enough, cool enough or ROCK enough? Like I said before, why the hell not? Kayleigh laughed uproariously, but then proceded to do the same with her free hand - the two of us rocked out in perfect symmetry. She lowered her hand from my shoulder and moved it to the small of my back, pushing me further towards the front of the crowd - a distinctly louder, muggier, sweatier and therefore stinkier part of the club, where oxygen was scarcer. A place where the price you paid for your proximity to the band was an occasional cider shower as exuberant young punks tried and failed to combine their interests in jumping around and holding alcohol.

'Now for your next lesson in punk rock! Time to mosh!'

And mosh we indeed did. This meant more jumping around, but in a more compressed area - then, when a little bit of space opened up, a fair bit of good-natured pushing and shoving. It was pretty intense. Then - ouch! - I received a Doc Martin to the back of the head. I turned round to see a young man being hoisted over the top of the crowd. It looked fun.

'I want to do that,' I told Kayleigh, clearly getting a bit carried away by this point (and being carried away is exactly what was about to happen to me).

'You want to crowdsurf? Are you mad?!'

'Possibly!'

'Good! Then let's go!'

She led me by the hand towards the back of the crowd. I swallowed the cooler air while I could. She tapped a stranger on the shoulder and, without saying anything, he locked his fingers together and crouched down. I put a foot into his hands and he thrust me into the air. The people in front of him put their hands on my back, lifting me and guiding me until I was horizontal. Pretty soon a sea of hands was in the air, either propelling me forward or getting ready to, should my wayward path veer towards them. Strangers' hands were *all over me*. I mean all over me. Clearly, your average punk rock crowd are a group of people who Never Mind the Bollocks when they're helping out a crowd surfer. I couldn't help but laugh aloud - I wasn't sure if I was ticklish or just giddy with the thrill of it all. As I neared the front of the crowd, a burly, bald-headed security guard grabbed me, briefly cradled me and lowered me gently to the floor, to safety. He ushered me towards the side door, which led to the toilets and took me to the back of the club, where I rejoined my Punk Rock mentor. I felt inclined to give her another hug. I wanted to give everyone a hug. I was 36 years old! And no one was judging me for these acts of juvenile abandon!

By the time the band went off the stage to milk the chanting and rhythmic clapping that preceded their inevitable encore, I was absolutely exhausted. It was the first time I had stood still for about an hour. My ankles ached and my shirt was sticking to my back. In all honesty, I didn't particularly want the band to return, but I had been shown such hospitality tonight that it seemed rude not to join in. *Shit-STORM! Shit-STORM! Shit-STORM!* I managed to muster up a few dregs of energy for the ten minute duration of their encore, but collapsed onto the nearest torn-up faux leather sofa when it was all over. Kayleigh joined me, even though she looked like she could have done the whole thing all over again there and then.

'So - how was it for you?'

How was it for me? There was a question I'd been asked many times before. The response was much the same. Sweaty. Noisy. Very, very satisfying. And now I was tired.

'So good!'

'Kayleigh! I didn't know you were here!' Two young men maybe fifteen years Kayleigh's junior leant down and took it in turns to kiss her on the cheek.

'Are you kidding? I never miss a Shitstorm gig! Daz, Potto, meet my friend Will.'

Daz pumped my hand and Potto fist bumped me. Or it might have been the other way round. They were like a punk rock Ant and Dec, interchangeable with their wallet chains and myriad piercings. They seemed nice enough, though.

'Great to meet you, Will,' beamed Daz / Potto.

'Will was a punk gig virgin before tonight - but he's been pogoing, moshing and crowdsurfing with the best of 'em!'

'Maximum respect, chief!' said whichever one had fist bumped me. I can't say it didn't feel good - maximum respect from the punk rock community! 'So you're a Shitstorm convert! Welcome to the club! Which one of our songs did you like best?'

Excuse me? Which one of *our* songs did you like best? Were they in the band or something? They might have been! Everyone here looked the same! Oh shit. Think quickly...

'Oh, man. You're gonna make me pick just one?'

I couldn't in all honesty distinguish one song from another. I hadn't been able to pick out a single lyric all night (though I'd made a mental note that if I could learn three chords and scream and snarl into a microphone, it might not be too late to start a one-man punk rock band before I popped my clogs. I'd simply recite Pi for every song in lieu of writing actual lyrics - no one would notice. I already had a name lined up). I'd hoped that complimentary little response would be enough to get me off the hook - but, alas, the three of them were staring at me, smiling, awaiting my choice.

'Ooh, you know. That first one you did. What was it called...'

'Oh, you mean 'Lamb to the Slaughter'?' asked the one who had shaken my hand.

I clicked my fingers. 'That's it! That's the one. 'Lamb to the Slaughter'. Of course. That one was rad.'

Nice work trying to sound cool, daddio. I think I got away with it, though, although not before the two of them had shepherded me over to the merch stand (that's right - I said merch stand) and persuaded me to fork over a tenner in exchange for the CD containing the afore-mentioned 'Lamb to the Slaughter' so I could enjoy it later at my leisure. Not really sure who outsmarted who there if I'm being honest. The one with the piercings in the sides of his ears told me I was all right and they explained that there was a club night about to start at the venue and asked I fancied sticking around and getting wasted. Kayleigh looked at me pleadingly. I had to admit I was tempted, but I looked at my watch. It was 11.30. I had vowed before the start of the week that I wouldn't let any of the dates spill over past midnight (I christened this the 'Cinderella Rule') - if it did, it would be encroaching on the next date's day. Somewhat less anally and more practically, it would mean I was tired on the next date - and that wouldn't be fair, would it? I made my excuses to the boys. Kayleigh asked if I minded her staying, but came to say goodbye to me outside the club. My ears were ringing.

'Kayleigh, I can't thank you enough for today. It's been so much fun. I've done things I never imagined in a million years I'd do.'

'You know, Will, someone once told me that life's not measured by the number of breaths you take, but the number of moments that take your breath away. I totally get that.'

I nodded and smiled. There was no goodbye kiss attempted by either of us, not even on the cheek. She lit a cigarette and waved me off, both of us smiling.

W: Evening, H!

H: A-ha! If it isn't Stephen King's long-lost Spanish brother, Juan. Yes, I'm still not done with the Juan jokes. So, get me up to speed.

W: (Chuckling) *Well, it's funny you used that word. Kayleigh was on it. Speed that is. She has turned into one of those adrenalin junkies, and her weapon of choice to accompany this pursuit is speed.*

H: *No way! Did you have any?*

W: *Nah. But she did manage to persuade me to join in with her other insane hobbies. She took me to a place called 'Thrillseeker's Paradise'.*

H: *Oh yeah, we've got one of them in Chicago. Okay, so Speed Racer's talked you into – what? Jumping off a bridge or something?*

W: *Not far off. We went climbing, bungee jumping and go-karting.*

H: *YOU?! Bungee jumping? But you're such a chicken shit!*

W: *Oh, it gets better. She talked me into going to a punk gig that night.*

H: *Punk? Don't you own a Phil Collins album?*

W: *No, no, no. God no. I own three.*

H: *So did you snog her?*

W: *Not this time. Didn't want to. She smoked.*

H: *So all in all you had a good date with Faggie Mae?*

W: *Yeah! It was one of the better ones so far. Not sure what to expect from Donna tomorrow.*

H: *If I'm on the right tracks you should be expecting a range of fabulous accessories and a guest appearance from Ken.*

W: *Oh stop it. She wasn't that bad.*

H: We'll see. Right, get some kip, you little rapscallion!

I may not see Kayleigh again - and, to be honest, may not particularly want to - but I believe a little bit of her spirit, her exuberance, her fearlessness, will be carried inside of me from now on . You only live once. And not always for as long as you'd hoped. You should take something from this little chapter of the book - this little chapter of my life - and do something well out of your comfort zone every now and again, just as Kayleigh does frequently. It doesn't have to be jumping out of a plane. Getting ON one would be something, if your nerves have prevented you from doing it before. It could be taking a dance class, just you and a bunch of strangers. It could be dying your hair pink even though you're fifty. And an accountant. Named Geoff. Don't forget, you're dying too - just a little more slowly than me I hope. Your time's short - and it was the moment you appeared in the world. In fact, do me a favour - put down this book and either do something scary or plan something scary RIGHT NOW. Go on. I'll be here when you get back. Okay, *I* won't, but my story will. We'll pick it up from where we left off. Go!

Saturday, 16th July, 2005

Welcome back!

So – the penultimate day belonged to Donna. Let's start with our backstory. We met when we were both in our early thirties - I was 32, and she was 31. She was working on the perfume counter at Debenhams and the first time I laid eyes on her, she was squirting scent into my then girlfriend's face (the girlfriend in question was Louise). As Louise and I walked away, Donna and I shared a lingering smile to go along with the lingering scent of *Obsession by J-Lo*. Maybe it was just her way of extending friendly customer service, but I was already besotted; already making plans to knock my dwindling relationship with

Louise on the head and make a move on Donna. After I had established whether or not Donna was single, of course. It wouldn't be easy. What need did I have to buy perfume? And for whom who would I be purporting to buy it? The girlfriend she'd already seen me with? I hoped mum wouldn't mind, but I chose to use her as my fake reason for shopping that day, and would ask Donna's advice. She told me I looked familiar; I told her I was shopping earlier that week with my girlfriend, then added that perhaps I should say 'ex-girlfriend now'. She gave me a sympathetic pat in the shoulder and said she hoped I was okay, that she could sympathise as she'd only broken up with her boyfriend a couple of weeks ago. It was as easy as that. I bought the perfume she suggested, figuring I would keep it and use it as a gift for the one after Donna (because even then I knew she and I were not in it for the long haul). The next day, I walked into Debenhams with a bunch of flowers, told Donna I hadn't been able to stop thinking about her and asked her out.

The funny thing was, even as our relationship progressed and she got to find out more about me, she never once asked me how come I was buying perfume for my dead mother. Maybe she forgot. Maybe she just never put two and two together. When you read on you will see that both seemed highly plausible.

It had clearly been a case of 'lust at first sight', and never graduated to anything more. It was never the case that I didn't fancy her - and that's something, I suppose – but nor was it ever the case that I felt connected to her, attached to her. We didn't last two months.

In hindsight, I should have started The Week with Donna – used her as the warm-up act to the main event. Knowing what I know now, I should never have followed Kayleigh with Donna, either. I had gone from this free spirited, wild-hearted cyclone of a woman to - well, I'm hoping this doesn't come across as misogynistic, but let's be frank, she was an airhead.

She had arrived at my front door with more a rattle-tap, rattle-tap than a knock-knock-knock. Whereas Kayleigh had changed beyond recognition, Donna looked exactly as I had remembered her - peroxide blonde hair scraped back in a ponytail. She wore pink. A LOT of pink. And jewellery. A LOT of jewellery. I think she was going for the rich-society-girl-about-town look. Two parts that and one part a character a five year old girl might be reading about in a fairytale. The heiress / princess look - it was just as horrendous as I hope I'm making it sound. A pair of sunglasses engulfed her face, inadvisable insofar as it was overcast outdoors, but advisable insofar as when she lifted them up to greet me, they revealed some fairly prominent crow's feet. She uttered her greeting in between chomps of her chewing gum. We hugged and she told me to grab my swimming trunks, saying she'd explain on the way.

What Donna had managed to put together was, essentially, a great girly day out, but of no interest to me whatsoever. It all started off with a spa morning, at a place called Elysian Manor - a converted stately home. I was to think of it as 'Man-pering' she assured me when I made my protests. I spend the lion's share of nearly every day in a relaxed state, so I wasn't exactly in dire need of R and R – being terminally ill is many things, but I haven't exactly found it stressful. What I will say is this – going to a spa is an excellent choice of activity for a hot-blooded heterosexual male out on the pull. Indeed I'm going to make it my next Top Tip:

Top Tip Number Five: Go to a spa!

I'd say the woman to man ratio was around 50:1, in that as there seemed to be around fifty women there and I was the only man. Now why the heck hadn't I thought of doing this when I was younger? I'm not suggesting all fifty of them were young and attractive (and there were lots of engagement and wedding rings on display) – but even taking all of that into account, the possibilities were abundant. And if nothing comes of your endeavours, you get to spend your day looking at ladies in swimming costumes and bathrobes! Of course, it was pretty much irrelevant that morning, partly because my pulling days were behind me and partly because I was with Donna. I either looked like her boyfriend or her gay best friend. With the lack of physical contact and the total absence of romantic chemistry, it was probably the latter.

It wasn't horrible - I will say that. The serene atmosphere? Attractive ladies dressed in white? Harp music? I felt at times like I'd arrived in Heaven a couple of years early. The place even had little angel statues and cherubs spitting water into the heated pool.

Some things I have to admit I liked - there was a 'Snooze Room', dimly lit and with bean bags and cushions (and that ubiquitous soft music). I actually got my head down for half an hour, clearly still a little frazzled from my punk rock antics twelve hours earlier. I treated myself to a massage, which, like the Snooze Room, had the added bonus of providing me with half an hour away from Donna's inanity. An attractive, petite brunette in her early twenties who spoke in soft, reassuring tones which blended with the generic flute music being piped through the speakers did the honours. I actually think I would have preferred some big, burly middle-aged woman – I spent the entirety of the far-too-pleasant massage focusing on not getting an erection rather than relaxing and enjoying it. Her hands were soft, her touch probing, and I wondered at the end if etiquette required me to buy her breakfast or meet her parents. And the outdoor hot tub was undeniably terrific, though I was transfixed by how exactly Donna's fake tan wasn't turning the water orange.

Some things, though, I just didn't like. I cannot see the appeal of sitting in a baking hot, steamy room with a bunch of strangers. Nor could I fathom out why there was a small queue in front of a little cubicle containing a rope which, when pulled, released a bucketful of ice cold water all over one's body. And some of the ladies didn't seem to move from the poolside loungers all day – I couldn't help but feel they'd paid an awful lot of money for a lie down.

'So how was your first spa experience, hun?' Donna asked as we walked back to her Ford Puma coupe car.

'I liked it! Thanks for treating me!' It wasn't a lie. The positives had outweighed the negatives. And whereas I was confident I wouldn't be going to any more punk gigs or bungee jumping off high platforms ever again, I couldn't rule out making a return visit to Elysian Manor. I definitely preferred it to the rest of the day.

We made a flying visit to her mum's house. I stayed in the car. Donna had told me there was someone she was dying for me to meet, with whom I was going to fall in love. Was she setting me up or something? Did she have a hot friend in there, ready to join in with the fun? She returned to the car with a creature more spoilt and annoying than the lady herself - a yappy little dog perched inside her Gucci handbag, looking as preened and pampered as its owner. I hate dogs. Always have. She must have known this? It must have come up? I have ended otherwise promising relationships with women besotted with dogs, for fear of being saddled with one. It can't just be me - the English language has given them some derogatory expressions. 'Dog tired' - do dogs get more tired than other animals? 'Dog ugly' - again, I can think of uglier creatures! Just off the top of my head - sloth, hippotomus and monkfish. 'Working like a dog'- I've never met a dog who's done a lick of work in his life! Mind you, I've met a few humans of whom I could say the same (although who was I to talk these days?). 'Dogged by illness' - as if a canine is to blame for your sniffles!

I could tell it (for despite knowing its gender, I cannot now refer to it as anything other than 'it') knew how I felt. When I finally managed to bring myself to stroke it, it snapped at me.

'Isn't she just adorable?'

'She is something else!'

It was a short drive into town, where we spent the afternoon browsing the exhibits at the local art gallery, Donna offering me her unique insights and theories behind each one. Not really. On her suggestion - her insistence - we ended up trawling around the local shopping centre, Donna letting out little squeals of delight at the over-priced scraps of material being peddled as women's fashion. I tried to alleviate the boredom as she was in the changing rooms by trying to spot a stray nipple or even flash of cleavage through the tiny gaps in the doors (she did have a smoking body underneath all the fake tan and bling). However, my enjoyment was ruined as soon as my glance fell on the dog, who was eyeing me from its bag on the dressing room floor. I was yapped at throughout. By the dog that is. Actually, by both of them. Often - too often - they were doing it simultaneously. Occasionally, I managed to squeeze in a word or a sentence fragment, but she was visibly uninterested in anything I had to say and carried on with her own line of inane chit-chat. In truth, I was probably equally oblivious to what she was saying. I amused myself by trying to estimate the ratio of communication. I would guess that the Donna to dog to Will ratio was approximately, on average, 40:15:1. Her speech was littered with those empty little Americanisms so beloved by the teens, which used to drive me mad when I was a teacher. Like! Totally! Like totally! Duh! OMG! Duh indeed. OMG indeed. Not that the teens loafing around the shopping centre sucking the life out of their giant McDonalds cups would have claimed any kinship with our Donna. They sniggered and pointed and gawped. Even with their complete lack of subtlety and sensitivity, she STILL seemed oblivious, far away as she was on Planet Donna. I walked at the maximum possible distance to her that I could whilst still being in her company / earshot. I wasn't sure which I was going to die of first - the testicular cancer or the sheer embarrassment. And all the time, that damn dog wouldn't take its beady little eyes off me.

'I think she likes you - don't you Precious?'

I wasn't sure if it was she was saying precious - the term of endearment - or whether that was actually its name. I never found out for sure, but I have written it with a capital because I suspect it was the latter. She was wrong - it didn't like me, and nor did I like it. I tried. Lord I tried. I tried tickling it under its chin, only to be barked at. I even - ugh - tried making the gurgly-wurgly cutesie baby noises Donna was employing.

Yes - this was a terrible, terrible date. I'd had impulsive Maria. Thoughtful Harriet. Wild-spirited Kayleigh. Hell, even crazy Suzie had been entertaining, in an insane sort of way. This was just boring and embarrassing.

'Now, today isn't all about me, is it?'

Oh thank God. Time for something a bit more Will-friendly.

'Your turn to shop!'

Or maybe not.

'Oh, no, that's okay, thanks.'

She stepped back and looked me up and down, completely ignoring what I'd just said. 'Babes, we HAVE to do you a makeover!'

I was offended. Didn't she realise I was wearing my sixth-best going out shirt today? What was wrong with the way I was dressed? Before I could voice my complaints, she'd dragged me into the nearest River Island and was frantically flicking through the clothes looking for something she thought would suit me. A tight-fitting salmon pink v-neck shirt had caught my eye and I was praying it hadn't caught hers - can you imagine the two of us stood side by side? Those teens would think all their Christmasses had come at once. Instead, she picked out a slim-build striped shirt and a skinny fit waistcoat (I wished for a moment I was overweight - River Island doesn't seem to cater for the fuller-figured gentleman and I'd be spared this humiliation). To go with it - a black skinny tie and a pair of tight ripped jeans. And to top the whole thing off, a pork pie hat. All of this might have been acceptable if I was half my age - it just wasn't me, and I didn't need to try it on to know that. But as she was ushering me towards the changing rooms, I apparently didn't have a choice. Great. Helen was right – Ken was making a guest appearance. It was me. I was the Ken to her Barbie. Actually, she was more like the little girl DRESSED as Barbie, playing with her Ken Doll, making him look fab-u-lous. Except I didn't feel fabulous. I felt stupid. Stupid and bored and trapped. I couldn't wait for this day to end. I looked at my reflection and sighed. *What were you thinking, man?* Praying no one else was around, I stepped out of the cubicle and waved my arms in a weak 'Ta-Dah' gesture (you'll notice 'Ta-Dah' came without its usual accompanying exclamation mark). Donna was sat crossed-legged on a high wooden chair. She tapped her fingers against her palm to applaud her creation. I turned to head back towards the changing room, dropping my fake smile as soon as my back was turned.

'Wait! You HAVE to accessorise! Here - try these on.' She handed me some brightly-coloured plastic beads, which I put on my wrist. Yes, I was wearing a bracelet. A man bracelet. I think a little part of me died inside, right there and then. It wouldn't have been the worst thing in the world if the rest of me had followed suit. I smiled, a little more weakly than before, and tried once more to get to the changing rooms. When I returned, Donna bundled up the clothes and dumped them on the counter. A pouty teen shop assistant, pale-faced, stick-thin and doe-eyed, looking for all the world like a clinically-depressed Manga cartoon character, rang it all up.

'That'll be £228.32.'

Wow. And not even a free 'please' thrown in to sweeten the deal. I looked at Donna. She looked at me. I continued to look at Donna. She continued to look at me. What - I was paying for this crap myself? It wasn't a present from her to me like the spa day? Unbelievable! I took out my credit card, trying my best to mask my sense of infuriation. I mean, it wasn't that I couldn't afford it - I just didn't want it! I would definitely be making a return visit to River Island on Monday morning, bringing the whole lot with me and getting my money back. That was the plan, anyway.

Donna turned to the girl on the till. 'Sweetie, would you mind cutting off the tags for us here? He's going to wear them now.'

Bugger.

The girl obliged and handed me the bags back. 'You can go back into the changing rooms if you like,' she drawled.

Gee thanks. I mulled over whether I was better off changing as quickly as possible - like taking a plaster off, only in reverse - or postponing the agony as long as possible. I went for the first option, this time not once looking at myself in the mirror for fear I might actually end up punching my reflection.

'Well, erm, thanks for that.'

'Don't thank me yet, babes! We're not finished!'

I gulped. 'We're not?'

'No! Our next job is to sort out those eyebrows! You deserve it! Now let's get you plucked.'

Oh I was plucked, all right. Seriously plucked. She took me to a beauty salon, where I was, inevitably, the only male customer. There was a theme to this day. Now, when she said I deserved it, did she mean I deserved to sit for ten minutes in eye-watering agony? Because that's what happened. In fairness, there are plenty of women who would concur that that's exactly what I deserved.

The lady with the tweezers and Donna were clearly familiar to one another.

'Donna, he's a handsome one, your new boyfriend! Especially now I've sorted out those caterpillars!'

I laughed, perhaps a little too vigorously. 'No no no! I'm not her boyfriend. Definitely not her boyfriend.'

Donna tucked her arm into mine. 'But he definitely could be looking this handsome!'

Lord help me. I looked at myself in the little round mirror next to me, which magnified my reflection - shaped eyebrows, trendy but unsuitable clothing and not to mention the light tan I still had from Monday's date with Maria. What was happening to me?

Donna's next suggestion was to take me to Toni and Guy's for an overpriced haircut, but it was here that I felt I had to put my foot down. I could take off these clothes, and I could live with these eyebrows, but if I ended up with a silly hairdo, there wouldn't be much I could do about it, other than have it all shaved off - and I wanted to look good for Mandy tomorrow. I diverted Donna's attention by suggesting lunch. We ate at Chiquito's, into which Donna easily (unfortunately) sneaked her dog-in-a-bag. My first job was to get a pint of Peroni - now THAT I deserved - but Donna stuck to mineral water.

'Good afternoon sir. Good afternoon Madame. What can we get for the lovely couple today?'

Oh God, not him too. I couldn't be bothered correcting him this time.

'Ooh, let's see. It all looks good, but I think I'll go for the enchiladas.'

'Just to let you know, sir, it's Double-Up Saturday. You can double the size of any main course for just a pound.'

My eyes widened. 'Well that's a no-brainer! I'll do that please. And what the hell, can you add a side of tortilla chips? Bring me the full works, dips-wise.'

'No problem. And you, Madame?'

'I'll just have a Caesar salad, please. Just a tiny bit of dressing for me if you don't mind.'

As the waiter walked away, Donna shot me a look pitched between stern and concerned. 'Babes, you've GOT to look after your cholesterol.'

I looked at her disbelievingly. I was surprised she even knew the word cholesterol (one of the few polysyllabic words she uttered all day). I was also amazed that she thought I would be concerned about my cholesterol levels. Something else beginning with 'c' was going to kill me long before that had a chance. It's the thinnest of silver linings, I suppose, but when you're dying you don't have to worry about the things that will kill you. As I'm sure you can imagine after my rants about Kayleigh, I'd never smoked a cigarette in my life, but if I wanted to, I could smoke forty a day. I could drink as much as I wanted, morning, noon and night if I wanted. And if I wanted a double portion of enchiladas, I was bloody well having a double portion of enchiladas. Cholesterol - pur-lease.

Our conversation - by which I mean the words she was speaking, with little pause for breath, let alone to allow me to respond - veered between the bland and the idiotic. I hadn't really wanted to talk about my illness with any of the Magnificent Seven, and thankfully Donna steered clear (it would have meant talking about something non-Donna related), apart from this chestnut:

'I mean, OMG, how lucky are you? When you think about it? If I had all that free time I'd watch Jeremy Kyle non-stop.'

If those same words had been spoken by, say, Maria, or Harriet, or Helen - because it's definitely something Helen would say, if they had Jeremy Kyle in the States - it would have been delivered with a great big dollop of irony. But I actually think Donna meant it. She actually wished she was dying so she could give up her job and watch daytime television. Mind you, I'll try not to get too sanctimonious - I can't really say I spend my dying days engaged in a nobler pursuit.

I amused myself as Donna was talking by conducting 'literally' count. One point for every time she said the word, and a bonus point if she used it incorrectly (in other words when she in fact meant to say 'figuratively', or just not bothered). Some genuine examples:

'Literally no one believed a word I was saying.' That was plausible. One point.

'Babes, I've got literally thousands of pairs of shoes.' I had to mull this one over a bit, but I decided even Donna could not own that many pairs of shoes or have the space to do so. Two points.

'I was literally over the moon when I got your message.' No, you most definitely were not. You have no aeronautical training. It is an idiomatic turn of phrase and one can no more be literally over the moon than it literally be raining cats and dogs. Two points.

'I literally didn't get a wink's sleep that night, I was so excited.' People don't tend to sleep with just one eye closed, so one point (awarded begrudgingly).

'OMG, I was so embarrassed, I literally could have died.' People die from being hit by a bus. People die from cancer. People do not die from embarrassment. Two points.

'This is literally the worst date I've been on in years.' Okay, I said that one. To myself, very quietly, when she was yakking to a friend on her mobile phone in between the courses.

I don't know if it was my general discomfort at this weird situation or the enchiladas I'd eaten (I'd wager it was a potent combination of the two), but almost as soon we'd left the restaurant, suddenly I needed the toilet. I made my excuses and dashed for the nearest ones which, somewhat inevitably given their location, were bustling. It would be futile at this point in the story to deny my idiosyncrasies - but surely we can't count a hatred of public lavatories as one of them? Surely that one's universal? Alas, my needs outweighed my reservations, so I took the plunge, so to speak. In front of me lay exactly ten different options (exiting not being one of them) - a row of ten cubicles. My mission would be to use the cleanest - and having glanced at the rota on the wall, we would be talking damage limitation since none had been cleaned for nigh-on two hours. This would require a hastily formed hypothesis based on previous experiences.

Let's number the cubicles, Number One being the closest to the entrance and Number Ten being the furthest away. And let me forewarn you there will be no number one / number two jokes in the following paragraph - this was serious business. There will also be no business jokes. Now, had the sinks been the first thing a fellow would have reached, even before the toilets themselves, my choice would have been easy enough - Number Ten. It's the furthest away! Number One would have been the most frequented due to its proximity to the entrance, and the usage of the others would have diminished the further down the line you walked. Most men aren't like me - they'll go for the easy option. Good for them. They clearly have no regard for the millions of multiplying microbes sharing their toileting experience. However, the sink was at the opposite end, just after the tenth cubicle. All rules were therefore off - some men would instinctively choose the cubicles near the sink, some wouldn't. There was still a slightly greater chance that the Number Ten would be less frequented than Number One, since a frightening percentage of men don't actually wash their hands at all after going to the toilet, rendering a trip towards the sink (and the cubicles near to the sink) pointless. But I reckoned the safest bets would be Numbers 7 and 8 - not directly near any of the 'hotspots' (Number One and Number Ten, near the exit and sink respectively) and just away from the middle toilets, which would represent appealing options because of their equidistance between the hotspots. Of course, I could actually forego all of this by going into the cubicles and checking their state of cleanliness - but wouldn't that have been a bit...weird? Besides, my situation was becoming increasingly urgent, so I was going to have to take my pick. I did a quick 'Eeny, meeny, miny, moe' and ended up putting this baby on po Number 8. I pushed the door open and faced my destiny. Apart from a few skids, it was as clean as I could have expected under the circumstances. I tore off enough strips of toilet paper to create a protective layer on the toilet seat and I was good to go. Even after my work was done and I'd flushed, I sat there for a while. I suppose it says something about how the day was going that sitting in a pongy public lavatory was somehow slightly preferable to continuing with my date.

And that's when I came up with my next plan of action.

I washed my hands (it was one of those unhygienic sinks where you had to actually turn the faucet - and thus share hundreds of other men's post-toilet germs - so I had to force the tap on and off by pushing it with my elbow. I'm not even going to bring up the matter of it being a bar of soap rather than a soap dispenser or that I had to pull on a door handle containing the germs of a thousand unwashed hands). Then it was action time.

So - the plan. Necessity is the mother of invention, and boy was it necessary for me to get out of this date. It's so easy in the mobile phone age to have an escape plan mid-date. You know the old routine - slip off to the toilet and text a friend asking them to ring you in five minutes with news of some crisis or emergency. We've all done it I'm sure. I prefer to set an alarm that sounds like a ringtone (clearly not advisable in quieter places where it's plainly obvious you're not actually talking to anyone). All well and good apart from the fact I had already used this routine with Donna, wherein I used the ruse of a concerned neighbour smelling a gas leak to escape a very tedious first date. A picture message sent by Donna the next night of her in her lingerie was enough to convince me that everyone deserves a second chance).

Listen, I KNOW this was bad. And I KNEW it was. But, in all honesty, I would have found something similarly despicable to do even if I hadn't been dying. In my moribund state, it was much easier to justify to myself - my days were numbered! Why should I have to spend one of them in the presence of someone whose company I really wasn't enjoying? When I returned to Donna's side, I let out a low moan from the pit of my stomach, which I clutched. I could feel the colour draining from my face - a surprisingly easy feat to achieve when I considered the possibly of seeing out the rest of this date.

'OMG, hun! You look awful! Are you ok? You've been gone for ages!'

'I'm ok...I think. It's just that every now and then I get these shooting pains in my annulus. I'm having a histogram on Tuesday as it's getting worse'.

Admittedly, annulus is a Mathematical term meaning the area between two concentric circles and histogram is a bar graph representing frequency distribution for certain ranges or values. Neither has absolutely anything to do with the human anatomy. It amused me, and I felt like I had deserved a bit of amusement.

'Owww! I think it might be spreading to my parabola' (another Mathematical term, meaning, if you're interested, the graph of a quadratic equation. I was really spoilt for choice with Mathematical words that sounded a bit like body parts).

Now, at this juncture, I had three options:

Option 1 - tell her that this was nothing to be too concerned about, that it was a regular part of my condition, but that sadly I would have to go home and take my medication. Tell her I had had a nice time. Maybe we could do it again one day?

Option 2 - go for the Oscar. Tell her I thought this was it. The end was nigh. I'd better rush home, say my goodbyes to my loved ones (which would consist of a phonecall to Helen if I were actually to do this), and call an ambulance. That way, there could be no possibility of having to make contact with her again. I could just ignore her emails and phonecalls. She'd think I was dead! Obviously, even by my standards, this would have been a terrible thing to do, bringing distress on Donna and tempting fate for myself.

Option 3 - do the gentlemanly thing. Tell her I was fine, that the pain had passed, and persist with the date.

I think you already know I chose Option 2. And boy, did I lay it on thick.

'Listen - ow! - I've had such a good time with you! It's been special! Ouch! Memorable! Oh God, the pain! I really feel as if we've made a,' I winced. 'Connection this time! Aargh!'

I kept my moans discrete enough not to attract the attention of the other shoppers and those bloody teens, who I could swear had migrated towards us.

'Babes, I feel it too!' Her voice quivered. 'Totally!'

'Look, I want you to know that if this turns out to be my last day on Earth, I just couldn't have dreamed up a better day!'

I almost broke out into a smirk, before it dawned on me that soon enough I could be having this conversation with someone for real.

'We're coming with you! Me and Precious. We want to be there with you, right til the end. Don't we, sweetie-pie?'

The dog seemed to be glaring at me again, with a look that seemed to say, *Look, I may be a dog, but even with my tiny dog brain, I'm not buying any of this. I'm smarter than her, you know.* Think fast, Jacobs. Think fast.

'NO! I mean...no.' I squeezed her hand, though the lies were making my own hand clammy. 'I - I want you to remember me this way. Goodbye, Donna!'

'Right, well then I suppose I'd better give you one final amazing kiss!'

She removed her chewing gum and plunged her lips to mine. I kept one eye open, gazing around me at the teens, now in fits of hysterics, and that bloody dog, now giving me a look more murderous than disdainful. Then I think I probably shrugged, thought 'sod it', closed that eye and enjoyed what was indeed an amazing kiss. You never know - it actually could have been my last kiss.

And so, just desserts for my deceptions, I began my Saturday evening alone and, ironically considering this was a week full of dates, dateless. My instincts were telling me to call it a night, to rest up for my final date tomorrow, really go all out to make it a good one - but I figured I'd be doing plenty of resting at some point in the near future. You know, for an eternity. So what the hell? I made a phonecall I had not made for some years. It was ringing. A male voice answered - it was him. That's right - a man. I couldn't believe I was doing this.

'Nige!'

'Big Willy! Wow - it's been a long time, man!'

'Too long, old pal! Too long. Listen, I've got some bad news and a proposition. The bad news is, I've got testicular cancer, and it's terminal. I've probably only got a couple of years left.'

'Oh my God, I -'

'So the proposition is - how about you and I have one last big night out? I'm still single, and I'm going to presume you are too, so what's say two serial ladykillers go and paint the town red?'

'Erm, give me half a second to mull that one over...Hell yeah!'

So - Nigel Mackenzie. I'm not particularly proud of this, but Nigel was something of a friend of convenience for me. He facilitated the lifestyle I wanted to lead - I needed to meet lots of women, lots of potential girlfriends, and if I was having a dry spell, what better place to, well, turn it into a moist spell than to hit the town? I obviously wouldn't have stood much of a chance on my own - who's going to talk to the sad, desperate loner? What I needed was a wing man - and that's basically all he was to me. I never met up with him in the daytime - only ever on nights out. He was fine with this arrangement - indeed, it was reciprocal. We could call each other on a whim, and be in town within the hour. I had known him since the last year of secondary school and what I liked about him back then was that he seemed more like he was 18. That remained true long after he actually was 18, and indeed I never saw him any other way. Mature and sophisticated he was not, but fun-loving and perpetually single he was: the recipe for a great wing man. I actually knew very little about him - our conversations would consist solely of the women around us and the alcohol we were drinking to help us meet those women.

Though our goals were much the same, his approach was more random, less systematic than mine. Basically, he would drink whatever he fancied, whenever he fancied it, in whatever quantities he fancied, then attempt to pull anything he - well - fancied. He would chat up loads of women, often clearly above his league. He had a very limited repertoire of chat-up lines, his favourite being to tell them his name, then adapting an already existing phrase, inform that, 'They call me Mac. And once you go Mac, you can never go back.' No one actually called him Mac, mind you, and very few went Mac, even after this approach. Those who did most certainly did go back, quickly and without fail. Without meaning to be derogatory or arrogant, I would say he's neither blessed with my charm nor my looks - but he wouldn't care. He would simply move on to the next one. Eventually, someone would fall for it – that was his philosophy, and he was dead right. He even had a hundred business cards printed out containing his name, catchphrase and telephone number to give out to the ladies he was attempting to pull, but decided after the initial run of a hundred cards not to get any more printed out, owing to the fact that they were being dropped on the floor and ending up in the hands of prank callers.

My approach - both to alcohol and to pulling - was more as follows:

Drinks 1 to 3 – a pint of lager. Sitting down. Scope out the situation. In sporting terms, this might be considered the pre-match warm-up. Any lager between 4 and 5% ABV is acceptable. Less than that and you might as well not bother; more and you're pushing your luck a bit.

Now time to step it up a gear.

Drink 4 - tequila shot. An injection of life into the evening. We're on our feet now. It's a little signal to any ladies around that we're not here to sit around drinking: we're here for a party.

Drinks 5 to 8 - a mixer. This will vary between nights but not within the night. The possible spirits are any renowned vodka, Jack Daniels and Bacardi and the possible mixers are lemonade, Coke and Red Bull. This does, of course, give nine different potential combinations, all of which are acceptable and all of which I have incorporated into my routine, though of course some are preferable to others - highest in the pecking order is Jack Daniels and Coke. Crucially, these must be single measures, never double - retaining a sense of control is paramount. They also provide a kind of sugar rush, an energy boost, so often much-needed at this point in the night - so obviously, low sugar versions of the mixers are not acceptable. It's usually at the end of drink 5 that I feel ready to put on my proverbial dancing shoes.

Time for a change at this point, as continuing in this vein would impede any potential performance later that evening. Brewer's Droop would, it goes without saying, be a disaster and the whole evening a wasted endeavour. Hence...

Drinks 9 and 10 - alcopop. As before, a variety is welcomed between but not within nights. I am now at the optimum point in terms of drunkenness; confident and unselfconscious, yet focused and coherent, so it's important not to lose the Dutch Courage into which I've invested my time and money. It's all about keeping the buzz going without actually getting MORE drunk, and alcopops are perfect for this. Plus, it's action time now - time to start talking to women - and the smell of alcopops on the breath is surely preferable to that of bourbon or lager. I tend to take my time with drinks 9 and 10, sipping rather than guzzling. It's at this point that, if I'm going to pull, I pull. It's also at this point that Nigel and I often become separated, and if we haven't said goodbye, that's fine. That's our unspoken agreement.

Drink 11 onwards - bottled water. This applies whether in the club or street or taxi. I must not have a hangover in the morning, just in case morning sex is on the agenda. If it is the case that I haven't pulled by now and I'm leaving the club, my hope is not lost. Now, it's no great revelation when I say that the outside areas of nightclubs are rife with potential lays – but would you know which kinds of women to look for? I do.

Top Tip Number Six: Go for the drunken criers. So very many women start off the night with a man on their arm and end it without. That was where I would step in.

The maths here (and it's as solid as any numerical equation you care to express) is as follows:

(Ladies + alcohol) – boyfriend = tears.

Tears means vulnerability, which in turn means a very strong possibility of rebound sex.

And that's the routine. Not that it arrived fully-formed, of course - it was the product of a period of trial and improvement, experimenting with different drinks and quantities. Sometimes I ended up too drunk; sometimes not drunk enough. I even once tried the 'Chumbawumba Path' - a whiskey drink, a vodka drink, a lager drink and a cider drink, in that order. The only thing I ended up with was a tubthumping headache. But as soon as I arrived at a winning formula, I stuck to it rigidly, religiously.

You know, I've told you all of that in the present tense, as if it still happens. I stopped going out with Nigel when I found out about the cancer. Whenever his name flashed on my mobile, I ignored it, and soon enough he stopped calling. Good old Nige, though – a couple of years apart was going to change nothing. The Deadly Duo were going to be reunited!

I found myself showering for the second time that day, raiding the 'Nights Out' section of my wardrobe for a suitably nice shirt (because I was definitely NOT wearing the River Island combo I now owned). I also found myself digging out a certain accessory I had not used for many years.

Okay, strange confession time now. I own a wedding ring. Not even a Hula Hoop one – a real one. A pretty nice one, too – 18 carat. I even had it inscribed inside with a shortened and paraphrased version of an Aristotle quote – *The circle is the origin of any and every marvel.* Now why, you might ask, would a man who has never been married, and never had the intention to GET married, own a wedding ring? Simple really. I'll explain the logic after I've made it my next Top Tip:

Top Tip Number Seven: Buy a wedding ring!

For a certain type of woman (and they're not normally the type you'd want to take home to meet your mum if she was alive), a wedding ring is like catnip. They see a decent-looking chap wearing one, and they just can't resist the challenge. It's a vanity thing – if they can pull someone who's happily married, who's evidently not looking for any action, then they've clearly still got it. So if I was in the mood for that kind of woman (because, hey, sometimes you fancy a steak dinner, and sometimes a greasy kebab is all that will do) I would dust off the ring and see what would happen. My ring is diamond cut, giving it that extra sparkle when the lights in the night club bounce off it. A word of warning, though - if you feel like trying out this particular strategy, remember to take it off at the end of the night. As I found out, it's easy enough to crash into bed at the end of a drunken night (alone or otherwise). You'll have some very awkward questions to answer the next day, if you bump into someone you know. And whatever you do, don't leave it on in the sun – you'll be left with a white wedding ring tan line. Again, some girls won't mind this – you're fresh on the market, so they'll want to snap you up while they can – but it will be off-putting for most girls. Most divorcees carry considerable emotional baggage, at least for a while, and who wants to help them carry that about? Anyway, I slipped the ring into my pocket, just in case I fancied a snog at the end of the night. I called a cab and away I went.

We agreed to meet outside the Paradise night club - formerly Cloud Nine, as it was the last time we were there. I arrived first. Nigel never seemed to change, and I presumed this would still be the case. He'd be wearing some utterly tasteless shirt – a strategy I'm going to allocate the honour of being one of my Top Tips:

Top Tip Number Eight – If you're not a looker, wear a noticeably terrible shirt.

Sounds mad, doesn't it? But it was a winning strategy for Nigel. His favourite was a shirt with rows of beer bottles all over it, but he had plenty of equally garish options. The beauty of this hideousness was that it was a talking point – an icebreaker. Women would come up to him and would say something sarcastic. *Nice shirt. Where* did *you get that shirt?* That sort of thing. They thought they were being clever, but it was Nigel who was the smart one – he'd lured the fly into the spider's web. He'd say something back to them, and suddenly a dialogue was happening. He'd anticipated their mockery and was more than ready for it with an arsenal of responses. Oftentimes after a couple of back-and-forths the women would walk away. Oftentimes he wouldn't get that far – they'd walk away or tell him to piss off as soon as he started trying to engage them. But sometimes – just sometimes – things would go further. He'd spin them his 'Once you go Mac' catchphrase; they'd laugh. He'd offer to buy them a drink, a drink would lead to a full conversation, a conversation to a hug, a hug to a snog and, just sometimes, a snog to a shag. The great thing about Nigel was that he was like one of those Bobo dolls – knock him down and he just got right back up again. So all those rejections hurt him not one iota, and those rare successes would be the only incentive he needed. I never had to resort to bad shirts, but I admired his tactics.

He'd arrived. He was paying a taxi driver and didn't seem to have noticed me yet. He looked different. His paunch was gone and he was wearing an actually very stylish checked shirt.

I shouted him. 'Nige!'

He looked over at me and beamed. He'd greet me, I was sure, with that annoying slogan from the Budweiser advert that everyone was saying in the year 2000 and absolutely no one was saying after that apart from Nigel – 'WAAAAAASSSSUUUUUPPPP!!!' Wait for it...

'Hiya, Will!'

Oh. We greeted with a manhug – brief, with firmly patted backs - and joined the short, fast-moving queue.

'Oh man, I'm sorry about - you know...'

'Thanks. But can we not talk about it, please? I'm just here for a good time. It's good to see you. The Deadly Duo - reunited!'

'Dude, tonight we're turning back the clock on your behalf. We're going in search of some serious tang.'

I winced. I had a good hunch what he meant, but I felt inclined to ask. 'Tang?'

'Yeah, you know: tang. Totty. TITS!'

'Women then...'

'Yeah! Tang! And tonight, Big Willy, my old mucker, you and I are tangsters!'

He pointed in the direction of a passing group of girls, making the noise and gesture of a machine gun. Quite rightly, they gave him a disgusted look and hurried past him. Before I knew it - and in all honesty, I could happily have waited longer, or better still gone home - we were at the front of the queue. We stepped inside.

Nigel made a sweeping gesture with his arm. 'And this, my friend - this is Tangster's Paradise!'

I couldn't decide which seemed more plausible - that Nigel had been concocting this slightly sexist brand of wordplay on my behalf as he was getting ready to go out, or that it was part of a well-versed repetoire, honed over the months we'd been apart. I decided upon the latter, imagining him adding to some sort of handbook containing a host of similar gems, to be whipped out whenever the situation called for one. In a funny sort of way, I could probably have related to that level of anorak-ish dedication.

As per our old routine, we bought our own drinks (which always seemed fair since Nigel without fail drank more than me). Ordinarily, he didn't stray far from beer, but this time he returned with what appeared to be something mixed with Coke.

'What's all this, mate?'

'This here's a double vodka and Coke: my weapon of choice these days. Much better for the waistline. Probably much worse for the liver, mind!'

Diminished gut? Rejecting the beer? Strange things were afoot here...

'Right, well, cheers! Here's to a good night!'

Nigel nudged me excitedly with his elbow as an attractive young lady was about to pass us by.

'I've been working on some new material! Check this out.' He tapped her on the shoulder. 'The name's Tom. Tom Bowler. Fancy your chances?'

She repressed a little smile but continued on her path.

'Hmm. Still tinkering with that one. I'm gonna have another go.'

He ushered me in the direction of two ladies, again attractive, again considerably younger than us.

'The name's Tom. Tom Bowler. Go on – stick your hand in there and have a rummage. You never know your luck.'

The two ladies giggled but moved away from us. 'Let's get a drink, Nige. The night's still young even if we're not.'

It was business as usual to begin with. We sat there, checking out the ladies present, the chit-chat inane and infrequent, as I worked my way through drinks one, two and three. The only difference was, I wasn't looking for a girlfriend this time, or even a one night stand; just a kiss. I felt a great deal more nervous this time - I didn't know whether it was because of the time that had elapsed since I last did this or because the girls seemed so very young, as did the boys who were pursuing them. I felt like a great Olympian who had come out of retirement for one last throw of that javelin, surrounded by all these younger, fitter athletes. Maybe it was the nerves that were making me drink so quickly - I had finished my third beer before Nigel had got through his first double vodka.

Routines are routines, though, so it was onto the tequila. Nigel, strangely, offered to buy mine as well as his own, and I watched him as he ordered. He seemed to spend ages shouting something into the barmaid's ear. The old dog! Had he started already?

So - we were on our feet, which put us in a small minority on what was a fairly limp and lifeless night considering it was a Saturday. I ordered my next drink. This was, I (correctly) imagined, to be my last-ever night out with Nigel, so I treated myself to a JD and Coke, and Nigel moved onto his second double Smirnoff and Coke.

By drink six I was really starting to feel it, so I had no problem having a dance. So what if hardly anyone else was dancing? That just meant I had a bigger audience. Nigel joined me, but he seemed a lot more rigid than I had remembered. I remembered a loose-limbed happy-go-lucky idiot, doing his big-fish-little-fish-cardboard-box routine regardless of the song, and throwing everything into it until he had worked himself into a sweaty frenzy. I wanted that Nigel. I implored him to speed up his drinking pace.

He rubbed his face vigorously with his hands. 'Look, Will, I'm sorry: I just can't do this anymore.'

I looked at him incredulously. 'What are you talking about?'

He fished around in his pocket, producing a golden band which he reattached to his finger. I knew straight away he wasn't keeping it in there for the same reasons I was. Great – it was the Harriet situation all over again.

'Will, I'm married. Got hitched a year ago next week.'

He opened his wallet and took out a picture of his wife, to which I didn't even try to feign an interest.

'Her name's Jessica. She's amazing. And I've got even better news: I'm going to be a daddy! We're having a baby boy in the New Year. Here, check this out.'

He fished once again in his wallet, this time producing one of those God-awful scan pictures, which to me always have the same effect as those Magic Eye pictures. I could stare at them for hours and still not see anything resembling a baby, though I know social convention states you're supposed to coo and marvel. This time, however, unlike the picture of his wife, I didn't even bother looking at it. Anger swelled inside me.

'Well, bully for you, Nige. How nice of you to present me with all this lovely news! You know, it's actually made my cancer seem so much more tolerable!'

I was drunk, and the alcohol was exacerbating my rage. I was being a dick, and I knew it.

'Why the hell did you even agree to come up with me tonight, hmm? What was all that tang shit about?'

'I came up with it in the taxi on the way here. I just wanted to have one final night out with you, just like in the old days. I suspected you were probably still single. I didn't want you to feel bad.'

'Regular Mother sodding Teresa you are, aren't you?'

'I was just trying to be nice. Please don't have a go at me. Look, Will, this life - it just isn't for me. Not anymore. Jess saved me from all of this; showed me there's a whole better life out there. I suppose - I suppose I've grown up. Look, my car's parked outside: why don't you let me give you a lift home?'

'You what? You can't drive! You've had three double vodkas!'

'No, mate - I've had three Cokes. I was just pretending. Same with the tequila. I asked the barmaid to just put water in my shot glass. Told her the story.

Sorry. I don't drink any more. I've been sober for over a year now, and I feel great.'

'Well a massive congratulations on your Happy Ever After. I'll decline your offer of a lift, thank you very much, and kindly ask you to sod off now. All I ever needed you in my life for was to be my wing man, and if you can't even be that, then you're of no use to me.'

He smiled. Not a sarcastic or bitter smile: just a smile. The smile of a man who had everything he wanted or needed; the smile of someone fulfilled.

'I'm so, so sorry about your cancer, Will. It should never happen to anyone, least of all someone our age. You know, I've started going along to church with the wife, and a lot of what they say there makes sense. I do believe there's a Heaven up there, a whole new chapter awaiting us when this one ends. I'm going to pray for you, Will.'

He stuck out his hand.

'Take care.'

I glared at him. 'You sanctimonious git.'

I turned my back for long enough for him to disappear, which thankfully he did.

Right, where was I? I could do this by myself. One more JD and Coke, then watch out, Ladies of Paradise. I practically necked it and ordered my first Smirnoff Ice. My vision was starting to get seriously blurred. That's how I'm going to attempt to justify my next gaffe, anyway. I approached an attractive blonde girl and began a rather slurred take on my 'Williams and Jacobs Market Research' spiel but was soon stopped in my tracks.

'Sir?'

Oh God, this sounded bad.

'Sir, don't you remember me? Sarah Winters from form 11A! You were my Maths teacher!'

'Sarah?' I did remember her; it didn't seem that long ago. 'How old are you?'

'I'm eighteen!'

I wrestled with my conscience for a second. Legally, what I was about to propose was absolutely fine. Morally, it was completely dubious. I can assure you that had I not had such a skin-full and been in such an emotionally heightened state, I would have taken the high road without question. Instead, I took the low road. The low, low road.

'Eighteen! Come here, you! It's so good to see you!'

I hugged her tightly; she did not reciprocate, and indeed looked slightly alarmed and intimidated.

'So - are you here with your boyfriend, then?'

'No, Mr Jacobs. I'm not...'

That was all I needed to know. I leaned in to kiss her. She pushed me away.

'Ugh, you creep! You must be three times older than me!'

Either I was looking rough, or her Maths was wobbly. If I recall her schooldays correctly, it was surely the latter. She stormed off. Unbelievably, I still hadn't given up the ghost.

'Sarah, wait! I'm...I'm dying!'

She looked back, narrowed her eyes and shook her head before disappearing to another part of the club. I downed my Smirnoff Ice and bought another. I could feel myself swaying as I stood at the bar. This wasn't going well, but I just couldn't give up. I had one more drink to go, and I WOULD get that kiss. This was not how I envisaged my swansong.

I approached a brunette, racking my brains for a chat-up line.

'Are you from Tennessee? Because you're the best a man can get!'

Oh no - that wasn't right.

'What? What the fuck are you talking about, you nob?'

She walked away from me before I had the chance to try my sentence again - although, let's face it, if you need two shots at a chat-up line, you're probably not going to be successful. It was at this point that I noticed a bouncer eyeing me from the corner of the club, speaking into his radio without blinking or breaking his gaze. I knew my card was marked. I should have gone home - but what about the routine? I couldn't stop now. I downed my drink and stumbled into the nearest group of girls I could see. I approached each of them one by one and just spurted out a chat-up line, giving each only a couple of seconds before moving onto the next one.

'I hope you know CPR, because you just took my breath away!' A grimace.

'If I could rearrange the alphabet, I'd put U and I together!' A look of disbelief.

'Do you believe in love at first sight, or should I walk away and come back?' A 'wanker' gesture.

And for the fourth lady, I saved my most impressive and bold attempt of all - I projectile vomited all over her dress. I was frogmarched out of the club, whereupon I stumbled into the nearest taxi.

I arrived home and, completing my routine, the first thing I did was down a pint of water. I put the kettle on and made myself the strongest cup of coffee I could manage, and dumped several heaped teaspoons of sugar into it. You see, despite the numerous rejections, one particular lady COULD salvage my night, and I needed to sober up a bit before I talked to her. I multiplied 274 by 78 in my head and spoke the answer out loud, partly to see if my thoughts were sufficiently clear and partly to see if I was able to speak properly. I passed on both counts, though I could not shake my slur.

W: Hey. Guess who.

H: Christ almighty, Will, it's late! I was beginning to think you'd kicked the bucket already.

W: Ah, sensitive and tactful as ever.

H: Oh, you know I love you. Are you pissed, by the way?

W: In the American sense? Yes. In the British sense? Also yes. I've been out with Nigel. He's changed. Then I tried chatting up, like, about a thousand women and they all said no.

H: You what?

W: Just remind me never, ever to go nightclubbing again.

H: And what about your date? How did that go?

W: Awful. The worst one yet. We went to a spa and did some clothes shopping.

H: You go girl!

W: I wanted to. So I pretended I was dying.

H: What a champ! It's womankind's loss that you never settled down. So no action today?

W: Erm...not quite. We snogged at the end.

H: Good God man, not again! I thought there was supposed to be no funny business going on this week?

W: She kissed me!

H: And you immediately pulled away?

W: Well, I...

H: I rest my case.

W: Anyway, last one tomorrow. Mandy.

H: Oh, I can't believe it's all coming to an end! What will I do for entertainment from now on? Good luck, mate. Keep me posted.

W: Will do. Love ya.

H: Love ya too. Keep your tongue in your mouth. Keep your dick in your pants. And keep smiling.

Sunday, 17th July, 2005

So – the final day! It was my last date of the week, and presumably of my life. As I drank my morning coffee in my dressing gown, against all odds relatively hangover free (there really is no justice), I recollected my first encounter with Mandy.

Our relationship started off with a bang...literally. Okay, I'm not too proud of this, especially when you consider what happened to my mum, but I had to be both creative and frankly rather reckless when it came to getting her phone number and asking her out. The first time I ever saw her was one sunny October afternoon, about eight years ago. We were having something of an Indian Summer. She was in her car, a BMW Z3 convertible, top down, and I was in mine – an altogether less sexy Volvo S40. We were side by side at a set of traffic lights. She was both ice cool and red hot, and I just HAD to speak to her. But how? How could I engineer a meeting between us? I had the time it took the traffic lights to change to formulate a plan. And lo, inspiration came to me. I did what I took to be the only sensible thing I could do under those circumstances – deliberately smashed into the back of her car. I'd let her drive off, then slipped into the lane behind her and followed her for a bit, trailing right behind her. As soon as she stopped at the next set of lights, I let my car run into the back of hers. It was a shunt more than a crash, and it caused no damage to either of our cars, but it was enough to make her get out to check out the damage. I gushed my apologies and asked if she wanted to exchange numbers, just in case there was any non-visible damage to the car. I crammed as much charm as I could into a one minute conversation. A couple of days later, I rang up under the pretence of being concerned - had she suffered any whiplash? Had her car been running alright? I asked if she believed in fate, because I hadn't stopped thinking about her since the smash - I told her I would love to see her again and that I hoped she didn't have a boyfriend. Such bravado! I had nothing to lose. She laughed, considered the idea for a few seconds then agreed. We met up that weekend and began what started off as a fairly casual relationship but ended up lasting for just a little over nine months – my longest-ever relationship. The thing was, I was never honest enough – man enough, I guess - to bring myself to telling her the truth, that our accident was no accident at all.

I enjoyed our time together. If she was occasionally a little feisty, it wasn't in the way Suzie would turn out to be feisty – she wasn't crazy or anything. Just a little hot-blooded – perhaps it was her Irish extraction. I wouldn't say she was high maintenance as such – but compared with someone like Kayleigh, who had been prepared to go along with whatever I wanted to do, I guess she was somewhat particular. She liked the finer things in life: the high-end restaurants, the overpriced hotels, the expensive jewellery. She was undoubtedly very classy, though – not like Donna – and very intelligent to boot. Compared with someone like Rhonda, she kept me on my toes somewhat, never giving me the impression she worshipped the ground I walked on, and I think that did me good. She'd had plenty of boyfriends before me, and maybe plenty after. And indeed, it was she who dumped me – a real rarity. She never really explained why – what goes around comes around, I suppose. I never lowered myself to the indignity of asking her either – I too would easily be able to find someone else. That I did – Tracey was in my bed within the fortnight.

By the time Day Seven had rolled around, I had learned to tell just by the knock what kind of day I was going to have. This one threw me, though – it was just a rather clumsy rat-tat-tat of the letter box. Funny – I would have expected Mandy to be a quick triple-knocker. Redhead, you see. I opened the door anyway and there she was – that same mop of curly flaming red hair. The same piercing green eyes. The same light smattering of freckles over the same otherwise porcelain skin. Only this time there was much less of her. And she was eating a packet of cheese and onion crisps. And she had a tiny scale version of Donna clamped under her armpit. Or so it appeared.

'Hello! Who are you?' she asked. Her voice was definitely higher and squeakier than I had remembered. 'Your hair's messy.' Hmm – certainly *sounded* like Mandy. Then a woman started running frantically up my drive.

'Gracie! How many times have I told you not to run off in front of me? That's very naughty!'

Ah – now *that* was Mandy. The resemblance was uncanny – like those Russian dolls. I was half-expecting an even tinier version to appear from inside of Gracie to complete the set.

'Will Jacobs. So…long time no see. You look – amazing, actually!'

'You were expecting the full-on bald head and frail figure coughing into his handkerchief, weren't you?'

'I think I probably was, if I'm honest. Do I get a hug then or what?'

I leaned over and gave her an awkward squeeze, never once taking my eyes off Mini-Mandy, who never once took her eyes off me. She just kept munching her crisps slowly, with a look pitched somewhere between quizzical and suspicious.

'Look, I'm so sorry about this. I had a babysitter sorted and everything, but she cancelled on me at the last minute. You know how it is…actually, you probably don't, do you? Do you?'

'No.'

'Thought not. I tried to ring you but I couldn't get any bloody reception and…anyway, I'm babbling. This is my daughter, Grace. Gracie. Hope you don't mind if she tags along today, do you?'

'No, not at all,' I lied. 'It'll be fun.' More lies. 'I mean, it'll be a bit different, won't it?' That one was true. 'Erm...hi Grace!'

She scowled at me. 'Gracie!'

You may think that, having been a teacher, I must like kids and have some sort of inbuilt paternalistic mechanism. You'd be wrong. I'd have been a primary school teacher if that had been the case. No, I was a secondary school Maths teacher, and in truth I always liked the numbers more than I liked the kids. Numbers follow rules. Besides, the pre-teens these days are just like the teens, and the teens are more like pubescent adults than proper teenagers. Let's face it, they're horny, half-hearted and prone to irrational mood swings – I had no trouble relating to them at all. But the little ones, like Gracie – well, they just scared the life out of me, and I had no idea whatsoever how to talk to them. So I did the first thing that came to mind – stuck out my hand to shake hers. I know – it was a bit stupid, but I panicked. She didn't shake it back, but instead placed a cheese and onion crisp inside it. I think that meant she liked me. I desperately racked my brains for a follow-up comment to build on my momentum.

'So...what's your doll's name?'

'Barbie.'

Barbie. Of course it was. I knew that. Then my blood ran a little bit cold as I tried to figure out how old Gracie looked and how long it had been since Mandy and I had parted company. It couldn't be, could it? I mean – she couldn't be, could she? And I couldn't – could I? So although I didn't actually particularly want to know the doll's name, I actually did want to know Gracie's age. I tried to play it cool, all the while aware that I had just been gazing at her for at least five very awkward seconds without speaking. Or blinking. Or breathing. There might have been a small gulp in there somewhere. But, just to recap, fully grown man staring at little girl. There was absolutely nothing right about this moment.

'And...how old are you?'

'I'm six years old and seven and a half months!'

'Phew!' The maths wasn't too hard to do there. Hang on – did I just do an internal phew? Or did I in fact say it out loud?

Mandy gave me a look. 'I'm sorry? Phew?'

Well that answered that one.

'Yes – phew. As in – phew, it's a bit hot out here, isn't it? Summer, eh?'

I could tell by the blank expressions on their faces, by the steady drizzle and by the summer jackets they were wearing that they didn't share my view. *Keep thinking on your feet, Willy. You can do this.*

'I mean, I suddenly feel really hot! It happens to me sometimes. Must be the medication I am on.'

'Of course, yes! You poor thing! Well, you better let us inside and get that air conditioning on.'

Phew!

Mandy looked terrific. With her long red hair, full lips and full curves, she looked like something someone might have painted on the side of a plane in the 1940s. I ushered both of them inside. There we were, the three of us, sat in the positions of the vertices on a scalene triangle, Mandy and Gracie close together but both looking at me, and I back at them. Clearly both Mandy and I believed the other one should kick off proceedings. It was actually Gracie who did so.

'Mummy, I need the toilet!'

'I bet you do my little cherub. It was a long journey, wasn't it? Will?'

'Oh – the toilet's just through the door over there.'

She toddled off, and the second she was out of earshot, Mandy snapped her gaze in my direction and started speaking to me in quick, hushed tones.

'Okay, here's everything you wanted to know about my daughter but were too afraid to ask. She's not yours, for starters.'

'Oh – that thought never even entered my mind!'

'Okay, whatever. Because believe you me, if she had been yours, we'd have either given our relationship another shot and been a proper family, or else you'd have been paying me some serious child support. As it happens, Gracie and I haven't got either of those things. Don't forget to wash your hands afterwards, sweetie!'

''Kay!'

'But in a way, it's partly because of you that Gracie was born in the first place. So maybe you should be partly paying child support!' She laughed nervously.

'Partly because of me? What are you talking about?'

'When we split up, my world pretty much ended for a few months.'

I wanted to interject and remind her that she dumped me, so why did HER world end? However, she was obviously building up a head of steam, and there was no way I was jumping in front of that train to try and stop it.

'I either wasn't eating at all, or I was eating all the wrong things to comfort myself. I stopped going out, but I didn't stop drinking – no, no, no. I was crying every single day, even at work. I missed you so much, it made me feel physically sick. Can you imagine what it feels like to feel sick every day for three months? I thought you were the one – I was sure of it. '

'But I don't see...'

'So anyway, I eventually started eating more and crying less – I was becoming a functioning member of society again. I started going out with my friends to nightclubs. I was determined to replace you. And that's when I met Antonio, who so did not replace you, but we began a relationship anyway. He was a complete and utter rebound. He was also a complete and utter weasel, much more in love with himself than he ever was with me. Not bad between the sheets, mind you.'

Her eyes drifted slowly away from mine and a tiny flicker of a smile appeared at the sides of her lips. I took 'not bad' to mean 'far better than you' and felt a momentary pang of jealousy and insecurity that I had no right to feel at that moment in time. She jolted immediately back out of her reverie.

'So anyway, within a few months of going out with him, I found out I was pregnant. He freaked out, flitted out back to Italy, and I've never been able to track him down since. Right – here she comes. We'll pick this up later. Here's my little princess!'

'Mummy, that man had a magazine with naked ladies in his bathroom! I could see their boobies and everything!'

Mandy looked at me scornfully and disbelievingly. I whispered to her through the side of my mouth: 'Don't look at me like that! You didn't tell me she was coming!'

'No, but I told you *I* was coming! Have some decency, man! Darling, that man has a name – remember, I told you earlier? It's Will. He's my friend from a long time ago.'

'Why have you got a boy for your friend? Girls are supposed to have girl friends.'

I grinned. 'Quite a few of those ladies in those particular magazines do.'

It was a spectacularly ill-informed joke, as the murderous look on Mandy's face proved.

'I'm bored. Have you got any toys, Will?'

'Oh God, I forgot to pack her colouring book and crayons. No, sweetie, he hasn't got any toys. He's a 36 year old man. I think you already saw what he does for entertainment when you went to the toilet.'

'But I want my TOYS! Take me home NOW, mummy!'

I'd heard *that* tone before many times. I'd even seen the same stamp of the foot. Clearly, the apple hadn't fallen far from that particular tree...

'No, no, no. There's no way in the world I am doing a three hour round trip just to pick up a few toys. I promised Will I would spend the day with him, and I want it to be very special, and I'm afraid, young lady, you're along for the ride.'

And that's when the tears started. Followed by the screaming. I learned at that moment that hell hath no fury like a red-headed six year old girl scorned. Fortunately, during my teaching days, I became quite the expert at the fine art of winging it. It was a skill I would deploy when arriving at work minutes before the bell went on Monday morning, dishevelled and exhausted from the weekend's antics, during which time I had failed to do any planning or preparation for the week ahead. New relationships had a particularly adverse effect on my lesson planning – they consumed all my time and attention, and oftentimes the temptation towards morning sex easily overrode the more sensible option of going into work a little earlier to set up for the day. So I'd simply wing it – just make something up on the spot. Usually I'd be making the lesson up on a minute-by-minute basis – and the funny thing was that they were usually my best lessons. I seemed to thrive on the pressure of it all. Anyway, I sensed I was going to have to dust off my winging skills here – steer the ship away from the iceberg towards which it was so obviously headed. Time to make a plan, and quick. Sure enough, and soon enough, a thought popped into my head. Well, a half-thought really. In fact, when you hear it, you'll probably agree that the fraction of thought was probably a good deal less than half and was, at best, one third of a complete thought.

'No hang on, hang on – I've got a Playstation! How would you like to play some video games with me, Gracie?'

And, just like that, the tears miraculously stopped. 'Yeah!'

Mandy shot me a congratulatory smile. 'Nicely done, Mr Jacobs! Clearly, I had underestimated you!'

'What are we playing? I can beat all my friends at Summer Dance Party. And you know that game Bunny Babies? I got all the way to Level 5! Oh, and I once won a gold ribbon in Penny's Pony Show!'

'Ah. Yes. Right. Well, I haven't got any of *those* particular games.' I quickly realised my error, but it was too late now. 'I've got Bounty Hunter. I've got Extreme Brazilian Streetfighting Gangs. I've got Mafia 4. And, erm, I've got Bounty Hunter 2: This Time it's Personal'.

Both Mandy and Gracie were staring at me. The room was deadly silent. I inflated my cheeks with air and let it out in noisy little puffs, desperately straining for something to do. When I'd had the brainwave of spending seven days with seven different women from my past, I'd thought long and hard about the possibilities, but at no point whatsoever had I envisaged myself trying and failing to keep a small child entertained. I scraped the barrel of my ideas and came up with Rock, Paper, Scissors. Jesus, it was going to be a long day. The game would, at least, eat up some time while I came up with something better. Gracie showed what would qualify as a morsel of interest in the idea (by which I mean her face remained expressionless and she didn't scream her disapproval), so we went with it. It was not successful.

So – Rock, Paper, Scissors. A quick visual guide for the uninitiated. The possibilities during play are limited indeed, and may be summarised thusly:

		Player 2		
		Rock	Paper	Scissors
Player 1	Rock	Draw.	Player 2 wins. Because, apparently, covering rock with paper somehow strips it of its rock-like power.	Player 1 wins. So remember – next time someone comes at you with a great big pair of scissors, seek out the nearest rock and attempt to blunt them. Warning – it may take a while.
	Paper	Player 1 wins.	Draw.	Player 2 wins. Okay, that one I can accept.
	Scissors	Player 2 wins.	Player 1 wins.	Draw.

So, as you can plainly see, there are exactly nine possible plays in Rock, Paper, Scissors, three of which are a draw, three of which result in Player 1 winning and three of which involve Player 2 winning. It's a game of pure chance. Right? If a person wins a game, it's not because they are more skilful, just luckier. Yes? And yet, I was something of a Rock, Paper, Scissors champion at Greenfields Primary School. During play, I would keep a mental tally of the moves my opponent had played, log them on paper afterwards and look for trends. If there was one to which they seemed more drawn, I would attempt to counter that by weighting my own choices slightly more towards the move that would defeat it. More often than not, it was to scissors that my opponents were slightly more drawn, presumably sub-consciously on account of the fact that scissors are arguably the most dangerous of the three. Although, admittedly, not those red plastic Primary School scissors – I'd say even a sheet of paper, with its ability to slightly slice your fingertip, is slightly more dangerous than those. So anyway, if it was indeed scissors they seemed to be using a little more frequently than the others, I'd use rock a little more frequently than the others. I'm not ashamed to say I would often be a kind of Rock, Paper, Scissors voyeur, sitting just within earshot and view, logging someone else's game on a little spiral notepad in preparation for my game with them. So that's one tactic. The other – and again the trick to this is the ability to keep a mental track of what's already happened in the game whilst focusing on one's current move – is to look for patterns. Few players make their choices purely randomly, even if they believe they do. If you wrote down the exact moves a player made during, say, a hundred plays – and, yes folks, I've done exactly that – you'd notice some sequences being repeated more than others. I used to use three of the colours in those four-coloured biros to colour code the moves, making the patterns really easy to spot. My reign came to an end when, possibly out of frustration and possibly due to the fact that I might just have been lording it a bit, Darren Kingsley seamlessly transformed the imaginary rock he was using into a very real fist, and bopped me on the nose. Fist beats all. I didn't play Rock, Paper, Scissors for a while after that.

So – I was prepared to dust off my old tactics in order to beat the little girl. I know that sounds harsh, but it would be a good life lesson for her. One day, long after I was dead and gone, she'd no doubt look back and thank me. I would soon learn her patterns and sequences. Things definitely got off to a bumpy start as Gracie played paper and I played scissors. We both let out a congratulatory 'yes' – clearly, there was some uncertainty over the rules. I explained I had won since scissors very obviously cut paper (though I demonstrated this with my fingers and her hands, just to clear up any confusion), but she insisted victory was hers. Her logic? Paper wraps around scissors 'so they're not sharp anymore' (which she demonstrated using her hands and my fingers, just to clear up any confusion). We called in the referee (not something usually needed during a game of Rock, Paper, Scissors), who didn't break the flow of the text message she was composing to confirm with not just a hint of disinterest that scissors did, indeed, beat paper. I resisted the temptation to make a 'ner-ner-ner-ner-ner' gesture;

(a) because I was 36 years old;

(b) because Gracie's mum was, after all, in the room and I was supposed to be showing her how much I'd matured;

(c) because I suspected my little redheaded opponent was probably perfectly capable of giving me a bop on the nose, as per historical precedent.

Gracie suggested we use that one as a practice go. In some ways, I felt loathe to say yes, but by gum I admired her competitive spirit, so I agreed.

We tried again. I played scissors and Gracie played rock. She seemed to have no problems conceptualising her victory this time. I'd lost that one, but – hey – at least we were rolling now. Except that on move three we both played rock, and instead of accepting the tie and moving on, Gracie waved her arms in the air and shouted 'woo hoo!'

I could feel my patience thinning a little.

'Why are you woo-hooing? You shouldn't be woo-hooing! This is most certainly not cause for a woo-hoo. That's a tie.'

I looked over at Mandy, ready to will her into convincing her daughter she was wrong, but her eyes were stilled fixed on the screen of her phone and this time she feigned no interest at all.

'I know! I'm not stupid! But I used a massive rock, and it smashed yours cause it was so massive and yours was so small.'

My right eyelid twitched involuntarily.

'Listen, we either play this properly using the proper rules, or we don't play at all. The rules are – rock beats scissors. Paper beats rock. Scissors beats paper. If we play the same hand, we tie. Got it?'

She narrowed her eyes and blobbed out her tongue. I took it as a yes. We played six more moves, one of them a tie, two of them victories to me and three victories to her, but mercifully none of them contentious. Now it was time to start figuring out her methods, start anticipating her moves. For her next move however – and for the sake of my sanity, the final move of the game – she held her palm out vertically and started wiggling her fingers.

'What the,' I chose my next word carefully '*Heck* is that?'

'It's fire. Fire beats everything. Gracie wins.'

Her attention still monopolised by her phone, Mandy called out, 'Oh, well done, darling.'

My blood was positively boiling. Apparently, Gracie's chart looked like this:

		Player 2			
		Rock	Paper	Scissors	Fire
Player 1	Rock	Draw (unless, of course, one player uses a bigger rock).	Player 2 wins.	Player 1 wins.	Player 2 wins.
	Paper	Player 1 wins.	Draw.	Player 2 wins.	Player 2 wins.
	Scissors	Player 2 wins.	Player 1 wins.	Draw.	Player 2 wins.
	Fire	Player 1 wins.	Player 1 wins.	Player 1 wins.	Draw.

I mulled over whether to introduce a fire engine to put out the fire, or just a bloody great asteroid to beat everything once and for all, but for the sake of the integrity of 'Rock, Paper, Scissors', I bit my tongue. Besides, she'd no doubt just play a bigger asteroid.

'Don't suppose you like solving Countdown Maths puzzles, do you? No, thought not. So by that same token, you wouldn't be at all interested in a bumper book of Sudoku? Right.'

My tone was petty, possibly somewhat sulky, though doubtless all of this was lost on Gracie who was, after all, six. I looked out of the window to see if the rain had let up. Maybe I could salvage the day by taking her to the park. Inevitably, it hadn't. I scanned my brain to think of anything else a little girl might like. Of course – chocolate! All females are pre-disposed to being pleased by chocolate, and I knew I had some in the cupboard. Just to keep things running nice and smoothly, I tried to pass it off as Gracie's victory prize. I went to the kitchen and took out my Tupperware box of assorted chocolates. There was a Mars Bar – probably a bit much for a six year old. There was a Bounty – not to everyone's tastes, so probably a bit of a risk. There was a Milky Way – that might do the trick. And – bingo – there was a Curly Wurly. They're tough old things, Curly Wurlies – definitely the most challenging of all chocolate bars. It would keep her busy for a while. I was tempted to offer Mandy one for the same reason, and save myself from another tongue-lashing. I instead offered a cup of tea, which she drank as we made small talk, about where she and Gracie lived (she had moved out of the area when a promotion came up at work), about what had changed where I lived, even about the bloody weather. I really wanted to get onto bigger things – the demise of our relationship, which still puzzled me. If one of the main objectives of the week was redemption, I certainly wasn't going to get that talking about catchment areas and unseasonal rainfall levels.

All the while we were chatting, I kept finding my eyes drawn towards Gracie, or rather the expensive suede chair on which she was sitting which, though described as off-white in the catalogue, was quickly turning a distinct shade of chocolate brown. She had discarded the wrapper in frustration and was now clutching onto the Curly Wurly with bare hands, the movement of her head reminding me somewhat of a lion attempting to tear chunks off a particularly tough carcass. The result was that the chocolate had melted all over her hands and, being six, her hands had gone everywhere. I surprised myself by not feeling as angry as I might have expected about this. After all, in the grand scheme of things, I had plenty of bigger things to worry about than cleaning my sofas.

The chocolate bar was gone. The small talk had dried up. This was turning out to be a long day. I eyed the clock discretely. The two of them had only been in my apartment for three quarters of an hour, and already the little girl was bored stiff. She was now fidgeting and I knew all too well from my teaching days that when kids get bored, that's when the potential for them to kick off is at its highest. But what to do? What I really wanted to do – the original plan – was to chat to Mandy. Talk about old times; heal up a few old wounds. Babysitting was never part of the plan. It was at that point that I came up with a plan to buy me a bit of free time with Mandy - and it was inspired by another of my exes, Harriet.

'Hey, I know, Gracie! How do you fancy doing a Scavenger Hunt?'

She screwed up her face at me; I couldn't tell if it was confusion or rejection.

'You know – like a Treasure Hunt! I'll give you a list of things to find in my apartment, then you go away and look for them! The more you find, the more points you get!'

She jumped up and down and clapped her hands together excitedly. I felt like doing the same.

'But there's one Golden Rule. You can look anywhere – *anywhere* – in the house, apart from this room! Okay? And, erm, maybe the bathroom as well.'

She nodded. So did her mum, which I took as a nod of recognition, a sign that she was on my wavelength. It was, if I say so myself, a minor stroke of genius. I grabbed the notebook from next to the telephone and started scribbling down a random list of items for Gracie to find:

1. Something beginning with 'J' (I first put Q, based purely on its high value as a Scrabble tile, but then realised she would soon find a quilt. I settled on J – worth three points less than Q as a Scrabble tile, and therefore a more common letter, but still in the 'safe zone' of letters – I could think of nothing offhand in my apartment which started with a J;

2. An animal (another safe choice – as you might expect, there were no stuffed animals up there, and of course no pets of any description. I supposed she might have found one in a newspaper or something, but even that would take her a long time);

3. Something that requires batteries (I imagined she would find plenty of examples in a scavenger hunt in her own mother's room, but I was safe. There was a remote control for my bedroom TV, but since I'd lost it several days earlier, we could both claim that as a victory if it turned up);

4. Something more than fifty years old (there were examples of this in the flat, but only a few, and she'd have to look really hard and really closely. I had the 1942 film *Casablanca* on DVD and *The Voice of Frank Sinatra* from 1946 on LP, to name just a couple. Even if she found those items, I'd argue over the technicalities and send her back - I mean *technically* the items themselves were pressed long after the film and album were made. There's no such thing as a fifty year old DVD. Unless, of course, you're reading this way into the future.

I really wanted to round it up to five items, but inspiration was not forthcoming – what I wanted even more was to get the little girl out of my hair as quickly as possible. I tore the sheet from its spirals and thrust it into Gracie's hands. She quickly disappeared out of the living room – and quickly reappeared into it before I could utter even a word of conversation with Mandy. She handed me the sheet back.

'Your writing is very messy!'

I looked at the sheet. Maybe I had created the list with a little too much vigour – it was rather scruffy, even by the standard of my less-than-perfect cursive skills. I rewrote the list, more slowly and more carefully, this time without joining the letters. I handed the sheet back to her.

'Good luck now!'

Once again she disappeared. Time to engage in some adult chat (which I admit does sound like a phone service which would cost 49p per minute, but that was really not what I was after. I just wanted to regain a sense of what it was like going out with Mandy, before you-know-who came on the scene).

'So then, Mandy, I was just thinking back to –'

'Some of these words are too hard for me! I can only read words if they're not too hard.'

Yes, she was back. I took the paper from her once again.

'Okay, sweetie, what if Will just reads you the list? Do you think you will be able to remember them all?'

'Yes! I've got a really, really, really, really, REALLY good memory and when I was Mary in the Nativity, I had millions of words to learn and I remembered them all!'

'Wow – that's – millions you say?' I resisted the urge to give her a quick lesson in Place Value, instead settling for an enthusiastic nod / smile combination. 'Good for you! Look hard, now! If you make a mess, that's absolutely fine. But remember – don't come back until you have found everything!'

I recited the list to her. Three times, in fact, just to be sure. She disappeared. I waited. I hoped. I listened. I could hear the clattering of footsteps in another room – finally, my chance had come!

'As I was saying, I was just thinking back to when you and I went out with each other and I have to admit, I'm still a bit baffled by it all. I mean, you say you were devastated by it all, but,' I tried the next three words in my head, shifting which one or ones had the emphasis. *YOU left me. You LEFT me. You left ME. YOU left ME.* That was the one. 'YOU left ME. Why?'

'Look, I can see one of the reasons you've got me here is to tie up all your loose ends, but – I just don't know. Something was – something wasn't – I mean, it was just, well...I'm sorry, Will. I just don't know.'

'Ah, well, I'm so glad we cleared all that up. Was there someone else?'

'No.'

'Did you love me?'

'Yes.'

'Were you IN love with me?'

'Yes.'

'Did you see a future with me?'

'Erm, no.'

'Did you want a future with me?'

'God yes.'

'Did you trust me?'

'Sort of.'

'Sort of?'

'Sort of. I didn't think you would two-time me, but I did think you'd chuck me as soon as someone better came along.'

I looked her up and down. Even dripping with that old-school Hollywood starlet glamour as she was then and still was now, I had to admit she was right. What the bloody hell was wrong with me?

She twizzled her hair round her finger and avoided my gaze. Then she threw her hands down onto her lap and her head up in the hair, forcing a strained smile.

'Jesus, why am I letting myself get upset about this now? It's all ancient history.'

We sat in silence for a good minute, though it felt like ten. Was I supposed to apologise here? Apologise for something I might possibly have done? I suspected she wanted to go back home. I REALLY wished we'd stuck to inane meteorological chit-chat. I also wished I hadn't given Gracie such an obscure list of items to find – things had become awkward in her absence, and she would at least give the two of us something to focus on that wasn't our failed relationship or the remnants thereof. Fortunately, she'd ploughed through the list with an impressive resolve, bursting back into the living room with a carrier bag to which she'd helped herself stuffed to the rafters with an array of items so random, they could have come straight off the conveyor belt on the Generation Game. She tipped the contents all over my laminate floor.

'Wow, that was quick!' She nodded at both of us and beamed, basking in her glory. 'Go on then, what have you got?'

But before Gracie could get down to sharing her findings, she had a more pressing question. 'Will, are you poorly?'

Poorly? What was she talking about? The cancer? Surely Mandy hadn't discussed that with her? And why was she suddenly asking?

'Am I poorly? What do you mean?'

'Have you got a sniffle or something?'

Both Mandy and I were gazing at her curiously, in anticipation. 'Erm, no, I haven't got a cold. Why do you ask?'

'Cause when I was looking under your bed for things for the treasure hunt, I found lots and lots of tissues. And they were all stuck together, with snot and bogies, I think.'

I slumped in my chair and covered my face with my hands.

'You didn't pick the tissues up now did you, honey pie?' I peeked through my fingers to see Gracie shaking her head. 'Good. Yes, babes, Will is sick. Very, VERY sick.' She whispered the next bit under her breath, through gritted teeth, eyes locked on me. 'In fact he could die at any moment. So just to be on the safe side, why don't you go and wash your hands again, in the kitchen this time, then when you come back we'll have a look at all the things you managed to find.'

She watched her daughter go before snapping her head towards mine. 'Will Jacobs, you are, in every possible way, a wanker.'

Hmm – not the first time I'd been called that this week. I let my hands drop but kept my head hung.

'I know. Look, I've really messed up here today. I didn't know you were bringing your daughter, obviously, and if I'd known, I might have had a bit of a tidy up of the old bachelor pad. I just – I just don't know how to deal with little children. I'm sorry. And all I've been looking for is a chance to talk to you. I know I wasn't very nice to you when we were together. I wanted you to see that I'm a bit nicer now. Do you want to just write this one off? It was good seeing you.'

'Oh no, no, no. You don't get out of it that easily. You're right. You were an absolute prat. And I deserve a nice day from you. Thing is, I come as part of a package, so Gracie gets to be part of that nice day. For what it's worth, I believe that you've changed, so prove it.'

Gracie returned.

'Right then, babes, what did you find?'

My sphincter tightened. I sensed this day was going to get worse before it got better. My mind raced, desperately scanning for items in my house which would be unsuitable for a small child. She rummaged through her haul.

'Something beginning with J is Jacobs! That's you! Look, it says it here – Will Jacobs.'

She thrust a phone bill into my hands. Holy crap. The girl was six, but daft she was most definitely not. She was a regular little Columbo, and I had to admit that though she had thwarted my original plans, I was starting to like her.

'I can't see any animals here, though.'

'I did find an animal! I found a mouse. On your computer, silly!'

She dangled the unplugged mouse by its tail and let it swing from side to side. My blood ran cold, as I tried to assess the likelihood of a six year old using a mouse to log onto and explore my computer, which was not password protected – why would it need to be? I lived alone! If Mandy thought the magazines were bad, she'd go positively ballistic if she knew what kinds of things were on my hard drive. I hurried the game along before she'd had a chance to report any findings.

'Ah, I see you found something with batteries in! My remote control!'

Result!

'Yes, and you hid it really well! It was right round the back of the chair in the other room.'

'Did you manage to find anything over fifty years old?'

'Yes. I found a picture of your grandad. I think he's more than fifty.'

I screwed my face up, befuddled. 'I don't have a grandad. I don't really have any family left.' *Grandad?*

'Well then who's this?' She thrust a piece of paper under my nose. I laughed. This one was going to be hard to explain. I angled towards Mandy for a safer bet.

'You see, there's this website, ageyourself.com. It shows you what you might look like when you're older. So this is me, pushing ninety.'

Mandy looked mildly confused. 'Why have you printed it, Will?'

'I don't know. No idea. Weird, isn't it? Really beginning to wish I hadn't now. Erm, well done, Gracie. You win.'

'Yay! What's next?'

What was next? I had no idea, but I knew it had to involve getting out of my apartment, and quick.

'Seaside! Why don't we go to the seaside?' I blurted it out. It was spurious logic - too wet for the local park, but not too wet to travel all the way to the seaside?

Gracie jumped up and down excitedly and started tugging on her mum's dress. 'Can we mummy? Can we, can we, can we? Please, please, please?'

Mandy seemed unconvinced. 'It's raining, darling. And haven't we done enough travelling today already?'

I figured I ought at least to have the courage of my convictions. 'Come on, Mandy! I haven't been to the seaside for ages. Let's go to Skegness. It's, what, an hour away from here?'

Two and a half hours later, we were there. The rainy weather had caused carnage on the roads and I may or may not have taken a few wrong turnings after declining Mandy's offer of using her Sat Nav. This earned me the new nickname 'Twat Nav', which Mandy uttered under her breath at an opportune moment when Gracie was distracted by a colouring book we had bought at the service station. She hadn't seemed overly-keen on the purchase, but had resigned herself to it when she realised the made-up stories she was requesting from me simply weren't cutting the mustard. They'd start off with a princess, called Gracie of course – so far so good – but the plotline would thin out a little as she looked for her Prince Charming. I guess that's not exactly my field of expertise, to which a host of women in this story would agree. I explained to her that I was a mathematician, not a storyteller, to which she responded that she was learning about Carroll diagrams in school, and they were invented by Lewis Carroll, who wrote *Alice's Adventures in Wonderland*. As I sat licking my wounds after being outsmarted by a six year old, I mulled over how like her mother the little girl was, whip-smart and always claiming the last word. We did try other ways to pass the journey – a game of 'I Spy' lasted for all of five minutes once we had exhausted the contents of the car and the unchanging countryside scenery. And a game of Celebrity Twenty Questions highlighted how little lay in the intersection of the Venn diagram that was Gracie and I's lives – she'd never heard of the people I was choosing as subjects – Einstein, Muhammad Ali and Richard Branson – and hers weren't even people – she picked a My Little Pony, one of The Tweenies and Shrek. When the colouring book lost its novelty, which somewhat inevitably it did quickly, Gracie turned to singing, either to the pop hits on the radio or, when the adverts were on or when it was a song she didn't know or didn't care for, a random children's song or children's movie song.

'She's a pretty good singer!'

'Yeah, pretty good. She has proper singing lessons. She does all the clubs going - all the after school clubs, all the Saturday clubs, all the Sunday clubs. Oh, she's faddy as hell, don't get me wrong. She's done everything from horse riding to chess to piano to archery and I don't think she's stuck with anything for more than half a dozen sessions before moving onto something else.'

'So why don't you make her stick with something? Get better at it? Practice makes perfect and all that.'

'Because I don't believe in practice makes perfect. It's nonsense. Has practising dating lots of women made you the perfect boyfriend? I could practise playing football every day for the rest of my life. It wouldn't make me perfect at it. It would make me better, but not perfect. But what Beckham's got is God-given talent. Something he was born with. I'm more interested in trying to find Gracie's God-given talent and I don't mind her trying and failing at a thousand things as we look for it. I mean think about it - she could be the greatest oboe player the world has ever known. She could be a future gold medalist Olympian pole vaulter. One of those could be her God-given talent. She could pick up that oboe, or that pole vault, and something magical could happen. We'll never find out, unless we try.'

'What, so you're saying you think we all have some kind of God-given talent, whether we've uncovered it or not?'

She shrugged. 'Maybe. I don't know. But I'll tell you something - everything Gracie tries, I try. If I'm picking her up from a piano lesson, let's say, I'll make sure I have a sneaky tinkle on the ivories before we leave. I'll sweet talk the archery instructor into letting me have a go before I hand over the cash. I haven't found my talent, if it's there, but I refuse to throw in the towel and say I'm too old to find it. In fact, if I were in your position, I'd be going hell for leather to try to do just that. I'd be trying anything and everything, just in the off chance. It's not like you haven't got the time on your hands.'

That was a bit direct. I blew a cynical snort of air through my nostrils.

'So I find out I'm a world-class shot putter.' Given a bit more time, I might have come up with an Olympic event slightly more plausible for a man of my age and physical strength, but I continued my rant undeterred. 'Then what? Chances are I won't even live to see the next Olympics. Or I find out I can play glockenspiel with the best of them. What do I do with that? Contact the Rolling Stones and ask them if I can come on tour with them before I pop my clogs? Dear Mick and Keith. I enjoy your music but cannot help but think it could be further improved by adding glockenspiel. Fortunately, I happen to be the best glockenspiel player in the world - but hurry! Because believe it or not I'm likely to croak it before you do!'

'Well, you're being a world-class tosspot at this moment in time, so perhaps you've found your talent after all.'

Jesus. I don't even think she was joking. Neither of us was speaking and the atmosphere had turned slightly frosty. This was so like Mandy! This sudden change of mood - it was her in a nutshell. *Are we nearly there yet?* Fortunately, we were. Unfortunately, it was still hammering it down, so we pulled our coats over our heads and scurried into the first arcade we saw.

Gracie relieved her mother of two handfuls of silver and made a beeline for those claw grabbers, trying to win a teddy bear you could easily pay for outright for not much more than it costs to have a few goes and lose. Mandy gestured towards an air hockey machine and she gave me the Clint Eastwood eyes from across the table. I tried to win using my knowledge of angles, figuring the best way to score a goal would be to knock the puck against the side of the table so that it would ricochet off at the same angle and into her goal. It was a much less successful strategy than hers, which was to ram the puck as straight and hard as she could. And boy was she giving that thing some welly - I sensed she was still slightly pissed off with me, either from our conversation in the car or from our former relationship in general. At 5-0 to her, it was nothing less than a whitewash. I was a sore loser, hanging my head in shame instead of congratulating her. She was not exactly a dignified winner, pointing both her index fingers at me and laughing.

Licking my wounds, I changed a trio of pound coins into two pence coins and we collected an empty-handed Gracie, who appeared to be handling her situation no better than me, pursing her lips tight and folding her arms. We dropped onto one of those horse racing games. You know the ones. Five horses. Blue and red have an equal probability of winning - a 2p bet on either of those will win you 4p back. Green wins 8p and yellow 12p. If you're feeling really frivolous, you could bet your money on the rank outsider, the white, which would pay out a whopping 40p. Whatever you bet on, a dramatic race usually follows as the five horses travel in a straight line towards the finish, the early leader almost never being the winner as some other horse gains ground and pips him to the post. It's actually great fun - I'm convinced you couldn't spend two pence in a more exciting way. I mean, in so many ways, it's dubious as hell - it's effectively betting for bambinos, and I'm amazed it's still around in this politically correct world of ours. Maybe that's part of the enduring appeal. They even provided little plastic footstools so that toddlers could reach up and have a go. I could see Gracie was choosing her horses randomly - probably as good as system as any, though I reverted to the system I adopted as a kid - two bets at a time. One on either red or blue (which I would alternate) and the other on white. By my reckoning, white would only come up about one race in every 25, so it wasn't the best of strategies. Mandy was placing her bets on medium-risk horses - always either green or yellow. I wondered if there was any deeper-seated logic behind that. Had I been a high-risk horse? She seemed to be faring slightly better than either myself or Gracie. However, ultimately, all three of us walked away from the machine empty handed. Of course we did.

Our next port of call, after changing another three pound coins, was those push-penny machines where you feed the slots with 2p coins until they're so stuffed that they spew them back out. Actually, maybe spew isn't the right analogy when you consider what end the coins are actually coming out of. Gracie was quickly engrossed. So was I, if I'm being honest. I had no intention of walking away from the machine in profit - who does? They wouldn't change the bloody coins back even if you did. I just wanted to hear the sound of those coppers crashing down onto the winnings tray.

I looked at the date on each coin before I put it in the slot, doing a quick calculation each time to work out how old each one was. 1991 - 14 years old.1985 - 20 years old. A shiny 2004 - a mere baby compared to the others. A rusty looking 1971 coin -34 years old. Only a wee bit younger than me. What kind of life had this little fella led? He was once shiny and brand new, just like that 2004 one. He'd seen decades come and go. Probably been in and out of thousands of people's pockets and purses, from millionaires to the tramps and everything in between. Probably been all over the country. He might have spent years on end remaining perfectly motionless, sitting in some little kid's piggy bank or stuck down the side of a sofa until he was rescued by a hand or a Hoover. And he might have had years on end of excitement - a new cash register to sleep in every night, or, like now, exciting afternoons tumbling through slot machines. If he was lucky, he'd just keep going and going, until his life ended naturally, gracefully, as he got taken out of circulation one day in the distant future along with all the other 2p coins still left. I mulled over keeping him, rescuing him, putting him in my pocket, but in the end I decided he'd have a more adventurous life taking his chances in this slot machine. He'd still be going long after I was gone.

Mandy's voice yanked me back to reality.

'It's weird, isn't it? For all the changes in the world over the last few decades, kids still seem to love these machines as much as we did when we were kids. Just look at Gracie. She's completely oblivious to us. For all she knows, you could have kidnapped me and be doing all sorts of terrible things to me right now.'

She narrowed her eyes and moved her lips somewhere between smile and pout. Was she flirting with me? The stirrings in my loins suggested I thought so. I giggled sheepishly and blushed a little. I could play flirty tennis with the best of them – my many telephone conversations with Helen had taught me how to rise up to the challenge when faced with a sharp-witted woman. But here? Now? With her daughter in earshot? I took the moral high ground and focused on her original point.

'Yeah, they're still popular as ever. Except, of course, kids are getting better value for money these days, when you consider inflation. What else costs the same now as it did thirty years ago?'

'Yeah you're right. Just give kids a couple of quid and let them loose on the 2p slots – seems to last a long time on these things! They're happy, bit of peace and quiet for the parent – everyone's a winner! About as cheap as babysitting gets really.'

'Hmm, a good nugget of parenting though that seems, it's flawed – look at little Johnny Wizzkid over there.'

I pointed to a young boy whose concentration was so intense that he had forgotten how to keep his tongue inside his mouth. He had mastered the art of simultaneously putting four 2p pieces through all four slots of the machine at once, pinching a coin between his thumb and index finger and one between his little finger and his ring finger, then using the same trick with the other hand. It was an act of dexterity if nothing else.

'In his naive youthful logic, he's thinking he's quadrupling his chances of winning. Of course, he's not. He's just quartering his playing time. If he was your kid, he'd be running back to you before you knew it.'

She shrugged. We kept stuffing the machines as we chatted, with an almost robotic rhythm.

'The beauty of the slots is that it's both fiendishly, almost idiotically simple – I mean, a chimpanzee could probably use its opposable thumbs to pick up 2p coins and push them through the slots – but it's also a game of strategy, if you want it to be.'

She rolled her eyes up towards the fluorescent overhead lights and avoided my gaze – not exactly an open invitation to continue my lecture, but I did so anyway. It was the same look I got from bored teenagers when I got over-excitable about a Maths theory, and that didn't stop me from finishing the lesson. This was a different Will from the one from the Will and Mandy days. Back then, if I occasionally feigned a moody distance, it was to mask the fact that I wanted to point out something terribly geeky, and if I'd opened my mouth I would have spewed a torrent of Maths and statistics - not exactly a turn-on for the ladies. At least I was self-aware. Nowadays I didn't care - I had nothing to gain and nothing to lose.

'How is it a game of strategy, you ask?'

'I didn't say anything...'

'Here's how! I think even toddlers quickly latch onto the fact that you push your coin in as soon as the top tray of coins is pulled to the back of the machine. Otherwise it just drops on top of the coins rather than in front of them, where it can give them that much-needed push off the ledge.'

'Hmm-hmm,' she replied, either distracted or bored or both.

'Well not always! Now and again, you want to deliberately let the coin fall on top of the others – what you're doing is building up your army, ready to advance onto the next layer. Strength in numbers.'

'Fascinating. Truly fascinating. Do continue. That's the response I would have given you if today was National Opposites Day.'

I ignored her. 'The machines usually have either two or three slots, and you're naturally drawn more to the middle ones, yes? Because there's nothing more dispiriting than the sound of those coins falling down the sides of the machine, where you can't collect them.'

'I can think of a more dispiriting sound right now.'

'Well, true though what I've just said is, I use a ratio-based system. For every three coins I put in the middle slot or slots, I put one in the slot on the furthest left. Then three more in the middle and one more on the right. Repeat *ad infinitum*. That way, the coins don't bunch up too much in the middle, where the sheer weight of them makes them difficult to shift. And that's something else people do wrong - they're psychologically drawn to the machines with loads of coins in, but that's slow moving traffic. You're much better off with the ones with fewer coins in. They move through the machine more quickly and more easily.'

Mandy stopped in her tracks. Her eyes widened and she stared off into the middle distance. Had I bored her into a stupor? I gazed at her, curious, and after a few seconds she burst into a fit of laughter.

'Mandy? Whatever's...'

'I've got it, Will! I've got it!'

'Got what?'

'I've got the perfect analogy for our relationship. You know before how you asked me to explain what had gone wrong for us and I couldn't? Well now I can! You were like a 2p slot machine!'

She gazed at me, still wide-eyed, her smile wide and open, too, as if she were waiting for some kind of acknowledgement or recognition. I told her she might have to elaborate a little bit, though I knew the explanation wasn't going to be flattering. It hadn't exactly started off that way, had it?

'You see, I just kept feeding you with 2p coins – each one was a tiny bit of my love, or time, or affection or whatever. And I did this in the hope that I would be rewarded by getting the same back. So I kept doing it – kept feeding you those coins. Kept investing myself in you. Kept telling myself that windfall was coming. And sure enough, it did – in dribs and drabs. A 2p here, a few coins there, but nothing like what I was putting in. But I STILL kept at it, because like this machine right here, those coins at the front looked sure to drop at any time. Then, after a bit, I'd put so many of those bloody coins in – invested so much of my time, given you SO MUCH of my love,' her voice was conveying a bit of anger now. 'That the only thing to do was just carry on, even though after a bit I could see full well that those coins weren't shifting. So I just kept at it until my money was gone. And that, Will – that was the point when I dumped you, when I simply had nothing left to give. Knowing my luck, the next woman that came along probably put a couple of coins through the slots and the whole bloody lot fell.'

Well not really. It was Tracey. But I took her point.

'You wasted my time, Will. You had no intention of being with me indefinitely. Nine months were – well, like I say, wasted.'

'Did you enjoy being with me?'

'Yes.'

'Did you walk away with at least some good memories?'

'Yes, I suppose.'

'Well then it wasn't really wasted time, was it?'

She had stopped playing. Her arms were by her side and she was looking out into the middle distance. Shit. I thought I'd salvaged the day. I didn't want it to end like this. Not that it WOULD end like this - it would end with a long, uncomfortable car journey, which was even worse. Fortunately, I'd already got my next move lined up. I pointed over to the dance machine in the corner of the arcade and nudged Mandy's arm gently with my elbow. Time to lift the mood, with the added bonus of the chance to get my revenge for the air hockey drubbing.

'You dancin'?'

She looked at me incredulously. 'You askin'? Hang on, let me try that again: YOU askin'?'

'Yeah, I'm askin'! No need to sound so surprised!' I shouted the little girl over. What do you think, Gracie? Me versus your mum? A little dance-off?''

The little girl shuffled around excitedly on the spot, imploring her mother to engage in competition with me. Mandy shrugged.

'Okay, mister. Let's do this. Me versus you. One dance. One winner.'

It had started to sound more like a Saturday night TV programme than a dance competition in a Skegness arcade on a rainy Sunday afternoon.

'Good luck mummy!'

'Oh don't you worry, darling. What Will doesn't realise is that you and I go to mother / daughter dance classes every Saturday morning.'

I had every right to be worried. I could vividly recall a wedding reception to which I brought Mandy along. It took little alcohol and zero persuasion to get her on the dancefloor, shaking her hips and flinging her hair about as several dozen men tried their best either not to gaze at her or at least to do it subtly enough not to ire their partners. Jesus, she was hot. And I attempted to dance next to her, far too sober to attempt to keep up with her, rigid and self-conscious and completely out of my depth. So yes, I had every right to be worried. And she had every right to be confident. Doubtless she could recall that night just as clearly as me. Little did she know I had an ace up my sleeve.Time for a spot of hustling.

'Oh no! You go dancing, do you? I wouldn't have agreed to this if I'd known. Is it too late to back out?'

Mandy flashed her daughter a smug smile. 'Yep!'

'Well at least give me a fighting chance. Can I pick the song?'

She laughed uproariously. 'Why not?'

I went through the pantomime of mmm-ing and aah-ing, of agonising over my choice, but in reality I knew exactly what I was going to pick. Britney Spears. 'Oops I Did It Again'. Awful singer. Awful song. I'd never danced to it in my life, and had presumed I never would. But it had to be that one. I fed the machine my pound coin, shook hands with my competition and we stepped up to the platform. Gracie watched the two of us with wide-eyed anticipation.

Okay, here's what happened. Rewind about quarter of an hour. As we played on the slots, Mandy had her back to the dance machine, but it was in my eyeline. The slots are a fairly low-brain activity, and I was finding as I was dropping the coins (and after I'd exhausted the novelty of giving each coin an imaginary biography) that my attention was being diverted by a teenage girl. Hang on, let me elaborate. She was dancing, for the second time, to that self-same Britney Spears song: doing a good job of it too, barely missing a step. I was oddly drawn to the pulsating neon screen showing her what moves she should be pulling off. And it struck me that it was a highly pattern-based sequence: very predictable and easy to learn. The platform upon which you dance has four large arrows, forward, right, backward and left, the screen showing which one or ones you should be stepping on. I'd noticed that the intro to the song - which is a slightly slower tempo than the rest of the song - had a somewhat irregular sequence but after that it was cyclical. Forward, backward, left , right, left, right, left , right, backward, backward, forward, backward, left, backward, right, backward, forward, forward, left, right. Repeat. Quite simple really. I found myself drawn into this pattern, chanting it in my head, much more interested in that than the machine into which I was stuffing my two pence coins. Forward, backward, left, right, left, right, left, right, backward, backward, forward, backward, left, backward, right, backward, forward, forward, left, right. It was almost hypnotic. Forward, backward, left, right, left, right, left, right, backward, backward, forward, backward, left, backward, right, backward, forward, forward, left, right. I'm recalling it now as clearly as I could then. Forward, backward, left, right, left, right, left, right, backward, backward, forward, backward, left, backward, right, backward, forward, forward, left, right. All I needed to do was memorise that intro, then I'd have the whole routine learned.

As the song faded out, I willed the teenager to have one more go, just one more go. Again, I'm quite aware that out of context, willing a teenage girl to dance to a Britney Spears song seems a little creepy, but let's overlook that. Anyway, she did. She had one more go. I admired her persistence; she was clearly not prepared to settle for anything less than a perfect score, and I could definitely relate to that. I concentrated as hard as I could on the screen, even suspending my slots session. The song, if you can recall it, has a sort of slow thudding keyboard riff at the beginning, and the steps mirror the notes. Simple enough in principle, especially if you know the song well, but the moves and the rhythm were just a bit more irregular than the rest of the song. It went left, forward, backwards, left, right, forward. I could do this.

I completely fluffed the intro, remembering the sequence but finding myself a second too slow each time. As soon as the cyclical pattern kicked in, however, there was no stopping me. Not that it was a walk in the park. All those months of not working had taken a serious toll on my fitness level - by the end of cycle two I was positively dripping in sweat, just as I had been at the end of that punk gig. I never imagined for one minute that this week would be so exhausting! Good job it was the last day today - I needed a rest! I was not to be defeated, though. My brain had worked hard – it was not about to be let down by my body. I would work through it. I did work through it. I could see through the reflection of the screen that what was a partisan crowd (i.e. Gracie) rooting for Mandy had swelled in size and half a dozen onlookers were watching the proceedings, which only served to boost my motivation. I gleefully watched my points rack up - after all, I had no need to watch the on-screen instructions. For a millisecond they matched Mandy's. Before long they were double hers. Then treble. By the end of the bout my score was quadruple hers, which I feel I can safely describe as a thrashing. I almost - almost - felt guilty to be trouncing Mandy so thoroughly in front of her daughter. If only she hadn't been so damned smug. I resisted doing a little victory dance as I stepped off the dancefloor-cum-podium, for fear of highlighting the fact that, in spite of what everyone just saw, I CAN'T ACTUALLY DANCE.

Thank you mathematics!

Mandy, more gracious in defeat than I, treated the three of us to a fish and chip supper as a reward, which we positively devoured. The mood was buoyant. All three of us seemed to be enjoying ourselves. Even the weather seemed to be changing for the better - by the time our plates were cleared, the last of the drizzle seemed to have ceased. It was chilly, and grey, but at least it wasn't raining.

'Right, come on you two. We're not coming all the way to the seaside and not going on the beach.'

'Are you bonkers? There's no one out there. It's completely deserted.'

'Yeah, so? All the better!'

I dashed into the nearest souvenir shop, grabbed three sticks of rock, a kite, a beach ball and a bucket and spade.

'Right - eat this, fly this, throw this and dig with this! Quick before it starts to rain again!'

Gracie beamed and the two of us ran to the beach, Mandy trudging behind us with a smiling reluctance. We passed the ball to and fro, getting about five minutes' value out of it before a gust of wind blew it out of our reach. I tried chasing it, which for some reason provoked fits of laughter from the youngster, but I quickly gave up the ghost as it started disappearing out of my eyeline.

This seemed like an opportune moment to break the kite out of its packaging. I hoisted Gracie onto my shoulders and she attempted to fly the kite as I sprinted along the beach. The kite whipped and flailed around us but failed to soar. Exhausted, I put Gracie back down on the sand but she was undeterred, refusing to believe that there was no more fun to be gleaned out of the windy weather.

She took from her pocket a little plastic soldier who was wrapped in a parachute and the two tied together with string. She explained she had won him (for it was a him and not an it - she had clearly already formed an emotional attachment) on the slot machines - he fell down with a bunch of coins. She threw him up in the air: he thudded quickly down onto the sand before his chute had had the chance to open. She tried again - the same thing happened. I tried - the same thing happened. I threw him up in the air with as much zest as I could summon - still the same thing happened! I had the bright idea to take him to the end of the pier and launch him from there. I explained my plan to Gracie, assuring her that although she would not see the little man again, he would get a glorious descent into the sea. She liked the idea. We ran (Mandy this time staying behind) and I launched him after a dramatic countdown. I envisaged a long journey for our military hero, as he was blown up and around by the winds before finally fluttering into the sea. It was really more of a plummet than anything, his chute still not opening until it was right near the water. To the unknowing onlooker - like the old couple who tutted at us and muttered something thankfully incomprehensible but no doubt judgmental - it really looked like nothing more than a fully grown man and a little girl littering by throwing a plastic bag into the sea. I cringed. It didn't take the soldier long before he returned to dry land, the tide bringing him quickly back, whereupon a dog off its leash grabbed him in his mouth and ran off with his prize. Sorry, little man. And sorry, little lady.

Both of us slightly crestfallen, we returned to the beach. Mandy rejoined us and the three of us wrote our names with our feet in the sand, as big as we could make them. As we stood back and marvelled at our creation, Mandy tapped her watch.

'Gracie, sweetheart, I'm really sorry, but we need to head back to Will's. We've got two long journeys ahead of us.'

Gracie sighed theatrically and let her head drop, but soon realised the futility of her display as we started walking away without her. She caught us up and tapped me on the arm.

'I like you, Will!'

She stuck out her hand for me to hold. I looked to her mum for permission. She nodded and smiled and we joined hands for the remainder of the walk to the car. By this point, some slithers of early evening sunshine had appeared. A bit late, perhaps, but certainly not unwelcome.

Within minutes, Gracie was sound asleep in the back, snoring gently, and the radio was humming to itself. Mandy and I weren't talking much, but it was an easy silence, not awkward at all. Neither of us was straining for something to say. She was awake, but her head was resting against the window and her bare feet were up on the car seat. When I glanced in the mirror, I could see she was smiling a little.

It was Mandy who eventually broke the silence. She bolted upright. 'Shag, Marry, Kill!'

'Excuse me?'

'Let's play a game! You've heard of Shag, Marry, Kill, haven't you?' I hadn't, and I let my silence explain as much. 'Right, basically, I will name three women. You have to decide which one you would shag, which you would marry and which you would kill.'

'Okay, I can see why you waited until your daughter was asleep before suggesting this. Nothing rounds off a family day out better than a game involving homicide and carnal lust.'

I realised I had erroneously described it as a 'family' day out – it had just slipped out. She didn't pick me up on it, so I quickly moved on.

'Before I play, I just need to establish a few things. I'm presuming that the marriage will involve sex, though I realise so many don't.'

'That's right, Bachelor Boy.'

'And there will be no repercussions for my murderous actions? No good marrying some glamorous Hollywood sex siren if I'm going to spend the rest of my days in prison.'

'You are entirely beyond the law and will be completely exonerated for your crimes.'

'Now, this shag. Can you elaborate on that for me?'

Mandy smirked. 'When a man and woman love each other very, very much, they – wait! I know I don't need to describe this to YOU of all people.'

'Yes, ha ha. No, I mean – let's talk semantics. Do I get just one session of sex? If so, how long do I get?'

'If I remember rightly, five minutes should more than cover it.'

Ouch!

'Okey doke, I walked into that one, but what about positions? Is it basically *carte blanche*?'

'Will, you're getting anal...'

'Well, that's what I was hoping for!'

She sighed theatrically. 'And I walked into that one...'

I took one hand from the steering wheel to stroke my stubble as I pondered the working of my next question. 'Do I get any special warm-up treats, if you know what I mean? And do I get to go again afterwards?'

She threw her hands in the air in exasperation. 'You're overthinking it, man! You're sucking all of the fun out of this delightful little parlour game! Right, just because I can see that you need this, here goes – you have half an hour, and you may do what you will.'

I nodded and paused but had yet to exhaust my line of questioning.

'This shag – when does it happen? Before I marry? I just want to make sure I'm not having any kind of extra-marital affair.'

'Right, because I'm sure monogamy has been right on the top of your love life agenda all these years. You have the sex and then you get married.'

'Right, last one, I promise. The kill part. Do I have to do the deed myself? And can I choose the method?'

'What the hell are you talking about, can you choose the method?'

'Well, I can't think of any celebrity I'd take any pleasure from killing in cold blood. Jamie Oliver comes quite close. I don't want to commit some gory murder. So, if possible, I'd like to choose a more humane method of doing away with them, please. A lethal injection, perhaps.'

'Okay, just to clarify – THIS ISN'T A REAL GAME. You won't actually be murdering anyone, any more than you'll be having a lavish Hollywood wedding or a steamy session with a celebrity.'

'I know, I know – just humour me.'

'Fine. You can choose your method of disposal. As you're a Shag, Marry, Kill virgin, I'll be gentle with you and give you a nice easy one to start with. But be warned, my friend – it will get harder. And you HAVE to give me an answer.'

I nodded, ready and willing for the challenge.

'Let's see. Carol Vorderman, Cameron Diaz and, erm, Yoko Ono.'

'Well, this isn't exactly a conundrum. I'd marry Carol, and we'd have beautiful Maths genius babies. I'd shag Cameron – she's very sexy, but seems a bit too wild to settle down with, and I'd kill Yoko Ono. I'm sure not many would mind.'

'Her son might. Very good, though. Let's take it up a gear. Next one: Catherine Deneuve, Brigitte Bardot and Marilyn Monroe.'

'Do I get to pick the era?'

'How do you mean?'

'Well, there's a world of difference between Catherine Deneuve circa 1965 and now. She was one of the most beautiful women on the planet in in her heyday, but I'm not sure I'd want to go there now. I mean, we're inhabiting a world here where sex with Cameron Diaz is very much on the cards, so plausibility isn't exactly key to the game. I'm chucking a bit of time travel into the mix is all.'

She chortled. 'I think I've learned more about you playing this game than in the entire time we were together. You're a pernickety little man, aren't you? Yes, you can choose the era. I think that one was a given stipulation in this case. Because sex with Marilyn Monroe in her present state would be a little weird to say the least.'

'That's true. Well, I'm going to have to compound Marilyn's troubles by doing away with her, I'll shag Brigitte and I'll marry Catherine. Do you think she would go for an ex-Maths teacher with ball cancer?'

'A HANDSOME Maths teacher with ball cancer! So you never know! Right, we're going to crank it up another notch. The *Friends* trio. Jennifer Aniston, Courtney Cox and Lisa Kudrow.'

'Damn you, Mandy! I have to kill one of those? They're all so lovely!'

She let out a pantomime villain's laugh. I explored the possibilities in my head, none of which quite sat right. 'Right, just to be clear, there's definitely no chance of killing two birds with one stone here?'

'You only get to kill one of the birds, you bloodthirsty beast.'

'No, I mean is there a chance I could marry one of them – where, clearly I can get sex on tap – then bring in another for that shag? A *ménage à trois*? You did say I could do anything I liked in that half an hour!'

'Fine. Have your threesome.'

I eventually plumped for marrying Jennifer, shagging Courtney and killing Lisa, but only for the crime of being ever-so-slightly less attractive than the other two and the oldest of the three – marrying Jennifer made good mathematical sense as she was the youngest and thus likely to live a little bit longer, so I'd be getting better value out of the marriage. It didn't occur to me at the time that, of course, unless any of them died in the next couple of years, all three would outlive me. Back to the game, though, and I reckoned I could follow Mandy's trail. She's just given me three certified hotties. Her next move would surely be to give me three unattractive celebrities.

'Janet Street Porter, Anne Robinson and Norah Batty.'

Bingo!

'Oh come on, now! Have mercy on me! I REALLY don't want to do the nasty with any of those women!'

'Therein lies the twisted beauty of Shag, Marry, Kill. You have to take the rough with the smooth. It's deliciously evil, isn't it?'

I had to admit, it was a great game – the kind of icebreaker that would have turned an awkward date into something a bit more fun. If only I'd known about it years ago. To that end, I'm going to make it my next Top Tip:

Top Tip Number Nine: On a first date, have a game up your sleeve. It doesn't have to be Shag, Marry, Kill – which as you will soon find out, comes with a health warning – but it could be.

'Right, I'm going to marry Anne Robinson. You stipulated nothing about *having* to have sex with the one you marry. We'll just have a loveless, sexless marriage where we don't talk to each other, other than through well-scripted put-downs. I might even ring up Cameron Diaz and see if she's still up for a bit of how's-your-father every now and again, just to keep things ticking over. In fact, forget all that – I'll just marry her then have it annulled straight away. You see, Mandy? THIS is why I get into technicalities! I'd shag Janet Street Porter but get really, really drunk beforehand – actually, just really drunk. I don't want to prolong things down there unnecessarily. And I'd put a paper bag on her head. And stick a photo of Cameron Diaz on the bag. And I'd kill Norah Batty! Although I've got to tell you I'm not mad keen on murdering a pensioner, fictional or otherwise – my life is really taking some dark turns in my dying years! Can't we just let time do its job with Norah Batty?'

'No. No, we can't. Besides, Yoko Ono is a pensioner and you already did away with her, so stop being so pious. Sorted!'

She went silent, but her eyes darted about as if she was contemplating something. Wow - had I finally had the last word? Had I won for once?

'Okay, smart guy. Try this one. What was the one before me called? Florence, was it? So – Florence, your mate Helen, and me.'

She wasn't smiling. Neither was I. Suddenly things had turned deadly serious. She was clearly trying to ascertain whether I was happier with Florence than I was with her and what exactly the nature of my relationship with Helen was. I considered jolting the car in the hope it would wake Gracie, but then realised this would result in two cranky ladies glaring at me instead of just one.

'Come on, Mandy! Let's not do this! You said the game had to involve celebrities.'

'No, you come on. And I said nothing of the sort.'

I replayed the start of the conversation in my head. She was right. Shit. Her eyes were practically burning holes in my temples. I realised suggesting resurrecting that game of 'Twenty Questions' from this morning would probably fall on deaf ears.

I pondered the possibilities systematically.

Possibility 1 – Shag Florence, marry Helen, kill Mandy

Even if this were my preferred choice, did I really want to tell the woman with whom I was sharing a car journey that I would kill her? This would also rule out Possibility 3.

Possibility 2 – Shag Florence, marry Mandy, kill Helen

Kill my favourite person in the world. Kill the person who had stuck by me through thick and thin. Kill someone I loved with all my heart and soul. Just not an option. So that would rule out Possibility 5, too.

Possibility 3 – Shag Helen, marry Florence, kill Mandy

Possibility 4 – Shag Helen, marry Mandy, kill Florence

Choosing this would have a flattering option for Mandy, but also an admission that I fancied Helen – I sensed Mandy was hoping for the former and fishing for the latter.

Possibility 5 – Shag Mandy, marry Florence, kill Helen

Possibility 6 – Shag Mandy, marry Helen, kill Florence

'Are you sure you want to do this?' No response. 'Very well. Here goes...I can't kill Helen. She's my best friend. And I don't have any burning desire to shag her, so I'd marry her. I know her the best. I think we could make it work. You're the sexiest of the three, so, erm, I'd shag you.'

Yeah, because that's just what every woman wants to hear, isn't it? *You're not marriage material, love, but I WOULD have it off with you. And whilst I don't like you enough to settle down with you, I like you enough not to kill you.* Suddenly, I felt very self-conscious about my wording, about the game, about everything. This wasn't fun. I started to mumble.

'You're, you know, well, I mean, it was always good with you. So, by default really because I've got nothing against her, I'd have to kill Florence.'

Also known as *Possibility 6.*

We sat in silence. This time it was an awkward one – a long, intense and protracted one. I suspected the only choice that would truly have satisfied her was *Possibility 2* – doing away with the person I now realised Mandy felt a threat to our relationship and marrying Mandy herself. No doubt she'd have given me daily grief for cheating on her with Florence. Maybe I should just have gone for that one and been insincere. I did her the courtesy of shutting the hell up. Or at least I tried to. Mandy wasn't letting me off that easily.

'You know what? I really thought you were the one. I'm as much of an idiot as you are.'

The One. I'd always hated that expression. She'd said it earlier on that day, in my apartment, and I'd let it slide. This time didn't feel like sparing her my lecture explaining why the phrase bugged me so. Maybe it was the impetuous side of me responding to the 'idiot' jibe.

'You didn't think I was the one, any more than I thought you were.'

'What? How dare you tell me what I did and didn't think, you pompous little prick?'

'Hear me out. Look, it's like this...'

I explained my way of thinking to her, although not in so many words. It's like this: there are six billion people in the world. Whether you're gay or straight, that leaves you three billion possible soulmates. If you're bi, it's six billion and you're just worsening your problem. Now, obviously some of them will be out of your age range, either too young for you or too old. So for argument's sake, let's call it a nice round one billion possible soulmates for you. How can anyone possibly say they've found 'the one'? The one in a billion? You've got a far greater chance of winning the National Lottery than finding 'the one'. What they mean is that they've found 'a one'. Someone who will do, who's good looking enough and has enough in common with them to delude them into thinking that no one else could possibly be more perfect for them. But unless you literally have found that one person out of one billion possible candidates who is that little bit more perfect for them than the other 999,999,999, then how can they be sure? That's why I wasn't 'the one' for Mandy, nor for anybody for that matter.

She wasn't impressed.

'Unbelievable. Unbelievable that you would let Mathematical probability dictate your love life. Well look where it's got you. Congratulations. You blew it, fella – big time.'

She turned her head sharply towards the passenger window. Fantastic. A lovely day was ending on a sour note. Nobody was speaking. I turned the radio up, quiet enough not to wake Gracie, but loud enough that Mandy and I didn't have to talk. I found myself vaguely irritated by the choices – a pop and R'n'B themed commercial radio station, a ponderous play on Radio 4, a football debate and some thumping dance music on Radio 1. I decided whether any of these was more palatable than the static that was ruining those stations playing songs I at least recognised, before conceding that the frosty silence was actually the most appealing option of the lot. I cranked it off. The silence only made me slowly angrier, though, and before long I felt the rather impetuous need to get something off my chest.

'I have to tell you something funny. You'll love this.' It wasn't funny. She wouldn't love it. And I knew it. 'You know how we first met when I crashed into you? And we always said it was fate that brought us together? WRONG! I saw you in your car, fancied the pants off you, and crashed into you on purpose so I could get your number! What do you think of that, then?'

She turned her whole body towards me.

'You did what? You absolute bloody dick. What were you thinking? You clearly weren't! You could have killed me, and yourself, just for a remote chance of getting in my knickers! You stupid idiot! And hang on - didn't your own mum die in a car crash? Unbelievable. So now you've decided to be honest with me, you might as well carry on in that fashion. Let me ask you this: I'm not the only ex-girlfriend you're meeting up with, am I?'

Rumbled again!

'Am I that transparent?'

'Yeah, pretty much. I just know what you're like. And these other women. Tell me. Did you do the same to them as you did to me? I'm just curious.'

'Do what? What do you mean?'

My agitation was increasing again.

'Drive them away?'

I didn't respond.

'Thought so. You know what I think, Will? I think the reason you end perfectly good relationships is because you're scared. It's not that you're bored, or that your feet are itchy or cold. You're scared of losing someone you love. Like you did with your mum.'

Whoah.

I flicked my indicator and pulled into a lay by. I switched off the engine, put my head into folded arms which were draped over the steering wheel and wept. Just sat there for a good five minutes and wept. Wept on my sleeve until it was drenched. Wept relentless, uncontrollable tears – worse than the tears I had cried for Rhonda, and much worse than the time I found out about the cancer. Mandy rubbed her hand up and down my back throughout. When I finally felt ready to lift my head, she embraced me tightly. I started the car and drove off. Nothing else was said for the rest of the journey.

As we approached my flat, a weak but nonetheless welcome attempt at a sunset had appeared on the horizon. And that's how we spent the final part of our final date – indeed, *my* final date. The week was at an end. I know what you're thinking – you're thinking, *Okay now, Will, this is all a bit clichéd. You've gone for the obvious setting sun / end of life metaphor.* I appreciate it's all a bit Hallmark-y, but that really is how it happened. As the last flickers of crimson were disappearing over the horizon, Mandy scooped her sleeping and very floppy daughter up in her arms.

After a brief toilet stop at my flat, she kissed me on the cheek and whispered, 'Goodbye, Will. Thanks for a nice day'.

She loaded Gracie up into her own car and drove off without waving or looking back. And, just like that, she was gone once again.

H: Mr Loverman!

W: Shabba!

H: So - your final date. Randy Mandy. I'm all ears.

W: Well, she brought someone along with her.

H: Hang about! Are you telling me you had some debauched three-in-a-bed situation? I can only imagine what your little one said!

W: What? No. Ugh. No - she brought her daughter along!

H: I see. Well that sounds like your idea of hell.

W: I mean, I thought it would be. It started off that way. We had a disastrous Scavanger Hunt in my flat. The little girl found...things. You know, like dirty tissues.

H: Oh no. You mean she found...your wankerchiefs?

W: Erm...yep. But then things sort of got better.

H: They couldn't have got much worse!

W: We started to bond. We went to the seaside and everything. It was...nice.

H: Oh my giddy aunt! Will Jacobs, serial womaniser, is actually a closet family man!

W: I wouldn't go that far.

H: I would! So the day ended well.

W: Well, it didn't actually end there. There was some shagging. Some marrying. Oh and let's not forget some killing.

H: Excuse me?

W: It's a game. We'll have to play it sometime. We had a few arguments in the car on the way back, but we parted on good terms.

H: Oh, that's good. So - you did it! Seven days, seven dates. Congratulations, young man! You gonna do it again? I bet you could easily dig up seven more victims.

W: Nah. I'll quit while I'm ahead.

H: Probably for the best. Are you going to see any of them again?

W: Nah.

And I didn't. There was, however, a small post-script to the Mandy story. I received a letter in the post, from the lady herself. It contained two pieces of paper. One was a handwritten note, which read:

Dearest Will,

I wanted to say thanks again for a really lovely day. Gracie now refers to you as 'Uncle Will' and she talks about meeting you all the time. Also, I've got a little confession to make. I took something from your flat. Well, borrowed it I suppose - I'm returning it, with a small modification. It shows what might have been. I wish you the very best for what remains of your life. Goodbye, Will.

Mandy

XXX

I unfolded the other sheet, curious. It was the ageyourself picture I'd printed, cut out and stuck onto another sheet; an ageyourself picture of Mandy as an old lady. We made a nice old couple.

Epilogue

So here I am, four months down the line from The Week. Still on death row and still alone – but don't pity me for that. Pity me for the dying bit if you wish, but not for the being alone bit. I pity those people who met their spouses when they were in their teens, like Pete and Georgina, who perhaps don't realise how unlucky they are. They've missed out on the experiences I've had – the highs and lows, ups and downs, good times and bad times. The euphoria felt at the start of the relationship is something they've only been able to experience once. I, meanwhile, have been lucky enough to experience it time and time again. And when a relationship comes to an end – in a funny sort of way, I love the intensity of the sadness. I love the fact that I'm *feeling* something. Sooner that than the blandness and numbness that must kick in after years of marriage. I love the way sad songs sound sadder, sound like they were written for me, about me. I pity the fact that those people who married their childhood sweethearts – and they're often so very smug about having done so – have missed out on the variety and adventures that the procession of women I've been with have brought into my life. Definitely don't feel sorry for me. Good, bad or indifferent, each of them has changed me to some greater or lesser extent. It could be something as small as introducing me to a new band I'd not heard of before, my love for which continued to grow long after the relationship had ended. If not a band, it could be a book, or a film, or a piece of artwork. In some cases, it could even be that, more than simply a band, book, film or piece of art, it's an entire genre that person has introduced me to, which remains a part of my life though the woman no longer does. Some of them have made me more trusting; some less so. Some of them have nurtured my fun side; some my intellectual side; some my romantic side. I have carried a bit of each relationship along with me to the next, and, cumulatively, each has contributed to the person I am today, and each can take whatever credit or blame they're due.

*****

And that was where Will's story ended - slightly abruptly and one Top Tip short of the ten he had promised. His tale didn't really end there, however. There was, in fact, a final twist in store for our protagonist – and it was me. Maria. I went back.

It was never my intention to fall for him again when we met up that Monday morning. Something just clicked, though. I kept thinking about him, starting the moment he left my house that evening and pretty much non-stop from there on. I knew it was stupid of me. He was dying. He didn't WANT a relationship. It was just a one-off. Things continued with Rob - remember him? - but it was a rocky road down which we were travelling. The frequency and intensity of our arguments increased, culminating in a huge drunken screaming match on New Year's Eve, 2005. I rang in the New Year alone, in tears. When I awoke the next morning, I knew what I had to do. I could take it no more - I had to see him.

I didn't ring. Just turned up on his doorstep. I didn't want to seem desperate — but how could I not when, in the nicest possible way, I desperately wanted to be with him? I told him about Rob; told him about my feelings. We kissed - again. I stayed over and it went on from there. What followed were fourteen difficult but largely blissful months.

We of course never had sex, but in its absence, we had romance and friendship. We made a much better job of it despite (or because of?) the abstinence. I knew it was stupid getting involved with him again. I'd had a perfectly healthy (if slightly psychotic and jealous) boyfriend — and I was trading him in for someone with a terminal illness? The truth was that Will and I had that magic ingredient, that spark, that SOMETHING that I didn't have with Rob. I knew that I was just letting myself in for a lifetime of grief when he eventually died, but I honestly felt it was a price worth paying. I wouldn't swap the pain I still feel on a daily basis for those fourteen months of a joy which I felt on a daily basis.

We — by which I mainly mean I - talked flittingly of marriage, with actual wedding rings instead of Hula Hoops, but in the end I finally conceded that, even in his dying days, commitment still terrified him more than death ever did. He met my parents for real on a trip to Australia — still clearly hungry for wacky challenges, he'd wanted us to travel to 26 countries, each subsequent one starting with the next letter of the alphabet. It was overly-optimistic, and between the fact that I could only travel in the school holidays and his limited time left, we only got as far as a wet weekend in Belgium, an amazing skiing trip to Canada and a boozy one-night stay in Denmark. Mum and dad loved him, by the way; I just knew they would.

Will had, it turned out, developed what is known as metastatic cancer, meaning it had spread to other parts of his body — specifically the lymph nodes in his abdomen. His condition worsened quickly — suddenly he was coughing all the time, often coughing blood, he was short of breath and he ached constantly. He managed to keep his health and his spirits up until the last couple of months. After that, he simply detereorated, and let death catch up with him. He died in hospital in my arms on the 2nd March 2007.

After a lot of deliberation, he'd decided eventually he wanted to be cremated. It was a somber, low-key affair, in which female mourners outnumbered male ones 3:1 (to use a bit of Will-speak). He'd prepared a list of people for me to invite – I didn't ask who they all were, and he didn't tell me. I noticed when I saw the list of attendees some months afterwards that five of the Magnificent Seven were in attendance, including myself. Harriet, Kayleigh, Donna and Mandy came; Suzie did not (and can you blame her?). Rhonda's mum even came.

Other than them, there were only a handful of others - the truth was that Will was not an especially popular person; he clearly put more effort into his girlfriends than his friendships. I had to talk my friend Izzy into turning up to make up the numbers a bit. Some of his old teaching colleagues were there – a fair few from the Maths department and a couple from the English department, where I had worked – I had got in touch with those. In spite of how nasty Will had been on their last meeting, Nigel turned up, as did Pete and Georgina – all good people, clearly. Of his family, his Auntie Barbara and Uncle Colin were there, alongside their own children, but that was about it. Not that he ever went looking for him, but Will's dad never made an emotional last-minute appearance in his life.

It was at the funeral that I met Helen for the first time – she managed to get time off work and a flight over from the States. Will would have been chuffed with that. She was lovely – I could see why he was so taken by her. I always wondered if there was a little more to Will's feelings for Helen than he cared to let on, either to everyone else or even to himself. I never dared ask him. And, well, you've read the book - you can draw your own conclusions. However, at the wake, after a couple of glasses of wine had lifted the mood and tongues were a little looser, I asked Helen about her memories of the day she met Will, back when they were starting university. She told me that she actually fancied him like mad and, had she not been so happily attached, she would have jumped into bed with him at the first opportunity. She told me that I was the first person she'd ever told that to, including her husband and, of course, Will.

It was several months after he died that I eventually found the stack of papers containing his story, on top of the wardrobe in his – our – apartment. It hasn't been an easy experience putting together Will's story – for starters, there were gaps in certain parts of the story, presumably ones he intended to go back and fill at some future point. Secondly, Will wasn't quite as well-organised as his charts and diagrams would suggest, and I found this story in quite a state of disarray – all jumbled up and out-of-sequence. I can only imagine that when I returned to his life that New Year's Day, he was still working on the story, but put it on the backburner or forgot about it. In completing his tale I've joined the dots as best I can, piecing together the tales Will told me during that final fourteen months and adopting his tone as much as possible. I may well have missed bits out; the bits he never told me. It was also difficult insofar as I loved Will, loved him to pieces, and at times the old green-eyed monster would pop out as I read about the other, many and varied, women in his life and the copious amounts of sex he had with them – I guess by not showing me the story he was shielding me. I suppose it upsets me to think that, just a couple of days after our date, when I couldn't stop thinking about Will, he was snogging exes in graveyards and shopping malls and playing Happy Families at the seaside. I was falling in love with him all over again the moment I left his side that Monday evening, whereas he was effectively straight out on the pull.

Of course, it was bittersweet bringing Will back to life in this way – his personality shone through in his words, and at times it was like he was in the room with me. I spent many a losing battle fighting back my tears. By the same token, though, reading bits of the story is therapeutic to me as it's an exercise in demythologising - when someone dies, or disappears from your life, it's so easy to turn them into something perfect in your mind, to filter out all the humdrum bits and all the bad bits and exaggerate all the good bits. When I read Will's story - and I do often, even if just for five minutes - it reminds me that he was a human being after all, frustrating and flawed as much as anyone else.

I cringed a little as I read his chat-up lines. The truth was, all the Maths he had invested in them – looking at all the success probability for each one, creating branching databases to prepare for different eventualities and so on – was just unnecessary. In my opinion, he massively over thought the whole thing. He was successful with women he met in pubs and clubs because he we was a bloody good-looking boy. Simple as that. He didn't need a system. I dare say that in most cases, if he was rejected, it was because the woman he was chatting up already had a partner. I can't imagine it being because they didn't fancy him, but then as someone who fancied him like mad, maybe I'm just blinkered or biased.

His story, of course, shows its age - bestdaysofyourlife.com has long-since vanished from public consciousness, swallowed up by the social networking sites which do the same job for free. I can't help but think his quest might have been a whole lot simpler had Facebook had been in popular existence then as it is now - but of course it probably wouldn't have been half as much fun.

And that just about brings us up to speed. I don't know what the future will hold for me – I'll miss Will for the rest of my life, but I'm still relatively young. I'm sure that one day soon, when I'm ready, I'll meet someone new. It's what Will wanted for me – he told me so many times. But this isn't about me. This is Will's story.

Oh, and regarding that last Top Tip - here's one in his honour.

Top Tip Number Ten – be sweet and kind and impulsive. Make a lady feel like a lady. Make her feel like she's the most special and important person in your universe at that moment in time, even if your plans for her don't extend past breakfast. I can tell you for a fact that that tactic worked with at least one of Will's many conquests.

Printed in Poland
by Amazon Fulfillment
Poland Sp. z o.o., Wrocław